PERUSIA

PERUSIA

Copyright © 2007 NJ Matthews

All rights reserved. No part of this book may be used or reproduced in any manner without prior written permission except in the case of brief quotations embodied in reviews.

Author's Note: This book is a work of fiction. Names characters, places, and incidents are the product of the author's imagination or are used fictitiously. And any resemblance to actual persons living or dead, events or locales is entirely coincidental.

Printed in USA

PERUSIA

BY

NJ MATTHEWS

*To Viv
Thanks
NJ Matthews
November 26/2007*

Library and Archives Canada Cataloguing in Publication

Matthews, N. J., 1932-
    Perusia / by N.J. Matthews.

A novel.
ISBN 978-0-9782564-0-1

    I. Title.

PS8626.A88P47 2007   C813'.6   C2007-900414-8

Other Books by NJ Matthews

Singularity

The Sophia

The Sign of Nun

Wee Johnnie Norrie

Dedication

This book is dedicated to my five grandsons, Jordan, Riley, Tanner, Spencer and Carson. They are all the 'light of my life' and any similarities between them and the five boys in this book are purely intentional.

And as for the women in my life, my wife Wanda, my daughters Colleen, Karen and Shelley and my sister Eileen, they will have to decide upon whom the character 'Lucia' may have been based (or not).

I would like to thank my good friend and mentor Reg Skene. Without his help I would still be lost in the morass of editing. His advice and suggestions have been of immense help in making my 'heap of words' readable.

NJM

© NJ Matthews   2007

Prologue

The mid-March skies are heavy with clouds that seem to press in upon the city. The smell of impending rain is in the air. Perhaps this is the reason so few people are milling about the streets.

A beggar conceals himself behind a statue and watches for any opportunity that might come his way.

It seems as though there is a pall over the city, a sense of foreboding. Even the stall keepers are at a loss for something to do as they stand behind their tables waiting for customers or perhaps the storm to be unleashed. Only one or two cries can be heard hawking their wares. Then even they become silent.

A lectica rounds the corner, carried by four stout men. It seems headed for the Curia Pompeii. It is obvious to the few onlookers that the golden litter holds a very important person. All know his name.

The beggar watches as the lectica approaches, biting his lip in anticipation. He carefully scans the streets and can see no one of authority.

Before the beggar can make his way to the litter he sees an old blind man struggle to it's side, forcing it to stop. The curtain in the side opens and an animated conversation ensues.

The beggar is too far away to hear what is being said, he skulks away angrily at the prospect of being outdone by another beggar, and a blind one at that.

The blind beggar leans heavily on his staff, slowly shaking his head as the litter moves on leaving him in the middle of the street. The old man's shoulders sag as he turns to make his way back to the walkway.

A Lictor comes out of the Porticus adjoining the Curia to welcome the important passenger. As he holds out his arm to assist the man inside to get out, it is pushed away almost disdainfully. With a wave of his hand the man dismisses the official and climbs the stairs to enter the Curia. Once inside it is evident that all of the others have arrived. Most are seated on benches awaiting the start of this meeting. Several men, sixty of his trusted friends, cluster around the seat he is to occupy.

He is intrigued by how quiet it is within the building. Strange, he thinks, given there are some nine hundred men here. The silence matches that of the streets, hardly the normal state of affairs.

The man sits in his chair and pulls the purple cloak around him to offset the chill in the March air. He is tired and would have rather been somewhere else this day. Perhaps he should have listened to his wife's urgings and simply missed this meeting. He knows of nothing momentous on the agenda today.

Before he has the opportunity to call the meeting to order, someone that he knows approaches him. He assumes it is to discuss some kind of petition before the meeting begins. There is always something being asked for.

The others move nearer. He stands as the petitioner comes toward him, surprised by how closely he approaches. With swift movement the petitioner grasps at his clothes, pulling them off his shoulders. Then he sees it, glinting in the light from the lamps, a knife held high. The knife stabs into his neck. He shouts and fights back the attackers but they don't stop. Instead they all reveal their knives and begin stabbing him.

He turns and sees the face of one of his best friends, knife in hand raised to strike. The knife pierces close to his heart and with that blow he resists no longer. He grasps the pedestal of the statue of Pompeii, his blood flowing over the statue's feet.

All those pressing around the man, fall on him, striking blow after blow with flashing blades. So bloodthirsty are they that some even strike each other in their zeal to share in the act.

When they finish, the conspirators look around them to find the place empty, all the others have left silently. No cheers for what they have done, no speeches, just empty silence.

The victim lies on the cold marble floor, his life draining from his body through 23 stab wounds, as the statue of his enemy Pompeii gazes down through sightless eyes.

At the age of fifty-five, so died Julius Caesar, and so began the chaos in the Republic.

Chapter One

Three years after Caesar's Assassination

The three boys, Pando the eldest, Tactus the middle one and Pico the youngest, crossed the fields of ripe grain on their way home from their tutor Castor's house.

They were excited at having seen the Roman Legions marching into Perusia earlier. But their early release from their studies and the fact they had no homework assignments, left them in an even higher state of excitement.

Tactus spoke to Pando.

"Why do you think that Castor was so upset Pando? It's not like him not to give us any homework."

Before Pando could answer Pico responded.

"What difference does it make, no homework is no homework."

"Be quiet Pico, I was talking to Pando."

"I heard Father talking about it with some neighbours. It has something to do with the Legionnaires coming to take land away for themselves. Everyone believes it's going to lead to trouble."

"What kind of trouble?" Asked Tactus.

"I don't know, father didn't say. But from the way Castor acted, I think it's serious."

Pico chased a butterfly and ran well ahead, not caring to be part of this discussion. He had more important things to do. Like catch a butterfly. Except that he lost interest in that adventure when a large gray rabbit jumped across his path and he veered in a vain effort to catch it instead.

"Pico you're never going to catch that rabbit, you'd have had better luck with the butterfly," said Pando.

"Tactus, why are you so quiet?"

He seemed preoccupied when Pando spoke to him.

"Did you hear me Tactus?"

"What, ah no I didn't, sorry."

"I said what's bothering you? You seem lost in your own little world."

"I was just thinking about all those soldiers and what's going to happen to the people who lose their land."

"Cheer up Tactus, it's not going to happen to us."

"How can you be so sure?"

"Just remember, we are of the "Equestrian Class', we would never be treated that way."

"I suppose you're right. I wonder what mother's making for supper tonight?"

"Whatever it is, I'm sure you'll like it. Maybe even a sausage or two."

"My very favourite."

The two boys laughed. Pico was so far ahead; he was very nearly at the front door of the house.

"Come on you two laggards, I beat you home."

He pushed through the door expecting to smell the aroma of the evening meal, but there was nothing.

"Mother, I'm home." He called out.

"In the kitchen." His mother answered.

When Pico entered he was surprised to see that his father was there too.

"What are you doing home so early?" Asked his father Marcus.

By this time the other two tumbled through the doorway and into the kitchen, they too were startled by the presence of their father.

Pando thought.

Something's not right I don't ever remember father being home this early. What is it I wonder?

"I asked why you are all home so early from the tutor's?"

Pando responded.

"When Castor saw the Legions advancing towards the city, he decided it would be better if we left early. He seemed very upset. What's happening father?"

"Nothing for any of you to worry about."

Pando could see the distress in his mother's face.

Have they had a fight? There's such tension, I can feel it.

It was as if Livonia could sense her son's anxiety. She forced a smile and said.

"Since you are all home early you can help prepare dinner. But before you do, get your homework done first."

Pico shouted and did a little dance around the kitchen.

"No homework, no homework. Castor didn't give us any."

Livonia looked at her husband, shrugged and said.

"In that case Pico, you can begin by taking the garbage to the shed."

"But why can't Leto take it out. What are slaves for?"

"I won't have you talk that way about Leto. We've always considered her to be part of the family not just our slave."

"Sorry mother, I didn't mean it the way it sounded. Where is she anyway?"

"She's left, her mother was ill," Livonia lied.

"So now we have no slave?" Asked Pando.

"You'll get used to it, she may be gone for some time," she said.

"Can't we get another slave father?" Asked Tactus.

"You heard your mother, you three can just pitch in until Leto gets back."

All three of the boys recognized that this discussion was at an end. They said no more about it.

Livonia whispered in her husband's ear.

"Marcus, don't take it out on them. It's not their fault, there's no way they can understand what's happening."

He nodded and left the four of them in the kitchen.

Even though it was still relatively early afternoon Livonia proceeded with the evening meal. Anything to keep busy, anything to take her mind off the worry for her family.

Pando filled the water containers in the kitchen carrying jars of water from the well in the courtyard. Tactus set the table in the dining area while Pico grumbled as he separated the lentils, good from bad, pebbles from lentils. He hated lentils, but said nothing.

"Is there anything else you need me to do mother?" Asked Pando.

"You could bring some more firewood in for the stove and then see if there's anything your father needs you for."

He did what he was asked and then found his father sitting under an olive tree in the courtyard.

Father seems deep in thought, I wonder if I should disturb him? I'd like to know what's happening, something is and I think it has to do with the Legionnaires.

Marcus looked up and said to his son.

"Come sit with me boy."

Pando did as he was asked and picked a piece of long grass, and stuck it in his mouth just as his father had. Marcus smiled.

After a long silence Pando spoke.

"Father, something is going on, I know it. I think I'm old enough to know if we are in some kind of trouble."

"Trouble, you think we are in trouble?"

"Well it's something, I don't know what, but things aren't right."

"You're very observant for one so young."

"I'm not that young."

"Barely fourteen, I'm sorry boy, but that is young."

"The Legion would take me at this age."

His father's eyes flashed as he said.

"Don't you even think about it. You think the Legion to be a glamorous life? Then you'd be a fool, death and destruction around you every day, it isn't just triumphal parades and pageantry."

"I didn't mean to upset you father. I have no intention of joining the Legion. I just wanted you to know that I'm old enough for you to count on me."

Marcus reached up and tousled his son's dark hair.

"My boy, I know I can count on you."

"Then why not tell me what's going on?"

"It's just politics Pando."

"Politics?"

"Yes, since Caesar's murder there has been great turmoil throughout the Republic with the loss of his strong guiding hand. There is much corruption on the part of many that would fill the void left by his death.

"Factions have developed, there are those like your mother and I who have always been faithful followers of the Great Caesar and the principles he put forward. Then there are the corrupt who want to enrich themselves.

"You know that the country is being run by a Triumvirate and as far as I'm concerned that's a recipe for failure. They fight amongst themselves and the Republic suffers."

"I don't understand father, what has that got to do with us?"

"Your mother and I have thrown our support to the Imperialist faction, those that seek a strong Emperor who can lead us back to Rome's rightful place in the world."

"And the others?"

"The Republicans who want the present state with all the corruption maintained."

It was then that they both heard Livonia's call for dinner.

There was little talk at the table, the boys sensed that both parents were preoccupied with thoughts they were unwilling to share with their children.

Marcus scraped up the last of his lentils with a crust of bread and leaned back in his chair, thinking about what might be had for dessert when there came a mighty crash.

The door to the house splintered into many pieces and flew inward as though smashed by an angry God. Standing in the doorway was a Lictor, a large man with wide shoulders and muscled arms.

He carried with him a 'fasces' a bundle of stout birch rods from which protruded an axe head, a sign of the legal authority bestowed upon him by the Praetor or Chief Magistrate.

The Lictor made his way through the doorway, almost filling the opening as he did so. Then followed three others of similar build and disposition.

In a loud voice the man said.

"This is the house of Marcus Merula and his wife Livonia, is it not?"

Marcus is on his feet. Angered at this intrusion he shouted.

"Yes it is and what business is that of yours. By what right do you break into my home and destroy my peace."

"I come by order of the Praetor Maximus to arrest you and your wife as Enemies of the State."

He held out the official parchment for Marcus to see. He responded.

"This is a sham, I'm not nor is my wife an Enemy of the State, we are loyal Romans."

"That's for the Praetor to decide at your trial, this document orders that you and your wife surrender to me and instructs me to transport you to prison."

"This is nothing but a lie, I refuse to go."

"I'm authorized to use force if necessary."

The other three moved menacingly forward, they seemed eager to take action against him.

Livonia screamed at the man.

"What about my children? I will not leave them. I must stay to look after them."

"That's no concern of mine, my duty is clear."

Livonia persisted.

"Let me make some arrangement for a neighbour to come in and look after them until this is cleared up."

"No, the children must leave this place. The property has been seized under the Proscription; your children have no right to stay here. They must leave forthwith."

"You can't do this." Cried Livonia.

The Lictor turned to his men and said.

"Shackle them both and put them in the cart. If they act up hit them with the cudgel till they're quiet.

"I'll get rid of the children take care not to do too much damage to those two. I've no more use than you three for Equestrians, but the Praetor will have your head if they seem abused."

Livonia screamed over her shoulder as she was dragged from the house.

"Pando take your brothers and go to your Aunt Junia in Rome, she'll help you. I love you all, take care."

Her voice trailed off into tears and they could hear their father shouting vainly at their captors. Then the groaning of a cart leaving and the sounds of gravel crunching under the wheels.

Chapter Two

It was dark as two brothers traveled north on the road from Rome to Perusia. Only the light from fires of other travelers was visible. There was no moon. Ludus kept looking back as if to make sure they weren't being followed. As he did he stumbled over a rock. His brother Viaticus caught him and said.

"Clumsy, I told you to be quiet and yet you make more noise than a chicken in the jaws of a fox."

Ludus ignored his older brother's comments and asked.

"Is going to Perusia a good idea? It's been three years since we've seen Aunt Livonia. Maybe they've moved somewhere else."

Viaticus sensed Ludus's anxiety. But was careful to conceal his feelings.

Mother and father arrested as 'Enemies of the State'? How that can be? Then thrown out of our own house, and our slaves taken, Perusia is the only place we can go.

"Viaticus, are you listening to me?"

"Yes, Ludus, but keep your voice down. I'm sure there are thieves and pick pockets on this road."

Ludus felt anxious. He strained trying to see through the gloom, imagining a criminal behind every bush. His stomach began to growl.

Perusia is a long way away and I'm so hungry. Aunt Livonia's cooking, always had too much garlic, Maybe they have a slave that does the cooking now.

The tears began welling up in his eyes at the thought of his mother in a dark prison. But he couldn't let Viaticus see them.

"Viaticus, I don't understand why anyone would want to arrest our parents, they aren't criminals. The official said they were "Enemies of the State' How can they say that? And what did he mean by Proscription?"

"The only thing I know Ludus is what I overheard father speaking about to our neighbours. He said that there was great turmoil in the Republic after the murder of Caesar. He said that the Triumvirate was never going to work. And that Octavian needed to be declared the rightful heir to Caesar.

"Old Cato tried to convince Father to be careful with his words. He said that to take sides at this point in history was folly Men had lost their lives for saying less.

"As for Proscription, I'm not sure what that means but it seems obvious that it's the basis for seizing our family property."

"Would they arrest him for saying that?" And why would they take mother away?"

"Remember what Cato said. 'Nothing is safe at this time; there is great tumult in the Republic. Men need little excuse to get rid of enemies, real or imagined'."

"Do you think they will kill our parents? Surely not, Viaticus?"

Instead of answering, He changed the subject..

"Perusia is a long journey and there's no way we can do it on an empty stomach. We need to find food"

"My belly is complaining with every step. Where will we find food?"

"We could steal it."

"Viaticus, Father would skin us alive."

"Maybe so, however, perhaps you could charm someone at that campfire up ahead. A young boy like you, surely some motherly woman would take pity on you."

"I'm not that much younger. Just two years but I would agree that is you have a lack of charm."

Viaticus hit his brother in the back of the head. Ludus was sure it was a good-natured smack but it still hurt. He knew that Viaticus was right and that he would have a better chance playing to the sympathy of a mother or better yet a grandmother.

Viaticus is big for his age, a man almost. In fact taller and broader than many men double his years, no he would certainly not instill anything like sympathy.

They moved quietly ahead. The smell of cooking reached their nostrils and the hunger pangs became more intense.

Ludus whispered to his brother.

"What is that smell?"

"Rabbit I think."

"Oh, I don't like rabbit."

"How do you know, you've never tried it?"

"Neither have you."

"They tell me it tastes just like chicken."

"Who are they?"

Just at that moment, both boys were struck from behind and fell senseless. When they recovered they lay before a blazing fire with two men staring into their faces.

Ludus looked up at the two men; Viaticus still groggy from the blow simply held his head. The men were a strange pair, one built like a tree stump. Almost as wide as he was tall. He had only one eye that didn't seem to move in it's socket. As a consequence the owner was forced to turn his head in the direction of whatever it was he was looking at.

The second one was taller, thinner and bald. He moved with quick bird like movements his hands seemingly in a continuous flutter. It was the 'tree stump' that spoke first.

"So just what were the two of you up to? Hoping to rob us I'm sure."

"Rob us. Rob us. That's a good one." Cackled the skinny one.

"Shut up Corripio. Leave this to me. You, the smaller one, answer me. What are you two up to?"

Ludus stuttered as he responded.

"Nothing sir, nothing at all. We were hungry, just looking for something to eat."

"You wanted to rob us didn't you? Steal our food and kill us. Isn't that so?"

"No No. Not at all, just let us go now and we'll not bother you further."

"You take me for a fool? Let you go? I think not, you'd be sure to come back and kill us." With that the 'tree stump' withdrew his sword and said.

"Corripio, quickly, tie them both up and if they refuse to stay quiet, gag them as well."

Both Ludus and Viaticus were trussed up back to back sitting on the damp ground. Corripio was swift; Viaticus couldn't help wondering how many other victims he had tied up in the same way.

They must have seen us and were waiting for us. Cutthroats, waiting to rob travelers and steal their belongings. Well they'll get a surprise; we've nothing to steal. Why didn't they just didn't kill us? The old one keeps looking at me. Why? I've seen that look before, when father buys a new horse.

Chapter Three

"Pando what are we going to do? It's dark and Rome seems so far away."

Pando sensed the tears in Tactus's voice. Pico had already cried himself to sleep, but if he and Tactus could just get some rest, he knew things would look better in the morning.

His stomach growled. They had had nothing to eat since the lentils at dinner.

"What's that noise Pando?"

"My stomach complaining."

"I don't mean that. Something's out there."

Tactus clutched at brother's arm, his grip hard enough to cause pain.

"I don't hear anything. It's just your imagination."

But Pando was not as sure of himself as he let on.

I heard something too. Just over there, but it's too dark to see.

Then nothing, just the sound of the wind.

Pando shivered as he strained to listen.

Why didn't I think to find some kind of weapon?

"Pando there's something cold and wet touching my back."

Pando saw nothing. He raised his head to see over Tactus.

Now I think I hear it.

"Pando, something is here with us, I hear breathing. I'm frightened."

Pando raised himself on to his elbows.

I see some kind of dark shape. Or is it just my imagination?

"It has a long tongue," said Tactus. "It's licking my back. What kind of monster is this?" Tactus shouted and pulled away.

Pando jumped to his feet, startling the creature. It jumped, hitting Pando squarely in the chest knocking him to the ground. Pando managed to grasp handfuls of coarse hair and twisted and turned, but the animal was too powerful.

Then Pico awoke and asked.

"Pando I'm trying to sleep you know. Why are you playing with that strange dog?"

The animal began licking Pando's face and growled playfully.

"It is a dog," cried Tactus.

The shaggy animal bounded among the boys nipping at their feet. Pico was still not impressed at being awakened, but a great lick to his face soon changed his attitude.

All three joined in a joyful romp with the animal in the dark.

"Pando, what do you think his name is?" asked Tactus.

"How would I know? He's a big brute. Maybe we should call him Brutus."

"I don't think you want to say that too loudly, Pando."

Pando hadn't thought about the name before he said it, but Brutus was known to be the name one of Caesar's murderers.

"Just 'dog' will have to do I guess," said Pando.

"Come here 'Just Dog'" called Pico.

All laughed, and Pando, took charge of the situation.

"Settle down now, both of you. We've a long walk ahead of us tomorrow. Save your energy."

He succeeded in quieting everyone even, 'Just Dog', whose presence was a comfort. They soon drifted into a dreamless sleep.

* * * * *

Pando woke from his sleep to find someone shaking his shoulders.

"Where's my dog?"

Pando jumped to his feet, his heart thumping in his chest.

The man was large, even larger than Pando's father.

Broad shoulders, thick legs, dark skinned, almost black. African I think. I've never seen a sword as large as he had.

"Do you hear me boy? Where is my dog?"

The voice was like thunder. The other two boys cowered behind their brother, unable to speak and too afraid to cry.

"The dog is gone, he must have left in the night," Pando protested.

The big man shifted his gaze to the two smaller boys and asked.

"Why are you three here anyway? Don't you know it's dangerous? Somebody might rob, you or worse, cut your throats."

His hand moved to the hilt of his sword.

With a trembling voice Pico asked.

"Why would you want to kill us? We haven't done anything to you. We never stole your dog."

"What have we here? A brave little man, hiding behind his big brother and making noises. Who said I was going to kill you? If I had wanted to do that it would have been done by now."

Pando couldn't take his eyes off this black giant. The three boys seemed frozen to the spot. The black man swung around to look behind him and, as the cape slipped from his left shoulder, Pando saw he had only one arm. The left one was severed just above the elbow.

As the man looked back at Pando he asked.

"What's the matter, never seen a one-armed black man before? Close your mouth boy."

He then fixed his attention on Pico and said.

"Since you appear to be the only one able to speak, why don't you tell me why you three are out here alone? Where are your parents?"

Pico looked to his older brothers; they said nothing, so he responded.

"We are on our way to Rome to visit relatives."

"As I said, you can speak. Too bad that you never say much when you do. Answer my questions boy."

"We don't know where our parents are. That's why we're going to Rome. We have an aunt and uncle and two cousins there."

"What do you mean, you don't know where your parents are? Did they abandon you?"

"They would never do that. They were taken."

"By whom?"

"I'm not sure. Some men."

"What's your name?"

"Pico."

"My name is Kashta. And you other two? What are your names?"

"I'm Pando and this is my brother Tactus."

"Can't Tactus speak for himself?"

"I can speak. When I have something to say."

The black man thundered.

"Impertinence begets discipline. Remember that."

Tactus's lip quivered and he struggled to prevent a tear from sliding down his cheek.

"Yes sir."

"Pando tell me your ages."

"Yes sir. I'm fourteen, Tactus is eleven and Pico is nine."

"Good. Now what have you got eat? I'm very hungry."

Pando answered.

"I'm sorry sir, but we have nothing. In fact we've been without food since dinner yesterday."

"Then you must come with me, this situation can not continue. You just don't understand your predicament."

"What do you mean sir?" Asked Pando.

"My name is Kashta. Use it when addressing me. You can't continue as you are. Because you've been abandoned by your parents, you could be sold into slavery. Then there would be small chance that you would ever seeing any of your relatives. We can look for my dog on the way."

"The way to where?" asked Pico.

"Just follow me, that's all you need to know."

His tone left no room for discussion.

"Can we get something to eat soon? I could eat an old shoe I'm so hungry, " Tactus said.

"I'll find you one of mine. It would make quite a meal for you. Let's find my dog."

"What's his name?" asked Pando.

"Fortis."

"What kind of dog is he?"

"A black one, a very big black one."

Chapter Four

"Sceleris," whispered Corripio.
"Are you awake?"
"I am now simpleton. How can I sleep with you poking me? It's hardly daybreak why do you disturb me?"

"I'm sorry Sceleris, it's just that I thought we should leave here before any of the others come. We would have some serious explaining to do about the two boys."

The older man thought for a few minutes rubbing his grizzled beard as he did so. He hated to admit that Corripio could be right about anything. But in this instance he was, Sceleris was not about to share this windfall with anyone.

"Rouse those two and we'll get on the road."

"But we must feed them Sceleris, they've had nothing since yesterday and while you and I can ride they must walk."

"Such tenderness Corippio. What is it? Do you want to adopt them?"

"If they take sick or look it, we won't get as good a price will we?"

"Alright, go ahead, boil up some pulse and be quick about it. Make sure you don't overfeed them, I want a profit on those two."

While Corripio busied himself making a fire Sceleris fed the horses. One was an old nag but Sceleris's horse had once been with the Legion. He was Sceleris's proudest possession. The fact he had won him in a crooked card game bothered him not at all.

As Sceleris measured out the grain he turned his one good eye to see Corripio helping the bigger boy to his feet.

Just look at the size of that one, hardly a child and yet not a man. He's taller than most and fine muscle definition as well.

Sceleris scratched at his beard as though it was infested, and perhaps it was.

To good for a slave, but as a gladiator, that would be something entirely different. If he is any good he could make me many times over anything I could get for him as a slave. But it will take training and that costs money.

He touched his face just below his sightless eye and remembered how things once were.

Corripio called him to the morning meal distracting him from his thoughts. All four sat cross-legged around the fire each supping from a wooden bowl. At least Sceleris and Corripio were eating the other two looked at the gray glob in their bowls and then at each other.

"What is this?" Asked Ludus.

"Breakfast, what do you think it is?" Growled Sceleris.

Ludus poked at the jelly-like mass with his spoon.

I'm terribly hungry, but I can't get this stuff down.

Viaticus on the other hand just shrugged, and wolfed it down, hardly tasting it.

"Not so bad Ludus. Just swallow it quickly, you'll hardly notice the taste."

Then he held his bowl out to Corripio and asked.

"May I have some more?"

Before Corripio could answer Sceleris bellowed.

"No, do you think I'm made of money? When you earn your keep you can ask for more."

Ludus choked down what he could of the meal and said nothing.

Corripio made sure that his master didn't see him as he handed a flask of water to them as Sceleris left to tend the horses,

"Here, drink some of this. It'll help wash down the pulse and the water will help swell the porridge. You won't get too hungry later."

With Sceleris mounted on his horse and Corripio riding in the wagon, the two boys brought up the rear. With hands bound by ropes and the ropes hooked to the wagon.

It was a sorry procession and none sorrier that Viaticus and Ludus.

Chapter Five

The afternoon sun beat down on them. The three boys were almost exhausted, but the heat didn't seem to bother Kashta. It was difficult for Pico in particular to keep up with the big man's pace. Finally he called out.

"Can we rest for a few minutes? I feel as though I might be sick."

"Keep moving, you can't rest out here in the bright sun. See that tree up ahead? We'll stop there."

To Pico the tree looked far away.

I think I'll die before I get there? Why is this happening to us?

Pando put his arm around Pico and said.

"Walk in my shadow Pico, it might help cool you. It isn't far. We'll soon be there."

Tactus was just as miserable but said nothing for fear of angering Kashta. Finally, they reach the shade, just as they did a light breeze came up the boys collapsed under the olive tree.

Kashta sat near them and removed a flask from within his tunic. He passed it to Pico and said.

"Here boy, have a drink, not too much nor too fast. Leave some for your brothers."

Pico was grateful and took care to obey Kashta. He handed the flask to Tactus and then to Pando. Fearful that there wouldn't be enough left for the big man; Pando took only a small sip before giving it back.

"Take more. What's your name? Pando isn't it? I have less need than you poor Romans."

Tactus resented the way Kashta had said 'you Romans' and before he could restrain himself blurted out.

"Are you less a Roman than we are?"

"Boy I am no Roman at all. I told you, I am a Prince of the Royal Blood. I am a Nubian, from an empire that has existed far longer than any Roman Empire. A country that exceeds Rome in culture, laws and achievements. Why would I want to be a Roman?"

Pando was astonished.

"You mean you don't want to be a Roman? I thought everybody did. Why are you here then?"

"I am not here by choice but rather as a matter of unfortunate circumstance."

The boys moved closer to Kashta. Each was waiting for the story to begin. When he failed to say anything more, Pico spoke.

"Won't you tell us how you come to be here?"

"That is a long story, I'm sure you would lose interest long before I ever finished it."

It seemed obvious to Pando that he needed to be coaxed into telling his tale.

"Please Kashta, we'd really like to hear it." Pando exclaimed.

"It was long ago, as many years as Pico here has been on this earth. I lived in a country so beautiful it is difficult for me to describe to you. Great snow-capped mountains rising above the lush green valleys with trees that bore exotic fruit.

"For as long as I lived there, I knew of no war or pestilence. Nothing disturbed our peaceful life."

His eyes misted over as he reflected on what once was and now seemed so far away.

Tactus spoke.

"It sounds wonderful Kashta so why did you leave?"

"As I said, it was not a matter of choice. One day I was sitting by a cool stream when I heard a noise in the bush behind me. Curiosity clouded my judgement and I went to investigate. I thought that perhaps an animal might have been injured, if it had, it was my duty to help.

"But as I cautiously moved through the bush I stumbled over something and the next thing I know I was being hauled up in the air in some kind of net. I couldn't get loose. As strong as I was I couldn't break the ropes of the net. I hung suspended in mid-air. Then I heard it.

"The laughter, loud raucous, it came from two men standing well below me. In the face of the older one I saw pure evil, I'll never forget that look."

He paused and from the expression on his face the boys were sure that he envisioned that face again as he retold the story.

Pico, his eyes as wide as saucers spoke.

"Then what happened? Why did they trap you?"

"It wasn't me they were after. It appears I was caught by accident. What they really wanted was an animal, a very special animal."

The boys hung on every word, for the moment they were transported from their own predicament to another more exotic place.

"What kind of animal?" Asked Pando.

"The King of the Jungle. Perhaps the biggest, strongest and most fearless lion ever. I saw him many times; we called him 'Lisimba'. In my culture all animals are seen as equal beings at least in spirit, Lisimba was greatly revered by my people."

"Did they ever capture him?" Asked Tactus.

"To my great sorrow they did. It was a terrible day." His eyes clouded once more.

"What happened then?" Pico's eyes grew even larger.

"Both Lisimba and I were put in cages and brought to Rome. I tried many times to escape but they kept me shackled.

"Lisimba was sent elsewhere I never expected I would ever see him again. Then things seemed to get better for me; I was taken to a place with other men, some foreign, others from here. The food improved and I had a clean place to sleep. Then I discovered why. I was to train as a gladiator.

"The men in the jungle were procurers of animals for the Circus Maximus, it seems I was just an unexpected catch which brought some additional profit."

Pando was enthralled.

"You were a gladiator? How fantastic, it must have been an exciting life."

Kashta held up the stump of his left arm.

"You think this is exciting?"

Pando felt remorse for what he had said.

"I'm sorry, it's just that all your ever hear on the streets is about the successes of the gladiators and not the injuries."

"Or of the deaths. But I resolved that I would never take the life of another just for entertainment. In fact I can see no reason short of defending myself or others from attack for ever killing anyone."

Pico looked at the stump and said.

"But surely a wound like that would be reason enough to kill your opponent."

"No, it was not."

"Please finish your story," pleaded Tactus.

"After I finished my training I was told that I would have my first battle at the Circus Maximus. Have any of you ever been to the Circus?"

They all shook their heads.

"Well it was sight to behold. It was a day much like today, hot sunny and with little breeze. The crowd in the Circus was said to be in excess of 150,000 people and all of them were looking for blood. It didn't matter whose blood, anyone's or anything's would do.

"The noise was deafening, I couldn't see from where I was placed, but I could certainly hear. I was told that this day even the Great Caesar was present.

"I grew anxious as the day wore on. Finally, I was called. Before entering the arena, I spoke to my father's spirit and asked him to watch over me then I climbed the stairs into the sunlight and walked alone to the center of the ring.

"Fresh sand had been spread to soak up the blood from the previous encounter. A mighty roar went up from the crowd as I stood, alone waiting for my adversary. In one hand my trident in the other a net of rope.

"I turned completely around in the ring and could see no opponent. Was this some kind of game?

"But then I saw a gate open at the opposite end of the arena, and there he was. Bigger than I had remembered, majestic in bearing and fearless. The crowd roared it's approval in anticipation of a certain blood bath.

"I was stunned, just standing there in the midst of this spectacle. For my foe was Lisimba.

"I could see Caesar and his party out of my left eye, seated in the Dictator's Box, covered by a canopy to protect them from the sun. I had seen his likeness before. His statues were everywhere in the city. The others with him I knew not.

"My attention was drawn back to Lisimba; he was walking slowly majestically towards me. As I began approaching him the crowd became even more excited. His tail twitched back and forth, his eyes seemed to penetrate me but I felt no fear.

"We came together and stopped each of us waiting for the other to make the first move and suddenly I knew.

"The noise of the crowd seemed to die out and I heard nothing but my own breathing.

"I reached out and touched Lisimba's great mane and he did not move. I could hear the crowd once more.

"'Kill him, kill him.' They all shouted in unison.

"But I did not, instead I bent down and whispered in Lisimba's ear and looked deeply into his eyes, yes I knew.

"Lisimba's spirit was Apedemek the Lion of the South.

"He lay down, just as you've seen my dog Fortis do and seemed content to lie at my feet.

"The throng was wild with anger, they wanted blood but they would get none from me this day. Suddenly, a man appeared coming up the same steps by which I had entered the arena, he was screaming as he approached with his spear.

"'You lazy good for nothing, kill the beast or I'll kill you.'

"It was the same man who had trapped me in Nubia, the evil one that I spoke of earlier, I never knew his name, but his face I will never forget."

"Then what happened?" Asked Pico, breathlessly.

"Lisimba arose and seemed ready to attack the evil one as he approached. The man raised the spear ready to defend himself from the lion. As he threw it I stepped in front of Lisimba and the spear struck my left arm, there was blood for the crowd at last.

"As I fell from the blow I could see Lisimba spring at the evil one, with one swipe of his great paw he struck out an eye and the claw cut the face to the bone. The evil one screamed and ran to the safety of the staircase by which we had both entered."

"Did Lisimba get killed?" Asked Tactus.

"No. Due to an intervention, I was granted my freedom from slavery and Lisimba was returned to the jungle of Nubia."

Pando looked at Kashta in wonderment.

"What a great story. Did you ever find out who it was that intervened?"

"Yes I did. Come now, get up we must be on our way for it's getting late."

"You mean you aren't going to tell us who it was?" Cried Pico.

"Better than that, you're going to meet him. Come on little man get moving."

* * * *

They struggled to keep up with Kashta, his long legs seemed to require two or more steps from each of them and even then they would fall behind.

"I don't see any dog," grumbled Pico.

"Keep a sharp eye out boy. That dog is my best friend we must find him."

Tactus could only think of how hungry he was.

Never mind any dog. Dogs could look after themselves, I'm sure of that.

"Please Kashta, can't we have something to eat. I'm starving," he said.

"We will eat when we get to where we are going," the big man said.

Pando had to admit he was hungry too but decided to say nothing. Pico however, persisted.

"Where are we going and when are we going to get there?"

"For such a little person you have a great deal to say. We are going to where I'm taking you and we'll be there when we get there."

Then he whistled and called out.

"Fortis, Fortis, where are you black hound? Why are you leading me on this chase?"

All they could hear was the wind whistling through the high grass and grasshoppers flying in their faces with each step. The sun was moving higher in the sky and the air was hot.

"I'm thirsty, can I have some water?" Whined Pico.

"What kind of soldier will you make? We've barely been on the road for three hours and you think you can walk all the way to Rome. What nonsense. When the sun stands above us we'll come upon a well, you can refresh yourself there. In the meantime, less talk more walk."

The three were downcast, no food no water their feet ached. Maybe Kashta was right, trying to walk to Rome is foolish. They trudged on not speaking. It seemed like hours but finally Pando spotted it.

"There it is, just up ahead. The well."

All three began to run towards it, threw themselves on the ground and began drinking the cool clear water.

"Not too fast and not to much," called out Kashta.

He pulled each of them back by the scruff of the neck and sat them down on their backsides.

"Listen to me or you'll make yourself sick."

He reached into a satchel strapped to his waist and removed a parcel. Something wrapped in a linen cloth. They couldn't quite see what it was. He broke of a piece and handed it to Pico.

"Here noisy one eat this and maybe your stomach will become quiet. I don't suppose that you could do likewise."

With that he handed a piece to the other two boys. All three looked at it suspiciously.

"You think I'm trying to poison you?"

He broke off a piece for himself and ate it.

Pando was the first to try it. Tentatively at first but then he tasted the sweetness. It was cake of some kind; he'd never tasted anything like it before. He looked at his brothers and with a full mouth struggled to say.

"It's good, really good."

The other two sampled it. They smiled at each other and devoured it.

"Can we have some more, please?" Asked Tactus.

"That's all for now, besides I must save some for Fortis, he will be very displeased if I have nothing for him when we find him."

"You would feed it to a dog before you would feed it to us?" Complained Pico.

"Fortis is of great value to me, you three are really more of a nuisance."

"Why are you so selfish?" Blurted Pico.

"Me selfish? Me a Prince of the Royal Blood of the Empire of Nubia. Selfish you say, you will pay me more respect than that my little man."

Pico stood trembling. It wasn't the first time his tongue had gotten him in trouble. But before the tears flowed Kashta said.

"Enough rest and nourishment. Time for you ungrateful louts to move on.

With that they continued their journey, to where they didn't know and all the while looking for an elusive black dog that would eat all of the sweet cake.

Chapter Six

Corripio scratched under his armpit, something crawling in the hair.

Is it lice? Just the kind of thing one picks up when there are strangers in our midst. The boys looked clean enough but you never can tell. Then again it might just as easily been Sceleris, he's never been one to take care in his personal habits.

The boys had been securely bound for the evening once again. He couldn't help feeling sorry for them.

I don't believe for a moment that their parents abandoned them.

They are almost fully-grown. Both are of good physique, strong and able to do much work. No, not abandoned, but it doesn't matter what I think. Sceleris will have his way.

Why should I care one way or the other what happens to them. I have enough trouble of my own.

I just regret the day I met Sceleris lying by the side of the road.

Corripio climbed into the back of the wagon and settled down to try to sleep.

* * * * *

"Viaticus, are you asleep?" Asked Ludus

"I think I was, why are you disturbing me?"

"How can you sleep? We should be trying to come up with a plan to escape."

"Escape? How? We are always watched."

"Viaticus, we aren't being watched now, they're both asleep."

"And we're both bound hand and foot. What do you expect me to do? And besides, if we do escape we have no idea of the direction to take to get to Perusia."

"We need someone to help us."

"Like who Ludus?"

"I think Corripio might. He doesn't like Sceleris any more than we do. Maybe he'd like to escape from him too. And he'd certainly know the way to Perusia."

"What makes you think he isn't just the same as Sceleris?"

"Remember when he gave us water back there? I'm sure he did that in spite of Sceleris. Maybe he was giving us a sign."

"You're a dreamer Ludus."

"It's worth a try. Don't tell me that you're just going to go along and be made a Gladiator or even sold into slavery?"

"Being a Gladiator might not be so bad."

"You're a long way from being one. I'm not saying you couldn't be but just consider being under Sceleris's thumb while you train."

"Yes that's true."

"One other thing big brother."

"What's that Ludus?"

"How many 'old' Gladiators do you know of."

* * * *

Sceleris stood behind the wagon relieving himself. The sun was just creeping over the horizon.

Going to be another hot day but I'd sooner have this than winter.

He shook the wagon violently with both hands causing Corripio to shriek like an old woman.

"What is it? What's happening?"

The skinny man stumbled to the front of the cart his hair and clothes in disarray. Sceleris gave the wagon one last shake and said.

"Get off your backside you old crock. I want my breakfast. It's time to get out of here. Go light the fire and get those other two moving."

Muttering to himself, Corripio went to the other side of the wagon where Ludus and Viaticus were pretending to sleep.

"Come you louts get up. It's time to move on. You'll get no breakfast if you don't move quickly."

"Corripio are you forgetting our bindings?" asked Ludus.

"Oh, yes. Just a moment, I need my knife."

He picked up his knife from the front seat of the wagon and made his way back to the boys. Sceleris called out to him.

"Don't you cut that rope you old goat. I just bought it and I don't need it cut to pieces."

"No, no of course not. I just need to use the point to loosen the knots."

What does he think I am a fool? Yes I suppose he does. I can think of several places on the person of my 'master' where I'd like to put this knife.

He knew he would do no such thing but he shivered with pleasure just thinking about it.

The knots had tightened with the turning and tossing of sleep so it took Corripio longer than usual to untie the ropes, being careful of course not to cut them.

Sceleris called out to him again.

"Corripio, get up here and get the fire started, I'm ravenous. Perhaps I should sell you to the bone yard and get a younger slave. What do you think?"

Ignoring the comment, he slipped the knife into a cord he wore at his waist so that he could use both hands to untie Viaticus. Only Ludus noticed it slip to the ground falling silently into the deep grass. It was obvious that Corripio had neither felt nor heard it fall.

When both were free he ran to Sceleris calling over his shoulder for the two to put the ropes in the wagon.

Quickly Ludus picked up the knife, it was small only about a hand's length but it was very sharp. He had to hide it quickly, the only place he could think of was within the loincloth he wore under his tunic. The blade protruded and rested against his leg. He'd have to very careful, if he fell, he was sure that it would be a fate worse than death.

Now they could begin to plan.

Chapter Seven

The sun was setting as Kashta and the boys approached a small farmhouse set back from the Roman roadway. It was almost hidden from view by the tall poplars that offered protection from the world beyond.

"Where are we?" asked Pando.

"You are at the end of the first part of your journey," Kashta answered.

I have no idea what he means. Does he intend to accompany us all the way to Rome? His thoughts were interrupted as Tactus asked.

"What is this place Pando?"

"I don't know, but I think we'll find out soon enough."

"What are we going to do about the dog? Don't you think it strange that we never found him or even heard him barking or anything?"

"I don't know Tactus, but Kashta doesn't seem to be concerned."

"When are going to eat? I'm hungry," said Pico as he hurried to catch up.

"Maybe we'll get something at the farmhouse. You should learn to eat when food is available," said Pando.

"But I did, then Kashta wouldn't give me anymore. Remember he saved it for the dog."

As they approached the house, a door opened and an old man stood framed by the opening. He seemed very old and slight of build. He leaned heavily upon a staff held in his right hand. He wore a toga that showed it's age, almost as gray as his hair. His beard and hair were quite long. But what really struck them, were his eyes.

The eyes were sightless the man was blind. Pando was reminded of the great marble statues he had seen in Rome. The eyes had no pupils, just the whites. It was as though the eyes were turned backward in his head.

The man stepped out and came towards them. When he spoke his voice seemed to resonate.

"Kashta, it is good to have you home and you've brought them with you. That's good, very good."

How can he see us? Kashta never spoke, how does he know he's here? How does he know any of us are here? Thought Pando.

The other two just stood there with their mouths open looking at those unseeing eyes.

"Come boys, come inside, you must be very hungry."

They didn't have to be asked a second time. Pando was first over the doorstep. As he passed the old man he felt a hand on his head.

"Welcome Pando."

Each of the others experienced the same thing. They were welcomed and addressed by name, by a man that could not see.

The house was smaller than their home but what interested the boys most was the smell of food wafting in from the kitchen. A smell so good that it set their stomachs to rumbling.

A small face peered around the kitchen doorway and even though Caecus's back was to him, the old man said.

"Oratio, come in and meet our guests."

Pando assumed the man was a slave and wondered at the introduction. But given the good manners he'd had instilled in him by his parents, he said.

"Hello Oratio, I'm very pleased to meet you my name is Pando."

"I'm afraid he is unable to answer you, for he has no tongue. But between he and I, we are enough to make a complete man. I am without eyes and have a tongue and he has eyes and no tongue."

Oratio laughed a silent laugh. Pando and his brothers didn't know where to look or what to say. Kashta broke the awkwardness when he said.

"Let's eat, I'm famished it seems as though two full moons have passed since I've eaten Oratio's wonderful food."

He ruffled the hair of the man's head as he passed by him to his place at the low table. Humble though the house was, the group ate in the style of the well to do, reclining on cushions and eating the various courses as brought to them by Oratio.

They finished with sweets, dates, small cakes and fruit. Even Pico, the notoriously picky eater devoured everything he was offered.

"Seems to me that the long walk did you some good Pico. I've never seen you clean up your plate like that before." said Pando.

Pico ignored his brother as he popped another grape in his mouth.

Kashta belched his satisfaction before saying.

"I must check on the animals and see how they have faired in my absence."

"Oh I think you will find that they have been treated well by Oratio as you just have my old friend. But go, satisfy yourself."

"May I come with you Kashta?" Begged Tactus.

"Yes but take care not to frighten the animals."

Tactus followed the big man to the out building just behind the house. Too small to really be called a barn it housed only one horse a few chickens and a goat. He followed Kashta around to the stalls where he made sure that each animal had adequate food and water.

As they left the barn, Kashta stopped and looked at the moon, it was a clear night and the air was warm with summer. Tactus stood and looked up too, unsure of what he was supposed to see. Then he asked.

"What are you thinking about Kashta?"

"Just thinking about home, that's all."

"But aren't you happy here? Caecus is your friend isn't he?"

"Yes he is. But tell me my little toad, are you happy here?"

"No, not really. I miss my parents, our house and my friends."

"Then why should you wonder at me being any different than you."

"I guess you're right. May I ask you something else?"

"You ask a lot of questions."

"Tell me about Caecus."

"That's not a question."

"I could make it into one."

"Hmm sounds to me like you're bound for the Senate."

"Please."

"Who is Caecus? That's what you want to know, right?"

"Oh yes please."

"Caecus is many things. He is my friend, a philosopher, and a prophet. Those things I know for certain. But he has told me that he is the son of a shepherd, that he was born in Greece and if we have both have enough wine he will tell me that he is really Tiresias."

"Who is Tiresias?"

"Tiresias, according to Caecus, was a sightless prophet born more than 1000 years ago during the dark ages in Greece. He has even told me how he came to be blind."

"How did it happen, please tell me."

"I think you are far to young to hear such stories."

"Please Kashta, please tell me."

"You are a curious one. Alright, but you must tell no one else."

"Not even my brothers?"

"No, not even them."

"I promise, I will never tell."

"When he was much younger he was walking in the countryside of his homeland when he had a startling experience."

Kashta paused and pulled a straw from the ground, to clean between his teeth.

"Kashta," pleaded Tactus.

"He came upon the Goddess Athena. I assume you know about the Goddess Athena?"

"Not much except that she was or is very beautiful."

"Well it turns out that Athena was taking her bath. She was naked of course and Tiresias saw her in all her nakedness. Athena became very angry and placed a curse upon him and struck him blind."

"Just because he saw her with no clothes?"

"Yes, but remember after all, she is a Goddess.

"Then what happened?"

"His mother Chariclo begged Athena to undo her curse, but she couldn't. Instead she picked up a serpent and commanded it to lick Tiresias's ears. And in so doing bestowed the gift of prophecy upon him."

"Do you really believe all that?"

"Do I believe that Caecus is really Tiresias and that he saw Athena naked and that she struck him blind. How would I know? I suppose stranger things have happened. Do I believe that Caecus has the gift of prophecy? Without a doubt, it was he that sent me to you because he could see the great danger you were in.

He is also the possessor of great magic powers that he can unleash to serve the good of man."

"You believe all of this to be true?"

"Yes and you would do well to consider how it was he knew you three stood outside his door, how he came to know your names and how he knew where I would find you."

Tactus stood in awe of what he had heard

Kashta was right. How else could Caecus have known these things other than by some magic means.

"Kashta, tell me, was Caecus the man who saved you in the Circus Maximus?"

"Yes, I owe him my life and now you know why I can't leave this place regardless of the pull my homeland exerts.

Chapter Eight

Viaticus and Ludus were covered in dust from the roadway, thirsty, hungry and unaware of where they were headed.

Each word they spoke to each other was like a barbed shaft, intended to hurt and solved nothing. The rope that bound their wrists chafed the flesh. Crusted blood mixed with the dust acted like an abrasive causing even more pain. If they didn't keep up with the jerking wagon, the tightening ropes would add to their agony.

"So Ludus, about this plan of yours."

"Shut up Viaticus they'll hear you."

"I doubt that, Sceleris is out in front of the wagon and Corripio likely can't hear anything over the rumbling of the cart.

"My guess is you have no plan otherwise you'd have told me.

"Perhaps Ludus, you enjoy the 'pulse'."

"Don't even mention that vile stuff. Even though my belly's empty you could give me a case of the heaves just thinking about it."

"So I'm right Ludus, you have no plan."

"Viaticus just shut up. The knife is chafing my leg; my feet are sore and my wrists and arms ache. Plan or not, we should escape tonight. Get as far away from these two as we can and see what happens."

"Brilliant, just brilliant, run for the sake of running."

"All right then, let me hear your plan Viaticus."

There was silence as the two lumbered along after the wagon. It seemed they had come to a mutual understanding without even speaking. Viaticus broke the silence.

"So be it. Tonight we'll get loose after they are well asleep and put ourselves in the hands of Juno and ask her to guide us."

The younger boy grinned and responded.

"And no more pulse."

* * * *

Ludus's comment about 'no more pulse' turned out to be inaccurate. They had it again for supper. But this time it was worse, Corripio had run out of salt. A sin that did not go unpunished by

Sceleris. He boxed his ears and twisted his nose until it bled. And then banished him from the campfire with nothing to eat.

Ludus and Viaticus ate the gruel in silence for fear they might suffer the same fate. In the darkness after they had finished, they watched the light from the fire play across Sceleris's ugly face. He was even more frightening in this light.

An occasional whimper came from somewhere in the dark.

"Shut up you mangy little animal. I can't even trust you with a simple task like remembering to bring the salt. I've a good mind to throw you down the next well we come across."

Ludus worried that Sceleris might be the one to tie them up.

Would he discover the hidden knife? Maybe it would be them thrown down the next well.

Then he heard him call Corripio.

"Corripio you brainless whelp, get over here and take these two and tie them behind the wagon. Make sure that you do it right or I'll skin you alive.

The thin man came shaking into the circle lit by the fire. With a trembling hand he motioned them to follow. Ludus was sure he could hear him say.

"Woe is me, woe is me. What have I ever done in my life to deserve such treatment?"

Corripio bound them as he always had, with their hands behind their back. Then he had them lay down back to back and tied their feet together. It was a very uncomfortable position. Sleep would be difficult, but neither of them had any intention of sleeping. Tonight they would escape.

They could hear Sceleris brow beating poor old Corripio, belittling him and grinding him down even further. Ludus felt sorry for the man, but there was nothing they could do.

Time passed slowly.

Will those two ever settle down and go to sleep? Thought Viaticus.

His bones ached, as he lay on the ground unable to stretch out. Ludus faced the fire and watched as it slowly died away. As darkness crept over the campsite, the deep snoring of Sceleris rattled in their ears.

"Viaticus, they're asleep I'm sure of it," whispered Ludus.

"Let's wait just a little while longer to be absolutely sure."

'The pain in my left hip is driving me crazy. I'm lying on the knife hilt. Let's see if we can't move our position so that you can reach it. There's no way I can get to it the way Corripio tied us up."

"I'll try Ludus, but I've got to loosen the ropes a little first. Move your hands this way so I can get closer to the knife."

"Fine but just be careful, the knife is very sharp and I'm afraid it's aimed at a very sensitive area of my body. I don't want to cut or worse yet, lose any body parts."

Viaticus couldn't resist saying.

"I'll do my best but if something goes wrong perhaps you could take up singing. I understand boys with high voices are in great demand."

Ludus responded with an elbow to the back.

"Take care little brother, remember I'm the one with the knife."

Viaticus was able to get some slack in the rope. Enough to move his hand under his brother's leg and feel the knife. He nicked his finger on the blade and pulled his hand back.

"What is it?" Asked Ludus.

"Nothing, I just cut myself that's all."

"Better you than me."

Finally, Viaticus was able to extract the knife from its hiding place. That was the easy part, now he had to orient the knife behind his back so that he could attempt cutting Ludus's bonds. He got the knife in his right hand and was able to hold it vertically. Carefully he felt the blade to make sure that it was facing away from his body. Then he said to Ludus.

"Carefully back up towards me and touch the knife very softly. Once you can sense the direction in which I'm holding it perhaps you can make an attempt to cut the rope. Just move your hands carefully in an up and down motion."

"What was that?" asked Ludus.

"I heard nothing."

"That's just it, Sceleris has stopped snoring.

Sweat ran down their faces and their hearts were pounding. They stopped what they were doing and waited for what seemed like an eternity.

Then, Sceleris began snoring once more, even louder than before. Ludus started his task again and when the rope was finally cut through he wanted to cry out but knew he couldn't. He set at once to cut the rope binding his ankles and legs. Then a hoarse whisper came from Viaticus.

"What about me?"

"In due time big brother in due time. Just let me massage my legs and arms and get the blood flowing again."

Ludus cut him free.

"That took long enough. Did you think you were the only one suffering from cramps? Come on don't dawdle, let's get out of here."

"Wait, I have one more thing to do." And with that he cut the rope into short lengths rendering it completely useless.

"There, that should get Sceleris's goat."

"Come on Ludus let's go. We'd better hope we never come upon Sceleris again in this life time."

* * * * *

Without a moon the darkness enveloped them like a dark heavy cloak. Progress was slow, as they had to avoid obstacles they couldn't see.

" Do you think they will follow us Viaticus?"

"No doubt. Sceleris will be angry at losing the prospect of selling us as slaves. His temper will drive him to follow us."

"And they'll be travelling in daylight, making their journey much easier than ours."

"Yes Ludus, so we need to make haste and try not to leave a trail that can be followed."

"Easier said than done, it's so dark I can't tell if I'm leaving a trail or not unless you mean the bits of skin I might be leaving behind every time I bump into something."

"Just stay off soft ground and don't break any branches."

"Viaticus, do you have any idea what direction we're headed?"

There was no answer.

"So, you don't do you?"

Viaticus was about to give his brother a smack when he heard something behind them. He put his hand on his brother's shoulder.

The noise again, someone was following them.

Viaticus whispered in Ludus's ear.

"If someone is following us he'll pass us here and we can jump on him. If he turns away then we'll just wait until he puts some distance between us."

"Suppose it's a wild animal?" whispered Ludus
"You mean like a rabbit?"

Ludus reached up and smacked his brother on the head. They heard another noise, closer this time.

Viaticus was sure he could make out a form. Maybe it was an animal he thought. Not all that big and kind of hunched over.

As the thing passed, Viaticus leaped upon it almost crushing it under his great weight. It let out a scream.

That didn't sound like any animal noise.

"Who are you and why are you following us?"

"It's me, it's me. Please don't hurt me."

Viaticus flipped Corripio over and sat on his chest.

"Where is Sceleris?"

"He's not here. I've run away just like you. Won't you let me go with you? Please."

"I don't trust you Corripio. I think you're just as bad as he is."

"How can you say such a thing? He's a beast. I'm a kind man, surely you don't think that the knife was left for you by accident. Besides, I can be of great help to you."

"You want to go to Perusia and I know the way."

"We can find our own way, we don't need you," said Viaticus.

"I don't think so, remember I've been following you and you're not going in the right direction for Perusia. You've been travelling in a circle.

"I'm sure you are unaware of the works of the great Archimides, if you were you would know that I'm telling you the truth."

Viaticus looked down at the little man squirming under him.

"What are you talking about and who is Archimides?"

"Archimedes was a famous Greek mathematician and he determined why it is that when men wander aimlessly they always travel in circles often ending up just where they began. He found that this oddity was due to the fact that all men are born with one leg just a tiny bit shorter than the other. Man needs points of reference in order to avoid this failing. In other words, you need to know where you are going. And I do. And you don't. So don't you see, you need me."

"Maybe he's right Viaticus. He wasn't as mean to us as Sceleris."

"I still don't trust him and I don't believe his story about the one short leg either."

"You don't think I'd lie to you do you? And please could you get off me, you are a very great weight you know."

Viaticus relented and got off Corripio. He extended his hand and helped him to his feet.

"Thank you. Now, unless you want to walk back into the arms of Sceleris, I think I should lead this party."

Grudgingly they conceded. Corripio did a little dance of joy and said.

"There's another reason I should lead the party."

"Why is that?" asked Ludus.

"Because I brought the food."

Chapter Nine

Tactus lay on the straw with both hands under his chin as he watched Kashta brush the horse in the stall. It was a very large horse, for even Kashta could barely see over it's back.

"What's his name?" asked Tactus.

"Fortitudo, I call him Fortitudo."

"That's a strange name for a horse."

"He has a big heart and fears nothing, the name fits."

Tactus fell silent, his large brown eyes watching what Kashta was doing. The horse stood patiently as he was being groomed.

I would really like to know more about his story. Maybe he'll get angry and send me away but I must know.

"Kashta, when you told us the story about the lion at the Circus, did you really mean that you could talk to it?"

"You find that so strange?"

"I've never heard of anybody being able to do that before, that's all. And when you talk to them do they answer you?"

"I would be very foolish indeed if I spoke to them and they didn't answer. Don't you think?"

"I guess so. Do you speak to Fortitudo too?"

"Of course."

"But I didn't hear you say anything."

"When you speak to animals it is not always necessary to use your tongue. Using the mind is just as important."

"I don't understand."

"It's difficult to explain."

"Could you teach me Kashta?"

"It's very hard to teach anyone. For one thing it has to be the right person. Animals won't talk to just anybody."

"What do you mean?"

"Well first of all the student must be pure of heart."

"Don't you think I'm pure of heart?"

"Just telling me you are doesn't prove anything. I can only tell over time, your actions and attitudes will show me."

"Oh please Kashta, please teach me how."

"You need to understand, that not everybody has the gift. Some people, no matter how hard they try, will never be able to do it."

Tactus was disappointed and appeared crestfallen until Kashta said to him.

"Come over here 'little toad' and I will give you a small test. We'll see if you're made of the right stuff."

Tactus didn't need to be asked a second time, he bounded over to the big man and looked up at him expectantly. Kashta picked him up effortlessly and looking into the boy's eyes and said.

"I want you to say nothing to Fortitudo, not a word. Do you understand?"

The boy nodded and waited for instructions. His heart was beating so loudly he was sure Kashta must be able to hear it. He didn't know how he was going to talk to the horse without speaking but he knew better than to ask.

"I'm going to take you around to the horse's head. When we get there, I want you to look into his eyes. You must try not to blink. I want you to try to concentrate on what is going on behind Fortitudo's eyes. Think of nothing else, just concentrate on what might be going on in the horse's head. Understand?"

He nodded again. Kashta held Tactus at the horse's eye level. The animal sniffed at him making the boy a little nervous. He was after all, a very large horse.

Tactus gazed into the soft limpid eyes and saw the gentleness there. He relaxed and began to concentrate on just what the animal might be thinking.

Then a strange thing happened. It wasn't as though any words were exchanged but Tactus knew what the animal was thinking. He began to giggle but quickly got control, fearful that Kashta might get angry with him if he didn't appear to take this exercise seriously.

Tactus then tried reversing the process, opening up his mind to the horse by responding to what the animal had conveyed to him.

It seemed to work, for Fortitudo began shaking his head up and down as though acknowledging what Tactus had said, or rather thought.

Kashta looked at the smiling boy and asked.

"So, what did you learn, if anything?"

"Oh I did. It worked Kashta, just like you said."

"Well, then tell me."

"Fortitudo said you forgot to bring him an apple this morning."

Kashta threw back his head and laughed loudly.

"He's right, so I did. And what did you say to him?"

"I asked him if he would like me to get him one and he nodded yes. You saw that didn't you Kashta?"

"I did indeed." He lowered Tactus to the ground and said.

"Off you go to the kitchen. Ask Oratio for an apple for Fortitudo."

Tactus was so excited and pleased at what happened he was almost at the door to the barn before he thought to turn and ask.

"Doesn't that mean that I am pure of heart Kashta?"

"It seems that may be so my little friend."

* * * * *

"Pico." Caecus called from the front door of the farmhouse.

"Have you seen Pando?"

"No, I haven't. Would you like me to go find him?"

"Yes and tell him to hurry. I must talk to him immediately."

Pando emerged from behind the barn. Pico ran to him and told him that Caecus wanted him.

"He seemed kind of upset Pando. You better hurry."

The boy sprinted to the door with Pico following close behind. As he reached the door, it opened and Caecus said.

"Come in Pando we need to talk. But I'm afraid, Pico that your brother and I must talk alone. Go see Oratio, he's in the garden, you can help him hoe the vegetables.

Disappointed, Pico stood there as the door closed in his face.

It's not fair. Why can't I be part of the discussion? Tactus is with Kashta and Pando is with Caecus and I get to hoe the garden with somebody that can't even talk to me. It's not fair.

* * * * *

"Pando please sit at the table."

He did as he was asked and Caecus took the chair opposite.

"Your cousins are in very grave danger and they seem unaware of it. You must go find them and bring them to me."

"But how Caecus, I don't know where they are and I've never traveled in the country alone before?"

"Yes I know that, but I can help you. Do you have the courage to undertake this quest?"

Pando wasn't at all sure, but he took a deep breath and said.

"Father always said that most important thing in a man's life is his family. I am obliged to undertake what you ask as a matter of honour. I will do it Caecus."

With that Caecus reached into the folds of his toga and removed something. He placed it on the table between them.

It almost took Pando's breath away it was so beautiful. It was an amulet of some kind, on a heavy gold chain. The stone was diamond shaped and of an intense blue colour with flecks of gold running through it.

"What is it? I've never seen anything so beautiful. What kind of stone is that?"

"It is called Lapis Lazuli, very ancient and very magical. This amulet will be your guide to help find your cousins."

"But how can this help me?" It's very nice but shouldn't it be a woman's adornment?"

"It will all become clearer in a few moments. But I must give you some instructions about the amulet. First, do not take it off once you place it around your neck. Not until you return here with your cousins. Second, protect it at all costs; do not let anyone touch it or take it from you. It is of great value and anyone that sees it will be aware of that fact. So you must wear it under your clothes at all times."

"I understand, but how will it help me?"

Caecus picked up the piece and held it up so Pando could see it shimmer in the light from the window. Then he pressed a concealed button on the side and the stone popped open revealing a small golden chamber inside.

"Oh, it's a locket. My mother has something like that."

"She has nothing like this Pando, believe me. Do you notice the shape?"

"Yes, it's shaped like a diamond, four sides and four points."

"Exactly. Each point indicates a direction, The top point is North the bottom South and the right side is East and the other represents West."

"But how does it work?"

"Patience my boy patience. First we must activate it. Put out your right hand palm up on the table."

Pando did as he was asked. Then Caecus took hold of the boy's hand and with a sharp knife, he quickly nicked Pando's forefinger drawing a good-sized drop of blood. Pando reacted by trying to pull his hand back but Caecus had such a tight grip on his wrist that he was unable to do so.

He brought the open amulet under Pando's finger and squeezed the blood into the golden receptacle. Then he snapped the amulet shut.

Slowly a change came over the gem, it seemed to emit a soft glowing light and Caecus said.

"There, it is energized, it's magic has been released. Put it around your neck. You will see that the chain is long enough that you can easily reach inside you tunic and lift it out so that you can see what it is telling you.

"Tell me which of the points is glowing brightest."

"The bottom one."

"Then that would tell you, that from where you are sitting in this house, you must go south to find your cousins. Now put the amulet inside your tunic next to your skin and tell me what you experience."

There was nothing at first. Pando was about to say just that when he felt it. A faint beating, was it his own heart or was it the amulet?

"I think I feel something, like another heart beat. Is that it?"

"Yes. And as you get closer to either of your cousins the beat will become stronger, if it fades you are moving away from them. Because all of you are of the blood of two sisters it seeks out such relatives."

"But won't my two brothers confuse the amulet?"

"No because the magic of the jewel has been set so it won't respond to relations as close to you as your brothers."

"Caecus this is marvelous, it's almost as if I'm in direct contact with my cousins. I can feel them.

But I have one question."

"What is that Pando?"

"Once I have found my relatives, how do I find my way back to here?"

"That is the easiest of your tasks. The dog Fortis will accompany you and while you may not remember the way, he will."

"You've thought of everything." Pando was feeling much happier now that he knew Fortis would go with him.

"When do I leave?"

"Now." Said Caecus.

"Go to Oratio, he has packed some food for you and the dog. Safe journey, I know you can do this. Just remember that a fox may change its skin but never its character."

With that puzzling admonition Pando left the blind man.

Chapter Ten

Caecus followed Pando out of the house and down to the barn. Pico and Tactus were both playing with Fortis. It was the first time any of them had seen the dog in several days.

"Look Pando, Fortis has come back," said Pico.

Tactus was rolling on the ground giggling as the big dog nibbled at his legs.

"Where have you been Fortis?" Tactus asked, ruffling the dog's ears.

"It's good to have him back again isn't it Pando?" He said.

Before his brother could answer Caecus spoke.

"Yes, it's good to have Fortis back with us, but I have something to tell you two."

Both stopped playing. They could tell from the gravity of the old man's voice that something serious was about to be said.

"I want you both to know that I'm sending Pando on an important mission. Both he and Fortis will be gone for several days. Tactus, you and Pico will stay with Oratio and me until they return."

"Pando why can't we come too?"

Pando could see the tears beginning to well up in Pico's eyes. He too felt the sadness of being separated from his brothers.

Then Tactus asked Caecus.

"You said that just the four of us would stay behind, what about Kashta?"

"He had to leave as well. We all must do what we must do. He will be back, trust what I tell you and ask no more questions."

The blind man leaned more heavily on his staff and stroked his wispy beard with the other hand.

"Come Pando, you must leave we have no time to waste. It is best if you travel mainly at night when it is cooler and you will attract less attention. Stay away from the main road and be wary of those that might do you harm. Say goodbye to your brothers and be off."

He turned abruptly and left.

Pando hugged Tactus and Pico. Even he could not hold back the tears. Pando couldn't help but wonder if he would ever see his brothers again. His heart was heavy but he did the best he could to lift their spirits by saying.

"I won't be gone long. Caecus says it's only about the same as three marathons. I'll run all the way and be back before you even miss me. And remember, I'll have Fortis with me."

"But where are you going and why does it have to be you?" asked Tactus.

"Caecus says that our cousins are in danger and I must bring them here. He says there is no time to waste."

"But what about our aunt and uncle can't they help Viaticus and Ludus?" asked Pico.

"Caecus just said that our cousins are in danger he said nothing of aunt and uncle. I suspect something similar may have happened to them as happened to our parents."

"Do you believe Caecus? Is he telling the truth? How does he know all of this Pando?"

"Tactus have you forgotten? Caecus can see the future he's a prophet we must listen to him. We have no other option."

"I just want to go home to mother and father," cried Pico.

Pando put his arms around both his brothers and said.

"That's what we all want. Perhaps with Viaticus and Ludus and with the help of Caecus and Kashta we can find our parents and somehow win their release."

Pando did not feel as confident in that statement as he hoped he sounded to his brothers.

"Now, I need to go. The sooner I leave, the sooner I'll be back,"

With that he headed to the house to get the food from Oratio. Even though Pando had not called the dog, Fortis trotted behind him as though an unspoken command had been given.

* * * * *

Caecus was awakened from his sleep by the sound of sobbing coming from the pallet where Pico lay. The old man arose from his bed, grasped his staff and made his way to the boy. He placed his hand on the child and could feel the wracking sobs.

"What is it Pico? Why do you cry so?"

Pico had trouble trying to speak the sobs made it difficult. Finally he managed to blurt out.

"I miss my mother. It's been so long since I've seen her I fear I will forget what she looks like." Now Pando's gone. What's happening to my family?"

Caecus shushed the boy and said.

"Come into the kitchen we mustn't wake Tactus."

They sat across from one another at the table. Fortunately for Pico, Oratio refused to sleep without a light so a candle burned between them.

"These are difficult times Pico but you must not give up hope. Remember that fortune favours the brave. I can tell you that you will never forget your mother or what she looks like. And as I look to the future, even though my vision is somewhat clouded, I see a glimmer of your family united."

"I wish I could believe you Caecus, but I'm afraid. What if they are dead? And if something happens to Pando, what will become of Tactus and me?"

"Your parents are not dead Pico."

"I think you would tell me that just to make me feel better."

"I am a man of honour I do not lie."

Pico could sense that Caecus was offended by what he had said.

"I'm sorry Caecus and I apologize, it's just that I so want to see my parents again."

The Caecus seemed to stare at the boy through his sightless eyes. Pico squirmed in his chair. Light from the solitary candle illuminated the old man. The flame flickered causing strange shadows to dance across the prophet's face. Caecus's eyes had always bothered the Pico. More gray than white and somehow rolled back in his head, he had difficulty looking at them.

Caecus reached out and moved the candle to the right as though he could actually see where it was. He reached for the boy's hands. Pico resisted the urge to pull back and allowed the papery flesh and bony fingers to hold his.

"Pico I want you to look into my eyes. Look deeply into them and say nothing."

He was tempted to turn away but forced himself to gaze into the stony orbs.

Then it happened.

The eyes began to change.

They're changing from the eyes like a statue to something else. But what? Mirrors. Are they mirrors? Yes mirrors, cloudy but they have definitely become mirrors.

The cloud began to lift in both eyes and he could see something.

What is it? Figures? Yes two of them. A man and woman. They're in some kind of a room. I don't recognize it.

It's clearer now but instead of seeming like a mirror the eyes are more like windows.

He could look in and see clearly now.

He almost cried out but remembered Caecus's admonition not to speak.

It's mother and father, she's just like I remembered her, I haven't forgotten.

Then Caecus's mouth opened and Pico heard his mother speak. His heart was so full he thought it might burst. He listened intently to what was said.

"I worry for my boys, particularly Pico. But Pando is a good boy and I know he'll watch over him. And Tactus too, my heart breaks for all of them. I miss them so. Its strange how we take such things for granted and only when lost do we recognize what treasures we have."

Pico had to resist calling out in the happiness of seeing her. Then he heard another voice coming from Caecus's mouth. It was his father.

"We will be a family again Livonia do not fear. Caesar's enemies cannot prevail. We must believe that this chaos will end and our world will be restored to what it once was."

Then Caecus's mouth closed and his eyes slowly returned to the normal granite stare.

Chapter Eleven

When Sceleris awoke to find his camp abandoned and Corripio missing his whole body seethed with anger. Unable to believe that Corripio had left him, he climbed inside the wagon calling out.

"Corripio, you poor excuse for a weasel come out, come out and face me now."

He turned over the blanket that the he normally slept on but there was no sign of him. Then he noticed that all of the food supplies were gone.

"That goat has left me nothing. I'll skin his smelly hide right off his body when I catch him. And Viaticus and Ludus as well. I rue the day I ever saw them, they have been nothing but trouble for me."

When he got out of the wagon and saw his new rope cut in short lengths he jumped up and down like a mad man.

"I will have my vengeance on all of them." He yelled to no one in particular.

"At least they've left my horse."

Untying the reins from a sapling he mounted and dug his heels hard into the poor animal's flanks. The startled horse took off at full speed almost spilling Sceleris from the saddle.

* * * * *

Pando was enjoying the run. His long loping strides covering the ground rapidly with Fortis easily maintaining the pace at his side. The moon was almost full giving him a good view of any obstacles ahead. He had taken Caecus's advice and was not running on the main road but through fields and groves of trees just off to the side.

The amulet bounced off his chest with each step. Giving him confidence that he and Fortis would find his cousins.

He thought about the brothers he'd left behind. It saddened him as he thought of Pico and Tactus's tears on their parting.

I'd better think about something else or I'll end up feeling even worse than they do.

His mind wandered as he ran, he thought of things his father had said to him. Then an old saying his father often used popped into his head.

'Gray hair is a sign of age, not wisdom.'

What made me think of that? Am I putting too much faith in what Caecus has said?

I had no doubt when the old prophet asked me to undertake this mission.

Why am I questioning it now? No, I'm sure that Caecus is a man of honour, look at what he did for Kashta. This is the right thing to do. Family is everything.

He was pulled back to the present by Fortis snapping at his tunic.

"What's the matter Fortis? You want to rest?"

The dog let go of the tunic and sat down.

"All right, let's rest, I could do with some water."

Pando took the flask off his shoulder and had a cautious sip.

I'm going to need to conserve this water. There's still a long way to go.

He cupped his hand and poured some into it. Fortis lapped it up gratefully.

The two sat quietly, enjoying the cool night air. It was a good for running, and they were alone, with only the sound of crickets breaking the silence.

* * * * *

Ludus, Viaticus and Corripio sat around the campfire having just finished their evening meal. The brothers leaned against a tree while Corripio lay facing them with his back to the fire so he could warm his backside.

"Ludus, I thought you said that after we escaped there'd be no more pulse?"

"Don't blame that on me. Corripio is the one that said he brought food. How was I to know all that old Sceleris had in the wagon <u>was</u> pulse."

Corripio then spoke up.

"Stop whining you two. Just tell me what you would have eaten tonight if I hadn't come along? Sceleris was so tight with his money he wouldn't waste it on anything more than pulse. At least not for us."

"You mean he had better food for himself?" Asked Viaticus.

"When he entertained his friends, other procurators he was trying to impress. They dined very well, very well indeed."

"Why did he want to impress the other procurators?" Asked Ludus.

"That's a long story."

"We've nothing but time and since there is nothing else to eat please tell it to us Corripio," said Viaticus.

"It happened several years ago. When Sceleris was a very prominent procurator for the gladiatorial games. You know the big ones at the Circus Maximus.

"He owned a slave a very big, strong slave. From Africa, he claimed he was a Prince of the Royal Blood of Nubia or something. A proud man and black, very, very black. As dark as night itself.

"Sceleris paid to have him trained as a gladiator, paid for all the equipment, his armour, his net and his wonderful headdress. He was all gold and black what a wonderful sight."

"Where did Sceleris get this slave from?" asked Ludus.

"He was on a trip to Africa, mostly to capture wild animals for the Circus. Sceleris had heard that there was a lion in the area and when he heard the natives describe him, he just had to have him. The natives had a name for the lion they called him Lisimba.

"He set a trap for him and waited in the jungle. As quiet as a mouse, he waited. And suddenly the trap was sprung but to his surprise he caught a giant black man and not a lion."

Viaticus and Ludus were listening intently, their mouths gaping in awe.

"Don't stop, tell us the rest of it," cried Ludus

"When he opened the net, the giant stood up and instantly grew a set of wings and flew away. And was never seen again."

He howled with laughter and began to dance around the campfire.

Viaticus jumped up and grasped Corripio around his waist and wrestled him to the ground and sat upon his chest.

"Tell us the rest of the story or I'll crush you like an ant."

"Get off me you horse," gasped Corripio.

It was then that Viaticus noticed a collar around Corripio's neck. He had seen it before. From a distance it looked like some kind of necklace, jewelry perhaps. But now up close, it was clearly a collar. He reached out to touch it.

"Leave that alone."

"What is it?"

"What's it look like?"

"A collar."

"It is, so ask no more."

"I can see writing on it Corripio. What's it say?"

"I don't know, I can't read."

"Then let me read it."

"No."

"You are in no position to deny me," said Viaticus.

And with that he held both of Corripio's arms under his legs and pushed his chin up with one hand.

Corripio knew that any struggle with the bigger Viaticus would be futile so he simply yielded and let him read.

"It says, 'This slave has run away from his rightful owner. It is unlawful to harbour or feed him. Return him to: Procurator Sceleris.'"

"Viaticus, we never put such collars on any of our slaves did we?"

"We only have two and they were more like family than slaves," said Viaticus.

"Corripio, I can see why you wanted to stay off main roads. If we are caught in your company we may be considered to be runaways too. Maybe we'll all be returned to Sceleris."

"You could be right Ludus. In any event, as long as Corripio is with us we can't expect to get any help from anyone. I think you and I should go on alone and let Corripio fend for himself."

"Oh please don't do that Viaticus. I've never been without a Master in all my life, someone else has always done my thinking."

"You mean you want me to be your Master?"

"Would that please you?"

"I've never even thought about being anyone's Master. No I don't think it would please me particularly."

"Why don't we just cut his collar off?" suggested Ludus.

"Oh no, you can't do that. It would mean certain death for me."

"Why?"

"Because that is the law. I must keep it on. Sceleris might still kill me if I'm returned, but there is always a chance that he might not. If I return without the collar then he must kill me, that's the law."

"Then I think what I've said is the best course, we must separate. You go your way Corripio and we'll go ours," said Viaticus.

"But you don't know the way." Said Corripio.

"We'll find the way won't we Ludus?"

Ludus nodded but his heart was heavy at leaving Corripio. After all he'd been instrumental in their escape.

* * * * *

Pando removed the amulet from his tunic, as he held it in his hand he could feel the faint pulsing like a tiny heart beat. The inner glow seemed more intense than it had in Caecus's house. He stood and took his bearings from the gem then he replaced the amulet next to his skin, comforted by the faint beating.

"Come Fortis. We've had enough rest we must push on."

Once again he stretched his long legs into any easy trot and settled into the next leg of his journey.

He enjoyed running. This quest would be no hardship for him. He'd run the marathon in many provincial games. This was much the same he thought, just a few more of them.

Fortis was running easily beside him. Neither was aware of what was running along just behind and downwind of them.

Chapter Twelve

Pico awoke with a start.
Was it a dream? Did I really see and hear my parents? Yes, I'm sure of it they're still alive. Caecus showed me, it's true even though he's blind he still can see. I don't understand it but I believe it.

He scrambled out of the makeshift bed and headed into the kitchen. His stomach was rumbling. Maybe there was some of that sweet cake left from last night.

Yes there it is on the table. Nobody will miss a small piece.

Just as he reached for it he got a smack on the top of the head. He turned to see Oratio wagging his finger at him. He quickly returned the cake to the plate.

"I was hungry it was only a small piece after all."

Oratio took him by the shoulder and pushed him towards the door. Once outside he made it clear by his gestures that Pico was to collect firewood so he could cook the morning meal.

Grumbling to himself Pico began foraging for pieces of wood, branches and twigs that lay about, he didn't notice Tactus approach.

"That's a good job for a little boy like you. I doubt you're much good at anything else."

Pico turned and stuck his tongue out at his brother.

"And I suppose since you are so much bigger than me that you have a much more important job is that it?"

"Well Pico I can talk to the animals you know. That's something that you'll never be able to do."

"Talk to the animals? Don't be so foolish. Nobody can do that."

"Well I can, Kashta taught me how."

"I don't believe you."

"Well it's too bad little brother that you have this big job to do or else I'd take you out to the barn and prove it to you. Here comes Oratio looking for his wood, better look lively or you'll get no breakfast."

Pico took the wood he had gathered and ran to Oratio. Oratio shook his head to indicate his dissatisfaction with the quantity. He pointed to a small outcrop of trees, and with rudimentary sign language let him know that he should continue.

Grudgingly, he made his way towards the trees watching Tactus out of the corner of his eye.

It isn't fair. Why is it that I have to be the youngest in the family? I never get to do anything exciting or important. Pando gets to go to Rome, Tactus gets to talk to the animals and I have to gather firewood, it's just not fair.

As he entered the wooded area he caught sight of Caecus standing quietly beside one of the trees. Pico was startled when Caecus asked.

"What's wrong Pico? I assumed that you'd be happy seeing your parents last evening."

"How did you know I was here Caecus?"

"Being blind does not mean I'm unaware Pico. I sense that you are unhappy, what is it?"

"Just being the youngest I guess. I'm always told I'm too little to do this or too young to do that."

"Ah I see. You think that the task given you by Oratio is beneath you is that it?"

"Not just that but that's part of it."

"That and missing your parents as well." He sighed and then said.

"Pico in life we must learn to overcome our disappointments. Take Oratio as an example, he has much more to overcome than you and yet he goes about his duties without complaint."

I must to agree that nothing has happened to me that's as bad as that. But still surely there must be more to look forward to than I can see now.

"I see you agree with me Pico and yes there will be more in store for you than you can see today. But patience is required, a virtue that the young seldom have."

Pico was surprised that the old man appeared to be able to read his thoughts.

I'll have to be more careful about what I'm thinking.

"Caecus could you teach me how to see the future?"

Caecus chuckled.

"Boy that is not possible for me to do. The Goddess Athena gave this skill to me. Only the gods can bestow such a gift, not a mere mortal like me."

"But Kashta taught Tactus how to speak to the animals."

"Yes so I understand. But that gift is of a different order than seeing future events."

Dejected, Pico bent to his task of collecting firewood and said no more. As he was about to head back to the farmhouse the old man said.

"Do not despair Pico for there is much other magic to learn if you are prepared to apply yourself."

"Oh Caecus, I'll do anything you ask of me."

* * * * *

Tactus stood outside Fortitudo's stall and held out the apple so that the horse could grasp it without nipping his hand. When the horse had finished his treat the boy gazed intently into the soft brown eyes. Could he do it again without Kashta being present?

Then it happened, the words were not spoken but Tactus heard them in his head nonetheless. It was clear, the horse has said

--Thank you.

He in turn said, in his head.

--You're welcome.

The big horse bobbed his head as if to acknowledge the words.

I can do it. It's remarkable. I wonder what stories Fortitudo might tell.

And once again the boy sensed the horse say to him.

--Oh I have many stories I could tell you 'little toad'.

Tactus responded.

--My name is not 'little toad'.

--But I heard Kashta call you that once.

--Yes you did, but my real name is Tactus.

--That may be so but I prefer 'little toad'.

--Whatever. As long as we can talk and you'll tell me your story.

Before Fortitudo could begin, Tactus heard another voice intruding in his head. It asked.

--And where is my treat?

Tactus turned and saw that the only other thing in the barn was Hector the goat.

--I said where is my treat? You gave Fortitudo an apple why have you brought nothing for me?

It <u>was</u> Hector. Tactus had brought an apple for himself but to keep peace in the barn he gave it the goat. The boy waited for a thank you but heard nothing.

--Don't mind him 'little toad', he has no manners at all.

The goat's beard jiggled up and down as he consumed the apple. Then Tactus heard.

--Mind your business you overgrown mule. It's bad enough having to share space with you and to endure your constant passing of wind. I really have no interest in hearing about your supposed exploits yet again.

Tactus felt it necessary to respond.

--Hector you are very rude and as for passing wind, you smell bad without having even that as an excuse. If you want any more treats I would suggest a little more in the way of manners or you'll go without.

--Thank you 'little toad'. Now where was I?

--You were about to tell me your story, I'd like to know how you come to be with Kashta.

--Ah yes. That was some time ago, let's see. I was in the Legion then and proud I was too. My master was a Centurion, and I led the column. Oh the banners and the trumpets we were a glorious sight.

Just then there was loud crash as Hector kicked at Fortitudo's stall.

--Enough, it's getting so thick in here I can't stand it. I'm going out to seek fresh air.

--Good riddance.

--Please Fortitudo, go on with your story.

--Yes, as I said I was once a member of the Legion and fought with my master in many battles. I was proud to have been with Julius Caesar's own Legion. What I wouldn't have given to be the great man's mount. Not that there was anything wrong with my master you understand. But it would have been such a great honour.

--How many battles were you in?

--Too many to count.

Tactus was beginning to get the impression that maybe Hector had been right about the stories, but he persevered.

--But how did you and Kashta meet?

--It was much later but before the great Caesar was murdered. My master and I were at the games in the Circus Maximus. It was at those very games that Kashta and I met. He was a gladiator who was to fight a great African Lion.

--Lisimba?

--You've heard this story? Asked Fortitudo, his disappointment evident.

--Kashta told me about the games, but not about you.

--I can't believe he didn't speak to you about me. Are you sure he told you about the games?

--Yes but please go on.

--Well, as you probably know that's how Kashta lost his arm and you must also know that the great Caesar freed Kashta. But that wasn't all he did.

--What else did he do?

--He gave a gift to Kashta for his courage.

--And what was that gift?

Tactus was getting a little frustrated. Why couldn't Fortitudo just tell the story without all these pauses? No wonder Hector gets annoyed.

--The gift was me of course. Caesar gave me to Kashta and I carried the wounded Kashta from the Circus to here, where Caecus nursed him back to health.

--That's a great story Fortitudo.

--Would you like to hear another?

--Maybe later, I'm sure that breakfast is ready and don't want Oratio to get angry with me.

Chapter Thirteen

"Are you sure we going in the right direction to get to Perusia Viaticus?"

"Why do you always doubt me?"

"I just wonder if there was any truth to what Corripio told us. You know, how people go in circles when they're lost. It seems to me that some of this countryside looks familiar. That's all."

Viaticus was not at all sure he knew where he was going and it didn't help having his younger brother cast doubts on his ability as a navigator.

"There's something else bothering me Viaticus."

"And what's that?"

"The way we treated Corripio. After all he's the one that made it possible for us to escape. He's the one marked as a slave not us. We cast him out without a second thought."

"You're too soft hearted Ludus. By allowing him to travel with us we were giving him aid, you know that's against the law."

"Tell me, is it because you don't think a slave's life is worth as much as ours?" asked Ludus.

Angered now Viaticus responded.

"Have you ever seen me treat our own slaves with anything other than kindness and respect? What's come over you Ludus?"

"I just feel badly. It's like we've left him to die. Shouldn't we go back for him?"

Viaticus's shoulders sagged as he said.

"If it's any comfort to you, I feel badly too and as for going back for him I don't think that is going to be necessary."

"Why not?"

"Because I sense he's been following us."

"He has?"

"Don't look around, I may be wrong. You stay here; I'm going to circle back. I think he's hiding in the bushes. Let me see if I can surprise him."

Viaticus crept with his big body as close to the ground as he could. He hoped the long grass would shield him from view.

But, if it wasn't Corripio who could it be? He was sure it wasn't Sceleris, why would he hide his presence? He'd simply ride up on horseback and capture them again.

As he got closer he could see an outline, not Sceleris too small for that, but maybe Corripio. He could almost reach out and touch the individual but instead he let out a mighty roar and jumped upon the smaller person.

Ludus heard the commotion and came running.

""Have you caught him?"

Viaticus was unable to answer his brother. He was too busy wrestling whoever it was. They rolled about on the ground creating so much dust that Ludus couldn't make out who was who.

Then there was a great scream. It was Viaticus.

"He bit me."

The scuffle seemed to be getting more intense Ludus had no option but to help. He jumped on top of both fighters and received a blow to his left eye that brought stars as well as tears to his eyes. He managed to get his arms around the waist of Viaticus's attacker and tried to pull him off. Receiving a vigorous kick to his shins for his effort.

Between he and Viaticus they succeeded in turning their attacker on his back with Viaticus sitting on top, straddling him.

The stronger pair prevailed and the stranger conceded and lay motionless on the ground. As the dust cleared it soon became obvious that the assailant was not Corripio. But who was it?

Viaticus leaned forward and shouted into the face of the intruder.

"Who are you and why are you following us?"

"My name is my business and I wasn't following you. Now get off me you big oaf."

"Not until you tell me why you were skulking in the bushes behind us."

"I wasn't skulking. What is it? You think you own this territory? I'm free to wander where I please. Let me up."

It seemed to Viaticus that he was not much more than a boy and very slight at that. He had to admit that for such a small person he'd put up quite a fight.

"I'll let you up but no more fighting. Do you understand?"

"I didn't start it remember and if there hadn't been two of you I'd have boxed your ears."

"Do you promise?"

"Yes, now let me up you horse."

Ludus was holding his eye, watching warily as Viaticus let this little whirlwind get up off the ground. He knew that his eye would likely swell shut and be discoloured for a week. He was relieved that there was no one he would have to explain it to.

"What's a young boy like you doing out here all alone?" Asked Viaticus.

"First, I'm not a young boy and second, what business is that of yours?"

"If you aren't a young boy then just what are you, a wizened old man?"

The eyes blazed and the person stood facing Viaticus with both hands on hips and feet spread wide apart.

"I'm a girl and you're a horse's backside for not noticing."

Ludus felt even worse about his black eye.

Viaticus's mouth hung open and he repeated.

"You're a girl?"

"Yes and proud of it." Her chin jutted forward in defiance.

Ludus spoke.

"But you shouldn't be out here alone. Something might happen to you."

"Yes like running into the likes of you. I can take care of myself."

"Perhaps you can, but can we make peace now? What's your name? I'm Viaticus and this is my brother Ludus. We're making our way to Perusia, we live in Rome and we're on our way to visit relatives."

She looked suspiciously at both of them. She was still standing in her defiant pose, but she had obviously decided they were no immediate threat.

"My name is Lucia and I'm from nowhere in particular and going to another nowhere."

"It isn't safe for you to be out here alone. There are evil men that could do you harm," Ludus said.

"Who said I was out here alone? And even if I was, I know how to take care of myself, I've been doing that for a long time."

Ludus continued.

"If you're not alone then who's here with you?"

There was a rustling in the trees behind them. Viaticus turned to face the threat. The branches parted and Corripio strolled towards them.

"Well gentlemen, we meet again. Such a surprise don't you think?"

"How long have you been following us? And what have you got to do with this young girl here?" asked Viaticus.

"That's not a very nice welcome, particularly after what I've done for you two."

Lucia was nodding her head in agreement as Corripio continued.

"Frankly, I don't think the two of you were making very much headway in your trip to Perusia, the direction you have been heading is much more likely to land you in the ocean.

"Many believe that there is safety in numbers. Don't you agree we'd be better off if we all traveled together?"

If the truth were to be known both Viaticus and Ludus were glad to see Corripio. Lucia however was another matter.

"How did you meet Lucia, Corripio?"

"Almost the same as you did although I must say that I didn't jump on her and try to beat her up."

"No, he was much more of a gentleman than you two."

"Corripio you know better than anyone the dangers you face having escaped from your master. And the trouble others could be in if they help you. That's why we separated from you," said Ludus

"Not very brave, the two of you." Lucia said.

Viaticus and Ludus hung their heads, she spoke the truth and they knew it.

"Why don't we let bygones be bygones and join up as a happy band of travelers that are prepared to share what we have and to help one another," said Corripio

Viaticus and Ludus looked at one another and silently agreed with Corripio's proposition. The older brother asked the question that had been on his mind since earlier in the morning.

"Corripio, do you have anything to eat? I'm starving."

Corripio laughed and said.

"Nothing changes including Viaticus's appetite. Yes I have your favourite, Pulse. But there is an additional benefit to joining up with Lucia; she is an excellent forager. She knows all of the edible plants that grow locally. She can find bird's eggs and all sorts of succulent tidbits. Why don't you and your brother gather some wood for a fire and I'll get some water from the stream.

"And if we ask her nicely, perhaps Lucia can find something to enhance our meal. After we have all eaten our fill, maybe Lucia might be persuaded to tell us her story."

Chapter Fourteen

The sinister figure stood in the shadow of the trees, watching the boy and the dog. It was the first rest they had taken since he had begun following them. He was glad that they stopped. He was beginning to tire himself.

As he followed them he was careful to avoid giving the dog any scent. Even now he positioned himself so that, what little breeze there was, carried his scent away from the two sleeping below him.

Caecus is up to something. Why did he bring three boys to his house? And why send this one on the road? He has to be heading to Rome. But why?

He must be carrying something, perhaps a message. But to whom and what does it say?

Somehow I must deal with the dog, separate him from the boy. But how can I do that?

Then he saw the dog rouse from sleep and lazily head out into the forest. He couldn't believe his good luck.

Now is my chance. I must find out what is so important that it has this boy running so hard.

He removed his sword from it's sheath, the sharp edge caught the moonlight. Silently he stole down the small hill towards Pando.

Good, he's sound asleep, he never heard a thing. I think it would be simplest to kill him as he sleeps and then search his body. I could do it quickly and be out of here before the dog returns.

But wait, what if he has nothing on his body? What if he has it committed to memory? Then it will be lost forever. No I must awaken him and then search him, if I find nothing then perhaps a little persuasion could convince him to talk.

He knelt beside the sleeping figure. The boy was on his back making it easy to clamp his hand over Pando's mouth and bring the sword point to his throat.

"Make not a sound boy or you die."

Pando looked up at the hooded figure crouched over him. Unable to see the face he smelled the putrid breath. His heart pounded and terror seized him.

Where is Fortis? Why has he deserted me?

"Boy, I must ask you some questions. I will uncover your mouth so you can answer but if you scream or shout you are finished. Do you understand me?"

To accentuate the statement he pressed the sword deeper into Pando's throat. Deep enough to draw a drop of blood but not deep enough to cause a wound.

"If you understand what I've said, blink your eyes else your eyes will see nothing more, ever."

Pando blinked.

Slowly the hand was withdrawn. The boy remained quiet, the sword still at his throat.

"What is your business and why is it so important that you must run?"

Another jab of the sword tip.

"I'm on my way to see my relatives in Rome."

"You're lying. Why would you run so hard just to see your relatives and why do you run at night?"

"I like to run, I run the marathon at the games every year. As for running at night, I do so because it's cooler and I have fewer leg cramps."

"You will have to do better than that. You make this seem like just a social visit to relatives when in fact you run with a sense of urgency that tells me you lie."

"I'm not lying, I'm telling you the truth."

"Tell me why Caecus has sent you on this mission and just what it is he wants you to do?"

"How do you know Caecus?"

"Shut up and answer me."

"I just met Caecus. He was good enough to give me food and water. He gave me no mission." Pando lied.

The man rose to his feet, the sword still at Pando's throat. He was a big man, Pando had not realized just how big until he stood up.

"Get to your feet and don't try anything."

Pando got up, there was no way that he could overpower this stranger.

"Take off your clothes."

"What?"

"You heard me take off your clothes."

Pando hesitated and got another poke with the point of the sword. He complied.

He stood in only his loincloth, facing the stranger. He hoped not to have to remove anything more.

"What's that hanging around your neck?"

Pando was aware that the amulet was glowing in the dark and he could feel the faint beating as it pressed against his chest.

He thought quickly and answered.

"A gift, a gift from my mother. A lucky charm you might say."

"Well it hasn't brought you much luck today now has it?"

The man was reaching for the amulet when it happened. Like a bolt of lightning from his left, it struck him. The force knocked him to the ground and sent his sword skittering across the grass.

A great roar came from the huge black beast. Pando could see the savage look in the great red rimmed eyes and the large sharp canine teeth as the jaws opened.

When they closed it was on the neck of the stranger.

Pando closed his eyes not wanting to see the carnage. He heard what seemed like a clap of thunder accompanied by the smell of smoke. Then it suddenly became quiet.

He slowly opened his eyes and saw, to his surprise, that the stranger was gone. Only the clothes he wore lay on the spot where he had stood.

Pando was transfixed unable to move.

What is this animal? Could it be a bear? The large head is swiveling in my direction, am I next?

But as Pando watched a transformation began slowly at first but then more rapidly. The shape was changing.

What is it?

He couldn't believe it. The animal was becoming smaller. Shrinking in size right before his eyes and the face, it was changing.

The face was Fortis.

Chapter Fifteen

The four of them sat around the campfire their appetites satisfied for the moment. Viaticus was surprised by the food that Lucia had been able to provide as though by some kind of magic. Neither he nor his brother had ever had mushrooms before nor had either ever heard of a weed that tasted like onions. She had even been able to find some kind of bird's eggs and made a refreshing brew with the root of a plant that he had never seen before.

He was also surprised at the utensils she had in the bag she always carried with her.

No question the meal was much better than having to eat pulse again he thought. He was impressed enough that he said.

"Thank you Lucia, I can't remember when I've enjoyed a meal so much."

She was startled by his comment; it was obvious that she was unused to such compliments. She turned her head away from him as though embarrassed by the attention.

Viaticus found her reaction strange but said nothing more. It was then that Corripio spoke.

"Lucia tell us how you come to be out here and on your own at such a tender age? Surely you cannot be more that 12 or 13?"

She poured herself more of the brew from the simmering pot and sat back as though considering whether or not she would answer the question. Instead she responded with a question of her own.

"Corripio I would like to know how you came to have Sceleris for a Master?"

"It is a story I'd sooner forget but I suppose it's only fair that I tell it.

"I regret the day I ever met Sceleris lying by the side of the road. There was so much blood I thought he was dead. All I wanted to do was see if the dead man might have anything of value upon his body. I could see no sense of it going to waste should that be the case.

"But when I turned him over and saw his face I vomited straight away. It was awful. One eye torn completely away leaving only the bloody socket, the skin on other side of his face was sliced to ribbons.

"It was then that a weak voice pleaded for help through lips that were beginning to bleed again as he tried vainly to speak. What was I to do? I know now what I should have done. I should have run away from that place straightaway.

"But no I could not. I was compelled by some force to stay and help this terrible remnant of a man.

"I built a makeshift shelter and ministered to him for many days. It was fortunate that I had worked in the service of a Greek physician. He taught me how to mix many remedies.

"The Greek had been attached to a Roman Legion, as his slave he taught me how to tend the wounds of soldiers. Therefore I knew how to treat Sceleris's injuries. There was nothing I could do for the lost eye, but I managed to stitch up the gaping wounds and applied tinctures.

"Gradually he recovered and with his recovery his strength grew and I must say so did his bad disposition.

"Instead of gratitude for what I had achieved I got nothing but criticism for what I had done to his face.

"I should have left him earlier but I could not for I had nowhere to go. My Greek Physician was dead, killed in a battle. I was now a slave without a master. I made the mistake of telling that story to Sceleris he laughed and said.

"Nothing to worry about Corripio, I will find you a place. After all, I'm a Procurator, fully qualified to transfer and sell slaves. Just leave it to me, I'll find you a place. Mind you, you're old and somewhat feeble and not likely to attract much of a price.

"The he stroked the stubble of his new beard and said.

"I have a better idea. I'll buy you myself. Yes that's it. You're now my slave with all the security that that provides.

"He laughed a great laugh and I shivered. I hate that man.

"It seems the story of my life that I do a good deed for someone and invariably it works to my disadvantage. Well, that's not going to happen with Viaticus and Ludus. Is it?"

Lucia sat silently, wrapped in her own thoughts.

Why is it I seem to know something of this? Of Corripio and the Greek, a fragment, a brief glimpse, as though I know this story.

"Lucia, it's time for your story now," said Corripio.

Pulled back to the present, she said.

"Perhaps these two might want to tell me what brings them this way? Particularly the big oaf who sat on me and almost broke me in two."

Viaticus blushed a little and said.

"I'm sorry if I hurt you, but I had no way of knowing that you were a girl."

"What's being a girl got to do with it? It never stopped my brothers or my father, for that matter, from hitting me."

"They beat you?" Ludus asked.

"Don't all parents?"

"Not ours, ours is a loving family. Neither one of us has ever been struck by our father and certainly not by our mother."

Lucia looked at them both the disbelief evident in her face and said.

"If the family is so loving then why were you abandoned?"

"We weren't abandoned, we were separated from our parents," said Viaticus.

"Separated, abandoned what's the difference? You're just splitting hairs. They didn't want you anymore or couldn't afford to feed you. That's the truth isn't it?"

Ludus jumped to his feet and yelled in anger.

"That's not true, my father is a prominent member of the community, we live well in our own villa. We have slaves and horses, we are not poor."

Lucia's eyes narrowed as she said.

"You say that like it's something to be proud of."

"What? That we are not poor."

"No fool, that you own slaves. Do you really think that owning another person is anything to be proud of?"

"All I meant was, that it is a measure of wealth that's all."

"That's all? She shouted.

Ludus sat back down in the face of this pepper pot's tirade as she continued.

"You two have lived all your lives in privilege and now that you are on your own you can't survive without someone looking after you. You cast Corripio out because he is a slave and yet without him you are two lost souls. Tell me why anyone should waste their time helping you?"

Corripio now interrupted.

"Lucia, calm down. These boys don't know any better. I don't see them as our enemy nor should you. If we don't teach them then how would you expect them to be aware of what is happening around them?"

She poured herself some more of the hot liquid and held the cup between her hands, thinking about what Corripio had just said. After a moment she spoke.

"Perhaps you are right Corripio, their ignorance is not their fault. I will tell them my story not to evoke sympathy but merely to educate these two dolts so that they do not continue unaware of the world around them.

"I come from a family of nine. I have five brothers and three sisters. I am the eldest of the group. My father is without a trade and as you can see my mother has no time to do other than look after the children.

"My father also drinks too much. This means that the meager amount of money he makes is further diminished by his habit. The children who are old enough are forced to forage for food or worse yet, beg for it.

"There is no money for tutors so no one is educated, no one can read and certainly no one can write. Each one of the nine is condemned to the same life as our parents, that of misery and want.

"What choices do my parents have? Very few and those that are available are distasteful. The most common choice is to sell some of their children into slavery. They make a bit of money on the sale and then there will be one less mouth to feed.

"But what to do if the child in question is unsuitable for life as a slave? What if it is sickly?

"You may already know the answer to that. Just simply abandon them, in the street or out on a country road. Leave them to die.

"Well in my case, I think you know what my parent's preference was going to be. I am not sick or crippled so I could look forward to being sold into slavery.

"Instead, I packed a few things and left my family home, such as it was. I vowed that I would never be anyone's slave. I was born free and free I will stay."

When she finished speaking silence enveloped the small group each seemed to be reflecting on what had been said.

Both Viaticus and Ludus were even more acutely aware of just how much they missed both their family and the comfort of their previous life. They wondered if they would ever see their home again.

* * * * *

Pando looked at the pile of clothes. There was no trace of any body just the clothes. The clothes confirmed that what had just taken place was not a dream.

Fortis nuzzled his hand; he withdrew it as though he'd been burned. What kind of beast is this? Looking into the dog's eyes only confused him.

How could this animal suddenly become so savage? This can't be the same beast he doesn't even look the same except for the colour of his fur. But, there are the clothes. It wasn't a dream and the nick in my throat that's real too.

Who was the man? And why was he following me? Caecus said nothing about the possibility I would be followed.

He looked around the area trying to see if anyone else was there but saw no one.

Fortis kept pushing at Pando's legs more insistently now. Pando bent down and took the dog's head in his hands and looked directly into the eyes.

No, not the eyes of a killer he thought. Then the long tongue darted out and licked Pando's nose and in spite of what had happened, Pando began to laugh.

Fortis pushed him again, with even more force.

"What is it boy? Are you telling me it's time to leave? I think you're right, I don't want to stay here any longer."

He put on his clothes and then withdrew the amulet from his tunic. As he held it he could feel his confidence return, he was comforted by the gem. Taking his bearing from the amulet he picked up the packet of remaining food and began a steady jog away from this place Fortis keeping pace at his side.

He ran easily and it wasn't long before his mind began to wander, back to his home and family. Would they ever be a family again? Then he could feel the pulsing of the jewel that lay on his chest, like another heart beat.

Yes, the heart beat of my family. We will all be together again I know it.

* * * *

Pico lay alongside Tactus neither was yet asleep.

"Tactus, are you awake?"

"No, I'm sound asleep. Why are you bothering me?"

"There's something I didn't tell you."

"About what?

"I saw mother and father last night."

"You lie. You were here last night. Why do you try to trick me? Is it because I can talk to animals and you can't?"

"I'm not lying, I did see them. And as far as you talking to animals I think that's a lie, so there."

"You are such a little child Pico. I don't tell lies. You're just jealous of me."

"No seriously Tactus I did see them."

"Where?"

How do I explain what had happened? Tactus will think I'm telling another lie only an even bigger one than he thought.

"Are you going to tell me or are you going to confess that you're telling lies?"

Pico began slowly and told the whole story to Tactus and when he had finished he asked.

"What do you think of that Tactus?"

"You don't really expect me to believe a story like that do you? You say you saw our parents in Caecus's eyeballs. Pish."

"It's true Tactus, why won't you believe me?"

Tactus smacked him in the head with a pillow and said.

"Go to sleep and dream something else up."

Anger burned within Pico. Why did no one ever listen to him? This was the curse of being the last born.

Chapter Sixteen

Pando was happy he had found a well on his journey, it was fortunate that dawn had broken otherwise he might have run right into it in the dark.

That would've been all I needed. Fall down a well with no one around. Not even Fortis could've helped me.

The cold water was refreshing. He was careful not to take too much at once. No need to get a bellyache he thought. Then he doused himself with water shaking the droplets out of his dark hair.

Fortis began pushing at his leg.

"Sorry Fortis, I guess you're pretty thirsty too."

He cupped his hands and dipped water from the well. The dog lapped it up eagerly his long tongue tickling Pando's palms as he did so.

He was getting tired from the exertion of his run, as well from the lack of sleep the night before. He tried to push the images out of his mind but it was impossible.

Chances are the man would've killed me even if I had told him of the mission.

The beast saved my life I'm sure of that but still, it was terrible. Why was the man after me? Surely not just because I'm trying to reach my cousins. What is there that Caecus didn't tell me?

He shook his legs to loosen up his muscles and was about to start to run again when he looked up into the cloudless blue sky and saw a bird circling overhead.

Get a grip. It's just a bird. There's nothing to fear. I must press on I've got two more hours before the heat of the day. Then I'll find a shady spot under tree and take my rest.

"Come on Fortis, let's get back on our journey."

The black dog fell in beside Pando, tail wagging and his tongue lolling out of the side of his mouth. Neither of them took any notice of the fact that the strange bird had broken off it's circling flight pattern and was now following them.

* * * *

Pico kicked at the stones in the farmyard, he was still angry with Tactus for not believing him. He noticed Oratio waving to him from the door of the farmhouse.

What does he want now? Probably wants me to peel potatoes or something like that. Might as well go and see what it is, I'm bored anyway.

Why is it that I'm the only one that doesn't get anything exciting to do? How long am I going to be the youngest? Forever I guess.

What's the point in trying to ask any questions of Oratio? He can't answer me anyway. I wonder what happened to his tongue? Maybe Caecus could tell me. Yes but he probably won't.

Pico stood looking at Oratio as he made gestures in an effort to tell the boy what he wanted of him. At first he couldn't understand the meaning of the body gyrations and facial expressions that Oratio was making.

Then almost as if a veil of misunderstanding was lifted, Pico could make out what Oratio was telling him. All without speaking a word.

"You're saying that you heard me telling Tactus about seeing my parents?"

Oratio nodded and added more visual signals all intended to carry on this strange form of conversation.

"Do I understand that you are saying that you believe me?"

Again, a nod from the mute.

How can this be? Somehow we're having a real conversation and he says he believes me. A smile spread over Pico's face and he asked.

"How did you learn to do this? I mean talk without saying the words."

Oratio moved his body, his arms his legs and the expression on his face all in an effort to communicate. But this time, Pico did not grasp the meaning. He shook his head.

Oratio then mouthed the word in an exaggerated fashion. Pico stared at the small man's lips and he repeated the word.

"Actor? Are you saying that you are an actor or were an actor?"

Again the head bobbed acknowledging Pico's understanding. The boy clapped his hands together and said.

"My father once took me to see a play. It was wonderful the actor could make you understand without saying a word it was like magic."

Oratio smiled broadly this was followed by more gestures.

"You were an actor in a Play? How wonderful, it must have been very exciting."

More movement, what's he saying?

"But it wasn't magic. Is that what you said?"

He nodded once more and then began to move like an old man. One carrying a staff, a blind man.

"You're talking about Caecus aren't you?"

Oratio was dancing with glee now he was almost as excited, as the boy was, at being able to converse with him.

"You say that Caecus is magic. No that's not right. You said Caecus has magic that's it isn't it?"

Another nod.

"If he has magic then why hasn't he made you able to speak."

All of the physical exertion on the part of Oratio was beginning to tell on him. He flopped to the ground and indicated to Pico that he had to rest.

But the last thing Pico wanted was to rest. This whole thing was as much a game to him as anything else. The boy continued to pepper him with questions but Oratio didn't respond. Then Pico asked the one question that he'd been wondering about ever since he met Oratio.

"Oratio, will you tell me what happened to your tongue? You weren't born that way were you?"

The little man's eyes flashed for an instant. Pico knew that he had asked a question he shouldn't have but he couldn't take it back now. He waited, would Oratio tell him?

Pico looked into the face sitting opposite him and knew instantly he would receive no answer.

"You're saying that the tale is too sad to tell. I'm sorry Oratio, I didn't mean to hurt you by asking."

Chapter Seventeen

They broke camp before sunrise and began their trek towards Perusia with Corripio taking the lead. Lucia was next, followed by Ludus and Viaticus. Neither of the two boys had slept well the previous night, they whispered to each other until Lucia had thrown a pot at them and demanded they be quiet.

Ludus was sure that Sceleris might capture them in their sleep, he was positive someone was lurking out there in the dark. His concern unnerved Viaticus too and as a result what little sleep they did get left them weary and did nothing to refresh them.

It had been Lucia's decision that they should not eat before moving on. She felt the need to keep the advantage of the distance between them and their pursuer as great as possible.

Corripio seemed full of vigour as he strutted easily in front of the small group. In fact he felt so good that he began to whistle. This was quickly terminated with a blow to the back of his head from Lucia.

"Don't be so stupid. We have enough trouble on our hands without signaling our exact location to those following us," she said.

"And just who made you the leader of this expedition?" Corripio asked.

"I did. So close your mouth and march."

He did as he was told; after all he had spent years learning to be an obedient slave. Why change now?

Viaticus's stomach began to rumble. While dinner the night before had been tasty it did not provide the bulk of his normal meal. He was so hungry that even the thought of the dreaded pulse was beginning to appeal to him.

"When are we going to stop to eat?" he asked.

Without braking stride Lucia reached to her left and pulled from the bushes some kind of plant.

"We're not stopping. Here eat this, it'll help stop your hunger pangs."

Viaticus looked at it, there were a few small green berries surrounded by a cluster of shiny green leaves. He was unsure of just exactly what he was supposed to eat. He picked at the berries just as Lucia said.

"Don't eat the berries, they'll give you diarrhea and I don't think I saw you with a change of clothes. Just eat the leaves and chew on the bark of the branch,"

He flung the berries to the ground. This is some breakfast he thought. He pulled off a few leaves and began to chew them. At first there was little taste and then his mouth began to burn. It was like a fire within his mouth. He threw the branch to the ground and yelled at Lucia.

"Are you trying to make a fool of me?"

"No, you seem entirely capable of doing that for yourself."

"Why is it you dislike me?"

"I never said I didn't like you. But one does get tired of your whining about food."

Viaticus was not just angry because of the trick she played. He was also angry that she considered him to be a whiner. Then Lucia asked.

"Tell me Viaticus, are you still hungry?"

He thought for moment and said.

"No, after that terrible stuff you gave me who could be hungry?"

"So then, it worked just as I said."

Ludus smiled to himself, he knew better than to make a comment. After all, his brother was more than a foot taller.

They trudged on without further comment until they came to a small stream. She held up her hand and signaled them to take a rest.

"Have a drink and fill up any containers you have."

Then she pulled out a small package from her bag. She carefully unwrapped the package and broke the contents into 4 equal pieces handing a one to each of them.

It was dense sweet cake of some kind, delicious but dry enough that they each had to wash it down with cold water of the stream.

"The water will cause the cake to swell up in your stomach so that even Viaticus won't be hungry for several hours."

He ignored her. The cake was good; he wondered how she came to have it. He hadn't seen her make it.

She must have brought it with her.

When they had finished Lucia stood and said.

"Corripio, I will lead from this point. You will follow me out to the middle of the stream and we will walk single file. That way we will leave no trail. When I decide that there is a place to leave the stream we will do so. But not until I'm sure that when we leave the stream it will be onto solid rock. Our trail will seem to disappear right here."

With no further comment she waded out into the stream and began walking against the current. The other three fell in behind her.

The water was extremely cold their sandals offered little warmth against the water. They trudged along no one speaking, just the splash of foot in water.

Viaticus's feet were numb but he made no comment, he was still stinging for having been branded a whiner by Lucia. He gritted his teeth and plowed on.

* * * * *

Pando was beginning to experience a pain in his side it was like a 'stitch' he'd experienced it many times in races before. He had 'run through it' at least once today. But he knew he would have to stop for rest soon. The lack of sleep the previous night was beginning to tell on his ability to run.

Even Fortis was starting to tire.

Up ahead, there's a shade tree. We can stop and rest there.

He laboured up the incline, his lungs burning. He dropped to his knees once he'd reached the shade.

He stretched out on his back and placed his arm over his eyes to shelter his face from the midday sun. In an instant he was fast asleep.

He fell asleep so quickly in fact that he failed to see the bird circling high overhead. A huge bird, its wings barely moving soaring on the warm air currents. Silent, moving closer now.

Fortis had moved a little distance from Pando as if to escape the heat of the boy's body. He too had fallen asleep very quickly, the bird unnoticed by him as well.

The bird looked down at the sleeping pair and made another wider circle as though looking for any other presence. It was low enough now that had Pando been awake he would have determined what kind of bird it was.

The ugliness was unmistakable; a long wrinkled neck with loose folds of flesh hanging from it. A beak, long and hooked, a dirty yellow colour with gaping black nasal cavities.

The legs were powerful with long crescent shaped talons that looked like they could slice it's prey with one swipe. Huge black wings with splayed feathers at the tips. So large that this bird could have carried away a whole sheep.

It was a vulture, the 'bird of death' the locals called it.

It turned, another lazy circle, losing altitude purposely, getting closer to it's prey. Then the bright shiny black eyes saw it.

Saw the amulet on Pando's neck. Shining in the sunlight, the tunic no longer concealing the jewel. Slowly the buzzard circled again coming even lower this time, it drifted up the incline against the wind so that Fortis would not get his scent.

The huge wings pulled forward stopping the forward flight and the bird settled on the grass not 15 feet from Pando and silently moved towards him.

Then in a flash he pounced on Pando's chest pinning both his arms just below the shoulders with the great talons. Before Pando could cry out the bird grasped the Lapis Lazuli in it's beak and pulled both it and the golden chain from his neck.

Then with a great thrust of the black wings it swiftly rose into the air, the jewel dangling from it's beak.

Pando cried out waking Fortis. The boy was in great distress; he'd lost the amulet. What could he do? He put his hands over his face and tried to hold back the tears. He'd failed, failed his cousins, and failed Caecus.

Then there was that noise.

"Fortis, what's wrong?"

The dog was in some kind of contorted position, the back was arched, and his neck was extending. Fortis was somehow transforming right before his eyes.

What's happening? The dog is changing shape. But what is it?

Then he saw. It was a great eagle, golden in colour, shiny plumage and glittering yellow eyes. With a beat of it's wings that sounded like thunder it rose into the air in pursuit of the vulture. The great wings of the vulture were no match for the power of the great golden eagle. The distance between them was closing fast.

Pando watched in intense fascination as the buzzard tried to outrun the great eagle.

What if the vulture drops the amulet? We'll never find it again.

As the eagle seemed prepared to dive for the attack, the big bird swerved and avoided what seemed inevitable. Pando could see the amulet catch the sun as the vulture tried to escape. He hoped against hope that the eagle could somehow get the amulet away from the other bird.

The eagle rose up high in the sky, it was obvious now that he intended to attack from above. There was no question that the eagle had the speed and power not possessed by the vulture. Surely he'll win out hoped Pando.

The eagle's talons sank into the back of the vulture; the shock of the impact sent them both tumbling in the air. Fortunately they have enough altitude thought Pando, maybe there's still a chance. But then he saw the amulet fall towards earth. Shaken loose from the beak of the vulture by the impact.

The eagle let the vulture loose and it continued it's fall, fluttering as though injured.

The great golden eagle beat it's wings in an effort to speed towards the ground and with a great swoop managed to catch the amulet before it reached the treetops.

Pando could almost feel the force of the air displaced by the wings as the great bird once again gained altitude.

He had lost sight of the other bird as it crashed through the trees, if not dead then badly injured.

The eagle circled and landed near him. Pando walked to the bird and saw the amulet lying at his feet. He held it and saw that it was still functioning, putting it on, he could feel it pulse against his chest.

He was so preoccupied with the recovery that when he looked up the eagle was gone and Fortis stood in his place, his tail wagging and his tongue lolling as usual.

Chapter Eighteen

The sun was beginning to set as Lucia, Corripio, Viaticus and Ludus finally clambered out of the water on to a large flat rock. While nothing had been said for fear of being accused of being a whiner, Viaticus was sure that everyone's feet must have felt like blocks of ice as did his. He resisted the urge to sit down take off his sandals and rub his feet.

He was surprised to see Lucia do just that as she said.

"Rub your feet and get the blood flowing. We can rest for only a short while, we must make camp before we lose the light."

Ludus's feet ached but like his brother he kept his thoughts to himself.

Lucia is so bossy, how did she get to be the leader?

His thoughts were interrupted as Lucia said.

"Let's move on, I don't like the looks of that cloud formation over there. We're going to need to build a shelter. There'll be no sleeping under the stars tonight.

"Follow me, do you see the gravel and rocks at the far end? Stay on that path; don't walk on any grassy areas until I tell you that it's all right. There must be no tracks.

"Now, let's go."

They moved silently, exhaustion becoming more apparent with each step. The light was slowly slipping away, surely they'd have to stop soon thought Viaticus.

After what seemed like an eternity Lucia finally said.

"Over there, see that rise and the clearing on top? That's where we'll camp tonight."

Corripio and the two boys collapsed to the ground when they had reached it.

"Get up you oafs. Didn't I tell you we have to make a shelter? Corripio, you and Viaticus find some branches; they must be large enough for poles and others with foliage to make a roof.

"Ludus, you gather wood for a fire and get it started. I'll go find something for us to eat."

Viaticus thought.

Could being in the Legion be any worse than this? And being ordered around by a girl, what if my friends ever find out?

Corripio got his attention by slapping him in the head with a long branch.

"Sorry Viaticus, that was an accident."

The smile on Corripio's face seemed indicate otherwise. But he let it pass. He was too tired to make an issue.

They returned to the campsite just as Ludus got the fire started,

"Well little brother, you've learned something on this trip. You couldn't do that before we left Rome."

Ludus blew on the flames encouraging the fire. Viaticus was right and if it hadn't been for Lucia, he still wouldn't know how.

There was a noise from the bush behind them and out strode Lucia proudly displaying their evening meal. Some kind of wild bird held up by the neck like a trophy.

"We'll eat well tonight. Good job with the fire Ludus."

His face reddened at the compliment, he avoided her eyes and looked towards the ground and said nothing.

"And you two, where's the shelter?

Corripio spluttered.

"We just got back with the material."

"Well get on with it."

Neither Viaticus nor Corripio moved.

"Did you hear what I said?"

Finally Corripio spoke.

"We don't know exactly how you want it made."

"What you mean is, you don't know how to make a shelter. Isn't that so?"

The two looked sheepish and didn't answer.

"What? You expect me to do everything around here? It seems to me that you'd be a very sorry lot if I hadn't happened along."

Angrily she instructed them just what she wanted done. And in short order they had a sturdy structure that would keep them dry when the storm hit. When they had finished, she said.

"Not bad. Mind you my little brothers and sisters could have done better."

With that she turned her attention to the bird. Cutting off the head and gutting it with two strokes of her knife. Making Ludus feel just a bit queasy. Then a flurry of feathers and the bird was ready for the roasting spit.

She gave Ludus the job of rotating the bird over the fire as she prepared the wild mushrooms and roots. She'd placed a pan under the bird and caught the drippings which she later used to cook the vegetables.

The meal was finally ready just as the last light from the sun disappeared behind the hills. Now they only had the light from the fire to see by.

She summoned them for the meal and they all sat cross-legged around the fire as she cut the bird in pieces and served each of them a portion. It was hot, greasy and surprisingly tasty. Then came the mushrooms and roots. They had no plates or forks so they held what was given in one hand and picked at it and ate with the other.

All in all a very messy procedure, but they were so hungry nobody worried about good manners. When they almost finished, Corripio spoke.

"Lucia, that was a fine meal. Thank you very much."

Not being close to a stream and wanting to preserve what water they had for drinking. The best they could do to clean themselves up was to wipe their face and hands on leaves and tall grass around them.

Ludus banked the fire for the night and they all gratefully retired to the lean-to for some much-needed sleep. It took almost no time before all were in a deep sleep unaware of the potential danger lurking in the woods behind them.

* * * * *

Pando was running easily, the cramps that bothered him earlier had passed even Fortis seemed to be enjoying the run. Pando's thoughts returned to the episode of the attack by the vulture and the strange event of Fortis's shape change.

He had heard of such things before but had never really believed them.

The stuff of tales told to children to make them behave.

But why had the vulture followed them? And what was this magic that Fortis possessed? Or is someone else exercising that power?

It must be Caecus; he must be behind all of this magic. But if he is that doesn't explain the vulture following us. It's almost like the creature knew I had the amulet.

And what about that man the night before? Who had sent him and why? He too had wanted the amulet. How did he know about it?

Why did he want it?

He shuddered as he remembered the event.

He could feel a tug at his tunic. It was Fortis.

"What is it boy? Do you want to rest?"

Fortis stopped running and sat down on the ground.

"I guess that's plain enough old dog. Let's rest then."

He took out his flask and shook it.

Not much left, I must be on the lookout for another well. I'll give some to Fortis and a small sip for me. I must conserve what I have.

The night sky was not cloudless but he could see a few stars overhead as he lay back. He thought about his brothers, his parents and his cousins. Would they ever be a family again? Yes he was sure of it. With Caecus's help we will, I must believe that.

He became aware of the amulet resting against his chest. The beating was more pronounced now, like a second heartbeat.

That means I'm getting closer. I wonder how much farther I have to go?

He sat up for a moment and took out the jewel and held it in his hand. It was somehow reassuring for him to feel it, to see it's magical glow of the purest blue colour he'd ever seen.

Yes the beat is definitely stronger now and the direction is glowing even stronger, I know I must be close.

He replaced the amulet inside his tunic and lay back; Fortis had crept up against his side making him feel safe. It wasn't long before he drifted off into sleep.

* * * * *

The thunderclap awakened the small camp. Viaticus sat bolt upright not fully awake. He had been stunned by the noise. Then the rain came, hard, on an angle, but fortunately from behind them. Surprisingly little water leaked in through the makeshift roof and the high ground selected by Lucia meant that the rain was not running through their shelter.

Viaticus sensed that something was wrong and it wasn't just the storm. He could sense that someone or something was out there. Even though it was almost impossible to see anything in the dark.

Then a bolt of lightning illuminated all around them. For an instant he could see Lucia's face next to him, eyes wide with terror. Just as quickly as the lightning the look was gone. But something was wrong.

"What is it Lucia?" asked Viaticus.

She said quietly.

"Something is here. I must find out who or what it is."

"I'm coming with you?" he said.

"No, stay here with the others."

Viaticus retrieved the knife that Corripio had dropped for them, he slept with it under his make shift pillow.

"I said I'm coming too, no argument, do you understand?"

She was surprised by the boy's forcefulness and she conceded. They moved close to the spluttering fire, standing back to back trying to see into the gloom.

At first they saw nothing and then Lucia let out a scream.

"There it is, over there."

With that Viaticus whirled to catch sight of it. It was big, just a shape in the dark. But a menacing shape and it was hurtling straight towards them.

"What is it he yelled."

Chapter Nineteen

"How long is it going to be before Pando comes back Caecus?" asked Pico.

"I'm afraid it will be a while longer Pico. He hasn't even reached your cousins yet."

Caecus, I don't really understand. Why did Pando have to go to get our cousins? You have magic, why didn't you just bring them here?"

The old man sat on the edge of the boy's bed and put his hand on his head.

"The magic I've been given doesn't work like that my boy. You see I am unable to take direct action with my magic. I can send someone to help another and influence the event in that way but I cannot suddenly take your cousins from where they are now and somehow transport them to this place. I do not have such skills."

"Caecus, I'm very confused by this 'magic' thing. Could you explain it to me?"

"Pico that is a very complicated subject and I'm not sure that you would understand the explanation in any event."

"Won't you try, please?"

Caecus could detect a note of exasperation in Pico's voice.

"Well I suppose we could discuss some of the basics. For example, there are two kinds of magic. There is the 'good' or white magic and then there is the 'evil' or black magic.

Only the pure of heart can practice white magic and it must always be performed for the good of people. For example, a possessor of magical powers must never use white magic simply to show how skilled he is, to show off so to speak.

The power should only be used to help others and never to enrich the magician. I've had people ask me to give them the name of the winning horse in a race at the games. They beg me and say. 'If only I knew I could bet on the animal and be rich beyond my dreams'. They have even offered to share their winnings with me.

However, if I did such a thing I would lose my powers forever and then would be unable to help anyone ever again.

On the other hand 'black magic' is the exact opposite. It is always used for evil purposes. To cast spells on people the magician doesn't like. For example, turning a man into some kind of beast, like a toad."

Pico screwed up his nose at the thought of being made into a toad.

"Which is strongest Caecus, white or black?"

"Not all magicians are created equal Pico. And each gets stronger with time, so the older the magician then generally the more power he has. That's the reason that it seems that 'good' does not always triumph over 'evil'."

"Do all magicians have the same powers."

"No, it wouldn't do for inexperienced or younger magicians to have all the powers available. They must develop the skills and sense to use each magical power granted."

"Even in the case of 'black magic'?"

"Of course, they attempt to do the most damage possible. Wasting the power is just as big sin in the eyes of black magicians as it is for us."

Pico sat quietly for a few moments considering how best to ask the next question.

"Caecus, how do you become a magician?"

"You truly ask a lot of questions for such a small boy."

"Won't you tell me, please?"

"In days long since past it was the Gods who gave such powers to mortals."

The old man stopped speaking and let what he had said sink in.

"But Caecus, I've never seen a God and I do so want to become a magician like you."

"Well there is another way."

"What is it Caecus? Tell me, tell me, please."

"Some of the very old magicians have been granted permission to bestow certain limited powers on those that are considered pure of heart and deserving of such an honour."

"Please let me be one of those Caecus, oh please."

"We'll see Pico, but first I must know that you are pure of heart and it wouldn't hurt if you ate your fish at dinner either."

* * * * *

The rain was coming down so heavily that Viaticus was having trouble seeing as the water streamed into his eyes. Lucia stood next to him, so close that their bodies were almost touching.

The thunder boomed and seemed to shake the very ground they stood on. Lucia grasped Viaticus's arm just as the lightning lit up the sky. Then they saw it, standing just outside their camping area. It was huge and hairy and then it seemed to disappear. At least they could no longer see it.

Not until the next lightning bolt illuminated the scene. There it was closer now, and seeming larger, small red eyes staring straight at them. Huge tusks curled up from inside the mouth that slavered and drooled on the ground.

"What is it?" Shouted Viaticus over the noise of the storm.

"It's a wild boar, as big as I've ever seen. Looks like it's getting ready to charge us."

Once again the light was lost and they could see nothing. The thunder and lashing of the rain made it hard to hear but Viaticus was sure he heard a snort and a scramble of hooves against the gravel.

"He's charging. Look out."

With that he pushed Lucia to one side, away from the attack. He could feel the coarse bristles scrape past his body and worse yet he could smell the stench of this ugly beast and was close enough to feel the left tusk brush his side.

The animal was struggling to stop and turn to charge again. The boar would be coming uphill giving Viaticus more time to do something.

There was a pause in the storm, and he could hear the beast snort and the scrabbling of the hooves on the gravel as the boar began his charge again. The lightning again and then the thunder, he could see the animal, even more terrifying than the first time.

He had almost forgotten the knife in his right hand. Viaticus had never killed anything in his life before. If there was ever to be a first time this was it.

He crouched low to the ground and just as the beast lunged at him it lost traction on the gravel. Viaticus stuck out the knife and as luck would have it the boar impaled himself on the knife jamming the hilt into the hard ground.

The blow was a mortal one severing the aorta and within seconds the great beast lay twitching upon the ground. With one final grunt all four legs stiffened and it was dead.

* * * * *

Pando awoke refreshed; he shook Fortis and said.

"Come on boy, it's time we got moving again."

He stood and removed the amulet from within his tunic and took his bearings. He couldn't help admiring the gem, his fingers caressing the shiny blue stone.

He could feel it beating against his chest.

Yes, I'm closer, definitely closer.

"I guess we'd better have something to eat Fortis, there's not much left, I'm not sure what we do when the sweet cake is all gone and we're getting low on water too."

He opened the bag and removed the package containing the food. When he unwrapped the package he was surprised to find that there was still as much cake as there had been yesterday.

How can that be? When we ate last evening it was almost completely gone. Strange. But then everything has been strange about this journey. There is definitely somebody looking out for us Fortis.

He took comfort in this fact and instead of considering it further he munched on a generous helping of the cake and washed it down with the water.

He made sure that Fortis received his share as well.

Chapter Twenty

Viaticus was stunned by the event and to see Lucia lying on the ground beside the giant boar. Has something happened to her? Is she dead? Or injured?

He pulled her by the arm to get her clear of the smelly beast. Then he heard her say.

"Take care you big oaf. You're scratching the skin off my backside."

No she wasn't dead. She didn't even seem to be the least bit upset. She just sounded like Lucia. There was another flash of lightning and then he could see her face, not nearly as calm as she sounded.

Is her toughness all an act?

"Come on let's take cover, there's nothing we can do about the meat in this storm," she said.

They returned to the lean-to to find Ludus and Corripio gripping each other unable to speak their eyes wide in terror.

"Are you both alright?" asked Corripio.

Lucia spoke for both of them.

"Yes we're fine thanks to Viaticus here. If that old boar hadn't fallen on his knife it might have been a different story though."

Viaticus knew she was right, he really hadn't made an attempt to stab the beast, it was all just a lucky accident. Still he thought he could detect a measure respect in Lucia's voice.

She continued.

"At first light we'll butcher the animal and take the choicest parts for our journey. The rest we can leave to the vultures. Wild boar is a fine meat, we'll dine like Senators all the way to Perusia."

Neither Ludus nor Viaticus could imagine eating the gross looking beast that lay just outside the lean-to. By the same token they knew that they would have no option, Lucia would see to that.

The fire was dying down, as was the storm. Ludus stoked it adding fresh dry tinder causing it flare up more brightly.

"Lucia, you're hurt. Let me have a look at that arm." Said Corripio.

Sure enough there was a gash some six inches long on her forearm with blood oozing from the cut.

"It's nothing," she said.

"Let me be the judge of that. Remember. I was the slave of on of the most famous physicians in Rome. I know about these things. If you don't want to lose you whole arm, you'd best let me attend to it.

"Ludus, go down to the stream and get some fresh water and bring it back here. I will collect the herbs I need from the forest. Day is breaking there should be enough light for me to see."

Viaticus and Lucia were left alone, he could see she was shivering from being wet and cold. He had no dry apparel to offer her and was unsure of just what to say. He didn't have to say anything, she spoke first.

"What made you follow me when the beast was about to attack? Are you really that brave or just foolhardy?"

Instead of answering her questions he said.

"That's a nasty cut on your arm. I thought you avoided the animal when he charged us."

"Not quite. I must say that but for you I likely wouldn't be sitting here talking. I suppose that means that I should say something nice to you like 'thanks'."

"Not if you find it so difficult."

"I do, but thank you."

That ended the conversation and both sat quietly awaiting the return of Ludus and Corripio. Ludus arrived first with the water and as Corripio had instructed him he emptied the contents into one of Lucia's pots and hung it over the fire.

"You all right Viaticus, you look kind of funny."

"What do you mean, funny."

"You just don't look like your normal self. Maybe it was the boar, did he frighten you?"

"Listen to who's talking." Said Lucia. "The boy hiding behind Corripio when all this was going on."

Ludus was embarrassed, she was right. He hoped that she couldn't see the redness of his face in the early morning light.

Finally, Corripio returned. He carried several branches from an assortment of bushes as well as some curious looking bark.

"Good the water is coming to the boil." With that Corripio dropped the bark into the rapidly boiling water. The bark turned the water to an appalling shade of yellow green and a sickly sweet odour wafted towards the lean-to.

He busied himself stripping the leaves from the branches. He carefully ordered them according to the bush they came from. When he was satisfied that he had enough, he removed his mortar and pestle from his bag and ground the leaves into a thick paste.

"Come closer to the light of the fire Lucia. I must be able to see what I'm doing." He commanded.

She snorted.

"It's much more important to me that I be assured that you also know what you're doing."

"When it came to potions and ointments I was even better than my master. He said so many times, rest his poor bones."

Reluctantly Lucia came and sat beside the fire, grateful for the warmth but unsure of the medical treatment.

Corripio took some moss that he'd gathered and wadded it into a pad and carefully dipped it into the boiling solution. Shaking off the excess he moved to clean the wound.

Lucia instinctively pulled back her arm but Corripio, anticipating this, had a firm grip and he persisted in the treatment.

At first it burned as much from the temperature as from the nature of tincture and Lucia let out a loud bellow.

"YOU FIRST BORN OF A FOUL GOAT. THAT HURTS."

Corripio ignored her and kept swabbing and as the dried blood was cleaned away the pain seemed to diminish as well. When the pain had disappeared completely he applied a thick coat of the paste from the pestle. He filled the gash completely and smeared some over the skin adjacent to the wound.

Lucia was amazed, the pain was gone, in it's place was a pleasing sensation and a scented aroma that seemed to relax her.

"Now Lucia, you must remain still until this paste gets very firm, that will protect the wound until it is completely healed."

"How long is that going to take?" She asked.

"The paste I applied knows how long it will take to heal you. When you are, the scab like paste you see now will fall away and you will know you are whole again."

Ludus was fascinated by the whole procedure. He said.

"I've never seen anything like that Corripio. Is it magic?"

"Some might say so, others say it is medicine. It doesn't really matter what you call it as long as it cures the patient."

"Could you teach me how to do these things Corripio?"

The little man seemed to grow about a foot in stature taking great pleasure in his newfound status.

"Of course I could teach you. It would take many years. The question is, are you smart enough to learn? Are you willing to apply yourself? The work is very hard you know and a great amount of study is involved."

Viaticus laughed out loud,

"Ludus study? I don't think so, all he ever wants to do is play sports."

"And what about you Viaticus? All you ever do is sit around thinking."

* * * * *

Tactus had just finished feeding Fortitudo his apple when there was a loud bang to the side of the horse's stall.

--It's Hector again 'little toad'. I do hope you brought him something he gets so jealous you know.

--Yes, yes. I brought him a carrot. Let me go give it to him.

The old goat stood watching Tactus approach, eyeing him warily his head lowered and horns at the ready as if to charge at a moments notice.

--Good morning Hector, how are you?

--I see nothing good about it and what do you care about me anyway?

--So that's the way it's going to be today is it? Why are you always so cross? I haven't done anything to you.

--That's just it you never do anything for me either.

--I brought you a treat.

--But you gave Fortitudo his first.

--Don't be so childish Hector. Here.

--What's this? That's not an apple.

--No, It's a carrot.

--What am I? Second class? Why is it that bag of bones gets a sweet apple and I get a crummy carrot?

Hector shook his head and stamped his feet.

--Maybe I should just eat the carrot myself, I like carrots Hector.

--You're as selfish as that old manure machine over there. Give me my carrot.

--Say please.

Hector shook his head and stamped his feet again.

Tactus was about to put the carrot to his lips when he heard a very quiet.

--Please.

--That's better. You know Hector, if you treated people nicely, you might be surprised at how much more you might get in the way of treats.

With three great bites the carrot disappeared and Hector said.

--Rats.

As he headed out of the barn Hector said over his shoulder.

--I'm going outside I suspect that the has-been horse is about to pass wind again and I can't stand it. Remember, next time I want an apple and I want it first. Let Fortitudo have the carrots.

--Tell me Fortitudo, is he ever in a good mood?

--Let me think. Yes I think so, it was, let me see, about fifteen years ago. I don't remember the reason though.

--I think it's very sad when someone is so cranky all the time. Do you know if something happened to Hector to make him that way?

--Not that I'm aware of, but Kashta might know. You could ask him.

--I will if I ever see him again. Why is he gone so long all the time?

--He has many missions for Caecus, but he never discuses them with me. They must be very secret and you know there have been even more of them of late.

--What do you think is going on Fortitudo, why all of this activity? Surely you must know where he goes.

--When I was in the Legion I always knew what was going on. But not here.

Fortitudo stood a little taller every time he spoke of his days in the Legion, holding his head up and throwing his chest out just a little.

--I miss Kashta, there are so many things I want to ask him about. I'd like to know more about Nubia. He makes it sound like a wondrous place. He has seen animals we've only heard about and I want to know more about them. And it seems to me that he has had many adventures. My life is so boring now.

--Well, I'm sorry if you find me boring 'little toad'.

--I didn't mean to hurt your feelings Fortitudo, I don't find you boring. It's just that I have nothing to do here.

--What about your brother Pico, surely you can find things to do together.

--Did you ever have a little brother Fortitudo?
--No why?
--If you ever did, you wouldn't have to ask why.

Chapter Twenty-one

Pando loped along the edge of the forest avoiding the road as Caecus had instructed him. His knees were beginning to ache with constant pounding over the hard ground. Perspiration soaked his tunic and the sun beat down on the back of his neck. The run was now becoming work he no longer enjoyed it.

How much farther do I have to go? And to think, I have to cover all this ground again on my way back. Well at least I'll have someone to talk to then.

"Sorry Fortis, I'm glad to have you with me but you're not much of a talker," he said aloud.

The dog just kept on running at his side, the pace didn't seem to bother him at all.

Pando was not just tired from the running but also from the lack of sleep the night before. The rolling thunder and lightning flashes in the distance had made it difficult to get any rest.

The amulet beat against his chest as he ran.

Is it my imagination or is it beating much stronger now? Yes, definitely stronger. I must be very close.

I have to be careful, if as Caecus says they are in great danger, then I best approach with caution. Otherwise I will place myself in that same danger and that won't help anyone.

But how can I seek them out and yet not expose myself until I'm sure it's all right.

A plan flashed in his mind.

I can begin to run in a circle around where they must be. If I watch the flashing glow within the Lapis Lazuli it will point to the direction where I will find them. Then by sensing the strength of the beat and by keeping it constant I'll maintain my distance from them. Once I return to this point I can began to close the circle and repeat the process.

That way when I do find them I will be sure that no surprise await us.

It'll be slow going in the forest but at least I'll be out of the sun. I don't see any other option.

Pando took note of a curious rock formation so that he could use it as a reference of completion of the first circle. Then he began at a slow trot.

"Come on Fortis."

* * * * *

So what's my decision? Do I go upstream or down? I must scour the edges of the stream. To see if I might find any clues as to the direction they took.

Yes, I see exactly where they entered, if I take that angle of the entry into account, then they must be heading north.

Sceleris dug his heels into his horse's flanks and entered the water. The animal slipped and almost fell nearly throwing him from his back.

"You old nag, I'll sell you to the tannery if you can't keep your feet better than that."

His mood got no better as the horse picked it's way through the slippery stones on the riverbed.

Corripio I should skin you alive for putting me through all of this. When I do catch you you'll think any previous beatings were mere caresses.

He continued muttering to himself as he proceeded with his single-minded pursuit.

* * * * *

Lucia had risen early and was busily butchering the carcass of the great beast. Even with only one good arm she wielded the knife with great skill and seemed oblivious to the stench that arose from corpse.

Ludus however, was not so lucky and as the smell hit him he headed for the bushes and heaved last evening's dinner into the brush.

Viaticus and Corripio were both able to suppress the urge to do the same thing, however they found it almost impossible to take their eyes off of Lucia as she worked.

She sensed that she was being watched and turned and said.

"Corripio fetch more firewood and stoke that fire. Viaticus, get your weak stomached brother and begin collecting our belongings so we can leave as soon as we've had breakfast."

Viaticus was astonished and said.

"You're going to cook that beast for breakfast?"

"You'd rather eat it raw?" She laughed.

Corripio scurried away intent on doing what he was told while Viaticus, stinging from her comments went after his brother.

"Come on Ludus, we've got to get ready to leave."

His brother came out of the brush wiping his mouth with the back of his hand.

"Did I hear her right? She's going to cook that thing for breakfast?"

"So she says."

"But I hate meat at the best of times. I certainly don't want any of THAT."

"Well you can always speak to Corripio, he never seems to run out of pulse," Viaticus smiled as he turned his back on Ludus.

The two boys collected what few supplies they had and packed them for travel. Corripio was busy stoking the fire as Lucia inserted a stout stick through the center of a rather large roast and readied it for the spit.

"Ludus, come over here." She called.

Hmm not even a please. He thought.

"I want you to lift that meat on to the spit. Then take this stick and insert it into the fork at the end of the wood I inserted into the meat. Sit here and turn the meat, rotate it so it doesn't burn."

"But I can't stand even to look at it." Cried Ludus.

"Just do as you're told, we all have to pull our weight if we ever expect to get to Perusia. And mind not to burn it. Do you understand?"

The unhappy Ludus nodded and sat at the end of the spit and rotated the roast over the fire.

Why am I here? What's happened to the life I once had? Has it gone forever?

An overwhelming sense of sadness gripped him as he thought of his mother and father and of the games he loved so much.

"You're burning the meat, keep turning the spit you oaf."

Lucia's harsh voice brought him back to reality with a jolt.

Who had put her in charge? Why do I have to take directions from her? I'm not stupid I know things too.

However, he did have to admit he didn't know nearly as much as Lucia and certainly not as much as Corripio.

"Why did you make the roast so big," asked Viaticus.

"Because I was afraid that somebody as big as you might have devoured a smaller one all by yourself."

Immediately she regretted her joke and said.

"I made it as big as I could because once cooked it will last longer than if it were raw. There's really no way we could carry uncooked meat in that sun."

What was it that happened to her in the past that causes her always to be on the offensive?

"How's the roast doing Ludus?" asked Viaticus.

"At least there's no sign of blood now. But I think we're going to need more wood, the fire's burning down."

"I'll go and get more. I know that meat is not your favourite thing to eat but I think even you must admit that it's beginning to smell pretty good."

"Yuck."

* * * * *

Pando was on his third lap around his circular path. I'm sure this is going to work, the beating has never been stronger. And I've not seen anything that I might consider a danger.

I'm tired but I must press on, one more lap then I'll stop for something to eat no sense making myself sick.

Just then Fortis stopped and stood very still.

"What is it Fortis?"

The dog lifted his head a sniffed the air. Pando could smell something too. What was it?

Then it struck him. He remembered the smell just as though it came from his mother's kitchen. It was the smell of meat roasting.

Chapter Twenty-two

"Do you think something has happened to Pando Tactus? He's been gone a long time."
"I don't know, I just hope he hasn't lost his way."
"Maybe we should talk to Caecus."
"What's he going to tell us Pico?"
"Well, he can see the future can't he? If something is wrong maybe he could tell us."
"Maybe you're right let's go find him."

The two boys found the old man in the first place they looked. Sitting under an old fig tree, seeming to gaze across the fields.

"Do you think he's sleeping Tactus?" Whispered Pico as they approached the figure.

"Hard to tell, I've never really seen him close his eyes."
"Why would he have to close his eyes? He can't see anything so I can't see the light bothering him."
"Call him Pico."
"No you call him."

At that the old man turned and seemed to be looking directly at the two of them.

"What is it? Surely you aren't afraid to speak to me?"
"No, no," stammered Tactus.
"It's just that we were wondering why it's taking Pando so long to get back here?"
"You fear that some misfortune has overtaken him. Is that it?"
"But since you can see the future, you'd tell us if that happened, right Caecus? Asked Pico.
"Pico you must understand that my ability to see future events comes unbidden. I cannot will the spirits to tell me what I may want to know. However, I feel sure that Pando is safe and that he will soon return with your cousins."
"But you don't know that for sure?"
"No Tactus I do not. It seems to me though that Pando has a brave heart and is strong of body and with Fortis at his side I'm sure that he will succeed."

While the answer was not exactly what the two boys wanted to hear, they took comfort in the words spoken.

"When will Kashta return?" asked Tactus.

"I cannot see him being away too much longer. Soon now I hope we will all be together, joined of course by your two cousins."

* * * * *

Pando continued tightening his circle around the area where he suspected his cousins might be. Then he noticed the spiral of smoke rising up through the trees. The smell of the roasting meat grew stronger and he thought he could hear voices.

That sounds like more than just two people. Could it be that Ludus and Viaticus have been taken captive? What do I do if they have? I must try to get closer without being seen.

I'll creep along the ground just under these bushes and try to make my way closer to the camp. I need to see who's there and avoid them seeing me.

Once I find out how many there are and what condition my cousins are in, perhaps I can come up with some kind of plan.

In his heart he wasn't so confident that any plan would be forthcoming.

It was then that he realized he was not alone under the bushes, right next to him was Fortis scraping along the ground just like he was.

If I can just move this branch I should have a clear view of the camp area. I hope the growling of my stomach doesn't give me away. That meat smells delicious, hardly a meal for breakfast but no matter, I haven't tasted meat since I left Caecus.

Fortis seemed overcome by the tantalizing odour, he bolted from the bushes and into the camp causing great disruption.

Ouch, what was that, it hurts. Everything has gone black. Now I see stars, like the heavens at night. I'm drifting away....

When Pando recovered his senses, he lay on the ground with an angry looking individual standing over him.

Who is this? What is this? A boy, a girl? Yes a girl. She has a large stone in her right hand raised as though ready to strike me again.

"Wait, Lucia. It's my cousin Pando. Don't hit him again," said Viaticus.

"What were you creeping around our camp for?" she asked.

"What? Why did you hit me? That hurt."

"I hit you because you were creeping around here like some snake. Who are you?"

"Like Viaticus said, I'm his cousin and Ludus's too. Just ask him."

But Ludus was too busy trying to wrestle the roast boar away from Fortis. But, the huge dog won and ran into the woods with his prize.

"Is that mangy cur yours?" asked Lucia

"No not mine, but he travels with me." Pando tried not to smile at the turn of events but was not very successful.

"What are you laughing at? Your dog has run off with all the food we had and you think that's funny?"

"I'm sorry but a dog is a dog."

"And you are no better than a dog." She raised her hand as if to strike Pando again but Viaticus stepped between them.

"Lucia, what he says is true, This is our Cousin Pando he lives in Perusia. We were on our way to visit them when Sceleris waylaid us. But I must say Pando I'm just as surprised, as Lucia is to see you here. Who sent you and why?"

Pando got up off the ground and embraced his cousin saying.

"That's a long story but first don't you think you should introduce me to the others."

Ludus came over looking a little sheepish after having lost the roast boar. They hugged each other and Ludus said.

"Pando you've grown since we saw one another last year. You're almost as tall as I am now. It's good to see you."

"And you Ludus."

Viaticus spoke.

"This is Lucia, your assailant. And over there hiding behind the tree is Corripio. If you believe that you've got a long story, wait till you hear ours."

Lucia let the rock she held slip from her hand, there seemed no doubt that the newest member of the group offered no threat to her. While the cousins talked Lucia reflected on the situation.

This is all I need another green kid. From the looks of him he's just as spoiled as the other two. It was bad enough with three of us together with four we are bound to attract unwanted attention.

But that stupid dog. He has to go I've no intention of foraging for him too. All that trouble and the roast is gone in the blink of an eye. I hope he chokes on it.

"So you say your parents have been arrested too Pando. No idea where they are?" asked Ludus.

"No idea. In fact Tactus, Pico and I were on our way to Rome to get help from your family when we ran into Fortis, the dog who ate your breakfast. Then we met up with his master Kashta."

Lucia pricked up her ears at what was being said.

Does he mean there are two more, another two brothers? I don't need that much trouble. And what's this with missing parents? A coincidence? Not likely, more a conspiracy I think. Trouble with the law? I need no involvement with the authorities. It's best that I just slip away from these hapless losers.

Corripio spoke.

"That was a dog? Are you sure? It seemed to me to be a rather large black bear."

He left the safety of the sturdy tree trunk and joined the main group.

"No he is a dog and generally very well mannered, I can only apologize for what happened," said Pando

"Well we can't eat your apology," spat Lucia.

"I have some sweet cake, I'd be happy to share with you."

Pando reached into the bag at his feet and retrieved the package from within.

Lucia laughed and said.

"There's not enough there to feed a bird let alone you horses."

Pando broke a piece off and offered it to Lucia but she refused to accept it. However, Viaticus did not. Then he broke another piece and handed it to Ludus. Both boys ate the cake and expressed their pleasure at the taste of it.

Lucia watched fascinated. Each time Pando broke off a piece, the cake got no smaller. She moved closer to watch as Corripio received his share and sure enough, the cake didn't change in size.

How can this be? I've watched with my own eyes and I see the cake being broken and given to each of them and yet there is always the same amount left. This is some kind of magic. Does Pando possess these powers or is there someone or something else out there watching over him?

Chapter Twenty-three

*W*hat's this? My good eye is acting up again, itching and burning. I don't have much of that ointment left that Corripio made for me. Another reason for me wanting him back. I can't afford to lose the little sight I have left.

Let's see, they're heading northwest at least that's the direction to Perusia if they were telling the truth. I'll gamble on continuing upstream. The water is shallow here my horse can easily outpace them. My only problem is being able to see where they leave the stream. I must concentrate.

At least the trees are offering some shelter from the sun, I've got to think, make a plan. Corripio will be no problem; he's been a slave for so long he couldn't make a decision for himself if his life depended on it. He'll be petrified at the sound of my voice and do exactly as he's told. The other two may be a different matter, particularly the big one.

And then there's the possibility that they've picked up another party. As I said, Corripio could never make a decision on his own and as far as the two boys are concerned they're too inexperienced to even know when a decision is required let alone what the right one might be.

No, I suspect I might be dealing with four instead of three.

I don't like the odds, four to one, even if two are a couple of kids and Corripio isn't any kind of threat but who's the other one or maybe there's more than just one.

He rubbed his good eye and began plodding up the stream scanning both banks as he went his horse occasionally slipping on the flat stones almost jarring Sceleris from his saddle.

* * * * *

"That cake was very good Pando. Where did you get it?" asked Ludus.

"I brought it with me, Oratio made it, he's quite a good cook."

Lucia was startled at the mention of the name.

Oratio, how is it I seem to know that name. This whole thing gets more curious by the minute. What can I have to do with any of this?

And why is it that the cake never seems to get any smaller when you eat it? Something very mysterious is going on here.

"I couldn't help but notice that the piece you have in your hand is still the same size as when we began to eat. Now we've had our fill and it's no smaller. How can that be Pando?" asked Viaticus.

"You noticed that too. I'm at a loss to give an answer, I never noticed until just yesterday. Mind you it was only Fortis and me eating it so I didn't really see it at first."

"Who's Oratio?"

"He's a servant to Caecus, Ludus. He does most of the cooking and looking after Caecus, he's blind you know so Oratio is always close by."

"He's a slave then?"

"No Viaticus, Caecus doesn't believe in owning slaves. Oratio is with him as a matter of personal choice."

Corripio swallowed his last bit of cake and said.

"Sounds like I might like this fellow Caecus very much. Will we get a chance to meet this fine man?"

"Corripio, I've been sent by Caecus to bring Viaticus and Ludus back to his farm. I for one would have no objection to having you travel with us. You too of course Lucia.

"I have no idea what the plan will be for my two brothers, my two cousins and me once we get there. I'm hoping he will be able to help us find our parents.

"I'm sure Caecus would make you welcome," said Pando.

Lucia was silent, not her normal state.

Caecus, why is that name familiar? What's happening here, it's like I have lived this time before? Some of this is clear and some clouded in mist.

Before Lucia could respond to Pando the bushes parted and Fortis came bounding into the small clearing. There was no sign of the roast but his tail wagged vigorously. With one leap he placed both front paws on Pando's chest and gave his face a mighty lick with his long red tongue.

"Ugh Fortis, you've got me covered in boar grease. Get off me you bad dog. Fortis, down get down you're getting the grease all over my clothes."

Lucia picked up a rather large stick and was about to beat the dog.

"Get off him you mangy cur or I'll knock out all your teeth, then see what you'll do with any other boar roasts."

"Don't hit him, he's just a dog. It's not his fault, it's just what dogs do."

Ludus moved to hold Lucia's arm when she said.

"He's a dog all right, a dog with no manners, perhaps I should box the ears of his master for not teaching him better. How would that be Pando?"

"Don't look at me. Fortis isn't my dog, just a fellow traveler. He may be bad mannered, but he is brave and beside that he's the only one that knows the way back to Caecus's farm."

Pando had no intention of relating Fortis's ability to shape change into other beasts. He felt sure if he said anything they wouldn't believe him, and in any event he couldn't explain it anyway. Some things were just best left unsaid.

Lucia continued, her eyes fierce and the stick still in her hand.

"Even if he isn't your dog you bear responsibility for him, you brought him here and he destroyed our food. The least you can do is take him down to the stream and wash him off. If you don't he'll stink to high heaven when the sun reaches it's high point. And maybe do something about yourself while you're at it, he's made a mess of you too."

Pando grasped Fortis by the scruff of his neck and began the walk down to the stream below saying nothing as he went.

She's a witch, how could Ludus and Viaticus have put up with her, she's so bossy. Even my mother never talked to me the way she has. I hope she decides that she doesn't want to come with us. I don't think I could stand 4 or 5 days of her nattering.

"OH this water is cold. Come on boy, in you get. If I have to do it so do you."

I don't know how much good this is going to do, I've got nothing to cut the grease, and the cold water certainly won't do it.

Maybe I'm wrong. Look at that, the cold water is making the grease congeal, I can pull it off in chunks and just let it float away downstream.

My legs are freezing and I haven't even started on myself.

"Stand still Fortis let me get the fat off your belly. What a messy eater you are.

"There, I think that's the best I'm going to be able to do. Go on get out of here."

The dog ran to the bank and found a grassy spot where he could roll and rub his body against it. Then stood and shook himself violently and ran up to the campsite.

Better than nothing I guess. Now, what to do with me just look at my tunic. I'd best strip it off and see how much grease I can scrape off.

He stood in the stream in only his loincloth as he tried to scrub the grease from his clothes. He had less luck than he'd had with Fortis. He worked so intently that he didn't notice the figure peering from behind a tree.

It was Lucia.

As the sunlight struck the amulet around Pando's neck her eyes widened and she gasped.

"The Lapis Lazuli."

Chapter Twenty-four

How can I tell if he's asleep or not? His eyes never seem to close. I'd like to talk to him but if he's sleeping he might get mad if I disturb him. But maybe he's not sleeping? Then I might sit here all day with nothing to do. This is really getting to be boring. Tactus spends all his time with that stupid horse and smelly goat, Pando's gone and I don't know where my mother and father are.

Could it really get any worse if he did get mad?

But before he could screw up his courage to do anything, Caecus suddenly said.

"What is it you want Pico?"

He jumped at the sound of his voice.

"I'm sorry if I woke you Caecus, I didn't mean to disturb you."

"I wasn't sleeping and if you didn't mean to disturb me then why are you here?"

"I wanted to ask you something, but if I am disturbing you I'll leave."

Caecus's voice softened as he said.

"It's quite all right Pico, ask your question."

"I was just wondering, how long have you been blind? Were you born that way or did something happen that caused you to lose your sight?"

"Why does that make any difference Pico?"

"It just seems to me that if you were born blind I would guess that you wouldn't miss what you never had. But if you once had sight and then lost it, I think that would be very difficult."

"And why might that be?"

"I just think how I would feel. Not to see the flowers, the birds, wild animals all the trees and of course all of the people. Like your mother and father, sisters, brothers, you know. It must be terrible."

"I understand what you're saying my little friend but you will learn as you go through life that mourning the things you don't have instead of enjoying all the other things you do have, is a waste of energy.

"I have been given many other things in this life. Things that others might take for granted. For example, I have friends, like Kashta, Oratio and you. At least I think you're my friend."

"Oh yes Caecus, I am your friend."

"Good then you see how lucky I am."

"And you have magic too."

"Is that what this is really all about Pico?"

He looked sheepishly up at the old man, hesitated for a moment and then said.

"Caecus, you did say you would teach me."

"I also told you that I would have to be sure of the reasons you might have for wanting to learn such things. To be successful in the pursuit of magic you must be pure of heart. Magic can never be used for personal gain, at least not the kind of magic I'm talking about.

"Not even to show off to others that you have special powers. Any powers that you may develop must be used to help others. Do you understand that?"

"Yes, yes Caecus, I do. Please teach me."

The old man scratched at his scrawny beard, tilting his head as though waiting for some kind of sign before answering the boy.

After what seemed like a lifetime to Pico, he said.

"Come over here boy and sit at my feet."

He did as he was asked and sat in anticipation. There was another long period of silence, and then Caecus pointed to a nearby fig tree. Pico's gaze followed the long bony figure, staring at what, he did not know. He was just about to turn to Caecus when it happened.

What is that? A puff of smoke, a bright flash. It's clearing now, what is it I see?

There standing just under the fig tree was something or perhaps, more properly, someone. But what or who? It seems to be about 3 feet tall with bright red hair and are those wings on its back? The face seemed human, but oddly so, covered with a leathery kind of pale yellow skin. A mouth, if indeed that was a mouth, was turned down in a scowl.

Pico's mouth hung open in awe of what he saw. He turned to Caecus and said.

"Caecus, what is that?"

"He is your new best friend. He's a Daimon, his name is 'Nog', and he's your Daimon now. Why don't you call him over?"

"But how?"

"Just call him by name and he will obey you."

Before he could, the Daimon spoke.

"Caecus what's this all about? I was right in the middle of something when you summoned me. I'm a very busy person you know."

"Well Nog, I'm sorry to have disturbed you, what was it you were so busy with?"

"Oh never mind, just tell me what's so all fired important."

"I wanted you to meet your new assignment. Nog meet Pico, Pico meet Nog."

To Pico's surprise Nog flapped his wings and silently flew to his side.

Now what am I supposed to do? Shake hands perhaps?

Tentatively he put out his hand out and Nog grasped it. Pico shivered at the feel of his skin, it seemed more like a reptile's cold like one too.

"Caecus, he's just a child. What do you expect me to do with him?"

"Nog it's not what you will do with him, it's what he'll do with you. He's your new Master, I would suggest you behave with respect if you don't want to fall further down the hierarchy and end up as simple gnome."

"Caecus, what's a Daimon? And what am I supposed to do with it or rather him?"

"Pico were you not pestering me to learn magic?"

"Yes, but not this kind."

"What, you want card tricks? Sleight of Hand?"

"You know what I mean Caecus, to have the power to change things. I'm young and small and not very strong yet. If I only had magic then maybe I could get my mother and father back."

"With Nog at your side you will have power Pico. However, because you are young and without experience in the world, this is the best way to teach you."

"You mean that Nog will have the power and he'll do whatever I tell him to?"

"Not quite. While Nog has been assigned to you, you must realize that he is an independent spirit. You can command him to do whatever it is you want him to do. If, however, Nog deems that the command does not come from your inner pure self, he is not obligated to obey.

"In addition, he will not act if he believes your motives are trivial."

"You mean I shouldn't show off."

"Exactly."

"Well then, what kind of powers does Nog have?"

"He has no power over life or death. He cannot alter historical events but he can help alter future events. He is your protector and will keep you safe even at the expense of his own life. You cannot ask him to bring your mother and father to you or you to them. But he has the power to communicate with them even though they will not know he is doing so."

"But how can that be? Won't they see him?"

"No, only you and I can see him and then only when we call him specifically by name."

"You mean he's invisible?"

"Just as I said."

"So then Tactus won't be able to see him."

"Is that so important."

"It's just that if he can't see him he isn't going to believe what I tell him either. He'll think I'm lying."

"Then perhaps it's best that you keep your new powers to yourself."

This isn't what I wanted. Tactus will never believe what I say or Pando for that matter. Tactus can talk to the animals, but wait, I've only heard him talk I've never heard the animals answer. Maybe he's lying, no he wouldn't do that?

"Pico, there are only two commands that you must remember in dealing with Nog. The first is to summon him simply call out 'Come Nog' and the second when you want to dismiss him just say 'Go Nog'."

"How long will it take him to appear Caecus?"

"It will be instantaneous, for he's always with you so he simply has to appear."

"That seems simple enough."

"It is, now I would suggest that the two of you find a quiet place and get to know one another. I think you will find that Nog can answer any questions you might have Pico."

"Thank you Caecus, while it's not what I expected, I will do my best not to disappoint you."

"Or me either I hope." Said Nog.

Nog and Pico headed for the meadow; it was a place Pico was sure they could be alone. *If I'm going to be talking to somebody that* nobody else can see I'd sooner that no one else sees me. Otherwise they might think it odd that I talk to myself.

"Do you really have to do that Nog?"

"Do what?"

"Hover like that, I find it a little irritating. Can't you just walk like a human?"

"But I'm not."

"Not what?"

"Human."

Chapter Twenty-five

Pando had little to pack up; in fact neither did his cousins it was Lucia that had the backpack. Graciously Pando offered to carry it for her only to be rebuffed rather brusquely.

"I was only trying to help, it looks heavy."

"I've had enough help from you and your two clumsy cousins, just fall in behind and follow. Keep up or you'll be left here."

I wonder what's biting her backside? Maybe Viaticus or Ludus knows.

"Lucia, Caecus said we should follow Fortis, he knows the way back. Shouldn't we let him lead us?"

"That fool of a dog, all he thinks about is his belly. The first sign of something to eat and he'll abandon us. Just follow me or go ahead on your own."

"Pando, maybe we should do as she says. We've done pretty well with her so far," said Ludus.

"And she knows how to cook. As long as we keep Fortis away from the food." Viaticus smiled.

Corripio was perfectly happy to follow Lucia's orders. After all it's what he was used to. He found he disliked making his own decisions, this being a free man wasn't all it was supposed to be.

They walked in single file through the wooded area and out onto a flat field ripe with grain. The sun was beginning to rise in the sky.

Lucia kept up a steady pace and didn't even seem to break a sweat whereas the other four were gasping for breath and perspiring profusely. They all wanted to take a break but were afraid to suggest it sure that they would be berated yet again.

As the sun seemed to hover directly overhead she finally called out.

"We'll stop here for rest and some food. Pando bring up your magic cake. Thanks to Fortis that's all we've got."

They found shade under a lone olive tree, an old tree with trunk so twisted it seemed like it must surely be in pain. Pando looked but could see no olives. They sat in a circle as Pando unwrapped the cake cutting a piece for each of them. And as before, the remaining piece grew no smaller.

That's a good thing, the pace we're moving at the cake is likely to be required for several more meals, thought Pando.

Ludus asked.

"Could I have some water Pando?"

"We are getting very low and I've seen no water since we left the camp this morning. We need to ration it, no more than two sips each."

"Are you the one in charge now?" asked Lucia.

"No it just seems the sensible thing to do, we don't know when we'll se water again."

"You may not, but I do," she said.

Viaticus asked.

"Where are we headed?"

"To Trebiae," she responded.

Corripio, rubbing his feet, asked.

"How much farther?"

"Two maybe three hours, depends how slowly you four walk."

"And there is water at Trebiae?"

"Yes Pando, lots of water."

Ludus was just getting comfortable lying on his back watching the cloud formations roll overhead when a pebble hit him in the hand.

"Get moving Ludus, there's no time for sleep."

What a witch, there is no fear that she will ever be someone's wife, nobody would have such a bossy woman.

Fortis continued at Pando's side.

So far so good, Fortis seems to be in agreement with the direction Lucia is taking. Fortis, you didn't get any cake, probably still full of roast boar. I don't think cake is good for dogs anyway.

Looks like we might be heading for a storm, those clouds look threatening. They help to block the sun so at least it's not so hot now. Lucia just doesn't slow down. How and why does she come to be here? A girl alone and on the road. It doesn't make any sense. She's not unattractive but so testy, she's all prickles, doesn't let anyone close to her. I wonder what's going on in her mind?

Just then Lucia stepped on a sharp stone; her thin sandals were of little protection to her small feet.

That hurt, but I can't cry out, mustn't show any sign of weakness. Don't limp, walk through the pain, it was just a stumble. Think about something else.

The Lapis Lazuli, I've seen it before but where? Why does Pando have it? I know it has magic but what is it? Where did Pando get it?

What's behind the disappearance of the parents? Am I getting involved in something that could present danger to me? All these questions and no answers.

Corripio, Corripio is it because you remind me of my oldest brother? Are you my brother? It seems a coincidence that my mother told me he was sold into slavery to a physician. The same story you told me. I can only assume that you tell the truth. Look my arm is healed now and barely a scar.

Why have these boys been singled out? For what purpose? There is magic here that was not with us before, why? Have the Gods taken an interest in them?

Viaticus saved me from the wild boar, was that just a coincidence? There's that word again, coincidence. No there is more to this than mere coincidence.

"How much further Lucia?" asked Ludus.

"See that hill up ahead? Just on the other side."

"That's good because we're just about out of water," said Pando.

Pando decided to sprint ahead, anxious to replenish his water container. The hill was further away than it first appeared and considerably steeper once he reached it. Even Fortis seemed to strain at the incline.

However when he reached the top and looked down into the little valley he was astonished at what he saw. There was water all right, lots of it. But more than that, he was awed at the beauty of the scene.

I can't believe it. The water is coming straight out of the ground; it looks like a pot being continuously filled to overflowing with streamlets coming together downstream to form a wide basin.

I've never seen anything like it and the trees; they're beautiful, cypress I think and poplar too.

The reflection of the trees surrounding the basin it's so clear and the reflection so vivid the trees appear to be growing down into the water like another world. The water sparkles so, I must taste it.

Cupping his hand he scooped up the cold refreshing water.

Wonderful. Maybe it's just because I'm so thirsty but that water tastes better than any other.

Lying on his stomach, he refilled his water container and was taken with just how crystal clear the water really was.

I can see the bottom covered in white stones; they seem to be all the same size. What's that to the right? I can't believe it. It looks like an underwater garden. It's truly like looking into another world the plants moving as though disturbed by a gentle breeze. Must be the current of the flowing water.

What's that? Tiny silver fish. They look like little birds flitting through the bushes. This is truly a marvelous place.

Then it struck him, the absolute silence. He couldn't even hear the water as it moved on its inevitable journey.

But the silence was soon broken by the voices of his companions.

"Where are you Pando?" called Ludus.

He stood up so he could be seen.

"I'm over here. Isn't this a wonderful place?"

Lucia was the last one to join them. Pando passed the water container around and they all drank thirstily even Lucia.

"What is this place Lucia?" asked Viaticus.

She paused and looked around before she answered.

"This place is called Clitumnus, named after the God Clitumnus, the river God. It is a sacred place honoured by many. You all would do well to remember that."

"But where is the water coming from, it just seems to pour out of the ground?" Asked Ludus.

Answering with authority, Lucia said.

"From the dwelling place of the God Clitumnus of course. From deep within the earth. It is his gift to us. It is ever flowing, pure and cold."

They all stood quietly, respectfully absorbing everything around them, they seemed unable to speak they were so moved by this place.

"Come with me, you must see something very special."

Lucia led the party around the broad basin, past some cypress trees and then they saw it. Just up a slight rise above the level of the water, it was a Temple.

A long staircase provided access to the second level entrance, obviously the main entrance although there seemed to be an entrance of the left side. This door, while at the same level as the main one, could be accessed from the ground level since the Temple was built into the side of a hill.

On the right side of the building were columns as might be seen in buildings in Rome but on a much smaller scale.

To the right of the staircase at ground level in a niche formed by the façade of the front entrance and the front wall of the Temple stood a large statue perhaps three times life size.

"This is the Temple of Clitumnus and that is his statue there to the right. This is a very ancient place so be respectful. Take time to say a prayer of thanks for what he has given us in this holy place."

Chapter Twenty-six

"Let's sit under that fig tree, the sun is very hot."

"Good idea, my skin is very tender you know."

Pico looked at the scaly skin and wondered how anything that looked like that could ever be tender. They both sat down in the shade, cross-legged, facing each other. Neither was prepared to begin, the silence was awkward.

Finally Pico spoke.

"So just what is a 'Daimon'?"

"Weren't you listening to Caecus?"

"Yes, but I'm not sure I understood completely."

"What's this? I've not just inherited a boy but a slow learner as well?"

"Why do you insult me? Am I not the Master here?"

"I'm an independent spirit assigned to you. So it would be as well that you treat me with some respect if this relationship is to work out."

I'm not sure that it's ever going to work out. This beast is just about more than I can bear. However, I did promise Caecus that I would try to work with him.

"I should tell you now that you may as well say what you're thinking because I know what's in your head anyway. And for the record, I'm not a beast."

Pico's face reddened.

How am I ever going to deal with him?

"Very carefully I should think."

Nog stroked his wispy red beard and stared at Pico with his piercing blue eyes.

"Now, what is it you want to know Pico?"

"Where do you come from and like I asked, what is a 'Daimon'?"

"Where do I come from? I am everywhere and nowhere, all at the same time. What am I? I'm what is known as an 'elemental' in the spirit world."

"You mean like a 'Demon', are you a 'Demon'?"

"No, you little twit. A 'Demon' is of the lowest order, driven by evil. My place is between the Gods and humans."

"Are there many 'Daimons'?"

"There is a 'Daimon' for every human."

"But how come I've just found out about you now?"

"Because your education has been grossly neglected and you've never called on me before."

"How could I call on you if I didn't know you existed?"

"Now that's a conundrum."

"What's a conundrum?"

"Silly boy. A puzzle you fool."

"Why is it you dislike me so much, we've just met?"

"I'm always cranky when I'm awakened from my nap."

"You were sleeping when Caecus called on you?"

"Yes."

"Were you sleeping long?"

"How old are you?"

"I'm nine, what's that got to do with anything?"

"Well that's how long I've been asleep. Ever since you were born."

"I don't understand. I thought you were supposed to watch over me, how can you do that if you're asleep?"

"Well, you never seemed to have much interest in me. So why not catch a few winks?"

"But you are awake now, right?"

Nog yawned and put his hand to his mouth as he said.

"Unless you're nothing but a nightmare I am."

"Nog can we start over? I'd like us to be friends."

"Yes we can. As long as you understand I'm not your slave and you're not my Master."

"I understand."

"So ask your questions."

"Why is it no one but me can see you?"

"You mean you and Caecus. All 'Daimons' are meant to be invisible. Caecus has given you the power to see me to help you grasp the idea of an elemental spirit.

"We are meant to influence our charge, keep them on the path of truth and try to prevent them from doing wrong. We can influence but we cannot change things. Only you and other humans or the Gods can do that."

"That sounds like my conscience. Is that the same thing?"

"Not quite. Your conscience resides inside your head but I operate outside your body. Mind you, we often work together."

"Caecus said you could communicate with my parents, is that really possible?"

"What he meant was that I could help you to communicate with them, much like he did for you earlier."

"Do you know where they are?"

"No, I don't need to. Our communication will seek them out wherever they are."

"Would you show me how? Please."

"Since you asked so nicely, I will.

"Now close your eyes and don't reopen them until I tell you to. I want you to draw from your memory a picture of your mother and father. I want you to concentrate until you see so clearly that they will seem to be here with us."

Can I do this? Last time it was Caecus's eyes. Is it possible I can do this myself? Things are rushing through my mind; everything's a jumble. Got to concentrate.

"Take a deep breath Pico. See only blackness behind your eyes."

See blackness, relax, and breathe out slowly. There the jumble is easing; it's getting dark, now it's very dark. I remember that day, I was so happy. My birthday, a gift, what I always wanted a bow and arrow. There they are, my father handing it to me and my mother is smiling at my excitement.

The image is getting clearer, I think if I reach out, I can touch them. However, I better not. They might go away.

What's that voice? It's Nog. Oh please don't frighten them away.

In a very quiet gentle voice, he could hear Nog saying.

"You need not speak the words, just think them. Your words will find them and they will understand and do the same."

--Oh mother, I miss you. Are you and father all right?

Better that I not say too much at once. I must wait to see if they get my message. Must concentrate on the image behind my eyes.

What's that? Is it my mother answering? Then he heard her voice.

--Oh Pico my youngest son, how I miss you. Be assured your father and I are in good health. We don't know exactly where we are but we are being treated well so don't worry. Tell me about Tactus and Pando, are they with you? Are they all right?

--Mother we are fine, please don't worry about us. Tactus is with me and Pando is going to be here soon. We are all safe and staying with a man named Caecus.

The image is beginning to fade, I must concentrate, bring it back. There that's better.

--Pico, tell me why Pando isn't with you now?

--Caecus sent him to bring our cousins Viaticus and Ludus here to join us.

--But why Pico?

--Caecus said they were in some kind of danger.

The picture, it's fading, tearing. I'm losing it. What's that strange noise? The picture is gone. I've lost them. That noise, what is it?

As he opened his eyes, Nog was sprawled on his back, mouth open and he was snoring loudly. That's the noise, Nog's snoring. He directed a kick at Nog's hip and awoke him; he sat bolt upright and spluttered.

"What is it, who's here."

"It's just me. I was talking to my parents and because you fell asleep I lost contact with them."

"Don't get huffy with me. After all when you've been asleep for nine years it takes a little effort to wake up completely."

"Can I go back and see them again?"

"Not today. We must wait until tomorrow."

I had better be careful with my thoughts; I can't afford to have him get mad at me.

"No you can't."

"Nog, I think that's enough for today, my brain is whirling at what you've told me and what we've done. And I think maybe you need more rest so we can start fresh tomorrow."

"Suits me."

"Then Go Nog."

Pico heard a strange sound. "Pfffffffft."

And Nog was gone.

I'm going down to the barn to see Tactus. I don't know about this 'Daimon' thing, it was good to see and talk to my parents but Nog is an arrogant little beast.

Suddenly Pico twisted in agony; somebody or something had pinched his backside, hard.

Hard enough to make his eyes water.

This magic business isn't all it's cracked up to be. I now seem to be in a position where I will never again be able to have any private thoughts.

This is not a good thing.

Chapter Twenty-seven

"Are you sure this is a temple dedicated to the God Clitumnus?" Asked Viaticus.

Lucia responded.

"Why do you ask?"

"I have seen the Temple of Jupiter in Rome. I used to pass it going to my father's work. This one seems somehow familiar, Mind you, I never got to go inside. Could it be that this is now Temple dedicated to Jupiter?"

"Well, that's entirely possible, the Senate often decrees new uses for old buildings. As I said, Clitumnus is an ancient God. Perhaps too old fashioned for our esteemed Senate. Let's go in and see if there are any other similarities."

As she moved to the long staircase, Fortis scrambled ahead of her, up the stairs and stood at the top on the landing. He looked down on her as if daring her to proceed.

"Looks like Fortis is interested in seeing inside too," said Pando.

"Pando get that beast out of there. He can't be allowed in, this is a sacred place," she said.

"What harm will it cause? What's so bad about a dog going into an old building?"

"Pando, have you no respect. Animals don't belong in places of worship. Get him down from there," she demanded.

No sense in getting her all upset I suppose, we're going to have to live with her a while longer.

"Here Fortis, come to me. Be a good dog. Come on boy."

However, the dog was resolute, he didn't move from his place on the landing.

"Pando, stop playing the fool to that cur, go up and bring him down." Lucia's voice was becoming shrill as her anger mounted.

Pando climbed the stairway, talking calmly to the dog with each step. Pleading with the animal to come down. He reached the top but the animal wouldn't move. Pando scratched Fortis's head and ruffled his ears, but he couldn't coax him to move from his spot.

"Pando, give him a smack and make him come down."

"I'm not going to hit Fortis Lucia. He's my friend and a brave one at that, he doesn't deserve punishment, he hasn't done anything wrong,"

"He's disobedient, that's enough reason to punish him," she said.

Then Viaticus spoke.

"Why are you getting so upset? You yourself said that this is an ancient place of worship and didn't the ancients worship animals? If that's true then why would you carry on so?"

"Shut up Viaticus, you don't know what you're talking about."

With that she picked up a stick and ran up the staircase almost pushing Pando off the small platform.

Fortis bared his teeth at her and began to growl, a menacing sound that Pando had heard only once before.

"Fortis, it's Lucia, why would you attack her? She's our friend."

The dog's jaws opened exposing the sharp canines as the lips curled back Pando was struck at how fearsome his good friend had become in just an instant.

Lucia raised her arm and made as if to strike the dog. Pando grasped her arm before she could make good on her intention. She screamed at him.

"Let me go. I must teach the beast a lesson. Pando, release me. NOW."

It was then that she felt something on her right leg. It was warm and wet. She looked down and exclaimed.

"He's pissing on me. The dog is pissing on me."

Pando looked down, still holding Lucia around the waist and by her right arm still holding the raised stick. She was right; he was pissing on her.

I don't remember Fortis ever drinking that much water.

When Fortis had finished relieving himself he turned his backside to Lucia and gave two scratches to the stone slab hurling several pebbles in her direction. Then descended the staircase, somewhat disdainfully thought Pando, to the laughter of the other three below.

Lucia's face was dark with anger; she still held the stick in her hand. Pando wasn't sure if he might be her new target.

"You all think this is funny. Have you no respect for this holy place?" She stamped her foot.

"Oh come on Lucia. Can't you see any humour at all in this?" Asked Ludus.

"I've a good mind to humour you with this stick Ludus."

Then Pando spoke, very carefully.

"Lucia the dog is just a dog, I don't think there was anything personal in what he did. If it helps I will apologize for his actions."

"I disagree with you. That beast intended to make a fool of me. And from the laughter of you lot, it seems he succeeded."

"Why would he do that?" asked Pando.

"He's your dog, ask him."

"He's not my dog. I've told you he belongs to a Nubian Prince named Kashta. He's a brave animal who has saved my life at least once. I owe him a great deal.

"I've only your word for all of that. As far as I'm concerned he's little more than a mangy street mutt."

What's wrong with this girl? Why is she so against Fortis? Peeing on her was not a good thing, but neither was the fact she was about to hit him just because he wanted in the Temple. Perhaps we should just go our own way. Fortis can guide us back to Caecus.

"Now I stink. And it will only get worse if I don't wash."

"There's lots of water here Lucia," said Pando.

"Are you stupid? I've told you. This is a holy place, I can't bathe here."

"Lucia, this stream mingles with other waters and ends up in the sea. Surely not all of it is 'holy'. It would seem to me that the holy part would be the water in the basin or pond, Could you not bathe downstream of the pond?" asked Pando.

Lucia turned sharply and thought.

I hate to admit it, but he is likely right. Besides, I can't stand the smell of myself. I have to do something.

She stormed down the long staircase; the little group at the bottom parted and allowed her through as though she was some kind of minor royalty.

She didn't speak or look back. She simply strode to the far edge of the pond. Relieved to be away from the laughing fools, she allowed herself to sink deeply into her own thoughts.

It is strange, with every step I can feel the tension leaving me. This is a beautiful place, so quiet. I can feel my spirit calm.

She allowed herself a little smile as she remembered what the dog had done. It wasn't really such a big thing.

Why is it that I have such animosity towards the beast?

She finally reached a place where the water spilled over and formed a rivulet that combined with others to form a stream that moved quickly away from this special place.

This should do. I must rinse my sandals in the cold clear water. That's better. Now I'll leave them on the grass to dry.

Oh the water is so cold; it's numbing my feet. The white stones at the bottom are so smooth it's like standing on a marble floor. What a marvelous place, the graceful cypress trees and the willows, but they can't be weeping, no, not here. I think they're bowing down to the spirits of this place.

It's a good thing that I'm wearing a tunic. It's short enough that he didn't hit that. I won't spend much time in this water, it's too cold just got to splash the water on my legs and make sure I scrub the urine away.

I feel differently, is it the water? Perhaps, anyway I feel at peace, it's like all the tension has left my body.

When she finished washing up she moved to the grassy bank and sat in the sun to allow herself to dry. Her mind drifted.

What is it that brought me here? How did I know about this place? I've never been here before and yet I know it, I know it well. What has brought me together with these people? Is this mighty Jupiter's wish? Is there something he wants me to do?

If that's so, please Jupiter give me a sign.

So much that has happened to me since starting this journey. A journey that seems to have taken place before. How can that be?

What is expected of me? Something is, I'm sure.

Time to head back to the others, I'm just about dry, a good thing too. Those clouds look like a storm in the making.

As she approached the Temple she could see that all of them were standing on the top landing of the staircase trying to figure out how to open the heavy door.

Well, not all are up there. I don't see Fortis anywhere.

She mounted the long staircase and arrived on the crowded platform.

"Do you feel better Lucia?" asked Viaticus.

"Much." She responded.

"Have you figured out how to open it yet?" she asked.

"Not yet." Said Pando as he twisted the large brass ring in the center of the door.

"Here, let me try," she said.

"One of these large bolt heads can be turned, that releases the lock on the brass ring, then you'll be able to turn it and the door will open."

They all stood in awe as the door swung open, just as she said it would.

"How did you know to do that?" asked Corripio.

"I don't really know," she replied honestly.

There was a light emanating from the gloom of the interior; that surprised all of them. They hung back each waiting for another to make the first move. Lucia was the first to enter.

"Come in, there's nothing to be frightened of."

Adding to herself.

At least I don't think there is.

"Where is that light coming from?" asked Ludus.

"Over there on the altar. It's the 'Light of the Eternal Fire', it must burn continuously to light the way for the God Jupiter," said Lucia.

It was not a large Temple, unlike those of Rome or even Perusia for that matter. The walls were damp and in some areas water trickled down the stone. There was an opening in the roof, directly over the altar meant to allow the ascension of Jupiter to his home in the heavens.

"Pando and Ludus, get those unlit torches from their niche on either side of the altar and light them with the flame. We need more light in here," said Lucia.

With that done, they were all able to see the interior more clearly. Behind the altar was a statue of a reclining figure of the God Jupiter. The flickering flames seemed to make the expression the face change as though it was alive.

"This place makes me shiver," said Ludus.

"Me too," said Viaticus.

Corripio was unable to speak at all.

As they stood looking at the statue, they heard a strange sound, a buzzing sound. It got louder and louder. Then they could see something rise from behind Jupiter's statue.

It was the largest fly that any of them had ever seen.

Lucia cried out.

"What is Lucia?" asked Pando.

"This is not good," she said. Her hand covering her mouth.

"Tell me what is it." Pando asked again as he moved away from the insect.

"It's Jupiter's Fly," she said.

"What?"

"I said it's Jupiter's Fly. It's a bad omen."

"What does all this mean?" Asked Viaticus.

Lucia drew a deep breath and answered.

"It means that there is a dead body somewhere here…or."

"Or what?" asked Pando.

"There will be a dead body here."

Chapter Twenty-eight

--Fortitudo, are you sure you don't have any idea when Kashta is coming back?

The horse shifted his great weight and leaned against the paddock causing it to creak under the strain.

--I'm afraid not Tactus. As you must know a Prince of the Royal Blood answers to no one, he goes and comes as he pleases. By the way, did you bring me a treat today?

Tactus reached inside his tunic and pulled out a carrot.

Fortitudo snorted.

--Is that the best Oratio can do today?

--I'm afraid so.

--I don't really fancy carrots you know. I much prefer apples.

--Perhaps then, I should give it to Hector?

--No, no, that's fine. I'll eat it.

The horse munched on the treat keeping one eye on the boy. When he finished and swallowed the last of the carrot he asked.

--What is it Tactus? You don't seem yourself today.

--I'm worried. Worried about my mother and father, worried about Pando, he's been gone such a long time.

--Oh Tactus, I'm sure you've nothing to worry about. Everything will work out just fine.

--I wish I could believe that Fortitudo, I just have this very heavy feeling in my heart. Why would anybody take my parents away from me? They didn't do anything wrong, I'm sure of that.

--I'm sure of that too Tactus. But these are very troubled times, ever since the Great Caesar was murdered.

"But what has that to do with my family?"

--Tactus, you are perhaps too young to understand but the Empire is in great turmoil at this moment, very nearly split in two. On one side you have the Imperialists and on the other the Republicans. They don't like one another very much.

Tactus thought for a moment and then said.

--You mean that because of politics my family has been taken away.

--What do you know of politics?

--Nothing, other than I've heard my father speak of it.

Fortitudo tried to pass wind silently, but failed. There was a sudden kick to the stall and a voice said.

--Stop doing that. You're not the only one that has to live in here.

--Sorry Hector, I couldn't help it.

--Go on with what you were saying Fortitudo.

--Well, if Caesar hadn't been murdered, by some vile Republicans I might say, we Imperialists would be in control today and the Senate would be free of dishonest politicians as we speak.

The goat kicked the stall again.

--Hogwash you Imperialistic fascist. You don't know what you're talking about.

--Go away Hector. I wasn't speaking to you.

--What's an Imperialist Fortitudo? Asked Tactus.

Before the horse could answer, Hector said.

--An Imperialist believes that one man, the Emperor, should control the whole country. These fools believe that they would be better off rather than having the power shared by responsible Senators.

--And exactly where, Hector, would one find these responsible Senators?

--Maybe the same place you'd find this god-like emperor Fortitudo.

--Are you a Republican then Hector? Asked Tactus.

--No you silly boy. Can't you see I'm a goat? Look at my horns, my beard, and my tail. Do I look like a Republican?

The horse snorted.

--The spitting image Hector.

None of this makes any sense to me, I can't tell if anything either one of these two tells me is true. They constantly bicker with one another. I think they do it just for the sake of argument.

--Can either of you tell me how this affects the disappearance of my mother and father? The boy asked.

Hector spoke first.

--I hate to admit that this bag of bones might be right about anything. But if your parents had chosen a side, whether Imperialist or Republican, it doesn't matter. Your parents could end up being a target of the opposition.

Then Fortitudo spoke up.

--The Imperialists are bound to win and your parents will be returned to you unharmed. I feel sure of that.

--You're like every other politician I've ever met. Just tell them whatever they want to hear, right?

--I'm not a politician. I'm a horse, in case you failed to notice.

--Maybe that's my problem. I'm looking at your back end, which must be why I mistook you for a politician.

* * * * *

Pico had escaped his kitchen duties by avoiding Oratio and sneaking out into long grass in the yard. He made his way to the shade of the furthest fig tree, sure that he could avoid detection.

I need to do some thinking I need to figure out just how to get along with Nog. My problem is, I need to be very careful just what I think about him. This is most disturbing. If I think anything that's negative, I'll end up all black and blue.

I'm beginning to think that I was better off when he was fast asleep.

I'll just stretch out here and think. Think what? This is just stupid, I may as well call him maybe if he sees me rather just hears me I will have a different impression on him.

"Come Nog."

Where is he? I hear a rustling up in the fig tree. There he is sitting up there on a branch, munching on a fig.

"What do you want of me Pico?"

"I just thought we should talk again. I'm not sure our first meeting went as well as it could have."

"Mutual Respect."

"What?"

"I said Mutual Respect. We both need to have it if we are to become friends."

"But I do respect you Nog, at least I try to. It's very difficult when you can read my every thought about you. It seems unfair when I can't read your mind."

"Nobody said it should be fair. It's the way it is. If you disrespect me, you'll get a poke. That's just how it works."

"To help me get used to this whole thing, do you think you could find another approach to remind me when I'm thinking improper thoughts? I mean something other than pain," said Pico

"Hmmm, let's see." Said Nog

"How about this, every time you have an improper thought your nose will bleed."

"That could be rather messy don't you think?" The boy asked.

" I suppose that's true. I know what we can do. When you do get into trouble, the first word that comes out of your mouth will come out backwards."

At least that won't hurt.

"Let's try that and see what happens," said Pico.

"Now that that's settled, what was it you wanted to see me about?"

"I'd like to find out more about the powers and what the rules are that would allow me use those powers."

"First, the powers are not yours, they are mine, given to me by the Gods. Second, you cannot use the powers directly except in special circumstances. You must ask for my help and the reason for the request must be self-evident. You must be able to convince me of the need for me to exercise these powers."

"I see, just like when I talked to my mother."

"Exactly, but in that instance I determined the need for and the benefit of using that power. Therefore, you can use it yourself without coming directly to me. You can invoke it by simply saying 'See Nog'."

"Thank you Nog, that's wonderful. Is it possible for me to see other people, like my brother Pando for example?"

"Not without coming to me first and making your request as I've said before."

"Can you tell me about your other powers?"

"There are several but the visualization is one of the most important ones. Another important power is to find lost articles, particularly things of great value. Then there is the ability to make things disappear and reappear somewhere else."

"This all sounds very exciting, I can hardly wait to get started."

"Started at what?"

"Why the magic of course. I mean your Powers."

"Sounds to me like you weren't listening to what I said to you the first time we met. This is not like some parlour game, it's very serious."

"Of course, of course. I'm sorry, I just got excited."

"Well then, enough for today. I'm going back to eating my figs. They are delicious."

"Go Nog." Said Pico
Pffffft.
Then he was gone.
Pico saw Tactus leaving the barn, he called to him.
"Tactus, over here, come on over."
The older boy made his way towards him, when he arrived, he asked Pico.
"What are you doing out here, aren't you supposed to be doing chores with Oratio?"
"Just taking a little rest. Have you ever tried eating a fig Tactus?"
"No, but I know I wouldn't like them."
"Here's one that fell on the ground go ahead, try it."
"You try it, I don't want any. How would you know they're delicious? I'll bet you've never eaten one either."
"No but there was an,..an animal here a short while ago, he seemed to like them.
"What kind of an animal."
"lerriuqs a."
"What kind of gibberish is that you're speaking."
"Nothing, just forget it.

Chapter Twenty-nine

There was a great clap of thunder followed by a bright flash of lightning and the rain began to fall. Sheets of rain soaked the little band standing on the top landing of the staircase.

"Looks like we're in for a real storm. Just look at those clouds it's almost as dark as night," said Viaticus.

Lucia turned, opened the door, and said.

"Let's go inside, that strike seemed very close by. It could be dangerous out here, and at least we can stay dry."

Corripio was the first one to go in, his fear of lightning overcoming his fear of Jupiter's Fly. Ludus followed but Pando stood on the landing and asked.

"But what about Fortis, we can't leave him out in this weather?"

"Yes, what about Fortis?" Echoed Viaticus.

Unexpectedly, Lucia responded.

"We have no idea where he is, but if he comes scratching at the door we can always let him in. Chances are he's smart enough to take cover and he'll come back when the storm is over."

Pando was taken aback at the sudden reversal in Lucia's attitude towards Fortis.

What's going on with her? First she gets frantic about Fortis entering this holy place and now it's all right if he does. I can't blame her for getting angry about Fortis pissing on her leg. I know I would too. However, Fortis didn't deserve to be hit with a stick either.

I can't figure this change in attitude out, maybe it's like father always used to say, 'women are like the weather, unpredictable and changeable'.

Pando was smart enough to keep his thoughts to himself and passed through the door with Viaticus following close behind.

Lucia pushed it shut with a loud clang.

It seems darker than it was when we first entered.

No light is coming in from the opening in the roof, just rain lots of it. Oh, another bolt of lightning, it almost lit up the whole temple. Have we made Zeus angry by coming here? I can feel the thunder in the pit of my stomach, but surely, we'll be safe here.

Corripio spoke.

"Lucia what shall we do? I'm frightened."

"We'll be fine here Corripio. We just have to wait out the storm and then we'll be on our way."

I hope I sounded convincing I'm not really as sure as I once was. What's happening to me?

Her thoughts were interrupted when Viaticus said.

"I'm hungry, when are we going to eat?"

"I still have sweet cake left and some water," offered Pando.

"Come to the front of the Temple away from the altar, that way we can stay dry. There's a lot of rain coming in through the roof, but I think there's a floor drain behind the altar that should prevent the floor from becoming too wet at the front. We'll be more comfortable," said Lucia.

The five of them sat on the floor in a circle and Pando passed around first the cake followed by the water flask. Each broke off a piece and handed the remainder to the person next to them until it returned to Pando looking as though it was untouched.

"This cake is really good Pando. I can't believe that it has lasted this long. Whoever made it must be a magician," said Ludus stuffing more cake in his mouth.

The others sat in silence satisfying their hunger and taking turns with the water flask when another flash of lightning occurred followed by rolling thunder.

Between the flickering light from the torches and the brilliance of the lightning flashes, the expression on the face of Jupiter seemed to change. From that of the benign to one of anger, or was it just imaginary?

As Pando reached for the water flask, the top of his tunic opened exposing the amulet. It glowed with an Inner Light that was brighter than ever before. Everyone saw it. Corripio spoke first

"Pando, where did you get that gem? It's beautiful and far too expensive to be wearing on the road. There are many thieves that would welcome the opportunity to steal it."

Unable to conceal it any longer he held it up for them to see.

"It was given to me by my friend Caecus to help me find my cousins, it was my beacon to them. This amulet along with my trusty friend Fortis brought us all together."

"Did he give it to you to keep?" Asked Ludus

"Honestly, he didn't say. However, my sense is I will return it to him when I next see him."

"What makes it glow like that?" Asked Viaticus.

"I don't know, all I can say is that it seems to have mystical powers. I don't pretend to know much about the stone aside from what it's called."

"You mean it has a name?" Asked Corripio

Before Pando could reply, Lucia answered for him.

"Lapis Lazuli."

"How did you know that Lucia?" Asked Pando.

"I don't know how I know, I just do that's all."

Corripio's eyes shone almost as much as the gem, he reached out his hand and asked.

"May I touch it."

Lucia jumped to her feet and shouted.

"NO. No man may touch the amulet unless the unseeing prophet determines that the person has a true heart. Grave consequences will befall any who do."

Pando was stunned; he turned to look at the girl.

Her eyes are closed, is she even here? What does she mean, grave consequences? Did I ever tell her of Caecus being blind? How does she know these things?

Corripio withdrew his outstretched arm, his hand shaking visibly as he did so.

Being a slave was so much easier. Life is just too complicated when you have to think for yourself.

Lucia sat down and quietly resumed eating her sweet cake as though nothing at all had happened.

Pando scratched his head looked at each member of the group and thought to himself.

This is all very weird. How does a young girl like Lucia acquire this knowledge and why? Why was she included in this group? Caecus said nothing about her or Corripio for that matter.

Moreover, what's going on with the amulet? Caecus said nothing of any kind of powers aside from being able to locate my cousins.

Probably a good thing I've said nothing about the man who followed me. Or the vulture episode. No way they're going to believe Fortis's ability to 'shape change', they'll think I just made it all up. I'm not even sure now that any of it happened.

Just then there was another lightning strike, close by and thunder again. In the brilliant flash, Lucia saw Corripio, sitting hugging his knees and weeping.

She moved to his side, the young girl consoling a man old enough to be her father. She put an arm around his shoulders and said.

"It's all right Corripio, everything is going to be all right. You'll see it will all work out. Please don't cry."

"Oh Lucia, I'm so ashamed. Here I should be the strong one comforting you, instead I'm just useless."

"That's not true Corripio, you're not useless."

"Yes I am. Oh, there's that buzzing sound again and it's even louder. Jupiter's Fly is going to get me. Oh woe is me."

"I don't hear any buzzing Corripio, I think it's just your imagination," she whispered.

"Oh Lucia, I should never have run away from Sceleris. He always looked after me. I don't want to be free anymore. I'm sure that's why I'm being punished now and I'm sorry that it's involved you and the others. I'm so sorry."

He was weeping uncontrollably now, his shoulders shaking with each sob. Lucia had to do something to try to convince him that things were not as bad as they appeared. So, she said to him.

"Corripio have you forgotten all of the beatings he gave you? Have you forgotten how he has demeaned you treating you like just another of his animals?

"This is not a man who cares for you or looks after you. He simply takes advantage of you. You are the one with the healer's skills and yet he's the one that takes all of the money for the cures you provide.

"These skills you have are the very thing that makes you worthy. Worthy as a free man, slave to no one. Don't you understand that?"

"Oh I don't know Lucia, it just seems to me that things have gone from bad to worse since I left him. I'm now a criminal in the eyes of the state and worse yet I've implicated you and the boys. I feel so worthless."

It was impossible for the others not to overhear the conversation between the two of them as a result Viaticus felt compelled to speak up.

"She's right Corripio, everything she's said is true. If it wasn't for you where would Ludus and I be now? Sold as slaves? Me learning to be a gladiator so I can face certain death in a Circus?

"Far from being worthless, Ludus and I owe you a debt of gratitude."

Corripio wept still, but less so. The rolling thunder seemed to diminish as well, perhaps the storm was over, or at least the worst of it thought Pando.

I'm still confused. Am I witnessing some kind of conversion here? From a street urchin to a mothering spirit right after being pissed on. Makes no sense to me.

I wonder where Fortis is. I hope nothing has happened to him. I've become very attached to that old dog even if he does do inappropriate things from time to time.

"There, see Corripio, the storm is letting up. Better things will come. You'll see," said Lucia.

They all heard a voice a very loud voice calling from outside.

"Corripio, I know you're in there. I know you can hear me."

"It's him, he's out there," said Corripio.

"Ignore him and maybe he'll go away." Lucia tried to cover Corripio's ears.

Again, he called.

"Corripio, I need you, come help me."

"Don't listen Corripio." She said still covering his ears.

"Corripio, I'm going blind. My good eye, I can see almost nothing with it now. Have pity, help me, please."

"He's a liar Corripio, you must know that. If he can't see then how did he follow us here?" She said.

"But he needs my help Lucia. I must go to him."

"No Corripio."

"But I must, don't you see."

Before he could be stopped he was out the door into the drizzle, just as Jupiter's Fly rose once more from behind the altar.

Chapter Thirty

Corripio closed the Temple door behind him leaving his new friends in stunned silence. Standing at the top of the stairs he peered out into the drizzle trying to see Sceleris. It was then he heard the voice again.

"Corripio, I'm over here, to your left. Can't you see me?"

I don't see him, but I can hear him all right. Wait, there he is. I see the bushes move. It's him, it's Sceleris.

He rushed headlong down the stairs, slipping when he'd reached the midway point and losing his footing on the slippery steps. He covered the rest of the descent on his backside, his tailbone connecting painfully with each stair tread.

I see stars. That hurt but I'm lucky I didn't break anything, at least I don't think I did. I must get up. Ouch, maybe I did break something, my back hurts so.

He struggled to his feet and made his way to the bushes where he'd seen Sceleris.

Yes there he is.

"Oh Sceleris, it's so good to see you."

"Get over here you poor excuse for a slave. Now it's good to see me is it? If that's true then why did you run from me in the first place?"

"They made me do it," he lied.

"How could two boys make you do anything you didn't want to do?"

"Oh Sceleris, I was careless. I got too close to them and the stole my knife. Threatened to kill me they did. Said they'd slit my throat if I didn't go with them to show them the way."

"Two boys could do that to you? You're a liar, come to me so I can give you the beating you deserve."

Corripio cowered at the feet of the bigger man and said.

"Please don't hit me Sceleris, I've told you the truth, really I have."

Then quickly changing the subject he said.

"Your good eye, it looks like you have puss running from it. You need immediate attention if I'm to save it for you. You don't want to be left as a blind man wandering alone do you?"

Sceleris shivered, as much from Corripio's words as from his clothes, soaking wet from the storm that had just past. Corripio stood up and peered into the weeping eye. He took a filthy rag from his pocket and carefully wiped the yellow mucus away.

"Yes Sceleris, it looks very bad, very bad indeed. I must apply some of my special salve right away."

"You have it with you?"

"It's in my bag in the Temple."

"You stupid fool, why didn't you bring it with you."

"I'm sorry Sceleris, I just didn't think. I heard your voice and I came running."

"Not thinking seems to be your strong point. If it wasn't for your curing skills I'd have killed you by now and been done with you."

"I said I'm sorry. I can go back in and get my bag."

"No, once you get in there I have no way of knowing whether or not you've had a change of heart. How many others are in there, just the two boys?"

"Ah, actually there are four others in there."

"What? How is it there comes to be four in there? Who are the other two?"

"Well, there's another boy, a cousin of the two boys. His name is Pando and then of course there is Lucia."

"Lucia, you mean there's a woman in there?"

"Not a woman Sceleris, girl about thirteen I think."

"Where did those two come from?"

"Pando apparently was on his way to meet his cousins when he met up with Lucia somewhere in the forest I think," he lied again.

"And there was no way you could escape from these children?"

"No Sceleris, remember what a strong one that Viaticus is, they kept me tied hand and foot most of the time."

"That experience will be nothing compared to what I do to you once we've finished here."

Corripio shuddered.

Perhaps if he knew about the amulet, he would be more kindly disposed to me. Maybe he wouldn't beat me. It can't hurt to tell him what I've seen.

"Sceleris, there is something important I have to tell you. Perhaps then you will think differently of me."

"I doubt that you would know if something was important even if the 'thing' in question jumped up and bit you on the ass. But go ahead and tell me and you'd better hope that I consider it important."

"Well, this Pando I spoke of.."

"Get on with it you fool."

"Well, he's wearing an amulet a Lapis Lazuli amulet. It looks very expensive."

"Is that so and where would a young boy get something of such value?"

"He said someone named Caecus had given it to him."

"Who is this Caecus, I've never heard his name before?"

"I don't know either Sceleris, but as I said, it looks quite valuable."

Sceleris wiped more puss away from his eye with the back of his hand, wiping it to his dirty tunic.

If I find a way to get this Pando to bring Corripio's bag to me, perhaps I can overpower him, kill him and get both the amulet and the salve.

I think I know just how to do that. He removed his knife from it's sheath and said to Corripio.

"Come here slave and do exactly as I say."

Sceleris stood behind the smaller man and placed one arm around his waist. His right hand held the knife that he brought to Corripio's throat.

Corripio could feel the razor sharp edge of the knife.

Surely he won't kill me. That knife, it's pressing against my skin I'm sure he's drawing blood.

I wish now I hadn't eaten that Sweet Cake, it's just rolling around in my stomach. Maybe I'll be sick and throw up. Or worse.

"Listen to me very carefully Corripio. I want you to call out to this Pando. Tell him to fetch your bag and bring it here. Do you understand?"

Careful not to nod his head Corripio whispered hoarsely.

"Yes, yes."

"Good, go ahead, call out."

"Pando, can you hear me?"

There was no answer. He called again.

"Pando, please answer me, it's important a matter of life or death."

"Very good Corripio, just remember whose life we're talking about."

Finally they heard Pando's voice through the door.

"What do you want Corripio?"

"I want you to bring me my bag. My medicines are in it. I need them to treat my patient."

"Why don't you just come and get it Corripio?" Asked Pando.

Sceleris gripped Corripio even tighter around his waist and growled.

"Tell him you can't leave me, tell him I'm too sick."

"Pando he is really ill, I need that medicine now, I can't leave him."

Another voice called out from the Temple, it was Viaticus.

"We see no reason to believe what you're telling us Corripio. Remember we know Sceleris. With the amount of time you're wasting in talking to us you could've retrieved your bag and be treating your 'patient' by now. This is nothing but some kind of trap."

Sceleris struggled out of the bushes dragging Corripio with him his knife still at his throat. He shouted angrily.

"Do you see this knife? It is exceedingly sharp, with one slash I can part this worthless head from this useless body.

If you want to keep Corripio alive, you've only to do as I ask. I want Pando to bring Corripio's medical bag to me here. No one else, just Pando.

If this doesn't happen by my count of ten, then his life is over and you all will have condemned me to go blind into the world.

Understand me, for I've nothing to lose."

* * * * *

Inside the Temple, Lucia, Ludus, Viaticus and Pando looked at one another each waiting for another to speak. It was Lucia who broke the silence.

"It may be a trap but can we afford not to try to help Corripio? What kind of people would we be to just let him die?"

"He created this situation himself, he could have stayed with us." Said Ludus.

Lucia her eyes flashing responded.

"So you're saying because he committed a stupid act he deserves to die?"

"No, of course not it's just…"

"Let's not fight amongst ourselves, I believe we must help Corripio," said Pando.

"But it's a trap, you know that Pando." Viaticus responded.

A loud voice from outside announced.

"THREE."

"We need a plan," said Ludus

Pando nodded enthusiastically.

"Exactly, and quickly too. Look, there's four of us and only one of him. I think if I take the bag down to Corripio and let him treat this Sceleris, we could rush him, and overpower the criminal if we all work together."

Lucia became excited at the idea.

"Yes, it could work, Sceleris won't be able to see anything while Corripio applies the salve and he'll be so intent on what he's doing he won't notice anything either."

The Voice again.

"FOUR."

Viaticus said.

"But we need something to tie him up with and we've no rope."

"I have the answer to that. There are young willow trees by the shore of the basin, while we get Sceleris under control, Ludus you can cut the smallest willow saplings and bring them to us. They'll be strong and supple enough to use as rope." Said Lucia.

And again.

"FIVE."

"Perhaps we should all say a prayer to the God Jupiter and ask for his help in making this plan a success," said Pando.

The four young people bowed their heads and stood in silence.

Chapter Thirty-one

Pando opened the heavy door a crack and peered out. Sceleris held Corripio firmly around the waist with a knife held to his throat.

"SIX," shouted Sceleris.

Pando turned back to the small group and said.

"I think he's serious, he means to kill Corripio if we don't give him the medicine."

My heart is thumping so loudly it might just jump out of my throat. Can I do this? I must, I couldn't bear to have Corripio's death on my conscience.

"SEVEN."

"Pando, here is the bag. Try not to get too close to Sceleris, just throw it to him. When Corripio begins to apply the salve, Sceleris won't be able to hold the knife at Corripio's throat and he'll be looking up towards the sky. That's when you must hit that beast with all your strength and knock him to the ground. That'll be our signal to burst out of the Temple and hold him down until we can tie him.

Do you understand?" Asked Lucia.

"EIGHT."

Pando nodded, took a deep breath and put his shoulder to the heavy door and stepped onto the landing.

"Oh Pando, please hurry, he means it. He'll kill me if you don't give him the medicine," cried Corripio.

The staircase was slippery from the rain so Pando moved down cautiously. At about the halfway mark Pando drew back his arm as if to throw the bag.

"NO." Shouted Sceleris, "bring it to me or he dies."

"Please Pando, the container the salve is in is very fragile. It could get broken, please do as he asks."

"Good thinking," whispered the one-eyed man.

There was little that he could do other than comply. Pando stumbled on the wet step and almost fell. He could hear Corripio suck in his breath.

The rest of the plan should still work.

He reached the last stair as Sceleris shouted.

"NINE."

"Bring it here Pando," Corripio begged.

Pando held out the bag at arm's length and approached the two men. Neither of them made a move towards it.

"Come closer to me," said Sceleris.

The boy was close enough now to smell the putrid breath of Corripio's captor. Then it happened, as quickly as a serpent strike's it's prey Sceleris released Corripio and grasped Pando so that his knife was now at the boy's throat.

Corripio sank to the ground, wailing like an old woman.

Pando struggled briefly but felt the blade cut into his neck, he had no option but to stay still.

Sceleris spoke.

"Well now, I understand that you have something of great value that you'd like to give to old Sceleris. Is that true?"

"No," he gasped.

"Corripio tells me you have a Lapis Lazuli amulet around your neck, so why do you lie to me?"

Pando glared at the cringing figure at his feet and said nothing.

Sceleris lifted the golden chain with the point of his knife until the gem was exposed. Even in the half-light after the storm it glowed magnificently. He loosened his grip on Pando and reached to grasp the jewel with his hand. Pando twisted free and turned just as it happened.

A brilliant flash, brighter than any of the lightning they had experienced during the storm. A loud 'crack' followed and the three were engulfed in a pall of acrid thick blue smoke.

Pando was stunned, his ears rang from the noise, he couldn't see because of the dense smoke and he saw spots before his eyes as a result of the flash.

He tried to move but his legs refused him and he toppled to the ground unconscious.

When he regained his senses he found Lucia looking into his face, concern evident in her expression.

"Are you all right?" She asked.

"I don't know. What happened?

"You best get up and have a look for yourself. I don't think you'd believe me."

She helped him up; he shook his head trying to clear the cobwebs. He looked around and then he saw him, Sceleris.

Or is it? Yes it's him all right; I'd know that face anywhere but something's wrong.

"Lucia, what's happened here?"

"You would know better than me. But I think he must have touched the amulet, did he?"

"Yes, yes he did."

"And now he's paid the price. In touching the gem he triggered powerful magic. I don't understand all of it but I think I told you that no one other than you should handle it."

Pando walked up to Sceleris or what used to be Sceleris.

This is most curious, it looks like him, yet he doesn't move, nor speak. There's something in the palm of his right hand what is it?

It's the amulet, just lying there. I must have it back.

Without thinking he reached in the palm and lifted it out, it looked the same as ever.

But that hand, it's as cold as stone. Let me touch it again. Yes it is, it's stone almost like marble. Sceleris has been turned into a statue.

Pando replaced the amulet around his neck and asked Lucia.

"Have you ever seen anything like this?"

"No never."

The both walked around the figure; every detail was just as it was in life, including the weeping eye. The knife in the left hand looked ready to injure but it too was now stone.

"Where are the others?"

"I sent them to gather wood from the forest."

"Wood from the forest?" He asked.

"Yes."

"But why Lucia?"

"For a funeral pyre."

"What?"

" I said for a funeral pyre, for Corripio."

"Corripio's dead?"

"Yes, I think as a result of this event. When the smoke cleared I found his body. I don't know what caused his death, perhaps fear or more likely the magic of the amulet."

"I'm sorry Lucia."

"Sorry for what?"

"Corripio's death, it seemed you two were quite close."

"You have no need to feel sorrow, it was nothing you did. He died as a result of his own actions."

Pando looked into her face and saw no emotion.

Strange, I was sure there was some kind of connection between them. But her coldness seems to indicate otherwise. Maybe this is just a reaction to whatever it was that happened here.

Could it be that it was the magic of the amulet that killed him. I don't have any doubt that the magic turned Sceleris to stone. But why didn't Caecus warn me? It could have been dangerous to the others.

If it hadn't have been for Lucia's comment in the Temple we could easily have had other people turned to stone. Was that just luck? No, I think that somehow Caecus has been watching over us all along.

Ludus and Viaticus returned from foraging for wood. Each carried a substantial armload taxing their strength as they staggered forward.

"We're going to need more than that." Said Lucia.

"Can we rest for just a minute, that stuff is heavy. How much more will we need?" Asked Ludus.

"Have you two never been to a funeral?" Asked the girl.

They shook their heads.

And you Pando?"

"No."

"You three have a lot of growing up to do. This lot looks all right, but try to find more dry wood, look under rock ledges, It would not bode well for the pyre to go out before the ceremony is completed."

Pando signaled to his cousins and said.

"Come, I'll go with you and help, it'll go faster.

"We three need to talk and I don't need Lucia interfering."

Chapter Thirty-two

As they left the site of the rather extraordinary event, the three boys gave the body of Corripio a wide berth. Fortunately for them, Lucia had covered the face with some kind of cloth so they didn't have to look at it.

Once out of Lucia's earshot Viaticus was the first to speak.

"Pando, what in the world went on back there?"

"I don't know much more than you do Viaticus, even though I was standing right there when it all happened. When the loud noise occurred, it seemed to knock me out. I remember nothing from that point until I found Lucia standing over me."

"Either she's very brave or very stupid. She rushed out of the Temple as soon as it happened. She didn't seem to have any thought for her own safety," said Ludus.

When they were far enough away from the Temple, Pando turned and said.

"I think there are some things about my part of the journey that I should tell you. You may not believe me, but honestly, it all happened just as I will tell you."

The three sat on a rock outcrop. Ludus and Viaticus looked at Pando prepared to listen to every word.

Pando sat quietly for a moment trying to decide just how to begin. When he thought about it, he realized just how outrageous his tale was going to sound. Would they believe him?

He cleared his throat and began his story from the beginning, with the arrest of his parents and his mother's request that they seek out her sister in Rome.

Neither Viaticus nor Ludus spoke, they just sat in rapt attention as Pando told them of Kashta and his dog Fortis and then the meeting with Caecus.

When he got to the part of Fortis, shape shifting into a bear and saving his life he saw a flicker of disbelief in the eyes of his cousins.

"I see that you have doubts about what I'm telling you. But you must believe that it's the truth."

"But Pando just how could the dog Fortis turn into a bear?" Asked Ludus.

"I have no idea Ludus. But I guess that it was some kind of magic for it happened again."

"What?" It was Viaticus's turn this time.

"Yes, I fell asleep under a tree and failed to notice we were being followed by a vulture. It swooped down and stole the amulet from around my neck. I cried out and awoke Fortis who saw what was happening."

"What did he do then?" Viaticus's eyes were wide in anticipation.

"He turned himself into a great Golden Eagle and flew after the vulture. The Eagle attacked the other bird and it dropped the amulet. I thought all was lost but then to my amazement the Eagle recovered it in mid-air and returned it to me."

"I can understand now your attachment to Fortis. Do you have any idea how he has come to have such great powers." Asked Ludus.

"Not really, all I can say is his master Kashta claims he is a Prince of the Royal Blood from Nubia. Perhaps Nubia is a place of great magic and Kashta bestowed the powers on his dog."

Viaticus spoke.

"Pando, up until just a short while ago we had nothing of a magical experience on our trip. However, I must say, we owe much to Corripio. Without his help, who knows where we would be today? Even though he was deceitful, I miss him."

Ludus echoed similar sentiments and added.

"I was so looking forward to learning more about the 'art of healing' from him and now that will never happen."

"Pando tell us more about the amulet. Did you know it had such power?"

"No, Viaticus. I knew it had magical powers but I was not made aware of just how powerful it was. Caecus indicated that it would lead me to you two and it did."

"Just what is happening to us all? Our parents arrested then all this magic and the death of Corripio, why?" Viaticus asked no one in particular.

"I agree with you, this is all very strange, why have we been singled out? What do you think Ludus?"

"It must be the will of the Gods, some higher power seems to directing what is happening. Let's just hope it's not just a game for their amusement."

"Viaticus, tell me about Lucia, it seems to me that she knows more than any thirteen year old should. She knew about the power of the amulet, remember. And why when she seemed to have a certain amount of affection for Corripio, did she show no emotion at his death?"

"I don't know much about her Pando. As I said earlier, after we separated from Corripio, we thought we would never see him again and then by chance we meet and he had Lucia with him.

"Frankly I think that was to our good fortune since, I'm sure Ludus would agree, we weren't doing very well finding our own way.

"Lucia took over and we were happy to let her. I don't know why she showed no emotion except that her character seems as strong and unbending as an iron bar."

"Now that Corripio is gone, she may not have the same interest in staying with us, I think we need to be prepared that she might go on her own," said Pando.

"But how will we find our way Pando if she does leave us?"

"The original plan was for Fortis to lead us back."

"Pando, do you know where Fortis has gone?"

"No, but he's done this before and always come back."

"Fortis doesn't seem to care for Lucia, maybe he won't come back this time," said Ludus.

"We'd better start gathering wood and getting back to the Temple. Lucia may not be experiencing the loss of Corripio, but I don't think that will make her tongue less sharp," said Viaticus.

Chapter Thirty-three

Lucia had scraped up clay from the banks of the sacred springs and working with her hands she fashioned the clay into an urn. It was crude but the best she could do under the circumstances.

She then took a stick and with her knife, she made it into a stylus. With the stylus, she engraved into the soft clay the following words in Latin.

'The remains of Corripio a Slave died on IX Sextilis in the fifth year
Safe journey to Elysium'

She took the remainder of the clay and made a cover for the urn. She tested it for fit and adjusted it so it just slid over the lip of the urn. Then she removed the lid and placed it alongside the vessel.

Not as good as it should be but given the circumstances it's better than having to bury him.

She moved to the corpse of the small man and looked down on the remains. Her heart was full of sadness.

Could it be that he was my lost brother? I will never know now, the least I can do is see that he has a proper Roman funeral. He deserves at least that much. I pray that your journey across the River Styx and your final judgement will allow you to enter Elysium and not be cast into Tartarus.

Surely the good things you have done will be taken into your account, your care of the sick and afflicted. Your forbearance in the face of slavery should surely count for something.

If only your concern for yourself had not led you into the final treachery. However, even then, you paid for that sin with your life.

I pray that you will get to Elysium Corripio.

Her silent prayer was interrupted by the return of the three boys each carrying a large armload of wood.

"We'll begin constructing the pyre shortly. It's getting late; we'll soon lose our light so we can't afford to waste time.

Each of the boys tried, unsuccessfully, to avert their eyes from Corripio's corpse. The suddenness with which life had left his body impacted them all. None of them had ever seen a dead person before.

Pando shook off the feeling by asking Lucia.

"No sign of Fortis yet?"

"Neither sight nor sound, perhaps he's gone for good," she answered.

"He'll be back, I just know he will. Probably chasing rabbits or something."

"Or maybe a wild boar, cooked or otherwise," said Lucia.

Pando hid a smile.

"Come, let's get busy with the building of the pyre."

None of the boys had ever had this experience before and were perfectly happy to take directions from her. She showed them just what area the pyre should cover and how to orient the wood to be most effective.

"Be sure to select the driest wood for the bottom rows."

She showed them how to interlock the lengths of wood to form a relatively sturdy platform and yet allow the free flow of air to feed the fire.

When they had used about half the wood, she raised her hand and said.

"Stop, that's enough for now. It's time to place the body on top of the wood. It should be easy work if we each take an arm or a leg. Take care when you lift him onto the pyre, we don't want to knock the wood over. Otherwise we'll have to start again."

Each of the boys hung back fearful of touching the body.

"Come on you babies, do you expect me lift him by myself?"

She already had a hold of one ankle lifting the foot. Shamed by the girl, the boys assumed their positions but each still hesitant.

Viaticus was the first, he grasped the left wrist, and Ludus followed grabbing the right one and Pando stood opposite Lucia taking the other ankle.

"Remember, lift him high enough to clear the wood and lay him in the center most spot. Ready? Now lift."

The boys were surprised at how heavy a lift it really was. Pando remembered his father saying something about 'a dead weight', now he thought maybe he knew what he meant.

"There, that's good. Now let me insert the urn before you resume building up the wood," she said.

"Where did the urn come from and what's it for." Asked Ludus.

"I made it and it's to receive Corripio's ashes. Do you boys know nothing at all?"

"But why put the urn in the pyre?" Asked Viaticus.

Lucia sighed and bit back another nasty comment. Instead, she explained.

"The heat of the fire will cause the soft clay to become ceramic much like the bowls your mothers use at home. The process for making them is the same. Out of respect for Corripio and to help him, hopefully, on his way to Elysium, the urn will convey his ashes on his journey."

"What's Elysium like Lucia?" Asked Ludus.

"How would I know stupid boy. I've never been there and hope not to go for a long time yet."

They all bent to their work, not speaking, just carefully piling up the wood.

"Pando, take care on the corners. If you don't interlock them as I've shown you, the pyre will collapse as it begins to burn. That will never do."

Lucia showed him again, just how to do it.

Finally the structure was complete; Lucia stood back and said.

"Well, it's not the biggest funeral pyre I've ever seen, but it'll do the job. Now we need to insert kindling in the spaces at the bottom of the pyre, twigs, dry leaves anything that will burn quickly and help the larger pieces catch fire."

"Looks pretty big to me. Why would it have to larger." Said Viaticus,

"The more important the person the larger the pyre." Then she commanded.

"Pando, would you and Viaticus bring two torches from the Temple, it's time we started the ceremony. Darkness is almost upon us."

The boys ran to the Temple, neither was overly anxious to enter it. Finally Viaticus twisted the secret bolt, turned the large brass ring and with a mighty heave, he pulled the heavy door open.

Even with the eternal flame and the two torches alight in their sconces, the place was eerie. Pando's stomach sank as he looked at the face of Jupiter with it's sightless eyes that seemed to stare at him.

Did the lips move? I could swear he's smiling at me. Or is it more like a scowl? The dampness seems to make his clothes look wet. The water seeps into the building right through the masonry walls.

They removed the torches from the wall and got out of there as quickly as they could. A loud buzzing sound followed them. They didn't stop to try to close the door.

"Lucia," cried Pando. "It's Jupiter's Fly it's following us."

"Quickly, give me a torch and you Viaticus, do as I do."

They lit the dry kindling and almost instantly the drier wood at the bottom caught. She knew that the pyre would be a success.

Jupiter's Fly buzzed even more loudly, hovering over the pyre, but as the flames licked higher, it had to move away, finally retreating back inside the Temple. The buzzing sounded angry as it retreated.

"He won't bother us any more. He is only present when a body is not cremated. He has no place here now," said Lucia.

The fire blazed hotly with the flames licking skyward. The heat forced all of them back a pace or two for fear their clothes might get scorched.

The center of the pyre was now glowing almost white, it looked translucent. The dark outline of Corripio's body could be seen within. The three boys turned away from the sight unable to continue watching the ceremony.

As he turned Pando thought he saw something at the edge of the clearing.

What is it? Something moved over there in the Cypress trees. Yes, it moved again. What is it?

His blood ran cold as he realized that it was the figure of a man.

What's he doing here? What does he want? Who is he?

Chapter Thirty-four

"There's someone out there." Said Pando.
"What did you say, I can't hear you over the sound of the fire?" Asked Viaticus.
He looked out to where Pando's finger pointed.
"I see it, looks like a man watching us. What should we do?"
Ludus and Lucia spotted the movement in the woods at the same time. The four stood rooted to the spot. Lucia's hand trembled as she held it to her mouth as though prepared to stifle a scream.
The figure moved slowly from the depths of the darkness of the woods. Finally as he come closer to the circle of light from the Pyre, Pando cried out.
"Kashta, is it really you?"
As the large man came closer it was evident that it was indeed Kashta. Viaticus was almost mesmerized by the vision of this huge black man dressed in clothes the likes of which he hadn't seen before.
I remember Pando talking about this 'Kashta' person but I had no idea he was so big. He makes me feel small. He only has one arm and those clothes, certainly not Roman.
Pando spoke.
"Kashta, it's so good to see you again, what are you doing here?"
The others seemed to relax at Pando's recognition of the stranger, all but Lucia that is.
Kashta moved even closer to the funeral pyre, ignoring Pando's question, he spoke.
"Why has there been no Invocation? Do you all expect the dead to row himself across the Styx?"
The heat from the fire was reaching it's fiercest causing the four young ones to back away. It was then that Lucia finally spoke.
"Why is this funeral a concern of yours? Did you even know the man?"
"I know many men, he among them. I take it by your tone that you believe that you are in charge here."
Her eyes flashed and her cheeks reddened. He was almost twice her size but she refused to be intimidated. She responded.
"I am in charge here because nobody else could be, no one else knew how."

Kashta allowed a small smile to play on his lips showing his startlingly white teeth, then he said.

"That was then, but now I am here and as a Prince of the Royal Blood of Nubia I will make the Invocation. Just stand quietly please. All of you." He said looking directly at Lucia.

The fire seemed to flare up at just that moment; it was now at its highest point with flames licking into the night sky.

Kashta raised both his arms into the air threw back his head and in a loud voice began the Invocation.

"MAY ALL OF THE GODS IN THE CELESTIAL SPHERE GRANT SAFE PASSAGE TO THE POOR MORTAL CORRIPIO. UNWORTHY AS HE MAY HAVE BEEN, WE BESEECH YOU TO ALLOW HIM ENTRY INTO HIS ETERNAL PLACE OF REST.
MAY THE POWER OF THIS FIRE PURIFY HIM
SO THAT HIS SPIRIT MAY PASS FREELY IF YOU SO WISH."

Again the group fell silent; each stood with their head bowed. Pando couldn't help but turn his head to catch a glimpse of Kashta.

How was it he knew Corripio's name? What is this tension between him and Lucia? I don't think that she ever met him before. Strange, the more life goes on the stranger it gets.

Kashta spoke.

"There is nothing to do now until the fire burns itself out. Even then we must let the ashes cool so that we can handle them and respectfully bury Corripio's earthly remains."

Lucia hotly responded.

"I know all of that, I made an urn to receive his remains. Why do you find it necessary to come along and interfere?"

He ignored her outburst and said.

"Now Pando, I haven't eaten in two days, can you find an old friend a crust or two?"

"I still have some of Oratio's Sweet Cake, will that do?"

"Ah, Oratio's Sweet Cake, I can think of nothing better."

He clasped Pando around the shoulder with his good arm and said.

"Lead on I'm famished." Then he turned to the rest of them and said.

"Nothing more to see here, come join us, we need to be properly introduced." Then as an afterthought he said over his shoulder.

"A very nice funeral pyre Lucia."

* * * * *

Tactus fed the last of the apple to Fortitudo and asked.

--Do you ever think it might be possible that you could give me a ride?

--Ahem, I'm not really sure little toad. After all I've been trained to carry Centurions and now a Prince. I'm not really sure if I could carry you even if it was allowed.

--What would be so different. I mean between carrying Centurions or Kashta, as compared to carrying me.

--Well size for one thing. I mean you are very small, I don't know how you'd fit.

--You think the saddle might be too big?

--Perhaps.

Then he added almost wistfully.

--I must admit that I miss the excitement of having a rider on my back. The rush that comes with battle, the noise, the shouting, and the clang of swords. I appreciated a congratulatory pat from my rider when we had done well in battle, and the extra ration of oats at the end of the day. But the best of all, the Triumphal Parades. The adoring crowds lining the roadways. I was always proud wearing the shining armour and having my Centurion well seated and ready for anything. Oh, we were a sight I'm sure. Now it's just the boredom, standing here in my stall, boredom, just boredom.

--Well, I'm sorry that I'm boring you Fortitudo. Said Tactus.

--No, not you. I didn't mean to hurt your feelings. I guess I just miss Kashta. We've not ridden together in such a long time.

Maybe if you let me climb up on your back it might make you feel better Fortitudo.

--But there's no saddle.

I could just sit on your back, without one I mean,

--But you might fall off, my back can be quite slippery you know.

--I'll hold on to your mane, I'll be careful.

--All right, but just this once.

* * * * *

"So tell me Pico, how are you and Nog getting along?" Asked Caecus.

"Fine."

"Just fine?"

"Well he is kind of.."

"Kind of what?"

"Prickly."

"Yes, that sounds like an apt description of him. What have you learned from him so far?"

"To be very careful what I'm thinking about."

Caecus chuckled.

"Particularly if you are thinking about him. Daimons are a strange lot."

Pico quickly added.

"But he has taught me how to see and talk to my mother and father.

The old man nodded and asked.

"Tell me some more about Nog."

"I need to make sure that I always tell the truth. Otherwise he's going to cause me some pain."

"Do you think your pain is more than that experienced by someone you lie to?"

"I never thought of it that way."

"Perhaps that's just what Nog is trying to teach you."

"Well, I have promised him I'll be more careful with what I say. But you know it is very difficult to always be truthful."

"With practice it will become less so."

* * * * *

--There, I'm up Fortitudo."

--So you are, but please be careful. If you were to fall off I might step on you and do you real harm.

Tactus had his fingers meshed in the horse's mane. He would never complain about the discomfort of having his legs spread so far apart over the animal's broad back.

I'm on his back; I'm actually riding a horse. Well maybe not really, but certainly almost. I wonder if Fortitudo might let me.

--Fortitudo could I ride you for just a little bit, just here in the barn.

--Oh, I don't think so Tactus.

--Please, please, just a little.

--It does feel so good to have a rider on my back. Perhaps just a few steps around the barn wouldn't hurt. Hang on tight while I back out of the stall. There, now I'll walk slowly to the end of the barn and come back. Hang on.

As Fortitudo cleared the stall he was immediately aware of how much bigger the horse felt and how high he was off the ground. Slowly the horse moved towards the far end of the barn. Tactus was amazed at how much Fortitudo's back swayed as he walked. It reminded him of a time his father had taken him on a small boat and the lake had become rough. The boat had swayed like this too.

Fortitudo reached the end and began his turn, Tactus could feel himself begin to slip, and he pulled hard on the horse's mane and righted himself.

--Ouch, that hurt, don't pull on it so hard.

--Sorry Fortitudo.

They were halfway back to the stall when the barn door opened. It was Pico.

"What are you doing Tactus? Do you want to get in trouble? You better get off before you get hurt."

"I will, I will. Once we're back in the stall."

Pico stood quietly and watched enviously as the two returned and Tactus dismounted. He came running to his brother saying.

"Promise me you won't tell anyone about this Pico."

Under ordinary circumstances that would have been easy enough for Pico to do, but these were no longer ordinary circumstances.

"Tactus, if anybody asks me if you were riding Fortitudo, I will have to tell the truth and say yes."

"Traitor, I wouldn't do that to you."

"But this is different."

"How is it different?"

"If I told you, you wouldn't believe me. What I can say is that I won't volunteer to anyone that you were riding Fortitudo."

"I don't understand you, you never had any difficulty in the past bending the truth."

"This isn't the past. Do you think he'd let me ride him too?"

Chapter Thirty-five

"So Pando introduce me to you friends."

Pando had retrieved Oratio's cake from his bag and handed it to Kashta. They had all moved back from the fire because of the heat. The flames shot high into the air sending sparks into the dark night sky.

"These are my two cousins, the ones I came to meet. This is Viaticus and beside him is Ludus, the younger of the two."

Then he turned to Lucia and said.

"And this is Lucia, we were fortunate enough to meet her on the road. That is we met her and Corripio on the road, that's Corripio on the pyre."

"Yes, Pando I know."

"But how could you know?"

"It doesn't matter, I just know."

Kashta held out his hand to Lucia but she refused to take it, eyeing him warily. The other two boys shook hands eagerly.

"What I don't know Pando is just how Corripio died, perhaps you might tell me."

The Pando told Kashta all that had happened including Sceleris's attempt to steal the amulet and what had resulted from his actions.

"Bring a torch Pando and let's go back to the scene, I'm most interested," said Kashta.

Pando led the way with Kashta at his side the others followed with Lucia bringing up the rear. When they reached the Temple, Pando walked to where the event occurred. The figure of Sceleris stood just as he was at the moment he grasped the amulet.

Kashta took the torch from Pando and walked towards the figure. He held up the light and walked slowly around what was left of Sceleris. It was as though the figure had been created by a master sculptor, the face captured in surprise, the missing eye and the other dripping some kind of mucus.

The light flickered over the statue, for that's what it was now, giving effect to changing expressions. At once Kashta recognized him.

"I know this man, or rather I knew him. Not by name, but by his actions and his treatment of me. What did you say he was called Pando?"

Viaticus answered for him.

"His name was Sceleris, he said he was a procurator of Gladiators for the Circus."

"Probably the only true words he ever spoke. Pando, this is the man I told you of, it was he who kidnapped me and brought me to this country."

Kashta held up the stump of his left arm.

"This was all his doing as well."

He handed the torch back to Pando and said.

"I'm still famished, let's find a quiet spot and have some more of Oratio's Sweet Cake."

The five of them made their way to a large flat rock near the pool where they sat and each had a piece of the magical cake and when they had had their fill, Pando wrapped the undiminished piece, and placed it in his bag.

Pando was the first to speak.

"Did you happen to see Fortis in your travels Kashta?"

"No I didn't, but don't worry about him, he'll find his way."

Lucia sat quietly watching this stranger and wondering what had brought him into their midst. She felt uneasy in his presence. She knew that he was a force, but what kind?

Is he to cause me more misery or is he one that will help me? What brings him to us, or more importantly who has sent him?

It was then that Pando asked the question that she couldn't.

"Why are you here Kashta?"

"To guide you back to Caecus of course."

"But I thought Fortis was to do that."

"As you have become aware on your travels Pando, there are dangers on this journey. Greater dangers than you have faced so far. Because of these dangers I have come to be at your side, all of you."

He made a point of looking directly into Lucia's eye when he made the statement.

Why is it I can't look into his eyes? Can he see inside me? I feel like he knows me, but how can that be? We've never met before. There is a power behind those eyes, eyes that have seen many things, things that are beautiful and things that are monstrous.

Why do I feel so frightened?

Pando spoke again.

"Kashta, do you know why Caecus didn't tell me about all of the powers of the amulet?

"Perhaps he felt you had no need to know."

"But we could have had a disaster, just suppose one of my cousins had touched it, or Lucia."

"But they didn't did they?"

"But the could have."

"Why worry about what could have been, concern yourself about what is."

Are there any other powers possessed by the amulet that I should be aware of?"

"Why ask me? Only Caecus can answer you."

"Then why didn't you tell me about Fortis's special powers?"

"I saw no need to tell you, you had no power to invoke them. Fortis accompanied you to protect you and guide you home. And he certainly did protect you."

"Yes he did and for that I'm extremely grateful, but Kashta it would have been a comfort to know."

Silence pervaded the small group, until finally Lucia spoke.

"You said you knew Corripio. Could you tell me how you came to know him?"

"I didn't say that I knew him, I said I knew of him."

"Then tell me what you 'know of him'," she added.

"Please."

"I can tell you what I know of him but I doubt that that is your real question. I think you'd rather know how I know of him and that I will not tell you."

Lucia got up and stamped her foot and angrily stormed away towards the still burning funeral pyre.

"I think it would be best if we all got some rest. Once we've completed the rest of the funeral ceremony tomorrow we must get on our way to Caecus."

Nobody argued with what Kashta had said, in fact a great weariness had overtaken all of the boys. Perhaps it was everything that they had experienced that day or the warmth emanating from the great rock they lay on or it could have been both. In any event they slept almost at once after laying down none of them noticed Kashta follow Lucia to the pyre.

* * * *

"Come Nog."

"What is you want now boy."

"I just want to talk."

"About what may I ask?"

"I'm trying very hard to follow the rules, you know about telling the truth and that sort of thing."

"Just let me climb down from the fig tree first. It's not too comfortable up here and besides my tummy is telling me I've eaten too many figs. Maybe some green ones too."

"I really don't like figs Nog."

"More for me then. Now why don't you ask your questions?"

"Well, is it always necessary for me to tell the truth?"

"Of course, what else is the truth for but the telling."

"I mean, even if I'm not asked for it do I have to tell a truth?"

"You're confusing me boy. I don't understand, give me an example."

"For example, my brother was riding Fortitudo earlier and I saw him. Do I have to go and tell Caecus?"

"Well of course, if Caecus asked you 'Did you see Tactus riding the horse', then you would have to tell the truth."

"But if he doesn't ask, do I have to tell him?"

"That would be something quite different, that would be a tattle-tale. However, if he's doing something dangerous and he might be hurt then you'd have to take action."

"You mean tell the truth."

Nog stroked his sparse red beard and said.

"Yes it would seem so."

"So then telling the truth depends on the circumstances, right?"

"So to speak."

"So the simple fact that I know something is true and say nothing doesn't make not saying it a lie, is that right?"

"Boy, are you trying to confuse me?"

"No Nog, I'm just trying to get things straight in my head. It isn't much fun getting poked all of the time."

"I resent that. Daimons are not mean spirited. I don't poke you simply to hurt you. How else can I direct you on the right path?"

"I don't really know, and I'm not accusing you of being mean. It's just that this thing called truth seems to be very slippery. Sometimes I think truth means different things to different people, so how is someone like me to know?"

"Pico, just remember, the truth is always the truth. You can't bend it or break it, it remains the truth."

"That's very complicated, let me try another example Nog. If I'm asked if a particular man is ugly and if he is ugly, how do I answer? If I say yes he is, and the man who asked me goes and says to the ugly man, 'Pico say your ugly' I have told the truth and caused hurt to the ugly man. If I said he wasn't ugly, then my lie doesn't hurt anybody, right?"

"Boy, I'm not in the mood for this right now, my stomach hurts. You sound to me like your future lies in the Senate; your logic about truth would fit very well there. But Philosophy is also a possibility.

Please send me away Pico, I don't feel well."

"Go Nog."

Chapter Thirty-six

Lucia stood staring into the fire, her eyes wet with tears. She didn't hear Kashta approach. She jumped when he said.

"Lucia, the fire is fine, we have an early morning tomorrow why not get some rest?"

She whirled around to face him.

"No one said I was going with you did they?"

"Why are always so angry, has one of the boys said or done anything?"

"No."

"Then have I done something to offend you?"

"I don't trust you and I certainly don't trust that mongrel of yours."

"Fortis, why he's harmless."

"Harmless? He pissed on me, the filthy beast."

A smile crept over Kashta's face.

"I don't think it's very funny. But I can see that you do. Until that dog and then you came along everything was fine but now I don't want to be around here."

"And you did nothing to offend Fortis?"

"How can you offend a dog?"

"He's not just any dog. He's a very special dog."

"Why? Just because he's yours."

"Perhaps, but if Fortis sensed the same hostility from you that I do, then maybe that's why he acted the way he did."

"There's no excuse for what he did."

"When I next see him, I'll speak very sharply to him."

He looks serious but I still don't trust him. Why is that? I've never seen him until just now. Why has he taken such an interest in these boys? Does he represent a danger to them? For that matter, why have I taken such an interest in them? I'm sure I'd be better off if I had never met them.

"Lucia, how is it you came to know Corripio?"

"I might ask you the same thing."

He held up his left arm or at least what was left of it and said.

"Corripio was in the stands at the games when this happened. Lucky for me, he rushed to me and applied a compress to the wound to slow the bleeding and allow time for Caecus to get to me.

"Then he just slipped away into the crowd, it was Caecus who told me his name."

"How did that happen?" She asked, staring at the stump.

"That's a long story, but it's your turn now, tell me of your connection to Corripio?"

"We just happened to cross paths on this journey. He was alone confused and unused to being free. I took pity on him and allowed him to join me."

"And that's all there is? Seems to me given all that you have done with his funeral pyre and urn, there must be more than that to the story."

"Why are you questioning me like this? I've done nothing wrong and yet you question me like you're a Praetor."

"Lucia it's just that I sense that Corripio was more to you than just an acquaintance. Remember, I told you I liked the man too."

The tears flowed down her cheeks, she was furious with herself for losing control. Gently, Kashta put his good arm around her shoulders and tried to console her.

A 'crack in her armour' but why is she so angry? Angry at the world and everything in it, it seems.

His voice was soothing now when he said.

"Tell me what it is? What's troubling you so?"

She sighed and like fish tired of fighting the angler she gave in and blurted out.

"I think Corripio may have been my brother."

"You brother?"

"Yes, I seem to remember but it was so long ago I'm just not sure."

"Could you be mistaken Lucia? You are very young."

"No, I sense it more than knowing for sure he was my brother."

"What about the rest of your family, what's happened to them?"

The words tumbled from her mouth, words that she had spoken to very few people.

Why am I suddenly telling this stranger my innermost thoughts? Why do I have this sense of distrust?

"That is an interesting story Lucia and sadly not a unique one. Many families have been forced to sell their children into slavery so the rest can exist. But it seems strange to me that you would feel the necessity to run away."

Lucia turned to look into the smiling face.

"I decided that rather than have no control over my future, running away was my best option. I have spirit; I'm not stupid. I felt I could make my way."

"I would agree that you have spirit Lucia, perhaps too much for your own good."

"What do you mean?" She bristled.

"You take offense easily, as you've just done. You push people away that get too close to you."

"Enough about me." She said, changing the subject.

"Tell me about yourself."

"That's a long story and it's getting late."

"So it's all right for you to question me, but you can't or won't answer my questions."

"Perhaps if you were less demanding and asked more pleasantly, I would."

She bit her lower lip and said.

"Please tell me about your life."

"That's better. Where to start? Well, as you've heard me say, I was born as a Prince of the Royal Blood in an empire called Nubia or as some call it 'The Land of Kush'."

"Kush? I've never heard of it, where is it?"

"It lies close to Egypt and shares the Nile with her. In fact Nubians once ruled all of Egypt. Much of the Egyptian culture was really ours, many people are unaware of that."

"You mean that Egypt was ruled by black people?"

"Does my colour make me somehow incapable of the greatness of an Egyptian or a Roman?"

"I meant no disrespect, it's just that I didn't know."

He continued with his story.

"We taught the Egyptians many things, their laws, their Gods, science and even the Pyramids."

"The Pyramids? Do you have Pyramids in Kush? I thought only Egypt had them."

"Egypt has but a paltry few, Kush has over 200. And even the Sphinx was our creation."

"I didn't know any of this Kashta. It sounds like a wonderful place. That leads me to ask why are you here? Why did you leave such a wondrous place?"

"I didn't leave of my own choosing. I was kidnapped by the man that is now a stone statue outside the Temple of Jupiter."

"Sceleris?"

"Yes, Sceleris. You asked about my stump earlier. It was because of him that I lost my arm and very nearly my life."

Lucia pondered what she had heard and then said.

"So, you are much like me, a wanderer trying to find your place."

"No Lucia, I know my place I always have. I stay in this empire because of one man, my friend Caecus. If it weren't for him, I may well have lost my way.

"Could he help me find my way?"

"Of that I have no doubt."

Lucia stood looking into the burning pyre; the fire was lower now, almost finished. Soon it would be time to bury Corripio's ashes, the final act in a sad life.

Would anybody ever remember that he was even here? Perhaps not, but wait, that's not true. I will remember him. A kind man, a weak man, a healing man. She turned and looked up into the face of the big man and said.

"Tell me something of your Gods Kashta. I find the Roman Gods confusing, there are so many of them."

"Yes there are and many of them come from Kush, and from Greece, with the names changed and sometimes their powers varied."

She looked confused and said.

"Then your Gods sound just as confusing."

"Perhaps but for me there are two that are most meaningful, there is Amun, the hidden one, the eternal God the father of all Gods and men.

And then there is Apedemek, the Lion of the South, Strong of Arm and guardian of The Royal Family.

I believe it was he in the Circus that day and that he saved me from certain death."

"But your not saying these are the only two?"

"No there are many other lesser Gods, but I keep these two fixed in my mind."

"I still find it all very confusing, all these Gods."

"Lucia, look up in the sky. Do you see all the stars up there?

"Yes, but what has that to do with anything."

"Do you see the brightest one, there in the western sky?"

"Yes I see it."

"Well then, just suppose that five men, or women for that matter, observed the same star but each called it by a different name, would that mean we have five different stars?"

"No, of course not."

"Do you not think that the same thing might be true of all the Gods?"

"I think that you may be wiser than you look."

Kashta laughed.

"I like you better when you're not so testy," he said.

It was her turn to laugh now.

Chapter Thirty-seven

"Are you going to ride Fortitudo again Tactus?"
"You didn't tell anyone did you?"
"No of course not. Well are you?"
" I think I kind of made him nervous the last time."
"Maybe he's just as worried as you are that somebody will find out he gave you a ride. He might get into more trouble than you if Kashta were ever to find out."
"You may be right Pico. But anyway, it was fun."
"You weren't scared?"
"No, of course not," then Tactus smiled and said.
"Well maybe just a little. When you're standing on the boards of the stall you kind of forget just how big he really is. Then up on his back you seem a long way off the ground. Maybe a saddle would make it easier but I doubt my legs could reach the stirrups."
"Did you bring him a treat?"
"Yes."
"And one for Hector too?"
"He'd just keep complaining if I didn't. I must say that he's a very cranky old goat. He never has a nice thing to say."
"Tell me honestly Tactus, can you really talk to the animals?"
"Of course I can."
"Will you teach me how to do it?"
"Kashta says you can't teach anyone, either you can do it or you can't." And lucky for me, I can."
"Can I try and see if I can."
"You can if you like, I'll even let you give him the apple."
What's come over Tactus, he's never been willing to share anything with me before?

Here's your treat Fortitudo, I hope you enjoy it. Perhaps when you're finished we could talk a little. There, that didn't take long, not a very big apple was it Fortitudo? When I come next time, I'll bring a bigger one. Would you like that?

Fortitudo, won't you answer me? He's not saying a word to me.
"Did you try to speak to him Pico?"
"I did what you told me to do, I said the words to myself but he didn't answer."
"Then I guess you don't have the gift Pico."

"Who cares? It's just a silly gift anyway. Why would anyone want to talk to animals?"

"Well you for one, at least up till a couple of minutes ago."

"Oh shut up Tactus, just shut up."

With that Pico spun around and stormed out of the barn leaving Tactus chuckling to himself.

--Where's my treat?

--Calm down Hector, it's right here, come and get it. There, isn't that a nice treat?

--Again with that mealy old carrot business. He gets an apple and I get something Oratio has obviously thrown away. Why is it I get no respect?

--You should be grateful for what you are given Hector, did no one ever teach you that?

--Is it too much to ask, just a little respect?

--Hector why do you always complain?

--You would complain too if you had my lot in life.

--Your lot in life? What have you got to complain about? You have a warm, dry place to live. You are fed regularly and as near as I can see, nobody asks you to do anything in return.

--That's what you think, remember, I have to put up with that old military windbag everyday. That's not easy you know.

--Hector that's not fair, Fortitudo is a brave horse who fought in many battles, what did you ever do that would earn you respect?

--I am a goat, and that should be reason enough to be granted some respect. I don't know why I waste my time talking to you; you're just too young to understand these things.

With that the goat aimed a kick at the boards in the stall, rattling Tactus's ears in the process. With his head held high he strode from the barn and out into the yard.

I must ask Kashta what it is about Hector that makes him so unpleasant. I don't think it's anything I've done to him. Everybody else here seems to be content with their lot, but not Hector.

Tactus returned to Fortitudo who had been standing patiently and listening to the two of them.

--Fortitudo do you have any idea why Hector is always so grumpy?

--I'm not really sure Tactus, I think he may have an inferiority complex. I think he longs to have some kind of an adventure that he could brag about. I know how much he resents it when I talk about all of the battles I've been in and the excitement I've had. I do my best to not talk about my exploits when he's around.

--Well I don't know what I can do about that other than talk to Kashta when he gets back. It's sad to see Hector so unhappy.

* * * *

Pico walked towards his favourite fig tree, he was deep in thought and didn't notice Hector leaving the barn.

Why is it that Tactus can talk to the animals and I can't? It's just not fair and then he makes fun of me besides. Brothers aren't supposed to treat each other that way. Mother even said so. Could he be lying? Maybe he's just making it up that he can talk to the animals. I'll bet Nog would know if he were telling the truth.

"Come Nog."

There was a rustle of leaves and a thud as a body hit the ground just next to him.

"Why is it you have to sneak up on a body?"

Nog got up and brushed himself off, straightening his clothing in the process. The remnants of his latest bout of fig eating were evident in his wispy red beard.

"What do you want now Pico?" He said indignantly.

"I just had a question I wanted to ask you, I'm sorry if I frightened you."

"You, frighten me? Don't be so silly. No one frightens a Daimon. Now what is your question?"

"Well, I just wondered…"

"Wondered what?"

"I wondered if you think that my brother Tactus can actually speak to animals? Or is he just lying?"

"Why does it matter to you whether he can or not."

"I just want to know."

"I think it's more than that. Are you jealous of him?"

How do I answer that? If I say no, I'd be lying and I'll get a smack. If I say yes then I'll admit to envy.

"Speak up boy, I don't have all day."

"It's just that I don't have anybody except you to talk to and I know you don't like it when I bother you. I'm just so bored waiting for Pando to return."

"That's not an answer to my question. A yes or no will do."

"Well I guess I am sort of envious."

"A truthful answer, there may be hope for you yet."

It was then that Pico noticed Hector standing a few yards away grazing on some sweet grass and he said.

"Maybe you could show me how to talk to Hector, he seems to be very unhappy too."

"First things first Pico. The answer to your question is, yes your brother can converse with the animals. He has a gift that you don't have."

"But that's not fair."

"Fair has nothing to do with it, it's just a fact. Now as to your second request, no I can't teach you to speak to Hector, as I said, you don't have the gift."

Pico hung his head despondently.

I don't care what Nog says it still isn't fair. And Tactus got to ride Fortitudo too. I have nothing.

"Seeing your parents is nothing?"

He'd forgotten that Nog could read his thoughts.

"I appreciate what you've given me Nog. It's just that if I talk to my family too often I'm afraid that I will cause them to worry about my brothers and I.

Perhaps I will just have to satisfy myself by talking to you."

"No, no, I have other things to do." Nog said hastily.

He stroked his beard and picked at his large ear with his forefinger. After a time he said to Pico.

"I think I have an idea that will satisfy you."

'What is it Nog, what is it?"

"Well by expanding the gift you already have, it's entirely possible that you could converse with someone else here."

"Who Nog, who?"

"I think you might find it very interesting to have conversations with Oratio."

"Oratio?"

"Yes."

"But he has no tongue."

"But if you speak as you do when you talk to your family and he does the same, then he has no need of a tongue."

"But what will we talk about? Cooking? What?"

"I think you may just be surprised."

"All right, I'll try it."

With that, Nog took his bony finger, the one that had just been inside his ear, and touched it to Pico's forehead.

What was that? It made me shiver.

"Now Pico, send me away and go see Oratio."

"Go Nog."

There was puff of smoke and that same sound. Pfffft.

Hector raised his head at the sound and looked in Pico's direction. He stood motionless for a time and with what seemed like a shrug returned to his grazing.

Let's see what happens, I hope Oratio will have something interesting to tell me. The only problem is that every time I get close to him I get another chore to do.

Oh well, maybe it'll be worth it.

Chapter Thirty-eight

Kashta took a step back and looked at the niche they had constructed of rocks collected from the edge of the pool. The decision to build it as opposed to a more traditional in ground burial of the urn was based upon the fact the available ground was laden with hard gravel and that they had little in the way of digging tools.

"That should work well, all we need now is to insert the urn and roll that rock in front of the opening to seal it."

Pando asked.

"Do you think the ashes are cool enough? And how do we separate Corripio's remains from the wood ash."

"Perhaps it will be obvious as to which is which once we look at the remains of the pyre," answered Kashta.

Lucia took one of the bags she used to pack her cooking implements in and used it to protect here hands as she lifted out the fired urn.

"This is very strange," she said.

"What is?" Asked Ludus.

"I put the urn and it's cover into the fire separately, but as you can see, the lid is now placed on the urn."

"Perhaps you were mistaken Lucia," said Kashta.

She bit her lip and resisted answering in her usual manner.

"If I had put the urn in the fire as you see it now, the lid would have fused to the bottom, making the whole thing useless."

She lifted the lid and was taken aback by what she found inside.

"It's almost full of ash. Who could've done this?"

Kashta moved so he could see inside.

"That is indeed strange and when you compare this ash to the remaining wood ash it is significantly different. I would say that the urn contains the remains of Corripio."

"But how did they get in there Kashta?" She asked.

"I am at a loss to say, perhaps wood nymphs, forest spirits, after all this is a holy place."

Lucia lifted the urn carefully and headed towards the niche.

She wasn't really satisfied with Kashta's explanation but she could see little point in delaying this final act. Painful though it may be for her, it had to be done

Corripio's death is a final thing, at least as far as this world is concerned. But I will hold him in my heart for evermore. The burden of being unsure of whether or not we are related will be with me always,

She slid the urn into its final resting-place and stood up. Viaticus and Kashta rolled the front stone into place, effectively sealing the niche. The five of them stood silently with heads bowed, then Kashta with his arms upraised spoke in his deep voice.

"Oh Great Amun Father of all Gods, please welcome our friend Corripio into the Afterlife. May your light shine upon him."

It was a simple prayer but Lucia was moved by it, she could feel her resentment towards Kashta beginning to ebb away. They stood in silence until Kashta finally broke it by saying.

"There's no more we can do here. We must eat and be on our way. We have a great distance to travel and it best be done in the cool of the day."

* * * * *

Pico was excited with the prospect of being able to have a conversation with Oratio.

He must have some exciting stories to tell. I suppose it will be impolite to ask him how he lost his tongue. But I am curious. There is something about him that makes me wonder if he has magic too. If he does I wonder what it is? Will he tell me?

He opened the door to the kitchen and saw Oratio standing with his back to him at the worktable in the middle of the room.

No sense in causing him a fright by calling him, I'll just move to the front of his table so he can see me. Then I'll try speaking.

"Oratio, how are you today?"

The little man almost jumped and then a smile wreathed his face. But he didn't give an answer.

"Oratio, my Daimon, Nog has empowered me to be able to hear you."

As soon as he had mentioned Nog he regretted it, he was unsure about telling anyone about him.

"Perhaps I shouldn't have said anything about Nog."

--It's quite all right Pico, I've met Nog and you know I'm not in a position to tell anybody anything about him.

"I understand you, this is wonderful. Do you have time for me to talk or are you too busy?"

-- I'll make time Pico. It's been so long since I've had the opportunity to converse with anyone I'm just overjoyed. Come sit by me at the table, I can work while you talk.

"I have so many questions I want to ask you."

--Go right ahead.

Now that he could, Pico was unsure of just what questions to ask. He wanted be careful not to offend Oratio.

"My brother Pando told me about your magical Sweet Cake, can you tell me how you make it?"

--Your brother? But he is away, how is possible that you could communicate with him?

"Another gift from Nog, he also made it possible for me to see and share thoughts with my mother and father."

--You are indeed fortunate to have a Daimon such as Nog. But as to your question, I'm afraid I can't tell you my secret about the Sweet Bread.

"But why not?"

--Because I don't know what the secret is. Caecus granted me the magical power to make the cake that's really all I know. It's not really very much different from the powers granted to you. You know that it works, but you don't know what the secret of it is.

"I see," he said somewhat disappointedly.

--Is that all you wanted to know about me Pico?

"No, no, there are lots of things I'd like to know. I just need to think about how to inquire."

--I can guess the first one on your mind. You'd like to know how I lost my tongue, right?

His face reddened, but it was true, he did want to know.

"Yes you're right, but if it's too painful I'll think of something else."

--One of the things I found after losing my tongue was the fact that having lost it meant I didn't have to talk about it. So, I have never really discussed it with anyone except Caecus.

"It's all right Oratio, you don't have to tell me about it."

--Not to worry Pico, maybe I should tell you about it. But you'd have to promise me to tell no one else.

Pico was thrilled with prospect of having a secret that no one else would ever know about, except Caecus of course.

"I promise, I promise, I'll never tell another soul, honest."

--I'll take you at your word my little friend. Now, where to begin? I think we can skip all the childhood things, there was nothing unusual about that particular time.

I should tell you though that I was not always a cook. In fact when I was younger I had some exposure to fame.

"You were famous?"

--Not too famous but I was gaining recognition as a poet.

"What kind of poems?"

Pico was not sure why he asked the question for he knew little of poetry and in fact spent his time wool gathering in Castor's classroom when the topic came up.

--Love poems to beautiful ladies, I didn't always look like I do now you now. In fact there were several young women who considered me quite handsome.

I think that's a bit of an exaggeration. Most of the women would be considerably taller than you are. But never mind.

"How many poems did you write? Do you still write them?"

--Too many to count and no I no longer write them.

"But why not?"

--Well you see, I sang my poetry, it was said that I had the finest voice in all of Rome. Perhaps an overstatement I'll admit, but nevertheless, some did say that.

"But what happened if you were doing so well?"

--I fell in love.

"What?"

--Yes, I fell in love. With the most beautiful woman I had ever seen. She was like a goddess and I worshipped at her feet. Pico, could you bring me that basket of potatoes from near the stove there?

Annoyed at the break in the story, Pico did as he was asked. He dropped the basket with a thud on the table and said.

"What was her name?"

--Her name, let's see now, what was it?

How can he forget such a woman's name? Is he just making this up?

--Her name was Aurelia, yes that's it Aurelia. I haven't spoken her name in so many years it seems strange for me to hear it again.

"So what happened between you?"

--Well, I was still a struggling poet living in a poor part of Rome and she was the charge of a very rich Senator, a very powerful man. It

174

was difficult to get to see her often, the best I could do was pay someone to smuggle my poems into her. Then one day she finally responded with a message of her own, brought to me by one of her slaves. Such fine delicate handwriting you just couldn't believe it. I was thrilled. While we couldn't see one another except for brief glimpses on the street, I was always sure of her love for me and I'm sure she knew of mine for her. But we had to be content with our correspondence. On one occasion her guardian intercepted one of my poems, he was furious with her and sent one of his biggest slaves to my small quarters and he beat me to a pulp. Aurelia was sent away to a relative in the country, I knew not where. My life seemed over, I'd lost my Aurelia, and I was bruised and battered. But what could I do?

"What did you do Oratio?

--What I knew best, I wrote some more poems.

"More love poems?"

--Not this time, I wrote poems about the Senator, but I had to do it very carefully, I never used his real name. For ridiculing him in public is against the law and punishable by death. So I cleverly used a name that everyone one could understand exactly who I was singing about. There were always rumours about some of his underhanded and crooked dealings. I put these to music and sang them in public and suddenly I became very popular, because it seems the public loves to see pompous officials made fun of.

"But you said that was a dangerous thing to do. My father has always told me that you shouldn't make fun of others."

--It turned out it was very dangerous, but I wouldn't listen to any words of caution from my friends. I was full of hatred for this man and what he had done to me by separating me from my Aurelia.

"Then what happened?"

--I had another visit from two of the Senator's henchmen. In the middle of the night they came to my quarters. One threw me on the floor and the other sat on my chest. The one on my chest put some kind of carpenter's tool in my mouth and caught hold of my tongue. I tried to scream but could not. He pulled out my tongue while the other cut it off with one swift cut of his very sharp knife. It was extremely painful, so much so that I must have fainted away. The two left me to drown in my own blood and I would have too had it not been for one man.

"Who was that?" Pico asked excitedly.

--When I came to, he was standing over me, and somehow the pain had ceased, as had the bleeding. I don't know to this day how he accomplished that, but I will be eternally grateful.

"But who was it Oratio."

--Why it was Caecus of course. He brought me here to recover and I've been with him ever since.

"Did he say anything to you that night?"

--Yes and it was very strange. He asked me where my tongue was. I looked all over my room but it wasn't there. Then he said, 'They must have taken it to make sure that your ability to speak is lost forever.'

"Who was this Senator Oratio?"

--Better that you don't know that Pico, you'll be safer that way. Now, enough of my story, help me peel these potatoes.

Chapter Thirty-nine

Pando and Kashta walked at the front of the small band with, for the first time, Lucia bringing up the rear. No one had spoken since they began their trip back to Caecus's farm. Finally Pando asked.

"Kashta, do you have any idea why Corripio died? I was there and saw nothing."

"But you told me you were knocked unconscious, perhaps it had happened during that time. Remember Pando, I had no opportunity to view the body. The pyre was already lit when I arrived."

"I saw no mark on his body Kashta, mind you we didn't remove his clothes. He just looked like he was asleep, his face was relaxed, I wasn't even sure he was dead."

"Well there seems little doubt that he was in fact dead. I assume Lucia said he was?"

"Yes she did."

"And then the three of you boys went into the forest scavenging for wood for the pyre?"

"Yes, she stayed behind and made the urn."

"Well Pando he is certainly dead but as to how he died, we may never know. Perhaps it was fright, I have seen that happen in the arena before.

Who knows what might have happened to you had you observed Sceleris's transformation, chances are, you were lucky to have been unconscious."

Pando shivered and they continued on in silence. After a time Pando was moved to ask.

"Kashta, how much do you know about the amulet?"

"I know that it possesses unimaginable powers, you are aware of only a few, but you have witnessed one of the most powerful.

"You must guard it carefully for there are others that covet it and would take it from you given the opportunity."

"But after what I've witnessed, would that even be possible. Wouldn't they just destroy themselves?"

"For some thieves that would definitely be true, but there others who have dark powers that make them immune to the forces within the amulet. You have already met two in your travels."

"You mean the man who was following me? And then the vulture."

"Yes."

"But how did you know about that Kashta? I haven't had an opportunity to tell you about these experiences."

"Pando, just accept the fact that I know many things." A slight smile crossed his face.

"Why didn't you tell me about Fortis being a shape-shifter."

"Would you have believed me?"

Perhaps not and had Caecus told me of the dangers, would I have gone? I would like to believe so. But it doesn't matter now; I must finish what I started.

"Who are these dark forces you speak of Kashta?"

"You will learn more about this when you next see Caecus. In the meantime we must all be vigilant."

Pando knew better than to pursue this matter any further; they all simply trudged on in silence.

* * * * *

Tactus left the barn and went looking for Hector determined to see if he could find out what was causing the goat such unhappiness. He found the animal curled up under an olive tree, snoozing in the shade.

"Are you asleep Hector?"

--Yes can't you see my eyes are closed?

"Why are you always so cranky? I'm just trying to be your friend, but you make it so difficult."

--Why do you want to be my friend? Nobody else does.

"You seem so unhappy that you make me unhappy too."

--So it's not really that you want to be my friend you just want to make yourself happy. Is that it?

"You may as well know Hector, I don't intend to give up. So tell me what is making you so grumpy and unhappy."

--I told you, no one gives me any respect.

"But you must earn respect, my father told me that. It doesn't come automatically."

--You know nothing about me. How can you say that I haven't earned any respect?

"Well that's true I guess, so why don't you tell me of the things you've done that should earn you respect?"

--Why do you care?

"I just do, so go ahead and tell me."

--Do you have any idea of the Goat in history? Of the role goats have played in culture and religion?

"No I must admit that I don't."

--You see what I mean, your like everybody else.

"That's not fair Hector. I'm just a boy, still going to my tutor; at least I was until all this happened. How can you expect me to know of such things?"

--Then you have never heard of Amalthea?

"Never."

--Amalthea was a she-goat that fed the mighty Zeus. I'm sure you've heard of him.

"Of course."

--Then there was the God Pan, but he was only part goat, his legs, beard and horns. And the God Azazel who symbolized life and creative energy was a goat.

"I had no idea."

--And the Scapegoat who takes on the sins of others, what would the world do without him?

Hector stood up and lowered his head. He said nothing for a few moments.

"What's wrong Hector? Hector can you hear me?"

--Yes, yes, I hear you.

"Then what's wrong?"

--There is a dark side to being a goat.

"What's that?"

--The sacrifice, it seems someone always wants to kill us as a sacrifice to their particular Gods. Take the Roman Lupercalia for example. Always with the killing of goats. Is it any wonder that I get depressed?

"Is that it Hector? Are you afraid that you will be sacrificed?"

--I'm always looking over my shoulder.

"But surely you feel safe here? Caecus would never let you be taken for sacrifice."

--No, not Caecus. But if in the dead of night if someone stole me away, who could prevent me from becoming just another sacrifice?

"But you're in the barn with Fortitudo, he would stop them."

--Oh piffle on Fortitudo. That nag sleeps so soundly he'd be no help at all.

"Whether you know it or not Fortitudo is your friend. He worries about you. Surely we can work something out so you'd feel secure."

--You really believe that old bag of bones cares about me? I don't think so.

"Come on Hector, don't be so negative."

Hector turned away from Tactus and with his head down and his tail between his legs began to slowly walk back towards the barn. Then he stopped and looked over his shoulder at Tactus.

--I know you mean well boy, but this hasn't really helped my disposition at all. I'm still depressed.

* * * * *

Kashta signaled the others that it was time to take a break. The sun was at its highest point but they still had access to shade. The five sat gratefully under some trees and Pando passed around the water container.

Lucia went into the forest to forage for something to eat. As good as Oratio's Sweet Cake was, she craved a change.

Let's see what I can find in here. It's not that I'm so hungry but I know I should eat something. Besides making a meal for the others will take my mind off things.

Not a whole lot here. What's that vine winding itself around that tree over there? Let me see. Well, well, it seems that we have some grapes and ripe too. They will be refreshing.

As she walked further into the woods her mind drifted to other things.

Could this Caecus person actually help me with these memories I have? Kashta certainly seems to think so. Why do I suddenly believe what he tells me? I barely even know him. Aside from that if he really could help me it would be worth continuing on with the group and meeting this man.

Even Pando speaks highly of him and I trust what he says. I can't live the rest of my life drifting in and out of memories that may belong to me or not.

What about this person Oratio? Who is he? And why do I have these recollections of him? I need to get some answers or I'll drive myself crazy.

Another reason to continue on is perhaps if I meet this Oratio the full memory of him will return. But will that necessarily be a good thing?

Then she felt a wave of emotion sweep over her. She struggled to hold back the tears.

Oh Corripio, why did you have to die? We had some connection I know. I sense that you were my brother and yet I'm not sure. To be alone is a terrible thing, family is everything and now I've lost you.

"What are you doing Lucia?"

It was Viaticus. She cleared her throat and said.

"I was foraging for some food for us. I thought you might like to have a change from Sweet Cake. Although come to think of it I still have some pulse if you'd rather."

Viaticus smiled at her and shook his head at the thought of pulse.

"No thanks, whatever you've found will be fine. I was worried about you and came to find you. When I came upon you it looked to me that you were very upset, I thought you were crying."

"You don't need to worry about me Viaticus, you know I can look after myself."

Then she added.

"But thank you for thinking of me."

He shrugged rather bashfully and said.

"You're welcome, would you like me to carry your bag?"

Chapter Forty

"Lucia that was a wonderful meal. You amaze me at what you are able to turn into delicious food."
She was surprised at how the compliment affected her. She was sure that she blushed as she said.

"Snaring the wild rabbit was they key to a good meal and the fire Viaticus built was just perfect. I'm glad you enjoyed it Kashta."

"Wasn't just me that enjoyed it, all the boys did too."

Each spoke up enthusiastically particularly Ludus, which was a surprise given that he was not a noted meat eater. Kashta continued.

"All around I'd say that this has been a very good day, we covered a good distance and although the weather was hot, we didn't waste much time with too many rest stops. From the looks of all of you, we best have an early night and get a good start in the morning.

"Viaticus and Ludus you give Lucia a hand cleaning up and you Pando can come with me and we'll scout a good place to lay down our heads for the night."

Pando was obviously pleased with this arrangement; the other two were not. However, each knew that it wouldn't pay to grumble.

* * * * *

"This rock outcrop looks like a good place to make camp Pando. It's high enough that it'll remain dry should it rain during the night and the rock will provide us with warmth stored from the sun."

The boy nodded his agreement and Kashta continued.

"We're going to have to set up a sentry system so that if anything comes our way we won't get caught by surprise. We must break the night into four parts. I'll take the first shift, then we can arrange with the others for the balance of the night. Given that Lucia has undertaken to keep us fed I think she can be excused from this duty."

"Oh I'm not so sure Kashta. Based on what I've seen of Lucia, she may well take offense at being left out."

"Why would she do that?"

"She doesn't like to be treated differently just because she's a girl."

"Let me talk to her, she'll understand what I'm saying."

Pando shrugged and asked.

"Are you anticipating that we might run into some trouble tonight?"

"I think it is just a good thing to be prepared, given your experiences when you traveled with Fortis I thought you'd be in agreement."

"No, I do agree, I was just hoping with you here we'd be safer than I was alone, well not alone exactly. I was lucky to have Fortis with me."

"No fear boy, We'll be up to any challenge."

"Kashta where did Fortis go? Do you know?"

"I sent him on another mission, you'll see him again soon, why do you ask?"

"No reason really. I like him a lot it's just curious, that since we met, I've never seen the two of you together."

"Just a coincidence Pando, Fortis and I are very close, closer than anyone could ever imagine. I depend on him to do things for me that I could not do myself. He is loyal and brave and I'm lucky to have him as a companion."

They made their way back to the others and by the tine they got there the cleanup was complete. To Pando's surprise, there was no disagreement on the part of Lucia with respect to Kashta's plan.

Of course he didn't really leave her out, it's just she got the last shift during which she could prepare breakfast.

They made their way back to the rock outcrop just as the sun disappeared below the horizon and darkness enveloped them. A fire was quickly started and all but Kashta stretched out to take their well-earned rest. It was only minutes before they had all fallen into a deep sleep.

Kashta sat with his back to the fire peering into the dark forest behind the weary group.

* * * * *

Pando awoke as Kashta shook him by the shoulders.

"Your turn boy. Keep a sharp eye out and don't drift off to sleep again."

With that Kashta curled up with his back to the fire and quickly began a quiet snore.

I'd better put some more wood on the fire; I wouldn't want to have to try to start it again. I've never been very successful at that and I certainly don't want to wake up Lucia to do it.

After that was done and the new wood caught, the fire crackled and burned brighter. Pando took up the same position that Kashta had. The heat on his body was comforting; the night air was becoming chilled.

Did I really sleep? It seems I just closed my eyes and Kashta was waking me. I must have, but I'm still so tired. I must stay awake.

What was that? I heard something out there. Or, am I just imagining it?

I don't see anything, just blackness. Wait, there it is again, a twig snapping, could be an animal I suppose. He reached inside his tunic and held the amulet.

Almost instantly he felt better, the anxiousness left him. He was protected, he was sure of that, or was he?

Yes, I do hear something. Should I wake Kashta? But what if it's nothing? I'll just look foolish.

Then he heard it, well not really heard it more like someone inside his head.

--Pando I want the amulet. Give it to me, you have no right to possess it. Bring it to me, and no harm will come to you

The boy ignored the demand and did not respond.

--Do not pretend that you didn't understand what I said. Give me the amulet.

Can no one else hear this? Is this all in my head? I must be going crazy.

Pando peered intently into the gloom of the forest. He could see nothing move then the rustle of a branch.

Whatever it is, it's coming closer. What should I do?

Suddenly he saw something, glowing in the dark. What was it?

Eyes, that's what they are. So bright and yellow. It must be an animal, but what kind?

--Bring it here now or I'll come and get it and you and all your friends will die.

Pando said nothing.

--You leave me no option but come and take the amulet. Your action has doomed both you and your friends.

The beast stepped from the shadows and into the circle of light from the fire. Pando's heart almost stopped when he saw this terrible thing staring at him. It was on all fours and crept slowly towards him.

He had seen nothing to equal this ugly animal if in deed it was an animal for it had the head of a lion, the body of a she-goat and the tail of a serpent of some kind.

Pando was stunned; unable to move he stood rooted to the spot. Then the words came again.

--Give me the amulet.

The great beast opened it's mouth and breathed fire, so violently that Pando felt the flames singe his clothes.

"Kashta, Kashta wake up, we are under attack."

The Prince was on his feet in seconds, fully awake and ready for action. His eyes widened when he saw the beast.

"It's the Chimera, stay back Pando."

Kashta moved towards the fire as the beast circled him waving it's serpent tail. It breathed flames scorching everything in its path.

By this time the others were up and huddled together in panic as the confrontation between the Chimera and Kashta was playing out.

"Pando take out the amulet and hold it up high." Kashta shouted.

He did as he was asked, distracting the Chimera from his pursuit of Kashta. The Prince reached down into the fire with his good right hand and seized a large glowing ember. He raised his arm over his head and shouted something in a language that none of them could understand.

The ember glowed white-hot and was so bright that it hurt the eyes to look at it, and yet it didn't burn Kashta. He hurled it with all his might at the great beast just as it opened its mouth to give another great roar.

Instead, the fiery missile penetrated the mouth causing the Chimera to stagger back screaming in pain. Then a great explosion followed that lit up the whole area as though it was the middle of the day. Great clouds of smoke enveloped them and when it cleared there was no evidence that the Chimera had ever existed.

Kashta sank to the ground and Pando rushed to his side.

"Kashta, are you all right? What about your hand?"

He held it up for him to see and there was no mark to be found.

"How can that be Kashta? That ember was so hot, it should have burned your hand badly.

All he said was.

"I'm much tougher than I look."

Viaticus ran to his side and asked.

"What was that thing."

"A Chimera, a supposed mythological creature, in the service of dark forces."

"It looked real to me." Said Ludus.

"Yes, there is little doubt that we have very powerful forces working against us, We must take even greater care." Said Kashta.

Pando looked at his friend with considerable admiration.

What would have happened to us if Kashta hadn't have been here? What were those words he said just before throwing the ember? Whatever they were, it was obviously magic for he not only demolished that terrible beast but he remained unharmed himself. I'm not even going to try to figure this all out.

Chapter Forty-one

No one got much sleep after the episode with the Chimera. It was very hard to settle down after all that excitement. Kashta decided that he would be the sentry for the remainder of the night. As dawn was barely breaking, he saw no point in delaying their departure any longer.

Kashta roused them all and said.

"Let's move on and put some distance between us and this place. We can stop for something to eat later. Better yet, Pando can pass out some Sweet Cake to save us some time."

There was no grumbling from any of them after the fright of the Chimera; this place held no appeal for them.

Pando ran to catch up with the big man. He was still shaken by what he'd seen. He needed to talk about it.

"How was it you were able to kill the Chimera? It was magic right?"

"I'm sorry to tell you Pando that the Chimera is not dead. Any magic I possess is not powerful enough to accomplish that."

"But he is dead, I saw it with my own eyes. You killed it.

"It only seemed like I killed it Pando. What really happened was that I was able to separate the elements of its being. Once it has had time to gather itself as a whole again, it's going be more than a little angry with us and me in particular."

"I don't understand."

"It's a hard concept to grasp, just accept my word, we haven't seen the last of the Chimera."

"But it can't be killed are we doomed to be pursued forever?"

"I didn't say it couldn't be killed, I just said my magic wasn't powerful enough to do it."

"Who has such power then?"

" I'm surprised you have to ask."

"Caecus?"

"Of course. And that is why we must hurry to reach him."

Pando said nothing more, they continued in silence but he looked over his shoulder regularly just to make sure nothing was behind them.

Viaticus turned to his brother and asked.

"What did you make of that strange creature? Were you frightened? How do you think Kashta was able to hurl that fireball at it and yet not get burned?"

"You sure talk a lot."

"Better than keeping it all locked up inside you don't you think?"

"Maybe, but frankly I don't know what to think. All I can say is that ever since we've started on this journey it's been nothing but one scary thing after another. I'd just like to get back to the way our lives used to be."

"Do you think that can really happen? Maybe this Caecus person can help us, I get the impression that Kashta believes so."

Lucia, who was bringing up the rear, listened to the two boys and then said.

"You both could have been dead or worse by now if it wasn't for the help you got from Corripio and now Kashta. Stop your whining and just get on with the march."

I think they're right, Caecus is the key. Although Kashta has magic powers, he seems to believe that Caecus's are superior. That was a very close call last night. I've never seen anything like that beast nor for that matter have I ever heard it described.

I've made my decision; I'm going with this group and meet this Caecus. If he is as good a man as Kashta says, then perhaps he'll help me with my memories or the lack of them.

Then there is Oratio. Can I find out why I know the name and what he means to me? I have this foreboding that my life will come to nothing unless I can solve these riddles.

* * * * *

"Tell me, what have you been up to Pico?"

"Oh Caecus, it's wonderful, Nog has made it possible for me to communicate with Oratio. We've just had a great discussion. He even told me how he lost his tongue."

"Did he really? Then you are most privileged, he doesn't share that with many people."

"It's really sad though. Is there no hope that he could ever speak again?"

"I'm afraid not, at least not now,"

"What do you mean?"

"Well, if we could have found his tongue after the attack it might have been possible to have found a way to re-attach it. But, alas, we never did find it and it's been so long now I'm sure that it has likely been destroyed."

"But if we did find it, could you fix it?"

The old man smiled as he heard how earnest his voice sounded.

"I could certainly try. Mind you it would take powerful magic even if we did find it. I wouldn't get your hopes up my boy."

* * * * *

"Fortitudo, I know why Hector is so cranky all of the time."

--Why is that Tactus?

"He says it's because he gets no respect because he's a goat, but that's not the whole story. I think he's concerned about someone turning him into a sacrifice to the Gods."

--Really?

"Yes, I think he feels that he has been unfairly singled out as a sacrifice simply because he's a goat."

--Hmmm, Tactus if that were true that would be discrimination wouldn't it? Nobody should be discriminated against just because they were born into a specific species should they?

"My mother has always told me that that isn't right. I know I wouldn't want to be discriminated against because I'm Roman and I'm sure you don't want to be discriminated against simply because you're a horse, right?"

--Of course not. No wonder Hector is always so grouchy. Do you think there is anything we can do to help him?

"Maybe I should talk to Caecus about it, he's a very smart man you know."

--Good idea Tactus.

* * * * *

"Come Nog."

Where is he? This is not like him; he always comes in the blink of an eye. I hope nothing's wrong. I'll call louder; maybe he didn't hear me.

"Come Nog."

"No need to wake the dead. I was having such a nice sleep, why did you have to wake me?"

He yawned and stretched to his full three feet and then dug into his left ear with his bony forefinger and extracted some blue earwax. He examined it carefully, rotating his finger to be able to view all sides. Then apparently satisfied he flicked the substance to the ground and turned his attention to Pico.

"What is you want of me boy?"

"You were right, I was able to communicate with Oratio."

"Of course I was right, I'm always right. Is this why you awakened me?"

'No, no, I just needed to know something."

"Get on with it boy, I don't have all day. I must get my rest."

That's all he ever does is sleep. Why does he need so much rest? He never does anything, Oops.

Pico never saw Nog's hands move, but he felt a sharp slap to the back of his head.

"Don't be cheeky boy, will you never learn?"

"Sorry Nog, I didn't mean to think that."

'You'll be even sorrier if you don't mind your manners. Now, why did you want me?"

"I found out from Oratio how he lost his tongue and then I talked to Caecus to see if there was something we could do to help him. It seems that if we could find the rest of Oratio's tongue then Caecus's magic might be powerful enough to restore it and he could speak again."

"I suppose that may be true, but what do you want of me?"

"Could you use your magic to help me find Oratio's tongue?"

"What would ever make you believe that my magic was better than Caecus's? If it had been possible to find the tongue don't you think Caecus would have done that right away?"

Of course, Nog was right and at once Pico was embarrassed that he hadn't considered this fact before disturbing Nog.

The Daimon could see the look of despondency on the boy's face.

I suppose I shouldn't be quite so harsh on the boy all he wants to do is help someone, an admirable trait. Perhaps there is a way that I could help.

"Maybe there is something I could do to help."

Pico's face brightened instantly and he said.

"Oh please Nog, please do. Tell me how, please."

"Well, I could circulate an inquiry through all the other Daimons at our next Lodge Meeting, just to see if perhaps the Daimon of either of the criminals who assaulted Oratio know anything."

"Do you mean those bad men have a Daimon too?"

"All mortals have a Daimon whether they know it or not and just because they don't know that doesn't mean the Daimon isn't present."

"Oh Nog, thank you so much for your help."

"Pico, this is really a long shot. It could take forever to get the message to the right Daimon. The other thing you should know is that if the men who did this are now dead then their Daimons would have been reassigned. Only the Gods would know where.

"Please try anyway Nog, Please."

Chapter Forty-two

"Hello Tactus. What is it I can do for you."
It always unnerved the boy when somehow Caecus was aware that he was close by.

"It's about Hector, Caecus, I was just speaking to him, or rather I was communicating with him. I think I've discovered why he's so cranky all the time."

"Have you now, and what might that be?"

"Well, it seems that he's afraid someone is going make a sacrifice out of him."

"And you think that's why he's so unhappy?"

"Yes."

"Tactus, I don't think it's all that simple. You must know, as does he, that he's completely safe here. Nothing is going to happen to him, he's well protected in this place."

"Then what else can it be?"

"I think you are partially right. However, his concern isn't just for himself, but for all goats. Over the ages goats have been singled out as a group to be used in sacrifices you see."

"Who singled them out?"

"It started with people of the 'old religions' and has somehow carried on down to this very day. Personally, I think it barbaric, but there is little anyone can do. Perhaps in time the practice will disappear."

"But in the meantime poor Hector is depressed."

"Maybe not for long Tactus."

"Why do you say that Caecus?"

"Well, for one thing, he has you for a friend. That's never happened to him before. There are many things as you go through life that we don't like and can't change but if we have friends those things are much more bearable."

"You really think that my being his friend can make a difference?"

"Yes I do, I really do."

I guess I'm just going to have to try harder with Hector. Now that I know he's not being grumpy for the sake of being grumpy maybe I can help him.

* * * * *

Viaticus fell back to walk with Lucia, there was a lot he wanted to know about her but wasn't sure of just how to ask. Sadness just seemed to hang over her.

What can I do to make her feel better? Ever since Corripio's death she seems to be even more unhappy. What was the relationship between the two of them? It must be more than a simple acquaintance. They barely had time to get to know one another before we met up with them. Did she know him before they met on the road?

Maybe if I talk to her and let her know she's not alone that will make her feel better.

"Lucia, what are you thinking about?"

She pointed her head and said.

"There's no room in here for you Viaticus."

He didn't understand the comment but was rebuffed by it.

"I mean there's so much going on in my head that it is impossible for me to share it with you or anyone else for that matter. Besides, why should you bother yourself about my troubles?"

"But isn't that what friends are supposed to do? I mean listen to the troubles of friends and try to help. But maybe the problem is that you don't consider me to be your friend."

"Viaticus, I do consider you a friend. Although I must confess that I've never had one and I'm probably not very good at being friends."

"You've never had a friend? I don't believe that."

"At least not that I can ever remember."

"You talk a lot about your memory, are your recollections really so bad?"

"My problem is not with bad memories, although I'm sure some are bad. My problem is with incomplete memories."

Viaticus was surprised and pleased with the way Lucia was taking him into her confidence.

"I'm not sure I understand what you just said."

"No matter, I don't want to bore you."

"Oh you're not boring me, far from it, I want to know all about you."

"Why?"

He blushed and tried turning away to hide it. She noticed and said nothing.

"Because I just do."

"Viaticus I know virtually nothing of you. I think it only fair that you tell me of your memories, your life so far."

"Not much to tell about me."

"So there you are, you question me about my past and yet you are unwilling to tell me anything about yours."

"Because it's boring."

"Let me decide."

"Well as you know, I live or at least lived in Rome with my parents and one brother. My father is a man of business in the city and my mother is at home looking after the family. That's about all there is to tell."

"You certainly make it sound boring. However I'm sure there's much more to your life than that. Tell me about your brother."

"Ludus? He's a brother, what can I say. Some times we get along and often we fight. Do you have a younger brother Lucia? If you do then you know what I mean."

"Thought we were going to talk about your life, now you've switched around to mine again."

Is she angry with me? Why did she speak to me that way? There must be something in her background that makes her so prickly.

"I just asked…"

"I know what you asked. The answer is no, I am the oldest in the family. That has it's own set of problems just ask Pando if you don't believe me."

"Didn't you say you came from a large family."

"Enough of my family, we were talking about yours. What kind of business is your father in?"

"He buys and sells land. I don't know much about it really."

"Is your family rich?"

"Rich? I don't think so. However since we started on this adventure, it has changed my opinion on how to define rich."

"What do you mean?"

"The way we've been living. I don't mean this in a negative way, but living off the land, no roof over our heads and our safety a question mark, it certainly makes it seem that we were rich back then."

"From my standpoint Viaticus, I'd say you were rich. I doubt very much that neither you nor your brother ever had be worried about being sold as a slave."

"No, that's true. It's hard for me to accept the fact that parents would ever do such a thing."

"Don't be hard on the parents, what would you do if you had no money and your family was starving? Death compared to slavery is a poor option. In many cases the slave owners treat the slaves better than the slaves families ever could. Don't take Sceleris as an example, he was an exception."

"Lucia, I think slavery should be abolished."

"That statement just shows how little you know about the country you live in. Without the slaves, both foreign and domestic, the country would collapse. Slavery is never going to go away."

They walked on in silence, Viaticus realized that he could never keep up his side of any argument with her. She is just too smart; it was obvious that he had a great deal to learn. He was still curious about her past and gave it one last try when he asked her.

"Lucia, what was Corripio to you."

Her eyes flashed and she asked him suspiciously.

"What do you mean, what was he to me?"

"It's just that I sensed your attachment to him being something more than that of a recent acquaintance."

There was no immediate answer; it was as though she was carefully considering her response.

"Viaticus, I don't know why, but I trust you. Please don't say anything to the others, promise."

"I promise."

"I have this sense that Corripio and I may have been related. At least I have a partial memory of him. Just as I was telling you, incomplete memories."

"Incomplete memories? I don't understand."

"That's all right because neither do I. All I can tell you is I remember something about Corripio, just not everything. I sensed that he might have felt the same thing too."

"Did you ever ask him about it Lucia?"

"No, there was no time. Really, I didn't know what to talk to him about. Perhaps I was more concerned about sounding foolish and now it's too late."

"You must have some idea of what the incomplete memory might have been."

"As I say, just fragments. I felt like he could have been related to me."

"What kind of a relation?"

"Perhaps a brother, an older brother."

The both walked without talking; Viaticus considered what she had said.

A brother and she can't remember if he is or not. How can that be? It would be hard for me to forget Ludus, mind you some days I'd like to but he is my brother, I could never forget him.

"You think I'm crazy don't you?"

"No, not a bit. It's just strange that's all. What other kind of memory fragments have you experienced?"

"I'm tired talking about this Viaticus, it's not helping me it just makes me feel worse."

I've said more than I wanted to. There's no way I want to get into Oratio and the fragments I have of him. Why does my life feel so incomplete? Why can't I just be like everybody else?

Chapter Forty-three

Pando awoke with a start; it was pitch black no moon and no stars. There wasn't even a breeze blowing, he was surrounded by silence.

Where is everyone? I don't hear any breathing; I can't see anyone anywhere. Did they all leave? If they have why did they leave me behind?

He sat up and hugged his knees and looked about, no sign that anyone except himself had ever been there.

Something has happened, I'm sure of it. They would never leave without me. Has the Chimera come back? Surely not, but what do I know about such a creature? If it had, the battle would have been fierce and I would've heard.

He reached inside his tunic and took comfort in the fact the amulet was still there.

If the Chimera came back I'm sure it wouldn't leave without this. But it no longer beats. Does that mean that my cousins have been taken far away or maybe even worse?

What was that?

To the left I think. Something moved someone or something is out there. Mustn't panic, stay calm. Think, what could have happened, what should I do?

My heart is thumping so hard I'm sure whatever is out there can hear it. Am I going to die?

Could I outrun whatever is there? Should I just lie quietly and perhaps it'll just go away? How could I outrun anything? It's so dark I'd run into a tree or something.

My head feels funny, what's happening to me? Strange thoughts are pushing their way in.

--So Pando, did you really think that I wouldn't come back?

"Who are you, what do you want?"

--You remember me, at least you should.

"The Chimera?"

--Of course, I'm not so easy to get rid of you see. Now bring me the amulet and I'll be on my way."

"No, I can't."

--And why not?"

"I must return it to Caecus."

--That old blind fool? What need has he for it? It's mine and I want it.

"You lie, it belongs to Caecus."

--It belongs to whoever possesses it. So just bring it to me and it will be mine.

Kashta said he separated the Chimera's 'elements', I assume he means that he broke it into tiny pieces. Is it possible that the beast could have collected himself so quickly?

--Did you hear me Pando?

"I can't see you, why don't you show yourself to me?"

--You don't need to see me, just put the amulet on the ground.

Why is it that it won't show itself? It was perfectly willing to do that last night and frighten us in the process.

"I think you're just another thief and not the Chimera at all. You just want to steal the amulet and sell it."

--Don't be so stupid, bring me the amulet. Now."

"I'm not stupid, if I give you the amulet then I have no protection from evil. Why would I ever do that?"

--You are making me very angry. Do as I say."

Pando didn't move from his spot, he heard the bushes moving and above the trees he saw a flash of light of some kind.

What was that? It looked like fire. There it is again. It's set some of the dry brush on fire. Now I can see, but what is it?

The Chimera, or at least part of it. Just the lion head kind of floating all by itself.

It hasn't been able to get itself all together yet, doesn't look nearly so fierce with just the head floating there even if it can still breath fire.

I have an idea.

"Ha-ha-ha."

--What are you laughing at you fool?"

"Me a fool? You don't know how silly you look suspended in the air that way with no legs or tail. Not nearly as scary as you were yesterday."

--You make fun of me? I'll eat you alive boy now bring me that amulet."

"No and I don't think you can come and get it since you've got no legs. Otherwise I think you'd have done that by now."

The beast roared and shot flames at Pando, but he was well out of range and while he felt the heat no damage was done.

I'm right he can't move he just hangs there. I must think how I can use this to my advantage.

I could run, but where?

--If you just place the amulet on the ground in front of you, I'll let you leave otherwise you will live to regret your decision. Not for long mind you.

"Where's the rest of your body? Did you misplace it?"

Pando laughed again, his stomach was churning but he was determined not to show it.

I wonder if I can trick the beast into telling me where everyone has gone? It must know and if I can find out then maybe I can run and escape and still hold on to the amulet.

It's worth a try.

"Tell me Chimera, where have my friends gone?"

--Now wouldn't you like to know that? And what makes you think I would tell you in any event.

"Would you tell me if I gave you the gem?"

--Of course.

"Then tell me."

--Give me the amulet first.

"No, no, I don't trust you."

--But you think I should trust you?

Pando was so wrapped up in trying to trick the Chimera that he failed to notice that, piece by small piece the she-goat body was beginning to appear.

"I'm an honest person, why wouldn't you trust me?"

--Who is to say that I'm not equally honest?

"This is getting us nowhere. I have an idea, you tell me the direction they left in and I'll remove the amulet from my neck."

--Will you put it on the ground?

"No, not until you tell me the direction."

--And then what?

"I'll hold it by the chain in my hand."

--What then?

"You tell me when they left."

--And?

"When you tell me, I'll lay the amulet at my feet."

--Will you step away from it then?

"Not until you tell me precisely where they've gone."

I know this is dishonest but once I know where they've gone I can snatch up the amulet and run to catch up. The Chimera still has no legs so he can't follow me at least I hope not.

Pando watched the Chimera's face intently, looking to see if he might catch a glimmer of the beast's intent. Again he failed to see the changes taking place with the Chimera's body. Now the long serpent's tail was almost completely reformed and hidden by the bushes and the darkness.

--So that's the way you see this working out?"

"Yes, don't you agree? Since neither of us trust the other, it seems like a logical way."

--Well, I've heard your theory. Now it's my turn.

"Go ahead, I'm listening."

Suddenly, without a word being spoken the silence was shattered by a noise that sounded like a giant whip cutting through the air.

Pando found himself ensnared in the coils of a snake. Not a snake really but the tail of the Chimera. The breath was being squeezed out of him and the harder he fought the harder the beast squeezed.

His arms trapped inside the coils were useless; all he could do was flail about with his legs.

Oh Jupiter. I'm going to die; I should have run when I had the opportunity.

"Help me, help me. Someone help me."

He could barely breathe now, things were getting black very black. He struggled to shout with what he was sure was his last breath.

"Kashta, Kashta, help me, save me."

The next thing he remembered was being shaken and none too gently.

"Pando, Pando, wake-up and stop kicking me. You're having a nightmare, just wake-up."

Pando look into the face looming above him, it was Viaticus, and it took him several minutes to catch his breath and get his bearings.

He sat up and said.

"It was a dream. Just a dream. But it was so real."

I feel so foolish now, everybody is here, and nobody left me. I should have known that. My heart is still thumping, what an ugly beast, I hope we never come upon him again.

"I hope I didn't kick you in my sleep Viaticus, if I did, I'm very sorry."

"It wasn't the kicks that hurt so much as your long toe nails. Remind me not to sleep next to you tonight."

"So Pando, you had a nightmare." Asked Kashta.

"It was nothing, just overtired I guess."

"Let me decide if it was truly nothing. Many things are revealed in our dreams."

Pando spoke quietly so as not to be overheard and told the Prince everything he could remember.

"Very interesting Pando, but I'm not sure it was just a dream. Not sure at all."

"What do you mean."

"I mean that it sounds to me like the beast got into your head. Now he is able to do that at will."

"You mean really in my head."

"Yes."

Pando shuddered and knew he would sleep no more this night.

Chapter Forty-four

No one could sleep after Pando's dream so at first light the little band headed back towards Perusia and Caecus's farm. They left without a meal so anxious were they to complete their journey before nightfall.

"Kashta, just how could the Chimera get inside my head? I don't understand," Pando asked as he walked at Kashta's side.

"There is much more to magic than you have learned so far, particularly the dark magic. Just trust me, the beast can do it."

"Can it read my thoughts."

"No, unless you are weak and allow it to."

"What must I do?"

"When it next comes to you, do not share any thoughts with it. It is a very clever beast and it will try to trick you into telling it what it wants to know. However, if you are resolute and tell it nothing it will become frustrated and in time will show itself."

Kashta said 'when' not if it comes again. I don't like the sound of that. Why have I been singled out?

"Kashta, is it because I have the amulet? Is that why the Chimera pursues me?"

"That's part of it, the rest of it will have to come from Caecus."

The rest of it, what does that mean?

"What do you mean, 'the rest of it'?"

"Sorry Pando, that's all I can tell you."

Pando knew better than to ask any more questions. They continued on in silence.

"Ludus, are you always so quiet?" Asked Lucia.

"I guess I'm not awake yet. With all that noise in the night, I thought we were being attacked. There was no sleeping after that."

"True, but then I haven't known you to be much of a talker anyway. Why is that?"

He shrugged his shoulders by way of an answer.

"Of course if you don't want to talk I understand."

"No, it's not that I don't want to talk to you, it's just that ummm."

"What?"

"You're a little uh." He struggled for a word.

"Go ahead say it."

"Forceful."

"Forceful? What do you mean?"

"You know, sure of yourself."

"Is there anything wrong with that?"

"No, no, It's just that I don't want to annoy you."

"Look Ludus, if you are annoying me believe me I'll tell you."

"Yes I guess you would."

"So what is it you'd like to talk about?"

Ludus was taken aback by her directness, but there is something he wanted know.

"Could I ask you something about Corripio?"

Her face darkened for a moment but then she replied.

"Yes of course. What is it?"

"Did you know anything about his skill with medicine? For example, how long it took him to become good at it?"

"You touch on a problem Ludus."

Is it too soon after his death for me to be asking questions about him? I hope I haven't caused her discomfort?

"If you'd rather not talk about it Lucia, I understand."

"No, it's not that. It's just that I know little of his history. We just met on this journey and while I won't deny that a closeness had developed, I don't know much about him."

I certainly don't think she's lying but this is so strange. I had the impression from watching the two of them that they were friends of long standing.

"What was you wanted know about? Maybe I can still help you."

"I was impressed with the way he was able to treat your wound, you know from the boar. I really hoped he might be able to teach me how to do that kind of work."

"That is noble work Ludus and I think you would be good at it. I've noted that you have a caring attitude and if you feel you have the mental capacity for it I think you can still do it."

"Really?"

"Yes, there is always room for another physician in this world, a good one at any rate."

Ludus could feel his cheeks warm and hoped that he wasn't showing any outward signs of his embarrassment.

"Do you have any idea how I could get started Lucia?"

"Kashta seems to have the answer to everything, why not ask him?"

With that Lucia dropped back to walk with Viaticus.

* * * * *

--Good morning Fortitudo.

--Good morning Tactus, how are you today?

--I'm fine, just fine. Fortitudo there's something I'd like to talk to you about.

The horse's head immediately became more erect. He shifted in his stall as if a centurion was about to impart a new battle plan to him.

--I'm at your disposal Tactus.

--It's about Hector. I've spoken to Caecus about him and his depression. Caecus has suggested that I make more of an effort to become Hector's friend. To see if I can't find ways to cheer him up and get him to stop thinking those morose thoughts about sacrifices.

--I think that's a wonderful idea my friend. How can I help?

--Well for a start, you know how I bring you a treat everyday?"

--Yes, and it's much appreciated.

--I wasn't looking for a thank you Fortitudo, please listen.

--Of course, very sorry, very sorry. Please proceed.

--Every morning I bring you an apple and only a carrot for Hector. He thinks this means I think more of you than him. But really it's because Oratio will only give me those two items.

--I'm not sure I understand.

--What I wanted to ask you is, would you mind if I gave you the carrot and Hector gets the apple for a while?

--Hmm, not very fussy about carrots you know. I much prefer the apple.

--But you're not depressed Fortitudo, wouldn't you give up your apple to help Hector?

The horse shifted in his stall as though considering the request.

--I suppose I could. Do you think if I do this, he might treat me with a little more respect?

--Fortitudo, it isn't a good idea to do something nice in anticipation of getting a reward. My mother told me that.

--I'm sorry I said that Tactus. Of course he can have my apple.

--Thank you, here's your treat.

--It's not very big is it?

Fortitudo, you're a strange animal, in some ways you can very generous and I've heard very brave. But in other ways you're very self-centered.

Come to think of it, I've met people very much like you.

Tactus bit his tongue and turned to leave the barn. He had seen Hector lying under the fig tree before coming into the barn.

--Hector, how are you this morning?

The goat raised his head to see who it was sitting next to him.

--Oh it's you Tactus. What's the matter, Fortitudo have nothing to say to you this morning?

--What do you mean Hector?

--I saw you go in to see him first, so I'm second choice, right?

--Hector, don't be such a grump. I've brought you a treat.

--I don't want a carrot today.

--It's not a carrot, see it's a nice juicy apple.

--And what did Fortitudo get? Some nice figs?

--No, he got a carrot.

--I don't believe it.

--I'm trying to be your friend Hector, here have the apple.

--Hmm it is a nice juicy apple. Why did you give it to me?

--Because you're my friend.

--Isn't Fortitudo your friend anymore?

--Is there any reason I can't have two friends?

--But Fortitudo is still your best friend isn't he?"

--Don't be foolish Hector.

--What do you mean?

--I mean you are both my best friends, I like both of you equally. Why can't you just accept that?"

--I don't believe you, that's why.

This business of trying to make a friend out of Hector is hard work. But Caecus says it's the only way to improve Hector's outlook so I must persevere.

* * * * *

"Nog, where have you been? I called you four times."

"Pico I told you I had a lodge meeting to attend."

"Where was this meeting?"

"In Egypt."

"Really? No wonder it took you so long to get back. Tell me, tell me, did you find anything out?"

"Just a minute, let me gather myself from my trip."

The little man shook himself and straightened out his trouser legs. An apricot pit fell out of the left leg and landed on the ground.

"That's better, I knew something was irritating me."

"Please Nog, tell me."

"I'll go one better than tell you, I'll let you meet the Daimon who was present when the crime occurred."

"You will? But I thought only the person the Daimon was assigned to could see him."

"Normally that's true, but in this case I got special dispensation for him to visit you. Pico, I'd like you to meet my good friend Tok,"

With that there was a puff of blue smoke and that same sound, Pfffft. And another being became visible. He was not unlike Nog in stature but entirely unlike him in appearance.

Tok wore a bilious yellow suit, which was badly stained with what looked like the remains of his last meal. Pico could smell him from where he stood, he smelled of cheap wine and rotten food.

"You'll have to forgive how Tok looks Pico. I'm afraid he overindulged at the windup dinner last night."

Tok held his head with his left hand and said.

"Did we really have to travel all the way from Egypt in one jump Nog? My head is still spinning."

"Tisn't the trip that makes your head spin Tok. Now straighten yourself up, I want you to meet my charge. Tok meet Pico, Pico meet Tok."

Pico wasn't sure if he was supposed to shake hands. But when Tok extended his, Pico had no option.

I wish I could wash my hand, this Tok seems very dirty. I can't believe that this is a friend of Nog's.

"Go ahead Tok, tell Pico what you told me about Oratio's tongue."

Before he spoke, Tok took a flask from his back pocket and had a long drink from it. He replaced the stopper and returned the flask to the same pocket. Then he said.

"Strictly medicinal Nog, you understand."

"I understand, now get on with it."

"All right, all right. To let you know who I am and how I know of these things I must properly introduce myself.

My name is Tok and I'm the Daimon of an unfortunate wretch by the name of 'Sordeo Occisor' a cutthroat criminal of the lowest order.

My charge is the worst kind that can ever befall a self respecting Daimon. Never was he aware that he even had a Daimon. I had no opportunity to modify his behaviour because he was a non-believer and never called upon me."

"Enough of all of that Tok, nobody here holds you responsible for what your charge did. Get on with what you know."

"All right Nog, just have patience, it's been a difficult time."

"Please Tok, tell me, it's most important to me." Said Pico

"Yes, yes. Well I was there the night it happened. The night that the poor man Oratio had his tongue cut out."

Tok paused and shivered, then continued.

"Occisor had a henchman with him who sat on Oratio's chest while my charge cut out the poor man's tongue. Oh, it was awful."

He removed his flask and took another drink. Nog was becoming impatient and said.

"Tell him who it was that ordered that such a thing should happen."

"Yes, yes. It was a very rich man. A very powerful man, he lived in Rome then, yes he did."

Nog was becoming increasingly agitated.

"Tell him what Occisor did with the tongue."

"He took it with him and gave it to this rich man. I was there when he gave it to him, but of course nobody knows that because ordinarily I'm invisible you see."

"We all know that Tok. Just tell him what the rich man did with the tongue."

"He took it and put it in a wooden box, a fancy wooden box all inlaid and everything. He said he would keep it to remind him that Oratio could never again say anything against him and then he laughed."

Pico couldn't believe what he had heard, but he needed more.

"And where is that box now."

"It's in Perusia."

Pico was dumbfounded.

"In Perusia? What is this rich man's name?"

"I can't say his name it's too dangerous."

"Say it Tok. Say it," said Nog.

"Lucius Antonius."

"The Tribune?" Asked Nog.

"Yes."

Chapter Forty-five

Nog dismissed Tok leaving he and Pico alone. By the puzzled look on Pico's face Nog knew that there would be questions. Before the boy could ask them Nog said.

"So Pico, what did you think of Tok?"

I'd better be careful what I say in answer to that. But why is he asking? If he can read my mind he already knows what I think.

"You're right Pico, you weren't impressed with him were you?"

"Well, he wasn't very clean was he? Do you trust what he told us to be true?"

"Don't be too harsh Pico. Remember what I said about how hard it is on a Daimon to be ignored by his charge. He has lived a very unsatisfactory life leaving him an unhappy being. However, I've never known him to lie to me."

"Then you believe the Tribune has Oratio's tongue?"

"Did you not hear me say that he doesn't lie?"

"Sorry Nog."

"What else do you want to know? I'm scheduled for an important game of Tabula."

"About the Tribune, why is he in Perusia? Doesn't he normally live in Rome?"

"Yes he does, but there are things afoot in Perusia, things that this cunning man would like to use to his advantage."

"What sort of things?"

"Things that you are too young to understand."

Why is it that they always say that? I'm too young to understand. I know a lot of things; I'm not stupid.

"I didn't say you were stupid Pico. It's just that these are complicated times. Best you ask Caecus."

I will talk to Caecus; he won't talk down to me. Honestly Nog, sometimes you can be so bossy.

Pico didn't even see the hand coming; it landed on the back of his head with a loud smack.

"Respect your elders Pico, did no one ever tell you that?"

"Sorry Nog, I didn't mean it."

"You are forgiven, just watch yourself in the future. Now, is there anything else?"

"Do you think it might be possible for us to recover Oratio's tongue from the Tribune?"

"What's this us business?"

"Wouldn't you help me? It would mean so much to Oratio."

"It would be a very dangerous thing to do and mean certain death or at least imprisonment if you were caught."

"So you won't help me?"

" I am your Daimon, the cause is righteous and for no personal gain to you therefore I would be committed to help you. Whether I like the idea or not by the way. However, you must discuss any such idea with Caecus before making any attempt at this."

"I will Nog."

"Now, dismiss me my game awaits."

"Go Nog."

* * * * *

Kashta was setting a very fast pace for his band of travelers anxious to reach Caecus's farm before nightfall. Pando's stomach was unsettled after a hurried breakfast of pulse followed by some sweet cake.

Even so, he managed to keep up with the big man even though it meant taking almost two strides for every one of Kashta's He looked back and could see the others struggling even more than he was.

"Kashta, everybody is looking tired back there. Can we stop for a short rest?"

"Not yet. There is danger in this place. We won't be safe until we reach the farm. I'll tell you when we can stop."

I don't see any danger; it's broad daylight we can see for miles in all directions. I see nothing. What's making Kashta press so hard now?

My head feels funny. Is it the sun? Should have brought a hat. But then no one else has a hat either and the sun doesn't seem to bother them. Maybe I'm coming down with something, I feel sick. That pulse didn't agree with me, maybe it had gone moldy, should have stuck with Oratio's cake. Now I have a sound in my head, what is that?

--Hello Pando. Did you think that I wouldn't follow you?

The Chimera, he's back and in my head. Kashta said not to share any thoughts with it. I must ignore it.

--You can't ignore me Pando, forget what the Black Prince tells you. He knows nothing of my powers. I want the amulet. Give it to me and I will leave you in peace.

I must think of other things. My mother that's it, I'll think of her.

--Your mother? Well she is very beautiful. You must love her very much. Do you ever want to see her again? If you do you must give me the gem.

I think you are an ugly beast. I think of Kashta destroying you and you are afraid.

--Think what you like, but know this, I fear no man. I want the jewel.

Pando looked back, everything was normal nothing out of the ordinary. The weary group simply trudged on.

--You worry about your friends and so you should. Perhaps you would reconsider your decision not to part with the amulet if they were under threat too. Pando you must understand that I'm a reasonable being. Just give me what I want and you'll never hear from me again.

Why should I do that? It doesn't belong to you.

--If you don't then you can look forward to one of your friends disappearing every mile of your journey until they are all gone, including the Prince.

"Kashta, it's back."

"The Chimera?"

"Yes, in my head."

"Fight it Pando, fight it hard. Be careful what you think of."

--What does he know Pando? He can't help you under the circumstances. Does he think he can get into your head and do battle with me here?"

I'll think of nothing, just blackness and maybe music, yes music that might help.

--You're annoying me, stop with the music, I hate music.

Good I've found something that distracts it.

--Stop it I said. That confounded racket is most irritating. How you humans consider that entertaining is beyond me. It just shows how really primitive you are.

I've learned something else. It can't control my thoughts only I can. I'm going to think about the last parade I was at. All the Legions marching, the drums and cymbals and trumpets it was loud yes very loud.

--Agghhh I can't stand this it makes my head swim. You haven't won yet Pando, I'll get what I came for, you'll see.

I think it's gone. Yes it is gone.

"What are you smiling at Pando?" Asked Kashta.

"It's gone, I made it leave."

"How did you do that?"

"You won't believe this but in an effort to prevent him from knowing what I was thinking, I thought about music."

"Music?"

"Yes and apparently Chimeras hate music. So much so that he left my mind."

"Very clever Pando."

"No, not clever, just lucky very lucky."

"On that note, I think we can all stop for a rest."

* * * * *

"Caecus, would you have a minute to talk to me?"

"Of course Pico, come in."

"I've found something out that might help Oratio."

"And what might that be?"

"I know where his tongue is."

"His tongue? How did you do that?"

Pico told Caecus of his discussions with Nog and how his friend Tok had been the Daimon of the man who committed the crime.

"And Tok said that the tongue is in Perusia."

"Did he tell you who it is that has it?"

"Yes, he said the Tribune has it."

"The Tribune, you mean Lucius Antonius?"

"Yes."

"And what would you like to do about that?"

"I would like to go and get it back for Oratio."

"That's an admirable goal Pico. But it would be a very dangerous endeavour for anyone let alone anyone as young as you."

"Everyone thinks I'm too young for everything. Please Caecus, I can do this, I'm very brave you know."

"I don't doubt your bravery Pico. However, the Tribune is a very powerful man he has many guards. They would not hesitate to arrest you or worse."

"But you are very powerful too Caecus. Couldn't you help me with your magic? And it would make Oratio so happy if you could restore his voice."

"Yes, I'm sure it would, however, it has been a long time since he lost his tongue and we have no way of knowing the condition of it now. Even if we were to succeed we can't tell whether or not we will be able to restore his speech."

"Please Caecus, please."

"Let me think about it Pico, I'll give you my answer tomorrow."

"Oh thank you Caecus."

"Remember, I didn't say that we would do this."

"No, I understand. There is one other thing."

"What's that Pico?"

"What's the Tribune doing in Perusia? Doesn't he normally live in Rome?"

"Yes he does but these are not normal times."

Chapter Forty-six

Pico was helping out in the kitchen, not through any desire of his own, but at the request of Caecus. He was bursting to tell Oratio his news but managed to hold back any hint of it. After all, Caecus had not really said yes.

Oh I hope he does say yes, I want so much to help Oratio. He's had such a sad life, who knows maybe he could even sing again?

I wonder why there are so many pots on the stove? Could it be that we're expecting guests? Nobody said anything; I'll ask Oratio.

"Oratio, are we having guests tonight?"

--I assume so, Caecus just said to set five extra places. Have you peeled all the potatoes Pico?

"Did he say who they were?"

--No, now what about the potatoes.

"Yes, I peeled them and sliced them just as you asked."

--Good, now you can do the carrots. Scrape them with a knife and rinse them with water.

Why am I doing all this? Where's Tactus? How come he doesn't have to help?

"Oratio how come you don't ask Tactus to help you?"

--Tactus is doing his share Pico. Didn't you hear that we just got a load of hay in from one of the other farmers? Enough to last the coming winter. Tactus is going to be very busy and with heavier work than you.

Pico smiled at this and then said.

"Do you think it's possible that Pando and the others are coming here tonight? And why five, shouldn't it just be three?"

--No sense trying to guess Pico, we'll just have to wait and see.

* * * * *

The group was keeping a torrid pace urged on by Kashta in spite of some muted grumbling. He was determined that they should reach Caecus's farm before nightfall.

"Can't we take a break Kashta, we're all exhausted?" Asked Pando.

"The sun is beginning to set, we'll lose the light before long. Just remember, danger comes with darkness."

"Are you worried about the Chimera coming back?"

"Do you believe it's ever really left us Pando?"

"But I can't see it anywhere."

"Trust me, it's here. I can sense it."

That doesn't make me feel very good. At least we're travelling in the open; the tree line is a considerable distance away. Why is Kashta pressing so hard? He can't be afraid of it can he? Surely not, he scattered it before I'm sure he can do it again.

Ludus called from the back of the line.

"Kashta, something is following us."

The line stopped and Kashta turned to look.

"I don't see anything."

"There, up in the sky, a big bird."

"Yes I see it now."

"Kashta, it's the vulture, the same one I'm sure of it. I thought the Golden Eagle killed it but it's back," said Pando.

"Perhaps it's just foraging for food. All of you stay here and I'll go back and see if it is a vulture. Stay down in the long grass so as not to be seen. I'll be back shortly."

With that he was gone. He ran swiftly, low to the ground, it was soon difficult to see him at all.

"Pando do you really think that it's the same bird that tried to steal the amulet?" Asked Lucia

"Hard to tell from this distance," he said.

"Too bad we don't have Fortis with us now," she said.

"I thought you didn't like Fortis."

"Pando, at a time like this I would like Fortis, believe me."

Viaticus shouted.

"Look, there's another bird up there."

It was the Golden Eagle its feathers shimmered in the glow of the setting sun. It soared around the vulture; shrieking each time it passed the larger bird.

"It's the Golden Eagle, the same one that saved the amulet before. He'll take care of the vulture just watch," said Pando.

But this time it was different. Each time the Eagle dove at the vulture, the bigger bird deftly avoided the sharp claws. It climbed above and behind the Eagle, then with a great beat of its wings plunged towards it.

The sharp talons raked the right wing of the Eagle causing the bird to flutter and fall.

There was a collective intake of breath by those watching below as they saw the Eagle plummet towards the ground.

Almost at the last moment, the great wings beat and the Eagle gained altitude, higher now than the vulture it turned and dove with wings thrashing the air, directly at the larger bird.

The Eagle was braced for the collision with both sets of talons extended it hit the vulture and grasped it by the neck then with a quick snap of its powerful beak it severed the head from the body. The Eagle released its grip and allowed the lifeless body to flutter to the ground and with a shriek it flew over the trees and disappeared.

A cheer went up from the little band with much hugging and jumping up and down.

"My Golden Eagle did it. He saved us," shouted Pando.

"Your Golden Eagle Pando? Since when?" Asked Viaticus.

"Never mind you two," said Lucia.

"Just be grateful we're all still alive and that Pando still has the amulet."

Pando reached inside his tunic, just to make sure.

Yes it's still there, thank goodness. Could this have been Fortis's doing? I didn't see him anywhere. It must have been but where did Kashta go?

Finally they saw Kashta approaching them; Ludus called out to him.

"Kashta, did you see that? The Golden Eagle demolished that vulture."

"Yes, I saw."

Lucia ran to him.

"What's wrong Kashta? You're bleeding."

"I'm all right, I fell and cut my arm, just a scratch."

"That's more than a scratch. Let me fetch my bag and get something to stop the bleeding."

He offered no protest and in fact was grateful for the opportunity to sit and rest for while.

Pando looked at the arm and wondered.

Something odd here. I'd swear that that was the same Golden Eagle that saved me the last time. But I saw Fortis shape change into that bird. This time Fortis is no where to be seen.

Kashta has a wound to his right arm. And the vulture injured the Eagle's right wing. Is that a coincidence?

Why is it I've never seen Kashta and Fortis together?

* * * * *

--Hector might I speak with you?

--What do you want oh mighty warrior?

--Is it really necessary for you to be so nasty with me?

--What do you want from me Fortitudo?

--I don't want anything from you other than to be your friend.

--What's all this 'sweetness and light' all of a sudden.

--Hector, can't we put aside our differences and be friends?

--Our differences are too great. You forget, you're a famous warrior and I'm just a goat.

--There's no need for all this sarcasm.

--Fortitudo, we've spent many years together in this barn during which time you've never even deigned to talk to me let alone be my friend. What's suddenly changed?

--Tactus was talking to me and…

--That kid should mind his own business

--He has your best interest at heart.

--What you mean is that he's made you feel guilty.

--No, I don't feel guilty. I don't think I've done anything wrong.

--You see, that's your problem Fortitudo. You never think you've done anything wrong.

--Hector you make it very difficult to be your friend.

--I never asked you to be my friend.
--I think you do this kind of thing on purpose.
--Do what?
--Antagonize people. You're afraid to get too close to anyone for fear you might actually come to like them.
--Not much chance of that with you.
--Well you may as well know this. I'm not going to give up on you. I will be your friend.
--You don't understand simple arithmetic.
--What's that supposed to mean?
--It takes two or more to make friends, one can't do it by themselves. And I only see one of you. Thank goodness.
--Look Hector, I'm trying to be nice to you.
--Nice, nice, when were you ever nice to me?
--Why just this morning. I gave you my apple.
--Your apple? No wonder I got a bellyache.
--Ungrateful. Well your carrot wasn't much either.
--There you go again. You did it again.
--What?
--Passed wind. That's your answer for winning every argument, just pass wind.
--I told you your carrot didn't agree with me. I'm sorry.

Chapter Forty-seven

"Glad to have you back Kashta."

"We are all happy to be here Caecus. It's been a long hard day, but my party was up to it. I must say though that we have five very hungry bellies. I hope Oratio has something delicious for us.

"I don't think he's ever disappointed you in the past has he Kashta?"

"Never."

"I think you should introduce me to our new guests before we go inside."

"Of course, forgive me Caecus. Let me introduce the lady first."

Kashta could see her cringe at the comment.

"This is Lucia, the two boys were most fortunate to meet her on the road."

The blind man extended his hand to her and said.

"Ah yes, Lucia, the friend of poor Corripio."

She was stunned at this statement.

How did he know of Corripio? We just got here and no one has said anything about him. He held his hand out to me and yet I didn't speak, how did he know where I was standing?

"You knew him?"

"Alas no."

What does he mean no? He somehow knows we were friends or perhaps more and yet he doesn't know him. How can this be?

Caecus looked at her with his unseeing eyes and said.

"Perhaps you can tell me more of him after we've had some dinner?"

Then he turned and said.

"This must be Viaticus. Kashta are you sure he's just a boy? He's bigger than many men I've met."

"Very nearly a man in all things with exception of life experiences. He has a pure heart and a strong body and is willing to learn."

"Admirable attributes." Said Caecus.

"And his brother Ludus."

"Ah yes, the athlete. But not just that, I understand you have an interest in medicine."

How can he know that? We all arrived together and no one has had a chance to speak to him without all of us being present. And just how did he know that Viaticus was big? Is he really blind? Or is he faking?

"Yes I do sir." Answered Ludus.

"A noble calling young man, I look forward to discussing your future prospects with you."

Caecus then moved to Pando and clasped his hand upon his shoulder and said.

"Pando, I'm so happy you've returned safely. And with the amulet in your possession in spite of other forces that tried to get you to part with it."

Pando moved to take off the amulet and return it to Caecus, but the old man restrained him by saying.

"No Pando, you must keep it on. You and I must talk later. In the meantime I hear your brothers approaching. I'm sure you and your cousins have some catching up to do."

Pico and Tactus burst upon the room full of excited boisterousness, much hugging and loud talk followed until Caecus said.

"You'll all have lots of time to visit and exchange stories but now our meal awaits. Please follow me into the dining room, we don't want Oratio to be offended by neglecting his wonderful meal."

And wonderful it was a strange assortment of meats and some vegetables the boys had never seen before. But the dessert was the high point for them all. Delicious pastries, exotic fruits that must have come from far off lands and refreshing cool sweet drinks topped off the meal.

The hungry travelers gorged themselves until they could not eat another morsel, then Caecus said.

"I think you will agree with me that we owe Oratio special thanks for this wonderful meal." Then he called out.

"Oratio, come join us."

Oratio appeared, somewhat apprehensively, in the doorway from the kitchen.

"My friends, this is the wonder worker who provided this marvelous meal for us. Oratio we all want to thank you."

The small man still standing in the doorway hung his head in embarrassment at the attention he was receiving.

No one noticed Lucia staring intently at the small man.

Oratio, why is it that I seem to know you? In my heart I feel it, but truly when I look upon you, I can't say that I recognize you. How can that be? I wonder why he's being treated like a servant or perhaps a slave here? Why was there no place for him at the table?

As though Caecus was reading her thoughts he said.

"Oratio is a humble man who doesn't like a fuss to be made over him. I asked him to eat with us but he refused. He simply said his place was in the kitchen."

Was he reading my mind? Is he truly blind? Those obsidian eyes reveal nothing of what's inside. Is Kashta right? Is Caecus truly a good man? I hope so. Oh Oratio, you trouble me so, why?

Oratio turned to leave but before he did so he stared intently at Lucia, she could almost feel his eyes upon her.

He knows me, I'm sure of it. But how, where? These memories, if that's what they are, are driving me mad. I must find a way to talk to Caecus alone and soon, I don't want to talk of this in front of the others.

When she looked back Oratio was gone. Then she heard Caecus say.

"It's getting late and I'm sure you're all very tired, I know you're all looking forward to a good night's sleep. Unfortunately, we don't have enough space in the house for all of you so I would ask the five boys to sleep in the barn.

Tactus has been very busy today loading up fresh hay for the winter therefore I'm sure you'll find it very comfortable.

Lucia I would ask you to stay with Kashta and me here in the house, Oratio will show you to your room."

Lucia was angered at being given special treatment.

Why do I have to stay here, just because I'm a girl? I'm as capable of looking after myself as any one of those five. I resent being treated as less than an equal.

Perhaps I shouldn't be too hasty with my anger; maybe his intention is to give me some time alone with him. He did say we'd talk later. It may just be a waste of time, but if there is a chance that he can help me I must take it.

* * * * *

Tactus led the way to the barn, he could hardly contain himself he was so excited about introducing his family to his two new friends Fortitudo and Hector.

"This is Kashta's horse Fortitudo, he has fought in many battles with the Legion before coming here."

"Fortitudo these are my cousins Viaticus and Ludus, of course you know my little brother Pico and this is my oldest brother Pando."

"Why are you talking to the horse?" Asked Ludus.

"I was just introducing you to my friend Fortitudo."

"What? You can talk to animals?"

"So he says." Said Pico.

Viaticus scratched his head and said.

"I've never heard of anybody being able to do that. Are you sure you're not just making it all up?"

"I'm not lying honest. Wait, I know, I'll ask him to scratch the floor with his right front foot. Watch."

"Please Fortitudo, do as I ask and scratch the barn floor with your right foot. Please, Please."

The horse stood still as though it didn't understand the request. Tactus was dying a thousand deaths as he waited.

--Sorry Tactus, I was just kidding.

They were all amazed when Fortitudo raised his right leg at the knee and made a very determined scrape at the barn floor.

"See, I told you. Do you believe me now?"

"Can you get him to do anything else?" Asked Pando.

"You still don't believe I can talk to him?"

"Well that wasn't all that much of a demonstration."

"Supposing I ask him to nip your ear Pando, would that convince you?"

Pando backed away from the horse and said.

"No, I believe you."

But he said it with a smirk on his face, which upset Tactus.

--What's going on here. Who are all these people and why are they here?

Tactus whirled around and saw Hector standing behind him.

"Hector these are all members of my family, we're all going to sleep in the barn tonight."

"Don't tell me that you can speak to the goat too?" Said Ludus.

"As a matter of fact I can."

--This place is getting unbearable. First I've got that militaristic old nag and now all of these strangers poking around. I think I'll go find someplace else to stay.

"Well I certainly don't hear either one of them talking." Said Viaticus.

"That's because you don't have the gift. Only I do and Kashta of course."

Pando looked dubious.

"You're telling me that Kashta speaks to the animals too?"

"Yes."

"Good then I'll ask him about it tomorrow."

"Pando, why don't you believe me?"

Before he could respond there was loud crash as Hector kicked the side of the stall once again.

"What was that?" Gasped Ludus.

"Oh that's just Hector, he's angry that you're all here, he's going outside to find a quieter place to sleep."

They all watched as the goat walked imperiously out of the barn door not pausing to look back.

"What's wrong with him?" Asked Viaticus.

"He's just an unhappy goat, that's all." Said Tactus

Ludus rubbed his eyes and said.

"That may be true, but I'm tired. Let's find that fresh hay and get some sleep. We can catch up with one another tomorrow."

Tactus led them to the haymow; it looked and smelled very inviting. The night was still warm so they simply flopped down upon the hay and didn't have long to wait for sleep to overtake them. Pando was the last to drift off as he did his best not to think about the Chimera.

Chapter Forty-eight

She sat opposite the old man in a room she took to be his study. Two tapers illuminated it; the flickering of which cast odd shadows on the plain walls. She was acutely aware of how vulnerable she was at that moment. He sensed her unease and reached across the small table between them and took her hand.

"There's no need to be nervous my dear, I only want to help you."

It's almost like he can read my mind. Can I trust him? Everyone else seems to think so but then they are all men or rather boys.

I don't see where I have a choice, if he can answer my questions then perhaps I can find peace in my life.

"Why don't you tell me what your concerns are?"

She answered.

"Why do I have to tell you anything? You seem to know everything about me without me saying a word."

"But I need to hear it in your words. I need to know how whatever is disturbing you is impacting upon you. My view of what may be a problem to you may not be the same as yours."

"Master, I find these things most difficult to talk about."

"I understand but before we begin you must know there is no 'Master' here, just equals."

"But you have so much more knowledge than me how can you not be the Master?"

"Because knowledge should free you not enslave you."

"I'm not sure I understand."

"Perhaps you will by the time we've finished. Now explain how I might help you."

"It's memories, incomplete memories. I remember things or parts of things but I do not understand how I come to know them."

"Such as?"

"Well Corripio for one. I seem to remember him as being an older brother and yet for the life of me I can't remember anything of our life together."

"Are there other such things bothering you?"

"Yes, I sense that for some reason I remember your servant Oratio."

"Please, I don't consider him a servant, he is a dear and trusted friend."

"Sorry."

"What do you remember of Oratio?"

"His name, it's a very odd name. But not his face and yet I have this strong feeling that we've met before."

"I see."

"That's all, you see?"

He ignored her and continued his questions.

"Is there anything else?"

"I know things and yet I know not how I know them."

"Explain."

"When Corripio died I knew how to build a funeral pyre and how to make an urn from clay for his ashes and how to fire it. And yet I don't ever remember even being to a funeral myself.

"And I seem to have an ability to find edible plants and cook them and yet I've never been trained to do so. I know something of the healing nature of plants too. Not as much as Corripio did, but still I was able to treat Kashta's wound."

Caecus said nothing regarding Kashta's injury. He just stroked his scant beard and said.

"And you see no logical explanation as to how you come to have this knowledge?"

"None whatsoever."

"Tell me about your family and why you find yourself alone in the world?"

She sighed and Caecus sensed she was close to tears. He reached across and pressed her hand to reassure her.

"I had the sense, perhaps more than a sense that my family were about to sell me into slavery. My family is large and had little money to feed us or clothe us. Oh, I don't blame my mother and father they were at their wit's end and could see no other option.

"I chose to run away because I did not want to be anyone's slave. My mother always said that my quick temper and high opinion of myself would lead me to ruin. Perhaps she was right."

"You don't think that do you Lucia?"

She thought for a moment and said defiantly.

"No I don't."

Is this really going to do me any good? Does this old man really know anything that can help me or is he just a charlatan? All this questioning is doing is making me feel worse.

"I have no intention of making you feel worse Lucia."

She pulled her hand away with a start.

This is weird; he does read my mind. Is nothing private? I must guard against my own thoughts.

"Is there anything else you'd like to tell me?"

"Not that I can think of at the moment."

"I see."

She watched Caecus as he tented his long slender fingers under his chin, then after a long pause he said.

"Lucia, I'm about to impart some knowledge that may help you to understand what has been happening to you. After I have done so you may have to make a very difficult decision should you want to change things in your life.

"The decision will be yours and I cannot help you with it. Of course you will be free to take no action and continue your life as it is now. Do you understand?"

"Yes I think so."

He nodded his head, cleared his throat and began.

"Tell me Lucia, what do you know of the Underworld?"

She was startled at the question. After a brief moment she replied.

"Not much really, my people are not particularly religious. I do know that the Underworld is where you're supposed to go when you die."

"That's correct and when one gets there the first thing seen is a beautiful white cypress and under that tree is a spring. This spring gives rise to the River Lethe one of the five rivers of the Underworld.

"The dead are encouraged to drink from the spring of Lethe, using what is referred to as the 'Cup of Forgetfulness'. The result of drinking from this cup is that all memories of the past life are wiped away so that the spirit can be reborn and start life afresh."

Lucia sat listening with her mouth open in amazement at what she was hearing, then she asked.

"So you're saying that I had a past life and somehow my memory from that was not eliminated before I entered this life?"

"It may be a little more complicated than that, but in general terms I could say yes."

"But why wouldn't I have taken the 'Cup of Forgetfulness'?"

"I can't answer that, it would just be speculation on my part."

"Speculation may be all I ever have, please tell my what you think happened to me."

"Well there is another spring in the Underworld, it's called 'Mnemosyne' or the Spring of Memory and if a spirit drinks from that spring then all past memories are carried into the next life. This spring was reserved for the 'Enlightened Ones'."

"But that can't have happened to me, I only remember fragments and I don't think I qualify as an 'Enlightened One', surely that would be someone like you."

"You are right, but perhaps the vessel was contaminated by containing some spring water from each. There is no way to prove that of course."

Lucia sat quietly thinking to herself aware that she might not just be thinking to herself.

What does all this mean? Can it really be true? I've never spent any time thinking about an afterlife or about reincarnation. It is a kind of explanation though. Could this be the answer? And if it is, what can I do about it now.

Lucia received another jolt when Caecus said.

"There is something that we can do and this leads me back to where we began this discussion. I can prepare a 'Cup of Forgetfulness' for you and we can perform a ceremony whereby you drink and we erase all memory of your past lives.

"The operative word of course is <u>all</u>; the fragmented memories you have now will be gone forever. You will be unable to recall any past relationship with Corripio or Oratio or anyone else from past lives."

"So you believe that Corripio and Oratio were somehow connected to me in another of my lives and not this one?"

"Seems reasonable, don't you think?

"Will I lose my memories of this life?"

"No, they will remain intact."

"Could I not drink from the 'Cup of memories' instead?"

"No."

"Why not?"

"Because as you said, you don't qualify as an 'Enlightened One'. Only they can drink from that cup."

"Then you're telling me that I really have no choice."

"No, you have choice. Do nothing and stay as you are or drink from the 'Cup of Forgetfulness'."

"But I've said to you I don't want things to stay as they are."

"I understand that Lucia but you must consider carefully. If you can truthfully say that the memory fragments you have now are worth nothing to you then we can go ahead with the ceremony.

"But consider this most carefully, memories are generally meant to be treasured and one should not discard them casually, even those that cause one pain."

"That's why you don't want me to rush this decision."

"Yes, remember, the process is irreversible."

Chapter Forty-nine

"Good morning Oratio. I guess you might like some help in preparing breakfast today. You certainly have many more to feed than usual."

--I was hoping you'd come here Pico, you're right I could use your help.

"What would you like me to do?"

--Well, if you could go out to the coop and collect some eggs that would be most helpful.

I hate that chicken coop; those stupid birds are always trying to peck at me. Why can't I get more important work? Even Tactus gets to unload hay and me; I have to forage around to find eggs. Well, I offered so I guess I'll just have to do it.

Pico took the basket and headed out to the chicken coop. When he opened the door the chickens began to flutter as though a fox had made its way into their midst.

"Ouch, that hurt. Get away you dumb birds, I only came for your eggs. I'm not going to hurt you."

Maybe Nog could help me here. It wouldn't hurt to try. Who knows, maybe he'd even like it in here.

"Come Nog."

He heard the sound and saw the puff of smoke through the cracks in the door.

--What is it you want Pico?

"Morning Nog. I just thought you might like to help me collect eggs for breakfast."

--Now why would I want to do that?

"Well, for one thing it would be a friendly thing to do."

--What's that got to do with anything. I'm not your friend; I'm your Daimon.

"You know Nog, I frankly don't see a whole lot of benefit in having a Daimon."

--You ungrateful little twit. Haven't I shown you how to hear Oratio and didn't I find out where Oratio's tongue is?

Sheepishly, Pico replied.

"Of course, you're right Nog. I'm sorry for what I said."

--You should be.

"Pico who are you talking to in there?"

It was Pando.

--Well, look at what you've done now Pico. What are you going to tell him?"

"No one Pando."

--He's not going to believe that.

"But I heard you Pico. What's going on?"

What do I tell him? He's never going to believe that I have a Daimon. I'm going to sound stupid that's all. But I can't lie either. What to do?

--Tell him the truth, what can it hurt.

"Nothing's going on Pando. I'm just collecting some eggs for breakfast. I'm sure you must be hungry."

He said, trying desperately to change the subject. Finally he whispered under his breath.

"Go Nog."

Again Pico could see a puff of smoke and hear the strange sound. However, apparently Pando could not.

"What did you say?"

"Why are you asking me all these questions Pando? I told you I was gathering eggs, that's all."

Pico came out of the coop with his basket almost full and closed the door carefully behind him.

"See, I've got lots of eggs."

"Yes you have, but you still haven't told me who you were talking to in there."

"I was talking to the chickens of course. If I didn't they would peck at me. It seems to calm them down." He lied.

Just as he walked up to Pando he felt a smack to the back of his head causing him to stumble forward from the impact.

"What is this Pico? All of a sudden you can't walk straight?"

"It's nothing, I just lost my footing for a moment."

The two walked back to the farmhouse together in silence for which Pico was very grateful.

Pico was surprised when Pando followed him into the kitchen.

"Good morning Oratio." Said Pando.

Oratio turned from his workplace and smiled at the boy and waved his hand in greeting. There was a momentary pause and then Pico was asked.

--Pico do you think you could ask your brother something for me?

This thing is going from bad to worse. How can I tell Pando that Oratio has asked me to ask him something? I know he wouldn't believe me about Nog so I'm sure he won't believe that I can communicate with Oratio.

--Pico I asked you something, please talk to me.

"Oratio, here are the eggs. Do think it will be enough?"

The small man nodded his head.

--Ask him what he knows about Lucia, please.

Pico tried to appear nonchalant as he asked his brother.

"Pando, this Lucia, she seems like a very nice person, how did you come upon her."

"When I met up with Viaticus and Ludus on the trail she and Corripio were with them. She and Corripio decided to join us on our journey here and I'm really glad they did."

Anticipating another question from Oratio, Pico asked.

"Why is that."

"Well she's very smart. She could find things to eat in the forest that we would never have thought of and she knew other things and so did Corripio."

"What kind of things?"

"Well Corripio knew about healing wounds and so does Lucia and best of all she can cook."

--Ask him how old she is?

"How old do you think she is Pando?"

"Why do you care? She's too old for you in any event."

"I'm just curious, she doesn't look old enough to know all those things."

Pico was getting more nervous as the conversation proceeded.

"My guess would be thirteen, maybe fourteen."

"Old enough for you Pando. Right?"

Pando could feel his face redden in embarrassment.

--Ask him where she came from, what town?

"Did she ever tell you where she was from Pando?"

"What is this sudden interest in girls Pico? When I left on my journey you didn't even like girls and now they're all you can talk about."

"Just curious Pando. And for your information, I think girls are a great nuisance nothing has changed."

"It will Pico, trust me."

Mercifully, Oratio could see Pico's discomfort and asked nothing more of him.

* * * * *

After a delicious breakfast they all left Oratio and Pico to clean up. When they were alone Pico said.

"Oratio, that was very difficult with Pando."

--Why is that?

"Because he would never believe that we can communicate the way we do."

--Why don't you just tell him about it. I think it's wonderful.

"So do I, but he'll just think I'm making up stories."

--But you never did that did you?

"Sometimes." He said with a little smile.

--Aha.

"Why are you so interested in Lucia anyway?"

--I'm not really sure. It's just that when I first saw her I had this feeling.

"What kind of feeling?"

--That I knew her, not that I recognized her, but that I knew her.

"I don't understand."

--That's all right, neither do I. Not completely anyway.

"Do you think it was from your younger days, you know, when you were a poet?"

--No, no, she's far too young to have known me then. You heard Pando say that she's only thirteen or fourteen.

"How long have you been with Caecus?"

--Fifteen years.

"Then could you have met her here?"

--Impossible.

"This is a puzzle."

--Yes it is.

* * * * *

Pando had been standing outside the kitchen door listening to the one sided conversation. Or at least he thought it was a conversation.

What's going on here? Is my little brother sick? Talking to himself, that's not normal. Maybe it's the separation from mother and father; he is the youngest after all. I worry about my two brothers. Tactus thinks he can talk to animals and Pico talks to himself.

What am I talking about? I've seen shape shifting animals, a man turned to stone, a black prince and how can I forget the Chimera.

It seems that we are losing touch with reality, do I even remember what reality is? I must talk to Pico, here he comes now.

"Pico, we need to talk."

The boy was apprehensive and asked.

"About what?"

"Something has happened to you since I left. You're not the same brother I left here."

"Yes I am."

"Not really and it isn't just you. Tactus has changed too."

"How have I changed?"

"Talking to yourself for one thing. I don't remember you ever doing that before."

Pico sighed and said.

"Come let's go and sit under that fig tree and talk."

He seems a lot more grown up. How could that happen in such a short time?

"Pando, I'm going to tell you about some things that have happened here in the last little while. I beg you to believe me when I tell them to you."

"Little brother, just tell the truth and I'll believe you."

Pico began by telling him of Caecus introducing him to Nog and how Nog helped him to be able to communicate with Oratio.

He told him of Oratio's early life and what had befallen him, all of it poured out of him. Then he said.

"Pando, I know all of this sounds like something I've made up, but honestly it's the truth as Nog is my witness.

"You must believe me, please. If you're in any doubt, ask Caecus, he knows of all of this."

Pando was stunned at what he had heard but he had a powerful sense that this was the truth. He put his arm around the boy's shoulder and said.

"I believe you Pico. I trust what you say."

Chapter Fifty

"Viaticus I've just come from Caecus, he asked me to find you and have you go see him at the farm house."

"Did he say what he wanted with me Pando?"

"No, but I wouldn't keep him waiting."

Viaticus began walking back towards the house, he really wanted to go to the barn and see Kashta and his horse.

Well, this should be interesting, I guess I can see the horse any time. Maybe I'll learn something of value from Caecus. I'd like to be able to understand just how he's able to 'see' when he's really blind.

Is this some sort of magic? The way Pando and Kashta talk about him, he sounds like a wizard. At least what I've heard wizards are supposed to be like. I've never believed all that stuff, I think it's just what parents tell their children to make them behave.

I must admit he certainly seems to have special powers and after seeing what happened to Sceleris and then the appearance of the Chimera, who am I to doubt magic.

He walked into the house and ran into Oratio just inside the front door. Without thinking he said.

"Caecus sent for me, do you know where he is?"

Oratio smiled and signaled with his finger for him to follow. Up the stairs to a small room.

Caecus sat with his back to the open door. Viaticus was surprised once again when he heard.

"Come in Viaticus, I'm glad you've come so promptly."

How does he do that? It really is unnerving.

Caecus pointed the chair opposite and said.

"Please sit here, I think you will be quite comfortable."

Viaticus looked around the room, it was quite dark with the drapes drawn and it smelled musty.

"I trust that you slept well?"

"Yes quite well, I don't think any of us realized just how tired we were."

"Yes, yes. Understandable, given the events you experienced in getting here."

Viaticus turned back to look at Caecus; it was impossible for him not to concentrate on the eyes.

Unseeing yes, but yet able to see more than most sighted people. How can that be? What does he want with me?

"Patience Viaticus. We'll get to that but first I'd like to know just what your understanding is of what happened with your parents."

"All I can tell you is that they were arrested."

"You're a man of few words."

"I speak only of things that I have confidence in."

"Meaning?"

"Rumours and speculation most often do not serve to clarify a situation."

"You mean you will not speak it unless you know it to be the truth?"

"Yes."

"Admirable."

The conversation stopped, Caecus knew that unless he pursued it, silence would continue so he said.

"Would you care to learn then just what it is that I know of what happened to your parents?"

"Yes."

"I have it on good authority that your father, a prominent business man in Rome was a faithful supporter of Julius Caesar. Isn't that so?"

"I could not argue with that."

"So faithful in fact that Caesar's enemies fearful of an uprising by those that opposed the murder of the Great Dictator, began arresting all of those they thought could be leaders of any revolt against them.

"Consequently they have been imprisoned in a secret location along with others of a like mind."

"Like my aunt and uncle, Pando's parent's?"

"Yes."

"Caecus, do you know where they are and can we get them free?"

"Mincing words is something you don't do Viaticus."

"My father always said, the direct approach works best."

"In most cases I would agree. However, you may find in the future that diplomacy is never out of place."

"Perhaps I'll come to understand what you mean, but for now could you answer my questions. Please."

The 'please' was an obvious afterthought and caused a smile to play on Caecus's lips.

"Yes I know where they are. As to your second question, that is more difficult and in fact is the reason I wanted to see you."

"I am here Caecus."

"The reason you're here Viaticus is that as the oldest of the group of five, it falls to you to make the ultimate decision regarding a plan to gain the release of your family members."

Why me? What has age to do in any of this? Surely the others should have some say.

"The others will be consulted of course, but the decision is yours Viaticus."

"What is this plan?"

* * * * *

"Come Nog."

Nog appeared with shaving lather on his face, he had no shirt and was naked from the waist up. He spluttered at Pico.

"Pico why is it you always seem to summon me at an inopportune moment?"

"Sorry Nog, but how can I tell when it's a bad time?"

The Daimon wiped the soap from his face with a small towel he had tucked into the top of his trousers.

"Have a look at my beard, is it even?"

"Looks all right to me."

"You gave me such a start, I was afraid that the razor might have slipped. Now what is it you want this time."

"Well, I was just wondering…"

"Get to the point boy, I'm getting cold without my shirt."

Boy, I didn't realize just how hairy his body is. He's certainly not the best looking thing I've ever seen.

There was a loud 'thwack' as Nog's towel snapped at Pico's ears.

"Ouch, that hurt."

"It was meant to. What have I told you about making nasty comments?"

"I didn't speak out loud."

"Might as well speak it as think it. It makes no difference."

"Sorry."

"Seems to me that 'sorry' is becoming your favourite word. Now speak up tell me why you called me?"

"I just wondered."

"What?"

"Could you show yourself to my family, you know my brothers and cousins. Just once."

"No. Why do you ask?"

"Well nobody believes me when I tell them that you've taught me how to communicate with Oratio. In fact they don't believe you even exist."

"Not my problem."

"Please Nog."

"The rules are that I'm invisible to everyone but you, and Caecus of course. I don't make the rules but like you, I do have to obey them."

Despondent, Pico hung his head and said.

"Go Nog."

* * * * *

"Hello Kashta, it's good to have you back."

"It's good to see you again 'little toad'. I understand you've been taking good care of Fortitudo in my absence."

"We've become good friends, I just wish I could do the same thing with Hector. I don't think he likes me."

"Hector doesn't like anybody."

"Not even you."

"Afraid not. He's just one unhappy goat. Do you know why?"

"Yes, I think so, he told me that he fears being taken for a sacrifice. He thinks that all goats are being discriminated against and that makes him feel very bad."

"I think you've made some headway with him Tactus. He's never told me as much as he's told you. Perhaps over time you will convince him that he has nothing to fear for himself. At least not here."

"I don't think that's his main concern. It's as much for his fellow goats as anything."

"I see. Maybe if you were to talk to Caecus he might be able to help. He knows much about ancient times when goats were much loved and revered. Perhaps a story or two of such times would help."

"I think it'll take more than that, but I'll try."

"You are a good friend Tactus."

The boy smiled then as he thought of what he must tell Kashta it was like a cloud passed over his face.

"What is it Tactus, what's wrong?"

"I have something to tell you, something that I did."

"Is this a confession of some kind?"

"Yes."

"What is it?"

"While you were away, I rode Fortitudo."

"You what?"

"I rode Fortitudo."

"But you could have been hurt, he's a big horse and you have no experience. Do you understand that it was wrong to do that without permission?"

"Yes and I promise I'll never do it again."

"Where did you get a saddle? I keep it locked up."

"I didn't, I rode him without one."

"Bareback?"

"Yes."

"That's even more dangerous."

At first Kashta was angry with the boy but then he came to realize what courage it had taken for him to tell him about it. His heart softened as he looked down into the face that was on the verge of tears.

"I've disappointed you haven't I Kashta?"

"No, on the contrary, I'm proud of you for having admitted your mistake."

"You're not angry?"

"No, but why didn't you tell me you have an interest in learning to ride?"

"I thought you might laugh at me."

"Never. Do you still want to learn?"

"Oh yes."

"Come let's get the saddle. We must do this thing properly."

* * * * *

What should I do? Drink from the Cup of Forgetfulness? Stay as I am? It sounds like such any easy decision, but it's not.

Memories are treasures, treasures of the soul can I just cast them out? Who was I in my previous life? Do I want to know? Why waste my time thinking about that, I can never know about my previous lives, no one can except of course the 'Enlightened Ones'.

Oratio and Corripio seem important to me; they are special memories could I really wipe them away? Do I even want to do that?

I have so many questions. I'd hoped Caecus could give me the answers but he just gives me more questions. He says the decision is mine, this is no help.

Is it possible that I may remember more of my past lives? It won't be if I drink from the cup. And yet, if I remember more will I be deviled more.

Oh Jupiter, help me.

Chapter Fifty-one

"What I'm about to tell you Viaticus must be kept in complete confidence. Should any of it leak out it could put your parents and your aunt and uncle in serious jeopardy.

"These are dangerous times; there are people in this world that would think nothing of ending the lives of others if they thought it would be to their advantage.

"Therefore, I must have your word that you will say nothing about this meeting to anyone.

"Do you understand?"

"How can I make such a promise without knowing first what it is that that you are talking about?"

Caecus quickly turned his head as though looking at Viaticus.

He has a very good point. His quiet demeanour is deceiving; there is much going on in his head.

"You're quite right in saying that Viaticus. Let's just say that should you have a need to discuss what is said here with anyone, that you talk to me about it first. Agreed?"

"Agreed."

"Good, now let me tell you about this plan."

"Before you do, may I ask why you have involved yourself in these matters relating to my family?"

"Are you critical of my interest?"

"No, not at all. It's just that from what I have been able to learn about the turmoil that is taking place in this country, prudence would seem to be in order. I for one don't know much about you Caecus."

This boy is far deeper than I first imagined. How could I have missed that?

"Viaticus, you're right to ask me of my intentions. Perhaps it would help if you knew my connection to the great Caesar and his assassination."

"For many years I was a trusted advisor to Caesar, he consulted me and sought my advice on many matters of state.

"I was able to use my skills to look into the future and provide him with guidance. I treasured my relationship with him; the bond between us was strong. I had great love the man.

"But I failed him."

"How did you fail him?"

"I failed to adequately warn him of his impending death on the Ides of March. My powers of persuasion were inadequate that day."

"But how can you fault yourself if he refused to take heed?"

"I failed because on the day it mattered most I was unable to convince him my vision was correct. He dismissed me. My message was somehow not powerful enough to have saved his life."

"I see."

"Do you? Then you might understand my interest in trying to save the Republic from the certain disaster that will come should the wrong man come to lead the country.

"These are the same sentiments expressed by your brave father and uncle and as a consequence they were arrested.

"If Marc Antony succeeds with his plan, it may well be impossible to gain the release of your family members."

"Then you take the Imperialist side."

"I take the side of Octavian."

"Why Octavian?"

"He is Caesar's rightful heir, legally adopted by the great man. A man who can follow in Caesar's footsteps and lead the Republic to even greater glory."

"But wasn't it Caesar who granted land in Perusia to the Legionnaires, dispossessing those who've live there and caused this turmoil?"

"No, it was done in Caesar's name but after his death."

"How could that happen?"

"A scheme hatched by Marc Antony and his brother Lucius. Conveniently they found a document Caesar had supposedly written before his murder.

"It was a forgery and meant to create an uprising between the Legionnaires and the town's people."

"But to what end Caecus?"

"In Marc Antony's absence, Octavian would be required to put down any such revolt with force and appear to be enforcing Caesar's will from beyond the grave.

"It could mean the start of a civil war and the discrediting of Octavian, with Antony coming to the rescue of the Republic.

"In fact, as we speak Perusia is under siege, we must do all we can to avoid a catastrophe."

"I think I understand."

"Good then let me tell you of my plan"

"It calls for a small group to go to Perusia and report back on just what is happening inside those walls. What kind of preparation has been made to defend the city?

"What is the mood of the people, not just the Legionnaires, but the townsfolk as well? What fortifications are in place?"

"You mean we are to spy?"

"Yes."

"But why would you need spies, you have magic? You know everything."

Caecus smiled and said.

"If only it were so. But there is so much turmoil in Perusia, so much anger, so much hatred that I cannot see clearly. I'm afraid that only someone who is actually there will be able to help."

"You want us to go to Perusia and become spies?"

"Who better, a few young boys, who would suspect you?"

"Who would go?"

"You, your brother and of course Pando."

"What about Tactus and Pico."

"I think they are too young."

"That maybe so but if I know them it may be impossible to prevent them from coming."

"Perhaps we should leave that decision up to the Field Commander."

"Who is that?"

"Octavian."

* * * * *

Lucia saw Pando sitting under the fig tree in the yard, he seemed deep in thought.

I need to talk to somebody; maybe Pando can help me. He seemed like a sensible boy and there really aren't any adults I can talk to. But how can I tell him?

Maybe all I need is some company right now, maybe not even talk about anything serious.

"Pando, do you mind if I sit with you?"

He looked up at the girl and saw that she seemed to be anxious about something.

"No, not at all. Come sit, it's quite nice here. So, how did your visit with Caecus go?"

"How did you know I saw him? She asked.

"Sorry Lucia, it was just a simple question, I didn't mean to upset you."

"I'm not upset, I just thought it was a private meeting."

"If you'd rather not talk about it.."

"There's nothing to talk about."

What's biting at her? I didn't mean anything by the question. There's definitely something wrong with her. Always challenging, never happy, I wonder what's really going on.

"I'm sorry Pando, I didn't mean to snap."

"That's all right. I won't ask anymore questions. If you feel like talking, I'll listen."

There was a long pause where nothing was said between them and then Lucia asked.

"What do you think of Oratio?"

"He's a great cook, but of course so are you."

She smiled at him and he thought how much prettier she was when she did smile.

"That's all, he's a good cook?"

"I haven't thought much about it, why do you ask?"

"It's just that he seems very familiar to me. I don't know why. I don't know if we've ever met but it seems like I know him."

"That's very strange."

"Yes, yes it is. It's too bad that I can't talk to him."

"Actually talking to him is easy Lucia, it's the fact he can't answer you that's so frustrating."

Is he making fun of me? I know he can hear and I know he has no tongue. No I don't think he is.

"Pando, do you know if he can write? Maybe I could communicate with him that way."

Should I tell her what Pico told me? I think he was telling me the truth but who knows. She seems to be really disturbed by something about Oratio.

"I hesitate to tell you this but there may be a better way to communicate with Oratio."

"She raised one eyebrow and said.

"Really."

"Yes."

"Well are you going to tell me?"

"It's going to sound weird but my brother Pico claims that he has found a way to understand what Oratio would like to say."

"Is this some kind of a joke?"

"I don't think he's lying to me, I can usually tell if he is you know."

"If that's true Pando, he could act as his interpreter, that could be of great help to me."

"The only problem Lucia, would be the fact that it wouldn't be very private."

"I just know I need to talk to him."

"I'll talk to Pico."

Chapter Fifty-two

Pando found Pico under the fig tree. As he approached, it seemed like he was talking to himself.

I don't know about poor Pico, I guess the strain of not seeing mother and father and my absence must be telling on him. I guess I can hardly blame him, I'd better call to him so it doesn't look like I'm trying to sneak up on him.

"Pico, do you have time to talk to me. Or are you going to have a little nap?"

Pico was little startled by the voice, but he was sure that Pando was too far away to have heard him talking to Nog.

"What do you want to talk about Pando?"

Pando sat down, wrapping his long arms around his knees, he said to his brother.

"Lucia would like to have a conversation with Oratio."

"How's she going to do that? He can't talk you know."

"I know that perfectly well, but I told her about your special skill."

"You had no right say anything about what I told you, besides, I thought you said you didn't believe me."

"I didn't say that at all Pico and you never said this skill of yours was some kind of secret. Unless of course you can't really do what you said you could."

"I can too."

"Then show us."

"How do I know that Oratio even wants to communicate with her? He might get very angry you know."

"Well you could just ask couldn't you?"

"But why should I bother Oratio with this. He doesn't like to talk about what happened."

"She's not curious about what happened to Oratio, he doesn't even have to talk about that if he doesn't want to. And I can tell her not to ask him."

"Then what is it she wants to talk to him about?"

"I'm not really sure, but I think it has something to do with the fact she thinks she might know him."

"I don't understand, either she knows him or she doesn't."

"Not quite so simple Pico, it seems there maybe something wrong with her memory."

"What? You mean she got hit on the head or something?"

"Who knows, but she needs you to help her, will you do it?"

Pico was flattered that his big brother needed his help. He was tempted to withhold his agreement but his curiosity was aroused. He wanted to know what this was all about too.

"Let me go and talk to Oratio and see if he is agreeable."

Pico ran towards the farmhouse while Pando decided that it might best to stay where he was until Pico returned.

The boy burst into the kitchen and startled Oratio who was standing with his back to the door.

--What is it Pico, you almost scared me out of my wits? I wish you wouldn't pounce like that.

"Sorry Oratio but something has come up and I just had to talk to you."

--Well, what's so important?

"Lucia, you know her, she came here with my brother Pando. Well she would like to talk to you and she would like me to be her interpreter."

--Why in the world would she want to talk to me?

"Pando says it has something to do with her memory, she thinks she knows you but she's not sure."

Oratio stood silently, thinking.

That's very strange. I have similar feelings but how would I have ever come to know her or meet her? I certainly have never met her since I've been here. And she's so young that she wouldn't have even been born before I came here.

"Oratio, did you hear me?"

--Yes, yes I heard you. But I don't know if I can be of very much help to her. It just doesn't seem possible that we've ever met.

"Maybe if you tell her that, it will help her to realize that she was mistaken."

--All right Pico, I'll listen to her and you can let her know what I think.

The boy ran back to his brother, pleased that he was to be a part of this meeting. Perhaps he could help Lucia and of course seem more important to his big brother.

"Pando, Pando, he said yes."

"Did he say when Pico?"

In his haste he'd forgotten to ask so he improvised.

"I think now would be good, we've already had lunch and it'll be at least 4 hours before dinner. He didn't seem too busy when I talked to him."

"You didn't ask did you?"

He hung his head and replied.

"No, but I'm sure it'll be all right."

                         *   *   *   *   *

Oratio held out his hand to Lucia, she took it and couldn't help but notice how soft it was. He held her hand so gently and yet firmly enough that she had some difficulty in withdrawing it.

--Tell her that I'm very pleased to meet her.

"Oratio's very pleased to meet you Lucia." Said Pico.

"Ask him if he has any memory of meeting me before."

"You can ask him yourself Lucia, he can hear, it's just that he can't speak."

She blushed slightly, she knew that, but this meeting somehow unnerved her.

--Tell her that I can't ever remember meeting her. Ask her why she thinks she has?

"He tells me that he cannot remember ever meeting you before. And then he asks, what makes you think that you have?"

"That's the difficult part, I don't know. It's just this strong feeling that I have. Is it possible that we met someplace other than here?"

She watched as Pico concentrated and looked at Oratio in silence.

A strange way to try to communicate but better than nothing I suppose.

--Pico I've been here for a very long time. Ask her how old she is.

"He tells me that he has been here for a long time. He wants to know how old you are?"

"I'm almost fourteen," she answered.

Oratio spread his hands and looked again at Pico.

--I've been with Caecus at least that long. I don't see how we could have ever met.

"He has been with Caecus, here in this location as long as that. So it doesn't seem possible that you've ever met."

She was crestfallen; the meeting was not going as she had hoped. Oratio saw tears were forming in her eyes. He reached out and touched her hand gently.

--Why is this so important to her Pico?

"Lucia, Oratio would like to know why this is so important to you?"

"I have a fragmented memory of my life, little bits float in and out of my mind and they seem important to me but I don't know why. It leaves me with the feeling of an incomplete existence."

"But what has that got to do with Oratio?"

Lucia was stunned at what the boy said.

Have I misjudged Oratio? I have the sense that he'd help me if he could.

--Pico, don't let her think that I'm so inconsiderate. I never made that comment.

The boy looked sheepishly at Lucia.

"I'm the one that said that, not Oratio."

Immediately her spirits were lifted. There was another long silence with Pico staring at Oratio.

--Ask her if she's spoken to Caecus about all this?

"Oratio wants to know what Caecus thinks?"

"I don't know if I'm permitted to tell anyone of what he said."

"Why not?" Pico said even before Oratio could make the same demand.

"He really didn't say I couldn't talk about it but I'm just not sure."

The tears were now flowing down her cheeks. Oratio reached out a gentle hand and dabbed them away with a soft cloth.

--Tell her that is doesn't matter if she tells me or not. I was just wondering if knowing would help me understand what's going on.

"Oratio doesn't want you to be upset, it doesn't matter if he knows what Caecus thinks. He just wondered if it might help him understand what's happening to you."

She stifled a sob and said.

"What could it matter, I'll tell you. Caecus believes that these memories may be from a past life. That when my spirit journeyed through the Underworld somehow my memory of my past life was not adequately cleansed, leaving me with these fragments."

Oratio jumped up and as he left the room he looked at Pico.

--Both of you wait here, I've got to get something. Something important.

Pico looked startled.

"Oratio wants us to wait here. He wants to get something from his quarters."

Lucia and Pico looked at each other and wondered just what it was that Oratio was going to get. Lucia thought to herself.

Maybe this was just a bad idea. Perhaps I should just drink from the 'Cup of Forgetfulness' and get this all over with, just live in the present and forget the past.

Her thoughts were interrupted by Oratio's return. He carried a scroll, dog-eared and worn from much use. Lucia reached out for the parchment, but strangely, Oratio withheld it.

--I'm not sure that my showing her this will help her or not.

"He tells me that he's unsure of whether he should give you the scroll or not."

"If he isn't going to let me see it then why did he go get it?"

Again a silence as the strange communication between Oratio and Pico took place.

--This scroll is very special to me. I have shown it to very few. I'm afraid that it may not help her and perhaps even make her sadness even greater.

"The document he has is very special to him, few have ever seen it. He's afraid that it may not help you, in fact he worries that it may cause you greater sadness."

"Can I be any sadder than I am now?"

With that, Oratio handed her the scroll. She unrolled it on the table with great care. She had a sense of the value of this document not just to Oratio but to her as well.

She began to read, it was a poem, a love poem. The words were beautiful they tore at her heart and soared from the page. She was overwhelmed as she read. She had the very real sense that she had read it all before but the words lay buried deep in her mind only now being recalled as she saw them on the parchment.

Her heart was full, she wept with joy at having recalled this poem from some dark recess and she said.

"It's so beautiful, I'd forgotten just how beautiful."

Oratio looked at her strangely and thought.

But how could she know of this poem? Only Aurelia ever saw it, I never showed it to another soul until now.
   Could it possibly be?

Chapter Fifty-three

The five boys gathered outside the farmhouse, all wanted to hear how Viaticus's meeting with Caecus had gone.

"What did he say can Tactus and I go?" Asked Pico.

"Well, he wasn't too happy about it at first, but I convinced him that it was important for everybody to be involved."

Tactus could hardly contain his excitement.

"When do we leave?" He asked.

"Not for a while yet, apparently there's going to be some kind of meeting here at the farm first."

Ludus was the first to ask.

"Meeting, what kind of meeting? And who are we meeting with?"

"He didn't say, just that we all had to be there."

Pando was annoyed that he wasn't consulted about all of this, asked Viaticus sharply.

"Who is it that we're supposed to meet with?"

"Caecus didn't say."

"Did he at least tell you when?"

"He said he'd let us know."

Pando continued.

"We are going to meeting with someone but we don't know who nor do we know when this is all to happen. Is that right?"

"I'm only telling you what he told me, you know that you don't question Caecus."

Pico pushed to the front and asked.

"Is Lucia coming?"

"No. Caecus says it's too dangerous for a girl,"

Pando laughed.

"Can I be there when you tell her that?"

* * * *

"Are you going away again Kashta?"

"Not that I'm aware of Tactus. Why do you ask?"

"It's just that I haven't seen much of you since you got back with Pando, I just thought you might be making plans to leave again."

"Don't worry little toad, I'll be here for a good while yet. Is there something you wanted to ask me?"

"Well, I'm sure you know about Caecus wanting us to spy on Perusia."

"I've heard, but do you think it's a good thing to be talking about it? After all spies are supposed to keep secrets you know."

"Even from you Kashta?"

"I think it's probably all right to talk to me, but you mustn't talk to anybody else."

"Oh I won't, it's just that I'm a little afraid and I don't want to say that to the others. They'll think I'm weak."

"Tactus you would be very odd indeed if you didn't worry at least a little. Tell me what bothers you most."

"Failing is what bothers me most. If we fail, I may never see my parents again,"

"So it's not for yourself that you're worried?"

"Maybe a little but a failure worries me most."

"Tactus let me tell you that I have no concerns about you and the others failing, I'm sure you will get the information necessary to help end the siege of Perusia. Just think; if you do that you will not only save your parents but the lives of many others in the town."

"But we are just boys Kashta. How can we hope to do what is asked of us?"

"You will succeed by making a careful plan and executing it exactly. You must have courage."

"But I don't think Pando or Viaticus know how to make a plan and the rest of us are too young."

"Don't worry about Viaticus and Pando, if they have trouble making a plan there are others that can help. But I doubt they'll need it."

* * * * *

Lucia sat alone under the fig tree, thinking about the decision she would soon have to male.

My discussion with Oratio really solved nothing. If anything it made the situation worse. Why did I recognize that poem? How could I? Yet it seems I've ever seen it before.

From what Oratio says, I wasn't even born when it was written and he's been here with Caecus all of my life.

This is really impossible. It's such a beautiful poem. It touched my heart, just as though it was written for me.

Poor Oratio, such a tragedy that he can't speak; I'm sure that there is much more we could discuss. What a horrible thing to have his tongue cut out.

What am I to do? Drink from the 'Cup of Forgetfulness' and wipe away all these memories and start fresh with experience from this life? Or stay the way I am and learn to live with these unexplained memories?

Is it possible that Oratio wrote that poem for me? If it was and I lost that memory, I don't think I could stand the loss.

If he did write it for me, what was our relationship when he did so? More importantly, will I ever find out?

Just then the dinner bell rang at the farmhouse distracting her from her thoughts. She slowly made her way to the house, not so much because she was hungry, as it was a reason to stop thinking about her dilemma.

* * * * *

The dinner was just about the best that any of them could remember having. Oratio had outdone himself. His attentiveness towards Lucia was unmistakable.

Each of the boys had to exercise great restrained in not commenting upon this fact. For they knew the wrath that Lucia might bring down on them if anything was said.

Lucia looked uncomfortable as Oratio hovered over her, but said nothing and even smiled sweetly at him much to the surprise of her travel companions.

Kashta spoke in his deep booming voice, each of the guests realized that it was the first time they had heard him speak indoors.

"Oratio, you have created a meal fit for a king,"

"Or a Black Prince." Interrupted Caecus.

They all laughed each acknowledging how much they had enjoyed the meal. It was then that someone knocked at the door.

"Ahh our visitor has arrived. Please let him in Oratio."

When he opened the door the light from inside flooded the small porch revealing a hooded figure standing in the doorway. The cowl of his robe obscured his face. But all could tell almost instantly by his bearing that he was someone of importance.

He stood alone on the porch as if awaiting an invitation to enter. Oratio bowed from the waist and with a sweep of his right arm silently bid the man enter. He did so.

Kashta stood and offered a military salute slamming his right forearm into his chest. The stranger returned the salute.

Caecus finally spoke.

"Welcome to my humble home. A place now significantly brightened by your presence. Oratio, please take our guest's cloak."

Lucia's hand went immediately to her mouth as if to stifle a cry.

Who is this? I've never seen a man so handsome he's like a God. The clothes while plain are obviously expensive. This is no ordinary traveler. And so young, if ever a man could be declared beautiful it would be him.

Her thoughts were interrupted when Caecus said.

"My friends I take great pleasure in introducing to you the Great Octavian, a member of the Triumvirate and a legend at such an early age."

There was a collective gasp. Each of them dumbfounded as Caecus introduced them by name. Incapable of speech, they merely nodded and shook the hand as it was offered. A firm grip of a large hand, the piercing blue eyes seemed to penetrate their very being.

Octavian turned to Caecus and said.

"Old friend it's good to see you again, it's been two years, my uncle's funeral as I remember."

"Your father's funeral as I remember," said Caecus.

Octavian smiled and said.

"One and the same."

"You came alone?" Asked the old man.

"I saw no sense in attracting attention by coming here in numbers."

He looked up and down the table at the expectant faces that turned towards him and followed his every move as he walked around them. Then he said to Caecus.

"This is the group you've selected for task? They seem very young."

"Yes they are young, but they have proven themselves to be brave and resourceful. Their age will work in our favour. Who will suspect a band of young children?"

Pando and Viaticus both flinched at being referred to as children.

"I understand that there are two families represented by those here, is that correct?

"Yes Octavian."

"I would like the eldest in each family to stand and make himself known to me."

Pando and Viaticus stood immediately.

Octavian motioned to them to come forward and face him. He spoke to Viaticus.

"By Your size I take you to be the eldest overall. Tell me if that's true and what your name is."

"My name is Viaticus and yes I'm the eldest."

"Where do you come from?"

"I come from Rome."

He turned to Pando and asked.

"And you, what's your name and where do you come from?"

"My name is Pando and I come from Perusia."

"Perusia, that's most useful, then you know the city well?"

"I've spent all my life there."

"Good, now tell me why you are prepared to undertake this dangerous mission?"

The two boys spoke as one.

"To gain the return of our parents," they chorused.

"Caecus has told me of your loss and I respect you for your honesty. Others might have been tempted to tell me they would do it for their country."

He walked around the two boys, stroking his chin as he did so. Then he stopped in front of Lucia.

"Why has no one introduced me to this beautiful young lady?"

Lucia could feel the heat of her face as she blushed profusely.

Chapter Fifty-four

T-- That was a very good apple Tactus, thank you. Tactus seemed to be far away, it was as if he wasn't even in the barn.

--Tactus, where are you?

--Oh, I'm sorry Fortitudo. I guess I was thinking about something else. I'm glad you enjoyed the apple, please don't say anything to Hector.

--Don't worry about Hector. What is it Tactus, your not yourself? What's bothering you?

--I don't think I'm supposed to say anything about it.

--You can tell me, who else but you and Kashta can converse with me anyway? Surely you trust Kashta? I won't even tell him if you don't want me to.

The horse shifted uncomfortably in his stall. Tactus sensed from his body language that he was annoyed.

--Well, we're being sent on a mission.

--A mission? What kind of mission? To where?

--Promise you won't ever let anybody else know?

--I've already promised.

--I'm sorry Fortitudo, it's just that I'm very nervous.

--About what?

--We're going to go on a spying mission, into Perusia.

--What? For who? Why?

--For Octavian, to try to find out the state of the city and it's citizens as a result of the siege.

--Octavian. What an honour.

--I guess it is, but I have a problem.

--What's that?

--Well, for one thing, I don't even know what a siege is.

--You've come to the right horse to find out my boy.

--Do you mean you've been involved in a siege before Fortitudo?

--Several.

--Then please tell me all about it.

--Pretty simple really. The City will be surrounded by forces, in this case, Octavian's, they will allow nothing in or out of the city. No food, no water and certainly no people.

--Then what happens?

--They wait.

--Who?

--The soldiers outside the city.

--For what?

--Tactus, is it really so difficult to understand. They wait for those inside the city to give up.

--And if they don't give up?

--There are only three options. Starve to death, surrender or fight.

--Two of those three options means that many will die doesn't it?

--Yes that's true but even in the event of surrender many will be put to death because of their involvement in the uprising. So I'm afraid there is no real possibility that this can end without bloodshed.

--Even if they surrendered?

--Oh certainly that would mean less killing but I'm afraid some is inevitable. And remember the main forces inside are themselves Legionnaires and they are not prone to surrender.

--Then what's to be gained by us going in to spy?

--My guess is that if Octavian knows which of those three options is the most likely he could select a strategy that would bring him success, end the siege and minimize losses on both sides.

--What would Octavian need to know? How would I know what would be important to find out?

--If the city is about to surrender, I think you will be able to tell that by the preparations inside the walls. If the people are hungry, if water is in short supply, if people are lying dead on the street, then they may think of surrender.

If they are well fed and no one is ill, then perhaps they are prepared to just wait and see what happens. I must say that I don't think that situation is very likely.

The thing that Octavian will want to know is what are the Legionnaires up to.

--What do you mean?

--I mean are they preparing to fight.

--How would I tell that?

--See what the cavalry is doing.

--What do you mean?

--The first line of attack if those inside are going to fight will be with the cavalry. They will come out of selected gates in the wall and surprise those laying siege. The foot soldiers will follow and great mayhem will ensue.

--So I should look for the cavalry mounted and ready to attack?

--Not necessarily, but you will see the horses assembled at particular locations close to the gates. This will be a clue to the intent of the defenders.

--Fortitudo, this all sounds hopeless.

--Then why are you doing this Tactus?

--Octavian says that this may be the start of a civil war and if that happens we will never see our parents again. What can I do?

--I think you must be brave and do this thing that has been asked of you Tactus.

--Fortitudo, I'm afraid I see nothing but death and destruction as a result even if we are successful. And that, plus the loss of my parents if we fail.

--Be of stout heart Tactus, I have an idea that may help you.

* * * * *

"Come Nog."

This time Nog appeared with the customary 'pfffft' sound and the cloud of blue smoke dressed in a toga of a saffron colour and golden sandals that were laced up his hairy legs to just below the knee.

"What is it this time Pico?"

"Have you heard about our great adventure?"

The little man snorted and said.

"Of course you foolish boy. I know everything you do and then some."

"Then you know we're going to Perusia?"

"What did I just say? Of course I do."

"Well, I was just wondering.."

"Out with it boy. What is it?"

"I was just thinking.."

"That's a bad sign, I'd just as soon you leave the thinking to me."

"Please listen to me Nog, this is important."

"Oh all right go ahead."

"You remember your friend Tok, you had him find the location of Oratio's tongue?"

"Of course, why don't you get to the point?"

"We're going to spy for Octavian in Perusia. You and I could try to recover the tongue and bring it back to Caecus so he could restore his speech. Would you help me do that? Please, please, Nog."

"What's this you and I business?"
"You'll be with me won't you."
"Do I have any choice?"
"Not according to Caecus."
"Don't get cheeky boy."
"Please help me Nog, it's very important to me."
"Why is it so important to you?"
Pico hung his head and looked at the ground as he spoke.
"I'm not entirely sure why, but there is something inside me that says that I must. Besides Nog, don't you believe it would be a good thing to do?"
"I cannot argue with the fact it would be a good thing to do but it will also be a very dangerous thing to do."
"Do you really think it's all that dangerous? Couldn't you just make yourself invisible and go in and get it? Nobody would be any the wiser until after we were long gone."
"Me steal it. I don't think so."
"But why not?"
"Because it's not what I do. I'm not a thief."
"It doesn't belong to whoever it is that has it now, so it's not like you'd be really stealing anything. We're just going to return the tongue to it's rightful owner."
"There's one other thing Pico."
"What's that?"
"I could never bring myself to touch that thing I have a very weak stomach." He said, belching behind his closed hand.
"Then I'll do it."
"You can't make yourself invisible."
"Couldn't you help me with that?"
"There is no way that I can give you the gift of invisibility at least not permanently."
"Even if I had it for just long enough to get the tongue. Please."
"It can be quite unpredictable. You'll be invisible one minute and visible the next, it's very hard to control at my level."
"What makes that happen?"
"Anger."
"What?"
"I said anger, if you have an angry thought while your invisible, poof! You're suddenly visible."
"I won't get angry, I promise."

"If you do, it could be then end of you, just remember who it is that has the tongue."

"I forget."

Nog threw up his hands and said.

"How could you forget. Lucius Antonius, the brother of Marc Antony and the sworn enemy of Octavian."

"Oh."

"Yes, oh."

"I still want to do it. I'll be careful really, really careful."

"I need my head examined."

"You mean you'll help me?"

"Do I have a choice, you'll just hound me until I do."

"Oh thank you Nog thank you."

"Before you thank me there is something you should know."

"What's that?"

"The location of the tongue."

"Yes, yes. Where is it?"

Nog hesitated before answering, the cleared his throat and said.

"Lucius Antonius has commandeered a house in Perusia."

"Well I guessed that much."

"It's your parent's house, your home."

Pico could feel the anger and resentment building within him, and then Nog spoke.

"You do that and you're instantly visible. You must control your anger.

"I will Nog just wait and see."

"That's just it, I don't want to see."

"Do you know where in the house it is hidden?"

"Yes, he keeps it in a special box, one given to him by his brother, brought from Egypt. It's inlaid with gold and ivory, he keeps it in the table your father stored his business scrolls in.

Chapter Fifty-five

"Did Caecus tell you when we are supposed to enter Perusia Viaticus?"
"Tonight, after dark."
"How are we supposed to get in without somebody seeing us?"
"We need to talk to Pando, Ludus. After all he knows the city better than either of us, I'm sure he'll have some ideas."
"He's just coming out of the farmhouse, we should talk now."
Viaticus waved to get the boy's attention. Pando acknowledged him with a wave and began to trot towards them.
"What is it? Asked Pando as he joined the two brothers.
"Let's go over and sit under the fig tree so we won't be overheard."
"Viaticus, there's nobody here to listen to anything we say."
"Just the same, we can't be too careful."
When the three were seated, Viaticus began.
"Caecus has told me that we are to enter Perusia tonight. Since you know the city better than either of us, I thought we should discuss just how we might do that."
"Yes, Caecus mentioned that to me too."
He smiled inwardly as he saw the expression on his cousin's face. Then he continued.
"The best place to enter the city is along the north wall. You may have noticed the barbacans located at intervals of approximately 100 yards along each of the walls that ring the city.
"My guess is that they will be manned as lookouts and likely these men will be armed so we must be very careful.
"The north wall is poorly maintained and the soldiers would not have had time to effectively repair all of the breeches. If we stay close to the base of the wall we won't likely be seen from above. We can creep along single file until we find a hole large enough for us to crawl through.
"I know such a spot, overgrown by bushes. I don't think that it will have even been noticed by anybody. So I should lead the way," said Pando.
While Viaticus was not pleased, he couldn't argue with the logic of Pando's statement. He simply grunted his agreement and Pando continued.

"Once we get through we should break up into two teams, we'll be less conspicuous that way. I would suggest that Ludus comes with me and that Pico and Tactus go with you Viaticus."

"And why is that Pando?"

"You are going to need someone that knows the city too. And Tactus is that person, he knows it well. And you as the eldest should be in charge of the larger group."

Is he trying to play me? As the eldest I should be in charge of this mission.

Oh get this jealousy out of my head. We all have to pull together in order to succeed. The important thing is to get all of the parents back safely. We have to get the information that Octavian needs so that he can prevent a civil war from breaking out.

It's not about me; it's about the success of this operation.

Viaticus spoke.

"That sounds like a good plan Pando. Now I think we need to look at just what it is that each group is going to try to accomplish once inside the city."

"I agree. I'd like to hear your opinions Viaticus and yours too Ludus. I don't see much point in duplicating our efforts."

Viaticus thought for a few moments and then said.

"I worry about Pico. Don't you think he's too young for this sort of thing?"

"Don't worry about Pico, he's much more capable than you think. A little boy can be a great distraction should you need one. And believe me, Pico can be very distracting. And another characteristic is that he is fearless."

"Yes, I believe that all right. But a little fear may be a good thing on this adventure," Viaticus said.

"So Viaticus, which elements do you feel comfortable looking after? If I may suggest something, Tactus is extremely good with animals, perhaps he could get some information on the readiness of the cavalry for example."

"Good idea Pando and perhaps Pico and I can get an indication about the city's provisions, food, water that sort of thing."

"Ludus, what are your thoughts?" Asked Pando.

"Octavian said he needed to know how the city is being fortified from within. Perhaps we could do that."

The two older boys nodded in agreement.

"Things may change once we are inside but I think those are the basics. Perhaps Pico can do a little begging so we can get an understanding of the conditions of the citizens," said Viaticus.

"I'd be careful with that. You send Pico out begging for food; someone might actually give him some. Knowing him, he likely wouldn't eat it and then where are we?" Pando said.

"You might be right cousin. Is there anything else?"

"Yes, Caecus wants to see you and Ludus."

"Now?"

"Right away."

* * * * *

Lucia walked out to the barn to see if Kashta was inside. She was angry and needed to talk to him. She opened the small door and saw him in the stall vigorously brushing Fortitudo's back.

He looked up when he heard the door.

"Lucia. What are doing here? It's very dusty."

"It doesn't matter. I have something I want to talk to you about."

He could tell by the way she was standing with one fist on her hip and her chin stuck forward that this was not a social visit.

"What's got you so upset?"

"I want to know why I'm not being allowed to go on this spying mission with the boys?"

How had she found out about that so quickly? Surely none of the boys have said anything, Oratio can't and Caecus wouldn't. She must have overheard a conversation.

"I don't know how you found out Lucia, but it just isn't the kind of thing a girl should be involved in."

"Why not? Just because I'm a girl? I can do more than any of those blockheads. I'm resourceful and I can get into places that they can't."

"Such as?"

"Well, a circle of women for example. Why would they want to talk to a group of young boys? Women are at the center of everything, how much food is there? What is the state of the family's health all those things that the would talk to another woman about."

"That may be right Lucia, but it doesn't change the fact that this mission is extremely dangerous, you could be hurt or worse."

"Any more dangerous than being on the road alone? You forget that I know how to look after myself."

How did I get involved in all of this? I didn't make the decision she couldn't go. Why is she acting this way towards me? I thought we were past all this, I don't have the time for such crankiness.

"I can't argue with you Lucia, you are resourceful. But you know that this wasn't my decision."

"But you have influence with Caecus."

"Why is it so important that you take part?"

"Because I want to help prevent a civil war."

"Or is it simply because someone has said no to you?"

"You question my motives?"

"Not really. I'm just trying to figure you out."

"Good luck! I've been trying to do that myself for as long as I can remember."

"Lucia, is it possible that you are putting yourself into harm's way for a particular reason."

"And what 'reason' would I have for doing that?"

"I don't know, but I think deep down inside you do."

"I thought Caecus was the philosopher."

"Do you know why you are so belligerent towards me?"

"I don't think I've been 'belligerent' as you say. Perhaps it's nothing more than a reflection of how you treat me."

"And just how have I treated you Lucia? Have I been unkind?"

"I don't want to pursue this discussion any further. Just tell me, will you go to Caecus and get him to change his mind about letting me go?"

"No. Go to Caecus yourself. It seems to me that you owe him a visit in any event."

"What do you mean?"

"I mean the 'Cup of Forgetfulness'."

She was startled by the comment.

He knows too much about me. Did Caecus tell him? He must have, else how would he know? Oh Jupiter help me, which way should I jump?

Is Kashta right? Am I intentionally trying to destroy my life?

Chapter Fifty-six

"Come in boys, thank you for coming so promptly."

Viaticus and Ludus took the two chairs placed opposite Caecus. Without knowing why, they shifted nervously in their seats and were startled when the door behind then slammed shut of it's own accord.

"Must be the wind," commented Caecus.

Ludus thought to himself.

More like some kind of spirit. I always find this place spooky. Why are the drapes never opened? And that smell from the burning candles, kind of sweet and yet it seems to sting the nose.

What is it about his eyes? They give me the shivers.

Ludus was brought back from his thoughts when Caecus said.

"I suppose you are wondering why I summoned you here this afternoon."

Both boys nodded.

"You and the rest of your little group are about to embark on a dangerous adventure. Dangerous not just to yourselves but to your parents and for that matter the whole City of Perusia.

"Dark forces are at work there, unpredictable forces capable of doing significant harm. This is serious business that will require your full attention.

"You ability to work together is imperative to the success of this mission. Do you understand what I'm saying?"

Viaticus answered.

"We're fully aware of what we must do. We will not shirk from our responsibilities."

Ludus looked at Viaticus with surprise and thought.

Fine for him to say but what do any of us know about these Dark Forces? I've seen the Chimera, if it's any example of what we may experience, I don't know how Viaticus can be so confident.

"Well said Viaticus, but I think you will need more than bravery to see you through this adventure. That's why I've called you both here."

He opened a drawer in the table and removed a leather pouch held closed by a drawstring at the top. He dropped it in front of the two boys, hesitating before he opened it.

"I'm going to give each of you something that may help you succeed in this endeavour."

With that he opened the bag and reached inside and removed the first object. A ring, a rather plain gold ring. Caecus removed a cloth from the bag and used it to polish the piece of jewelry until it shone brilliantly.

He reached for Viaticus's right hand and placed the ring on the third finger. It fit perfectly, just as though it had been made specifically for him.

Viaticus held his hand out at arm's length and studied the ring; it had a flat surface much as any other signet ring might have. But it had no jewel; instead there was a small engraving cut into the surface. It was hard to distinguish just what it represented.

"Why do you give me this ring Caecus?"

"Wait, I'll make all that clear after I've dealt with your brother."

He reached into the bag again and removed a bracelet, also made of gold, but in this instance it contained at its center, a large ruby. He polished this with the same cloth and it too shone with a brilliance to match the ring.

Caecus took Ludus's right arm and placed the bracelet on the wrist. There was a loud 'click' when the clasp was snapped shut. Then Caecus spoke.

"These two pieces of antiquity cannot be removed from you body by anyone other than me. Go ahead and try."

Both boys struggled to remove the jewelry but could not. Viaticus could not even turn the ring on his finger.

"What are these for Caecus? Are they to protect us on this mission?" Asked Viaticus.

"Yes, but perhaps not in the way that you may think."

Viaticus looked at the old man and thought.

Why is it necessary for him to always talk in riddles? Why can't he just make his point directly?

Ludus asked.

"Are these things magic? Will they prevent us from being injured, or worse?"

"Yes, these things have magic but as I said before, not necessarily the kind you normally think of."

Viaticus was becoming somewhat agitated.

"Caecus, what good will these things be to us if we don't know how to use them?"

"Have patience Viaticus. When the time is right you will know. It's not the case of you using them but perhaps the other way around."

"I'm thoroughly confused Caecus," said Viaticus.

"I would ask you to consider this. Perhaps the true magic is within the two of you and not in the jewelry at all. Consider that these artifacts may simply release that magic."

Ludus and Viaticus looked at one another and then at Caecus who said.

"You must put your faith in yourselves."

* * * * *

"Nog, can you show how this invisible thing will work?"

"Pico, it's really very simple. I will give you a word to say and once said you will be invisible until you repeat the word. Unless of course you become angry while invisible, then everyone will be able to see you.

"Would I become visible all at once?"

"No, it will depend on how angry you are. Very angry and 'Poof' your completely visible. Slightly angry and perhaps only your feet are visible."

"Will this stay that way, I mean with people able to see my feet?"

"If you get rid of the anger, you'll be invisible again."

"That doesn't sound so difficult. Can we try it please? Just for the practice."

"Well there is one other thing you have to know."

"What's that?"

"You have to remove all of your clothes first."

"What?"

"Of course, it's only your physical body that is made invisible, not your clothes. It wouldn't do much good for you to disappear if your clothes were still walking around."

"You mean I have to be naked?"

"Yes."

Nog hoped that this fact might end Pico's interest in recovering Oratio's tongue, but he was wrong.

"All right, let's try it. What's the magic word?"

"Are you sure that you really want to do this Pico?"

"Yes, yes. I want to help Oratio, he's been so sad."

Nog heaved a great sigh and said.

"I need my head examined, but all right. But before we begin there is something you need to understand."

"What's that?" He said impatiently.

"You need to memorize the word,"

"Of course, but even if I forget, you'll be there, you can get me back."

"That's not the way it works. You must say the word, both to disappear and to reappear. Otherwise you will stay in the state you're in after saying the word. No one else can say it for you."

"I'll memorize it, now can we try it?"

"There's one other problem."

Pico was getting exasperated.

"What is it now?"

"When I tell you the word, I'm going to disappear."

"But you say it again and get back, right?"

"Yes."

"Good, then let's do it. What's the word."

"Caxtazaro."

And with that Nog disappeared. That is his body disappeared but his weird Saffron toga and golden sandals, laces and all, were still there as though suspended in air.

It looked so funny that Pico could not suppress his laughter. And then he heard.

"Caxtazaro."

Suddenly Nog was back, just as he had been.

"So what's so funny?"

"Oh nothing Nog. Can I try it now? But I'd like to leave my clothes on if I may. Just like you did."

"All right, but just remember what I've told you."

Pico could feel the excitement build within him. This was real magic and he was going to do it. Then he said loudly.

"Caxtazaro.

He was a little" disappointed that he felt nothing.

Why didn't it work? Did I do something wrong? Maybe I should say it again.

He raised his arm and then he noticed that his arm wasn't there. He could see his tunic move but not his arm. Then he tried the other and then looked down at his legs.

"It worked Nog, look it worked."

"Yes I can see that, why are you so surprised?"

"I'm sorry Nog, I should never doubt you."

Nog moved out of Pico's line of vision and stopped to pick up a slender stick from the ground. He moved behind the boy and gave him a sharp stab in the backside with piece of wood. The boy howled in pain.

"What did you do that for Nog? That hurt."

"Are you angry Pico?"

"Don't you think I've a right to be?"

"Look at your hands boy. What do you see?"

Pico looked down and was surprised to see all of his right hand and most of his left floating in the air as if detached from his body

"Now, do you understand what I've been telling you? If that sort of thing happens when you're stealing Oratio's tongue it could be very embarrassing, it may not be your hands exposed. Not only that, but it could be the end of you."

"Yes, I see what you mean. Now how can I make my hands disappear again?"

"Get rid of the anger, think nice things. Think of how good I am to you."

Pico struggled and he had little luck until he concentrated on his mother and his warm and tender feelings for her. Then just as quickly his hands disappeared.

"I understand now Nog, let me come back."

"Just say the word."

Pico could feel the panic arise within him. He'd forgotten it.

"Nog, I forgot."

"You forgot? I'm a Daimon for a dunce. How could you forget?"

"I just got excited, I'm sorry. Please Nog."

"Caxtazaro."

Nog's clothes stood empty again. Then Pico said.

"Caxtazaro."

"Caxtazaro." Said Nog. His clothes were filled once more as were Pico's.

"Pico, I may have made a grave mistake in teaching you this."

"I'm sorry Nog but after that, I'll never forget Caxtazaro again."

And his clothes stood empty again.

Chapter Fifty-seven

Caecus stood on the porch of his house bathed in the light from within the building. He looked out upon the five boys gathered before him. Each knew that Caecus could not see any of them.

The anticipation of the impending mission added to the excitement of each of them. Finally the old man spoke.

"I don't have to tell you how important this assignment is, the return of your parents is paramount.

"But this much more at stake here. The future of the Republic could rest on your young shoulders."

As he paused in his speech, Fortis trotted up casually beside him and nuzzled the old man's hand.

"I know each of you are brave in your own ways, as is my friend Fortis here. But I am unable to foretell the outcome of your adventure because of all the turmoil and agony that exists within the City.

"So we can only hope and pray that all goes as planned and that each of you return safely. Take no unnecessary risks, watch out for each other and be brave of heart.

"Fortis will go with you, he is keen of eye and as brave as a lion, he will help keep you safe."

The old man's body seemed to sag as he finished speaking. Fortis left Caecus and ran to the group taking up a position in the lead next to Pando.

As they made their way out of the farmyard they could hear Caecus say.

"May Jupiter watch over you and bring you all back to me safely."

* * * * *

They were fortunate to have a clear night with a near full moon as the small band marched on towards Perusia.

Fortis trotted on some twenty paces ahead, while Pando and Viaticus marched side by side, neither of them speaking. Pando was surprised by just how quiet everyone was none of the usual pushing and joking one might expect of a group of young boys.

Then, just ahead, twinkling lights were visible. They could see Perusia rising up at the top of a steep hill. Pando held up his hand as a signal to stop.

"Let's stop. Once we start climbing the hill we won't be able to rest.

"Gather 'round me so I can tell you what the plan is to get inside the city wall."

Viaticus had reconciled himself to the fact that Pando was best suited for this part of the task and listened intently as he touched his new ring on his finger. Pando continued.

"Caecus has told us where Octavian's forces are positioned outside the wall on the south side. There are three operational gates in that portion of the wall whereas only two on the north side. And these two have been all but filled in for centuries, so there is no possibility that the Legion inside has been able to restore them.

"Octavian's men will be placed some distance back from the wall so that they can't be attacked from the barbicans.

"That should mean that the Legion inside will be massed at the gates to the south leaving the north wall with little or no protection.

"The north wall is where I remember an opening covered by bushes where we played. If my memory is correct it should be large enough for all of us to get through. Even you Viaticus."

Viaticus smiled and said nothing.

None of them had seen Fortis come back, he sit listening intently to what Pando had to say. None of them, including Fortis, noticed the furtive figure following some distance behind. Whoever it was had the benefit of a downwind breeze.

Pando stood up and said.

"Let's move on, we've a steep climb ahead."

* * * * *

As they got closer they could see the campfires of the Legionnaires, just about where Pando had predicted. They were stationed between the three large gates in the ancient Etruscan walls that rose up bathed in the stark moonlight.

Torches were evident at the top of barbicans; at least those that were close enough for them to see.

Voices of Octavian's men could be heard carried by the slight breeze. They were impossible to make out because of the distance. But it was a reminder of just how delicate this endeavour was. After all, their mission was secret; they could be considered any enemy by either side.

* * * * *

The figure that followed had closed the gap between them as they approached the north side of the wall. But no one was aware.

Pando spoke to Viaticus.

"I don't see a light in any of the barbicans so far. I think what Caecus has told us is right. There is little or no fortification on this side.

"We need to move in closer to the wall so I can find the opening."

Viaticus waved to the others to move closer to the base of the wall.

As they did so, Ludus stepped on a loose boulder that rolled away from him twisting his ankle painfully in the process. He cried out.

"Ludus shut up. You could wake the Underworld with that shriek," said his brother.

Ludus was writhing in pain upon the uneven ground.

"Do something, do something. It hurts."

The other four crowded around him, no one sure of what to do when someone pushed through.

"Get out of the way, let me have a look."

"Lucia. What are you doing here?" Asked Pando.

"I said get out of the way. Do you want to get on with this mission or not?"

All backed out of the way.

She examined Ludus's foot. He winced painfully each time she touched it.

"Just a sprain," she said.

She opened her satchel and removed a jar of ointment, then taking off his sandal she smeared the ankle with the medication.

"Stay still for a few minutes until the salve penetrates the skin."

She wiped her hands on a rag from her satchel and said to Pando.

"What are you looking at? You didn't really think you were going to get away with leaving me behind did you?"

"But Caecus said you weren't to come."

"How would I know that? I never asked him for permission."

"Then who gave you permission?"

"No one, I didn't believe I needed any permission."

"You know you could be in great danger," said Viaticus.

"Why? Because I'm a girl?"

Just then Fortis returned to the group to see what the delay was.

"What's that stupid dog doing here?" She asked.

Pico spoke up.

"He's not stupid. Caecus sent him with us. What have you got against Fortis anyway?"

"Did you forget? That filthy beast pissed on my leg."

"Do you ever think that your problem with Fortis is of your own making?" Asked Viaticus

"It wasn't me that relieved myself on his leg." She said indignantly.

"Enough arguing, quiet down. Have you all forgotten why we are here?" Asked Pando.

Finally, Ludus spoke.

"My ankle, it's all right now. It doesn't hurt anymore."

"You see, it is worthwhile having me along."

Changing the subject Pando said.

"Come on, let's move. I have to find that opening in the wall. Follow me single file and watch that you don't trip over anything."

They crept slowly along with Pando searching behind every bush as they went. It seemed to take forever but finally Pando whispered, somewhat loudly.

"This is it. It's still here."

All of them crowded around him as he pulled back the branches to expose the blackness of the opening.

Viaticus was the first to speak.

"I'll never get through there. The bushes are so overgrown there's hardly enough room for Lucia to get through."

Pando thought.

He's right, I don't remember the bushes being this big. Perhaps if we try pulling at some of the branches we can make enough space.

"Come Viaticus, help me to pull up some of these shrubs."

"That won't work. Just look at how thick those branches are. You need a sword or better yet an axe to cut through them."

"We have neither," Pando responded.

"What? How could you have come so unprepared?" Lucia was livid.

"It wasn't like this when I was last here," Pando was despondent.

"Whoever it was that said you should lead this mission Pando was sadly mistaken about your competence," Lucia said icily.

She didn't notice Fortis quietly approach her from behind. When he got close enough and was about to lift his hind leg, Pando shouted.

"No Fortis. Come here."

The dog lowered his leg and obediently trotted over to Pando's side.

"He was going to do it again, wasn't he?" She said.

"Forget about it, he didn't do anything. Let's just get on with trying to solve this problem."

Lucia reached into her satchel and pulled out a small axe, a hatchet really. It shone in the moonlight, the edge glistened, it was obviously very sharp.

"Here, use this. At least one of us came prepared for the unexpected. Give it back to me when you're finished. If that dog bothers me again, he'll be hopping around on three legs."

Pando hacked away at the brush, the axe worked well and in a short time he had cleared enough space that he could squeeze through.

Probably still not big enough for Viaticus. If I can just get this big one out of the way then I'm sure everyone can get through.

There that should do it.

I suppose I can count on being harassed by Lucia about not being prepared for evermore.

He backed out of the opening and said.

"That should be big enough for us all to get through. Once on the other side of the wall we will need to reorganize the mission considering we have one more person now."

Lucia was the only one to comment.

"Give me back my axe."

Fortis scurried through the opening and disappeared.

Chapter Fifty-eight

Once everyone was through the opening Pando said.

"Since we have an extra member of our team, we'll have to reorganize ourselves slightly.

"Tactus, you and Viaticus head to the south side of the city and see what you can find out about the status of the cavalry.

"Pico, you and Lucia go to the city center and find out what you can about the food situation and get a sense of the mood of the citizens.

"Ludus, you'll come with me."

"Why are you putting me with Pico?" Questioned Lucia.

I might have guessed she would have an objection about going with Pico. I don't have time to play games with her, might as well put an end to it now.

Pando spoke sharply to the girl.

"You have three choices Lucia. Do as I ask, go into the city alone or go back to the farm. I really don't care which choice you make.

"Just bear in mind, Pico knows the city better than you can ever hope to so going in alone doesn't make much sense.

"Maybe you'd be happier going back to the farm, frankly, that would make the rest of us happy too."

Lucia was astonished at Pando's forcefulness. Then she stuck out her chin and said.

"I'm going, come on Pico."

She turned and pulled Pico by the hand.

"Lucia, let me go, stop treating me like a child." Pico pulled his hand away and ran ahead of her. Lucia glared at Pando over her shoulder as she turned to follow the boy.

Pando ran after them and stopped them saying.

"Look, remember why we're here. Stopping acting like spoiled children.

"Do you both understand your task?"

Pico said.

"Don't worry Pando, I know exactly what to do."

Lucia said nothing, her head down glowering at the ground.

"Lucia, did you hear me?"

"Yes." She said grudgingly.

"Good. Then go and good luck. Make sure you're both back here at dawn."

Pico waved at his brother as he and Lucia disappeared into the darkness.

I worry about Pico. He's so young and being fearless is not always such a good thing. Lucia is resourceful and smart if she just wasn't always so cranky.

Anyway, I think they'll make a good team, Lucia will make sure that Pico doesn't take any unnecessary chances.

He returned to the others and asked.

"Have any of you seen Fortis since we got through the wall?"

"It's so dark he could be sitting right beside us and we couldn't see him." Said Ludus.

"You're right." Pando tried a low whistle and sure enough Fortis came bounding up to them.

Pando grabbed the big dog's head and held it close to his face saying.

"Don't go straying away, do you hear? You're coming with Ludus and me, stay close."

With that, they went there separate ways each agreeing to be back before first light.

* * * * *

Pando and Ludus made their way towards the Town Square. It would be a good place to obtain information. To find out just what the state of affairs within the walls truly was.

Ludus turned to Pando and said.

"Looks like we might lose our moon. You can hardly see the stars for the clouds that are moving in."

"You're right, but we should find things a little better as get into center of town. The street torches will be lit and it's still early enough that there should be people about."

They continued on in silence, only the sound of Fortis's panting and the cicadas seemed to float on the cool night air.

They rounded a corner and saw light up ahead. A fire of some kind Pando thought.

Can that be a campfire? But why on a city street? That was never allowed vagrants would be arrested.

It was just then that Ludus stumbled over something and almost fell. Pando ran to him and asked.

"Are you all right Ludus? You didn't re-injure your ankle did you?"

"No, I'm fine. But what is it?"

They both leaned down for a better look.

"Ludus, it's a man. At least I think so. Help me turn him over, he must be hurt."

The two boys struggled to get the man turned onto his back. They gasped in horror. It was Ludus who spoke first.

"He's dead. Oh Holy Jupiter."

The man's body was swollen about the abdomen; the mouth lay open as if in agony, his eyes bulging from his face.

Pando felt as though he was going to be sick. He moved back from the body just as the smell hit him. Reeling backwards he grasped Ludus.

"This is terrible, what do you suppose happened to him?"

"I don't know." Answered Ludus.

Both moved away from the body, closer to the center of the road. They both agreed that the victim was beyond any help they could give him. Their only option was to continue with the mission.

They walked on contemplating what they had seen, and then Pando spoke.

"Could be starvation I suppose. Mind you I've never seen a man who starved to death before."

"Nor I. Said Ludus.

"When you consider that no food has been allowed in for weeks, it's definitely a possibility."

"I don't doubt that you're right Pando. If so then we are likely to see more bodies on the way."

As they approached the light from what appeared to be the campfire, both boys grew uneasy unsure of what awaited them.

Ludus spoke first.

"Do you think we should stop and talk to them?"

"It's what we're here for, but I don't like the idea anymore than you do."

But before they had a chance to make any choice at all, it was made for them. A rough voice behind them said.

"What is it you two are up to? Out to steal what little food we have to eat?"

Before they could answer or turn to see who it was, both boys received a sharp jab in the back. A spear thought Pando.

"Don't turn around, just keep going straight ahead towards the campfire, so we can get a better look at you."

They had no option other than to comply.

As they got closer, an old woman sitting by the fire looked up at them. Her greasy gray hair was plastered to her head like a skullcap; one eye seemed to have a yellowish film over it. Ludus thought.

This is the ugliest old woman I've ever seen. And she smells almost as bad as that corpse back there.

"What's this son? You bringing company for dinner?"

She cackled at her own humour.

"I found them sneaking up on our camp mother. Probably going to try to steal our food."

"They make poor thieves then don't they? Since we've nothing to take." She laughed again.

Pando spoke.

"We are not thieves, we were simply passing by when this man, your son I take it, stopped us."

The man with the spear came into the light of the fire. Pando was surprised to see it was someone about his own age, dressed in filthy rags. His face was gaunt, his mouth slack showing blackened teeth.

"Where are you from? Not hereabouts I'm sure." He said, poking Pando in the stomach with his spear.

"Doesn't look like you've missed many meals, or your partner either for that matter."

Ludus lurched back trying to avoid any contact with the spear.

Pando's mind was racing.

What do I say? I have to come up with some kind of story.

"Did you hear me? I said where are you from?"

Before Pando could invent a story, the old woman interrupted.

"Leave them alone, can't you see they are just boys like you?"

"Just like me? Do I look like them mother? My belly's touching my backbone and you say I look like them?"

"Mind your mouth boy."

Ludus noticed an iron pot on the fire, steam rising from within. He asked.

"I see you're cooking something ma'am. Could you tell me what it is?"

"Stone soup."

"Stone soup?"

"You deaf?" Asked the son.

For which he received a cuff on the ear from his mother.

She picked up a medium sized stone from the ground in front of the fire. It was bleached almost white. Carefully she lowered it into the simmering pot. Then she said.

"It would taste much better if we just had some salt."

Under his breath the son said.

"A piece of pork would help too."

"How long have you been without food?" Asked Pando.

Her good eye watered as she said.

"I can't remember when we last had a good meal. We once had a prosperous farm. But that's gone now, taken by the Legionnaires."

Her son spat upon the ground at the mention of the soldiers.

She continued.

"It was long before my two babies died, they got sick and we had no milk and one night they just died, both of them together.

"And then my husband died, that was him you came across up the road. He just wandered off and died.

"It's been weeks, maybe more since we've had enough to eat."

Sadness overcame both Pando and Ludus. Why had all of this happened? What can we do? Thought Pando and then he remembered.

He reached inside his tunic and removed a small package; it was Oratio's sweet cake.

The son eyed him suspiciously.

"What have you got there?"

"It isn't much but I'd like to share it with you and you're mother."

"What good is a little bit of cake like that going to do."

"Just wait and you'll see. Some say the cake is magic."

The old woman watched with her one good eye as Pando carefully broke the piece in half and handed a piece to her.

In turn she took the piece and broke it in half again giving half to her son. She was amazed that the remaining piece she held in her hand was the same size it was before she broke it.

"Eat it slowly because it's quite rich." Cautioned Pando.

The mother and son did as they were told.

"It's delicious." Said the old woman.

The son was dancing from one foot the other as he ate.

"I can't believe it, not only delicious but it's never ending. A Never Ending Cake.

The stone Soup was forgotten, the Never Ending Cake was thoroughly enjoyed and Pando and Ludus learned much of the state of the city over the next hours.

Chapter Fifty-nine

Pico was moving so quickly that Lucia was having trouble keeping up but she wasn't about to ask him to slow down.

It seemed to her that they were heading east, but she had no idea why Pico seemed so purposeful in his actions. However, she was sure he knew exactly where he was going.

At last she said.

"Pico, is it necessary to run to where we are going? Aren't we supposed to be collecting information about the state of the city as we travel?"

"We'll have time for all of that on our return."

"Return from where?"

At some point I'm going to have to tell her about where we're going and why. I just hope her feelings toward Oratio are strong enough that she will be in agreement. She's so hot-tempered she might just spoil the whole thing.

Perhaps I can explore her feelings a bit and get an idea if she will support what I'm doing.

He ignored her question and posed one of his own.

"Lucia, what do you think of Oratio?"

She was shocked at the question.

Why is he asking that? Does he know something? He's just a child he can't know anything. Unless he listened in on my conversations with Caecus.

"I don't understand what you're asking."

"Well, you wanted me to interpret for you. I can only assume that he means something to you."

"It's just that I have this feeling that we've met before. I just wanted to find out if he felt the same thing."

Pico looked at the girl.

"Well it certainly seemed like he did. He showed you that scroll didn't he?"

"I must admit that the poem was very familiar, but it still didn't really confirm anything to me," she said.

Pico stopped moving and Lucia almost bumped into him in the dark. Looking very serious he asked.

"You didn't answer my question. What do you think of Oratio?"

"He seems like a very nice man. A very talented one too from what I could gather from his poem. Why are you asking me all this?"

"Do you like him?"

"Pico, stop asking stupid questions."

"They aren't stupid. Just tell me."

"Of course I like him, he seems gentle and kind and it doesn't hurt that he's a marvelous cook."

Pico was just about ready to take a chance and tell her about his particular mission to Perusia. But not quite.

"Don't you feel sad for him and all the terrible things that have befallen him?"

"I would guess that worse things have happened to others."

"Then you don't feel sorry for him or have any interest in trying to help him?"

"How could I help him? Of course I feel sorry for him, but what good does that do?"

"So does that mean you would help him if you could?"

"You think me so mean Pico that I wouldn't?"

"Lucia, why can't you just answer me directly?"

"Of course I would help him if I could, but I see no way that I can."

Pico could feel the excitement course through his body.

"Suppose I told you that I know where his tongue is?"

"You what?"

"I know where his tongue is."

"How do you know that. Besides, what good is such knowledge?"

"Caecus can restore his voice if he has the tongue. When Oratio was attacked it was Caecus who saved him. He looked for the tongue then but the villains had taken it with them."

"How do you know all this Pico?"

"Oratio told me."

"And how did you find out about the location of Oratio's tongue?"

"Because I'm a very good detective."

Lucia was astonished to see Pico's head bob forward just as she heard a loud smack.

"What was that? She said.

"Nothing, nothing." Pico said, rubbing the back of his head.

"What do you mean, 'you're a good detective'?"

"No, that's not true, I lied. But if I told you how I really found out, you'd think that was a bigger lie. Let's just leave it that I did find out."

She shrugged and said.

"And now that you know this, just what do you propose to do?"

He took a deep breath and said.

"I'm going to steal it back and take it to Caecus so he can restore Oratio's ability to speak."

"But that's not why we're here. Did you get permission to engage in this venture?"

"From the same person who gave you permission to come along Lucia."

"In other words, no one gave you permission."

"No."

"If anything goes wrong, we're both going to be in great trouble."

"I'll take the blame Lucia, it's my idea after all."

"I'm not worried about blame. It's just that this could be very dangerous. If we get caught…"

"Not we Lucia. Me."

"Are you not afraid?"

"Haven't you heard, I'm fearless. Besides, I have a secret up my sleeve,"

"What's this secret?"

"Can't tell, otherwise it wouldn't be a secret."

They resumed their travels, at a somewhat slower pace. There was silence between them as Lucia contemplated what the boy had told her.

After what seemed like hours, Lucia broke the silence.

"Are we there yet?"

"We're getting close, very close. We must be extremely quiet from this point on. Whispers only."

Lucia was about to say something when Pico held up his hand to quiet her. He pointed up ahead; she could see a light.

"What is it? She whispered.

"It's the house, just up ahead."

"How do you know that, it's so dark?"

"I should know it, I was born and raised there."

"That's your house?"

"Yes."

"But who lives in it now?"

"Lucius Antonius."

"The Tribune?"

"Yes."

"You can't go in there Pico. They'll kill you as soon as they see you."

"I told you, I have a secret. Come."

They crept forward concealing themselves in the high bushes surrounding the house. Lucia whispered.

"It's a very large house Pico, your father must be very rich."

"I don't know, I've never really thought about it before. Not really rich, just like our neighbours really."

"From where I come from, this is rich, believe me."

"Follow me Lucia, the catch on the back door doesn't work well. It's my best way in."

They made their way as silently as they could to the back of the house just as the moon hid behind a cloud making it extremely difficult for them to see.

Lucia could feel her heart thumping in her chest.

This isn't such a good idea. But I can't let Pico see that I'm afraid. Pando was right, he is fearless.

Pico could see a man and a woman standing in front of a window talking. They were too far away to hear what was being said.

"Someone's coming." Whispered Lucia.

They ducked their heads down so that they could just see over the hedge. Pico whispered.

"A sentry. We must wait and see if there are any others."

Just as he said that, a second sentry appeared around the other corner of the house. They met and exchanged a few words that Pico and Lucia could not hear. Then turned and retraced there steps again.

Pico watched as this action was repeated twice more. Giving him an idea of how much time he had when neither soldier was at the back of the house.

"Pico, I think this is far too dangerous. There's no way you can get in there without being seen," she whispered.

"Not to worry, they aren't going to see me."

"What do you mean?"

"That secret I told you about. I've learned to make myself invisible."

"What?"

"Yes, but before I can do it you have to turn around."

"Why do I have to turn around?"

"Well you see, I can't turn my clothes invisible."

"So you mean you have to be naked?" She smiled.

"It's not funny, it's the only way. Please turn around."

She did as she was asked and heard the rustle of clothing dropping to the ground. Then she heard.

"Caxtazaro! OK, you can turn around now." He whispered.

When she did, all she saw was Pico's tunic and sandals neatly piled on the ground.

She was amazed and said.

"Are you still here?"

"Yes."

She reached out to try to touch him. He immediately responded.

"No, don't do that."

Instead he reached out and grasped her hand.

"That's remarkable. How did you learn that?"

"That story is for another time. Watch for the sentries."

They waited until both soldiers disappeared around the corner of the house. Then Pico said.

"Lucia, there's just one thing."

"What is it?"

"Whatever you do, please don't make me angry."

She looked puzzled at the request. He said again.

"Please Lucia, don't."

Chapter Sixty

"Follow me Viaticus, I know a way where we don't have to go through the town center.

"I want to get to the south side where the cavalry should be located. I think it's important that we do that as quickly as we can."

"And why is that?"

"Well, I've been told that if the Legionnaires do launch an attack, it will be the cavalry that will move out first.

"Therefore if we know the readiness of the cavalry we might have some idea of when the attack may come."

"Who told you all this Tactus?"

"You don't know him, but trust me, he has a great deal of experience in such things."

Viaticus didn't pursue it any further instead he trudged along with Tactus. He was surprised that there were so few people out on the streets. It was still fairly early and the weather had not yet turned cold. He asked Tactus if he knew why this might be.

"I don't really know Viaticus. When I've been down here with father at the same time of night, it's usually bustling with activity.

"It's as though everybody is waiting for something to happen."

"I don't mean to offend you cousin, but I must say that your city stinks. I thought Rome was bad enough but, ugh, this is terrible."

"You're right, it smells like something is rotting somewhere close by. Be careful not to step in anything."

The turned down a street that was bordered on either side with stone walls rising up above them connected with soaring archways. Pitch torches at intervals down the street cast weird shadows that seemed to dance menacingly above them. Tactus could not resist a backward glance, but saw nothing.

"I'm not sure I like your short cut Tactus."

Tactus didn't answer but picked up the pace substantially.

It's eerie with no people on the streets and I see only a few lights in the windows above.

What's that over there in that alcove? Is it a man or just garbage thrown out to rot? Well I'm not going over to look.

But he couldn't take his eyes off the spot. He looked over his shoulder for one last look after they passed shadowy doorway. The object never moved, at least he was sure it hadn't

"Tactus, slow down, there's no need to run is there?"

The boy responded.

"We still have a way to go and don't forget we have to work our way back too. There's no time to waste."

They continued on in silence. Viaticus had no problem staying even with Tactus, his great long legs could've left Tactus far behind had he wanted to.

"Do you hear that Viaticus?"

"Yes, sounds like people. We'd better approach with care we don't know how we'll be received."

They rounded a corner and then they could see, but what was it? It looked familiar.

"What do you think they're doing Viaticus?"

"From here it looks very much like the pyre we built for Corripio, however, it's many times larger. If it is a funeral pyre it must be for somebody very important."

"Yes, I think you're right. There are certainly a lot of people involved. I wonder where they got all that wood?"

Viaticus thought for a moment and then said.

"It looks like furniture, broken pieces, for the most part, some tree branches as well. There is quite lot more to put on the pyre from the looks of that pile on the right.

"If we are cautious this may be an opportunity for us to join in unnoticed and help. That way we may be able to get answers to some of our questions."

"That's a good idea Viaticus, let's do it."

Carefully they made their way to the fringe of the crowd. They seemed to be working with some urgency to complete the pyre. Both boys simply fell into line and began carrying wood from the pile and placing it on the pyre in much the same way as they had for Corripio.

They listened carefully to the conversations taking place. The two men working alongside Viaticus spoke about the dead man.

"He was a good man and now dead before his time."

The older man responded.

"What choice did he have? But I agree with you, he was a good councilor, always looking after the people. You don't find many like him."

Viaticus was puzzled.

What do they mean, he had no other choice? I wonder how he died, something to do with the siege maybe? He seems to have been well thought of.

"With the mess we have here now, what need to do we have of councilors anyway. Octavian is to blame for all of this."

Tactus wanted to speak up in support of Octavian, but knew he could not.

The boys just simply continued carrying firewood and listening.

"Yes that's right, it's all Octavian's doing. And he the son of Caesar, the one who proclaimed that we should be given land as a reward for past service to the Empire."

"Octavian has strangled this city. No food for 6 weeks, even the stray dogs have been eaten."

Tactus was shocked.

They've eaten dogs? What kind of people are these. They're worse than savages.

The older man stumbled and fell; the other stopped and helped him to his feet.

"Are you all right?"

"Yes, yes. If I had any sense I should end my own life as Councilor Fabius did, then you could just throw me on the fire with him and put an end this sorry life."

"Never mind old man, things will get better."

"Don't talk nonsense, how can they get better?"

"As we speak, the cavalry is getting ready to attack. Once they burst out of here, you and I can melt away and never even be noticed.

"My brother is a member of the cavalry, he says they can break through and rout Octavian's forces."

"A pipe dream my boy, a pipe dream."

Tactus signaled to Viaticus.

"We must leave now so we can see if what he says is true."

The two boys slipped away as quietly as they had come, fortunately, they left unnoticed.

They kept close to the stone walls, deep in the shadows so that no one saw them. Finally, out of sight of the crowd, Viaticus spoke.

"How much farther Tactus?"

"I would guess perhaps 6 more blocks and we should be there."

"And what do you propose to do when we arrive?"

"Well, I'd just like to make sure that what we've heard is true."

"If it is, then what?"

Tactus stopped and looked into his cousin's face.

Should I tell him what Fortitudo told me? Will he believe me? No one, except Kashta, believes I can communicate with animals. Why should he? I don't see any option, I need his help, I must confide in him.

"What is it Tactus."

"I'm going to tell you something I'm not sure you're going to believe."

"Tactus, with everything that has happened to us so far, I'm just about prepared to believe anything. Tell me."

"I've learned how to communicate with animals."

"You mean you can talk to them?" He asked incredulously.

"Not really talk, not with words and everything. More like we each can understand whatever it is we want to say without actually saying the words."

Tactus waited expecting disbelief from Viaticus. When he didn't say anything, Tactus asked.

"Do you believe me?"

"Like I said Tactus, since Ludus and I left Rome, we've experienced so many strange things, I have no reason to doubt you. But what is it that you propose to do once we get close to the cavalry?"

"Well. Fortitudo, Kashta's horse, suggested a plan that may help prevent a battle from developing and it could save many lives."

"A horse told you this?"

"Not just a horse. Fortitudo once belonged to a Centurion in the cavalry, he has fought in many battles and knows the strategies used."

"And just what is his plan?"

Well, there's no turning back now. I may as well tell Viaticus the whole thing.

"Fortitudo says that there is likely to be at least 4 cavalry Centuries. A Century is approximately 80 to 90 strong."

"I thought a Century was a hundred men."

"So did I, but Fortitudo says it's just a name, the numbers vary."

"Doesn't make any sense, but go ahead."

"Each Century is led by a Centurion and all of the horses in the Century take their lead from the Centurion's horse.

"So his suggestion is for me to communicate with each Centurion's horse and convince them of the fact that Octavian is trying to prevent the outbreak of a civil war that could destroy the Empire."

"And you say a horse told you all this?"

"You said you'd believe me."

"Sorry Tactus, please go ahead."

"Fortitudo told me that in most cases the horses have more brains than the Centurions on their backs. So if those four horses decide that they don't want to be a part of a civil war, the other horses will refuse as well."

"Then what happens?"

"Well as you've heard, it appears that the plan is to have a cavalry charge through two of the gates on the south side wall to start the battle. If I can convince the four horses and they in turn lead the others to follow them, then they will effectively block the gates.

"If they don't go through the infantry can't follow and the whole thing will be a failure."

"But what happens then Tactus?"

"According to Fortitudo, the Legionnaires will consider the refusal of the horses to advance to be a bad omen and will give them an excuse not to engage in battle.

"He says that all of these soldiers are very superstitious."

"Tactus, who am I to say this won't work. But tell me, how do you know which horse is which?"

"Oh that's easy, the Centurions horses are all decorated with breastplates and medallions, they'd be hard to miss.

Viaticus shook his head in wonderment.

"Come Tactus, let's get to the south wall."

Chapter Sixty-one

"Pando what made you think to bring some of Oratio's cake?"

"Honestly, I just thought we might get hungry while we're in Perusia. I knew there was no likelihood that we'd find any food here."

"I can't believe things are so bad. People dying for lack of food, even little children," said Ludus

"This is a war, just as if there was open fighting. You and I don't know much of war, mostly the big parades and celebrations afterwards."

"Well, I can't see how there'll be any celebration when this is all over."

"You're right Ludus. We'd better get moving over to the south wall to see what we can find out about the infantry."

"What is it that we're supposed to do once we're there?"

"Just see how ready they are. How many men they'll be able to muster. Don't forget, the Legionnaires have been suffering too."

They continued on in silence contemplating all that they had been told by the woman and her son. Both of them, although they did not speak of it, were determined to do what they could to help end the siege and return the community to a more normal state.

After some time Ludus spoke.

"Pando, I was just thinking about Oratio's cake."

"What about it?"

"It's very remarkable. From that one piece of cake that you gave the woman, it's possible, because of its nature, you could end up feeding the whole city and avoid starvation of many people."

"I hadn't really thought about it in those terms Ludus. But I suppose it's conceivable, except for one thing."

"What's that."

"It would depend on all people sharing and that's not a trait that everyone has."

"But just think about it Pando, an end to hunger."

"Don't you think people might get a little tired of the same thing at every meal."

"As compared to having nothing, I don't think so."

"Ludus that's a very noble idea but, once hunger ceases to be a problem the public will begin demanding variety. It's just human nature."

"Maybe Oratio could invent other foods that have the same kind of magic."

"I don't think Caecus would agree with you."

"Why not?"

"He says magic is only to be used in extraordinary circumstances not as a spectacle for everyday consumption.

"Mankind is more than capable of growing enough food to feed themselves as well as the less fortunate. There is really no need for magic under these circumstances."

Ludus could see the logic in what his cousin had said; still he took comfort in what help they'd been able to give the woman and her son.

* * * * *

Viaticus and Tactus arrived at the south wall and managed to climb up on the roof of a fairly tall building, but not without the scraping of knees and elbows in the process.

They crept to the edge and looked down on the scene below. It was as Fortitudo had said it was a classical organization of the Cavalry for an attack.

Two columns of horses were being organized behind the two outside gates in the wall. The infantry was beginning to assemble behind the middle gate.

The idea was to have the cavalry make a simultaneous charge through the gates on both flanks of Octavian's men. Once the flanks were contained and any means of retreat was cut off; then the infantry would be unleashed through the middle gate.

Tactus watched the scene unfold and realized he had little time to try to implement Fortitudo's plan. He must get down there immediately.

"Viaticus, I must get down there now."

"I'll come with you."

"No, you'll attract too much attention. Look, see those boys down there? They're about my age and they're feeding the horses. If I can slip in there with them it will be an ideal opportunity to communicate with the lead horses.

"If you're with me, I would hardly think the two of us would be unnoticed."

"Then what am I to do Tactus? Just sit and watch?"

"You will be my means of escape should I get found out."

"And just how will I do that?"

"If I get in trouble, I'll signal you, then you create some kind of diversion with lots of noise, that'll let me get away.

"We can meet in the Town Square. You remember, the funeral pyre, there were lots of people there. We'll just mingle with them and make our way back to the meeting place."

Viaticus was not happy with the arrangement but he could see preparations proceeding down below. There is little time he thought.

'All right, but take care little cousin."

Tactus smiled and with a wave he was off.

* * * * *

Even though the evening air wasn't all that cool, Pico shivered in his nakedness.

One more pass by the sentries then I think I can get inside. I'll have to be careful, the back door sometimes squeaks when it's opened.

What are those two doing in there? That's my father's study that's where I have to be. I'm so nervous.

But why? They won't be able to see me. I just have to be very quiet. And quick, just get the box and leave.

Wait, I can't do that if they're in there. What would they think to see a box float across the room? What can I do?

--Pico it's me.

--Is that you Nog?

--Yes now listen and don't interrupt. Once you're inside, the room I mean. I will find a way to get both of them out of there. When they leave, get the box, don't wait to look inside, just get out of there, then you and Lucia get back to the meeting point.

--Yes Nog.
Just then he heard a hoarse whisper.
"Pico are you still here?"
"Yes Lucia, what do you want?"
"What are you waiting for?"
"The box is in the room where those two people are. It would look pretty strange to them if desk drawers started to open and close by themselves don't you think?"
"Then what are you going to do?"
"Wait."

Pico was just as anxious as Lucia, but knew he had to wait for whatever is was that Nog was going to do, happened.

I can see the two of them, but I can't hear what they're saying. My guess is that they might be arguing she's shaking her finger in his face.

Wait, something has happened, What is it? I couldn't see anything take place.

They're both standing now, each covering the lower half of the faces with their hands. They're running from the room. Now is my chance.

Pico ran to the door and slipped inside before one of the sentries returned. The door to the room he wanted was closed. He wondered why.

He opened it just enough to enter, then he understood why it had been closed.

The stench was awful, it was making his eyes water. He thought he might become sick. He began breathing through his mouth and that helped.

He made his way to his father's table. It didn't look as he remembered it. Everything that might have reminded him of his father had been removed.

A great sadness came over his heart; he was near to tears as he thought of the fun he had had in this very room. Then he remembered his true mission and caught hold of his emotions.

He opened the first drawer and found nothing.

Could it have been moved to another place? Is this all for nothing? Nog has never given me any bad advice it must be here.

He opened a second drawer and still saw nothing.

But wait, what's under that papyrus scroll? Yes there it is, just as Nog said it would be.

Pico picked up the box and put it under his arm. He was tempted to look inside but remembered Nog's warning.

It was then that he heard it, footsteps in the hall.

He was caught; no time to get out the window and someone is at the door now.

I know I can't be seen, but the box floating in the air is a dead giveaway that something isn't right.

Just as the door was beginning to open, he made his decision.

I'll hide behind the draperies to the left of the window. All I can do is hope whoever is coming won't stay long.

From where Pico was standing he could lean from behind the drape to see who was coming in.

It was the sentry and behind him, both covering their faces with damp clothes were the two people he had watched from outside.

The woman spoke.

"The smell is terrible, just as if some creature has crawled in here and died. Mind you I shouldn't be surprised at that, given the slovenly way this house was kept by the previous tenants."

Pico could feel his anger rise at the woman's comments and how they reflected on his mother. His mother was a wonderful homemaker; this woman was a liar.

Then Pico suddenly realized the danger he had put himself in because of his anger. He looked down and could see his feet slowly reappearing. He shuffled backwards as much as he could, trying to conceal his toes behind the drape.

I've got to think nice things. No anger, just nice things, my beautiful mother, I must concentrate on her and how she makes me feel.

It's working; my feet are disappearing again.

The woman spoke again.

"Here, I'll open this window and help air this place out.

"You, Legionnaire, check every corner of this room, if something has died, I want it removed immediately."

Pico pressed himself as far away from the window as he could. He saw an arm come through the opening in the draperies. Fortunately she didn't attempt to open the drape fully. Then she unlocked the double window and pushed them outward.

What a stroke of luck, I've only got to wait for the right moment and I can escape through the window.

It was then that it happened, Pico inhaled some dust loosened when the drapes were moved. He had the irresistible urge to sneeze. It was torture trying to hold it back, but the woman stood right in front of him.

He squeezed his nostrils shut with his free hand. It wasn't working; the urge to sneeze grew greater. Finally he could hold it no longer; he sneezed.

But he had stifled it to a point where he was sure no one heard, however it was at the expense of his eardrums. They popped so loudly that he wasn't sure he wouldn't be deaf forever.

He held his breath; nobody seemed to have heard.

Then he saw Nog at the window.

--Pico, slip me the box, but be careful. That way you can just walk out of the room anytime you want. Nog whispered.

--Nog was that you that created that terrible smell?

--Yes.

--What was it?"

--I don't know, perhaps something I ate?"

Pico slipped the box into Nog's hands while the others were preoccupied in another part of the room.

Heaving a sigh of relief, Pico stepped out from behind the curtain and sauntered across the room. He enjoyed seeing the consternation on the faces of the people looking for the source of the odour

He did a little dance as he passed each of them taking great care not to touch them, then walked out through the open door.

Chapter Sixty-two

Tactus made his way through the crowd of people that had congregated along the south wall. So many people that he was hardly even noticed.

He moved closer to the cavalry Centuries and saw that feed was being off-loaded from wagons.

This may be a chance for me. If I volunteer to help feed the horses then I'd be able to tell the horses of Fortitudo's plan.

I'm surprised that there is any feed for the animals, rationing must be severe. At least they haven't been reduced to killing of the horses for food.

That man over there, he seems to be in charge. I'll ask him.

"Excuse me sir, but do you need any help in feeding the horses?"

The man looked at him as if he were a strange beast that had just dropped out of the sky. Then he said.

"And why would you, obviously a local boy, want to help us?"

"I love horses and when I grow up I want to be in the cavalry," he lied.

"Do you now? Then by all means you may help.

"Here take this bucket and get some feed out one of the sacks over there. Not too much mind you. There's no more for the animals to eat than there is for us humans."

Tactus was elated.

He stood in line behind others that were helping to feed the horses. He could see the meager amount being put in each pail and even at that the grain was already sprouting.

Looks like just enough to make them sick. But if that's all there is I suppose it's better than nothing..

Tactus took the pail and headed towards where the animals were tethered. He was in luck; the Centurions' horses were all together, fastened to a line of rope at the front of the rest.

He wasn't in time to begin feeding the first horse. Someone else was already doing that. He took the second in line, a splendid roan stallion that was stamping his feet in anticipation of the meal.

When Tactus held it up to the animal's muzzle, the horse drew its head back at the offering.

--I know it's not very good, but it's all there is.

Startled, the animal instinctively moved away.

--What's your name?

--How is it that you know how to communicate with me.

--A good friend taught me how.

--I've never met anyone that could.

--Well as you can see, I can. What's your name?

--Ducis, my name is Ducis. This food is terrible, surely they don't expect me to fight with this garbage in my stomach?

--Fighting is what I've come to talk to you about.

--Who sent you?

--I have a friend named Fortitudo, he suggested I talk to you.

--Fortitudo, that 'old bag of bones'? How do you know him?"

--I met him on a farm where I'm staying at least I am for now. I'm surprised to find that you know him as well.

--We served in many campaigns together, until he was 'put out to pasture'. How's he doing?

--Well, very well.

--But what has he to do with your being here?

--As I said, he's a good friend on mine and both of us have great concern over what's happening in Perusia.

--As do I. none of us has any desire to fight against our own kind.

--Fortitudo suggested I come and tell you of his plan to avoid a battle.

--Sounds like him, always scheming. But I'm prepared to listen.

Tactus gave him Fortitudo's plan in great detail, all the time watching the big animal's eyes. For that was the best way for Tactus to gauge what his response might be.

When he had finished, he asked.

--Well, what do you think?

--We are sure to be beaten in the process, but that would be a small price to pay for avoiding a civil war.

--Good then I should talk to the others.

--No need for that, I'll look after them. It's easier for me and I won't need any long explanations of just who I am.

Tactus was elated. He'd achieved what he came for. He continued to feed other horses until he could find a way to slip away and rejoin Viaticus.

* * * * *

Lucia was getting impatient standing outside the window. She could see the three people inside moving about the room as if looking for something.

Do they know that Pico's in there somehow? What are they looking for?

Just then she saw the back door open slightly and close almost as quickly.

He made it. He's out.

She resisted the urge to call out. Instead she picked up Pico's tunic and held it out at arm's length.

The box settled to the ground and the tunic was taken from her grasp.

He must have put it over his head. It's really strange, I can see his outline but nothing of the rest of him.

Hoarsely she whispered.

"Pico, you did it."

Then another whisper.

"Caxtazaro!"

She looked at Pico's face in the moonlight. He was smiling broadly and his chest was thrust forward proudly.

"Yes Lucia, I did it, I did it."

"I'm very proud of you Pico."

He blushed for as nearly as he could remember that was the nicest thing she had ever said to him.

He picked up the box and held it carefully and asked her.

"Do you want to see it Lucia?"

"Ugh, no."

"But we have to. How do I know this is really the right box? Maybe I've gone to all this trouble and when I give it to Caecus there's nothing but useless junk inside."

"You look Pico, I don't want to see some blackened shrunken piece of someone's body. Ugh, it makes me shiver just to think about it."

The two of them had moved some distance away from the house as they talked. Pico held tightly to his hard won treasure and thought.

Do I really want to see this thing either? But I have to. I would be so embarrassed if I brought the wrong thing back.

Just at that instant, the clouds cleared from the nearly full moon. He had to open the box, he steeled himself for what he might see and then gingerly, opened it.

There it was lying in the bottom of the box.

Not blackened, not shriveled. It was as if it had just been removed from Oratio's mouth.

Pico watched, fascinated as the tongue moved.

"I think it's trying to tell me something."

"Don't be so gross Pico."

"No Lucia, look."

"I don't want to see."

She slammed the lid shut almost catching Pico's fingers.

"You got what you came for, now let's get back to the meeting place."

* * * * *

Pando and Ludus headed into the town, as they approached the Square they could see an assembly of people forming.

Something is going on, they needed to find out just what it was. They stayed back in the shadows with their backs to the rough stone walls of the old part of town.

The overhead archways obscured the moon; the pitch torches placed infrequently along the narrow streets cast the only light.

"What is it Pando? What's going on?"

"I can't see because of the crowd of people."

They crept closer, when they reached a point where the street opened onto the Square, they both saw it."

"A funeral pyre," said Pando.

"So many people and yet so little noise. Odd, don't you think Pando?"

"I would guess it's out of respect for the dead Ludus."

"I wonder who's funeral it is?"

"Let's get closer and maybe we can find out. From the size of the pyre it must have been someone very important."

They made there way to the edge of the crowd and then saw why there was little noise. Standing on a balcony overlooking the scene in the Town Square was a man in flowing robes A Priest, about to give an oration dedicated to the deceased.

A sonorous voice seemed to float on the night air.

"We have gathered here this night to help Jupiter's servant make his successful journey to the Underworld.

To help him to cross the river Styx and from there to journey to where the Gods direct him to go."

Pando sensed another presence, the Priest's voice seemed to fade into the distance, the crowd suddenly stilled.

It was like he was in another place entirely, but he wasn't there alone.

Then he heard it.

No not heard it, sensed it.

--Pando, you didn't think that I was gone forever did you?

--What do you want of me?

--You know what I want, I want the amulet.

--It isn't mine to give.

--It's so simple Pando, just bring it to me.

--Get out of my head

--And if I don't?

Music, that's it, I must think of music. Loud music.

Chapter Sixty-three

"So Tactus, tell me how things went?"

The boy's face was flushed with excitement; his eyes wide with the anticipation of what he hoped would come.

"Viaticus, it went better than I could have expected.

"As luck would have it, the first horse I took the feed to is an old friend of Fortitudo. Can you believe it? They even fought in battles alongside one another."

"So you actually talked to this horse?"

Tactus could sense the disbelief in Viaticus's voice.

"As I said, it's not really talking. Not out loud anyway. But were able to communicate and he's agreed to help with Fortitudo's plan."

"Does this horse have a name?"

"Ducis."

"That's a strange name. What does it mean?"

"It means 'Leader'."

"Well, if that's so, it would seem you found the right horse."

Tactus went on to tell him of his meeting with Ducis and how he would contact all the other horses.

"But how do you know they will all agree and go along with you?"

Tactus realized that there was no real way for him you be sure of that.

"I have faith in Ducis."

"But you've just met him."

"Let's just wait and see. We have a good view of everything from up here on the rooftop."

"So what you're saying is that a cavalry charge is really going to happen."

"Yes, and from the preparations I saw when I was down there, it'll be sooner rather than later."

* * * * *

"There was nothing really scary in the box Lucia."

"I just think it's really gross. Someone's tongue in a box?"

"But it's Oratio's tongue. Don't you want him to get it back? Just think he'd be able to talk to you just like the rest of us can."

"It's still gross."

"Well I'm happy we got it, and I'm sure that Caecus can restore it and Oratio will even be able to sing again."

"I don't really understand you Pico."

"What do you mean?"

"You hardly know Oratio and yet you took a tremendous chance in getting that 'thing' back. I could understand it if it belonged to one of your brothers or your cousin even, but why Oratio?"

"He's my friend and friends are important. But it seems you don't think so, is that why you don't have any?"

"What do you mean? I have lot's of friends."

"Really? I've never heard you talk about any of them. Why is that?"

He's right, I have no friends and now I have no family either. All I have are fragments of memories. I don't even know what they mean. What's wrong with me, why don't I have any friends?

"Did you hear me Lucia?"

"Yes I heard you."

"Don't you want to talk to me about your friends?"

"Why are you picking on me Pico?"

"I'm not picking on you. You just seem so unhappy all the time that I thought it might help if you talked about it."

"I'm not unhappy."

"Yes you are, just look at the way you 'bark' at everybody. Just like you're doing to me now."

Lucia decided to change the subject.

"Pico, you're telling me that you did all of this just because Oratio is your 'friend'?"

"Of course."

"What's he ever done for you?"

"That's not the point Lucia, you don't do things for friends and then expect something back as payment."

"So you did this just out of the goodness of your heart, is that it?"

"Why do you belittle an act of kindness? I've seen you do the same thing."

"No you haven't."

"What about Corripio?"

"What do you mean?"

"Pando told me about the funeral. You didn't have to do that. You could've just buried the body."

"No I couldn't, then his spirit may not have been able to cross the River Styx."

"Why would you care about that? What's that got to do with you?"

"I had to help his spirit on its way."

"And that's not an act of kindness? By the way what did you get in return? I mean aside from the feeling of comfort in having done something good."

"Oh shut up Pico, just shut up."

But he ignored her and continued.

"You've done other good things too. Like healing Ludus's ankle tonight. You didn't have to do that."

"Yes I did, otherwise we'd' still be trying to get inside the walls."

Why can't he just leave me alone? Some of the things he says are true but it doesn't change anything. So called friends can turn on you, disappoint you. I'm better off without them.

"Lucia, I want to ask you something."

"What?"

"I would like to be your friend, will you let me?"

* * * * *

--Pando, I'm creeping into your brain. Once I'm there you'll be unable to think about music or anything else you might think will drive me away.

--No, no, I won't let you.

"Pando, what is it? You look like you're in pain."

"It's nothing Ludus, just a headache."

--You think you have a headache now, just wait.

Something touched Pando's hand, something wet. He looked down.

"Fortis, I'm so glad to see you. Where've you been?"

"Probably in hiding Pando. With food in such short supply somebody might have decided to make a meal of him," said Ludus.

--Do you think that mangy black cur is going to save you Pando? Trust me, he won't. Just bring me the amulet.

--No, I've told you, it's not mine to give. If you want it then ask Jupiter to give it to you.

--Stupid boy, bring it to me.

--Why have you not made yourself visible to me? How am I to know that you are not just in my imagination?

"Pando, what's going on? You're just standing there staring into space. Are you all right?"

"I'm all right Ludus, just stand away from me, there is danger here."

"It's the Chimera isn't it?"

--You see Pando, your cousin isn't stupid. He knows I'm here without seeing me.

"Tell me Pando."

"Yes, he's here but he's afraid to show himself."

--ME AFRAID! He shouted, but still did not reveal himself.

There was a noise like a strong wind rushing by and then some unseen object struck Pando. It almost knocked him off the rooftop where he and Ludus were standing.

The boy was motionless.

"Pando, what happened? Pando talk to me."

But there was no response; Ludus could see the colour draining from Pando's face.

Is he dying? No, he can't be, not Pando, he feels cold, Oh Jupiter help me. What's that? I feel something.

--Hello Ludus, you and I haven't had much to do with one another up to now. But that's about to change. If you don't want to end up like your cousin, you must do as I say.

--What is it you want of me?

--Reach down and take the amulet off the neck of your cousin.

--No, I will not.

--Do as I say.
--No it's a trick.
--What do you mean, 'a trick'.
--You think I don't know that I'll be turned to stone if I touch it?

What was it that Pando told me would drive the Chimera away? Yes that's it, music, and very loud music. Pando said he thought of loud music.

--Stop that racket.

Instead Ludus thought of the massive parades he and Viaticus and his parents had attended in Rome. Triumphal Parades of the returning Legions from far off lands with cymbals and drums, yes lots of drums and trumpets and flutes and chimes all making a wondrous noise.

--I said stop it boy, you're going to live to regret this. I'll be back.

With that Ludus's head cleared and he tended to Pando. Fortis sniffed at Pando's head and then his chest. The dog uttered a low growl and backed away from Pando.

Ludus was astounded by what happened next.

What's going on here? Something seems to be wrong with Fortis. Is he ill? His back is twisting strangely, what's happening?

The beast seemed to grow in size right before Ludus's eyes, and then it rose up on its hind legs and stood upright. The shoulders spread, the tail disappeared.

It was becoming a man, suddenly Ludus realized.

"It's Kashta," he shouted.

* * * * *

"Look Viaticus, their horses are being assembled for the charge. I was right."

"Yes, it appears so Tactus."

They both watched as the Legionnaires mounted, all were fitted with shiny armour but none more so than the Centurions each was wearing the sculpted musculata befitting their rank. The horses pranced in eager anticipation but of what? A battle or a revolt?

Tactus and Viaticus waited impatiently for the commander to give the order.

Were they going to witness the end of the siege or the start of a bloody civil war?

Chapter Sixty-four

"Kashta, how did you do that?"
"That is of no importance now Ludus. Pando is gravely ill and we must do all we can to save his life."

"Did the Chimera do it? He was here you know."

"Yes, it was the Chimera. Why he chose not to make himself visible is anyone's guess. But as nearly as I can understand, a blow struck Pando from the Chimera's tail."

"The tail is coated with a poisonous substance and if I don't get him to Caecus immediately there will be no chance to administer the antidote. Pando will surely die."

"Then let's go Kashta."

"No Ludus, you don't understand. I need you to stay here and distract the Chimera."

"But it's gone."

"Not for long, once it's cleared it's head it'll be back trying to get the amulet."

"But what can I do by staying?"

"As I said, distract it, so it doesn't follow us."

But how can I do that, it's the amulet it's after and that's around Pando's neck?"

Kashta stood silent for a moment, the words of the priest floated up from below reminding them both of the funeral taking place in the Square.

"Ludus there is something you must do if we are to save your cousin."

"Tell me, I'll do anything you ask."

"You must remove the amulet from Pando's neck and place it on your own."

"But I can't do that. I'll be turned to stone."

"Ludus you must understand, that will only happen to those who are not pure of heart. From what I know of you, I think that you'll be safe."

Ludus thought.

Am I pure of heart? Can I really say that? Can anyone? What am I to do? I can't let Pando die. But then I don't want to die he either.

Without realizing it he touched the bracelet he wore on his arm. The one Caecus had given him.

What power is thing supposed to give me? Caecus never really told me. Does he believe I'm pure of heart? Would he have given me the bracelet otherwise?

None of that really matters. What matters is that I must save Pando. How could I live with myself otherwise?

"What's your decision Ludus?"

"I must do it. I can't let Pando die."

"Even at the expense of your own life?"

"I can only trust that my heart is pure."

"Good then, take it off Pando and put it on."

Nervously, Ludus bent over the still form of his cousin.

This is serious, his lips are turning blue and his breathing is so shallow I'm afraid we might lose him before Kashta can get him to the farm. I must do this.

Ludus placed his forefinger on the gem and held it there. And nothing happened. He didn't turn to stone.

Without realizing it, he had been holding his breath, now he released it in a burst.

He unhooked the clasp and removed the amulet, placing it around his own neck. Then Kashta spoke.

"You're a brave boy Ludus, I'm sure that Pando will be most grateful to you the next time you meet."

With that Kashta lifted the still form and gently put him over his shoulder. The big man seemed to hardly notice his burden as he turned to Ludus and said.

"I must go now. Take care in your dealings with the Chimera, it is a slippery crafty beast. Watch out for any traps he may set for you."

"But what should I do?"

"You have a good brain, use it."

And with that he moved into the darkness and was gone.

The ceremony for the funeral of Councilor Fabius continued. Ludus seemed to sense it might be coming to an end as he saw several of the mourners bringing torches to stations around the pyre

One of the torches was handed to the priest, obviously he would start the fire, but there was yet one more prayer to be recited.

--So Ludus, we're alone at last.

The boy was startled by the fact the Chimera was back; still the beast was not visible.

--What do you want from me?

--You are not that stupid.

--I'm not giving you the amulet, it's now been entrusted to me.

--So, you're prepared to die for that piece of jewelry?

Ludus touched his bracelet once again. It was hardly comforting for he felt nothing.

--Would you really kill me?

--Do you think yourself so important that I wouldn't?

--I just wonder, if you're prepared to kill me, why didn't you just kill Pando when you had the chance and take the amulet?

--You're just full of questions aren't you?

--I'm beginning to suspect I know why.

--Are you really so clever? I doubt it.

--I don't think you have any intention of killing me.

--Oh and why might that be?

--Because I don't think you really want me to give you that amulet at all.

--That's a rather stupid statement.

--Is it? I don't think so. I believe that if you touch it you'll be turned to stone. As anyone with an evil heart would be.

Anger now.

--You think you're so clever. Well then just think about this. If you do not follow my demands to the letter I will leave you here and go to your cousin and finish what I started. He will die because of your stubbornness.

-- So, Chimera, I'm right. You need me for more than just passing over the amulet. Tell me, what else is there.

--You must willingly follow me to the Goddess Ate and personally hand her the amulet.

--And turn her to stone?

--Stupid boy. She possesses great powers, greater even than those contained within Jupiter's Stone.

--Stupid am I? Seems to me that you need my cooperation in any event. You can't accomplish this without me.

--I can kill your cousin.

--True, but what then? Kill me? And then what?

--Has anyone told you are a frustrating child?

--I seem to remember my father saying that. But I might have a solution for you.

--You, a solution? Don't be silly.

--Then you don't want to listen?

--Oh why not? I can always scorch your backside later. What do you propose?

--Are you good at riddles?

--More stupidity. Of course I'm good at riddles. Why?

--Well, I will give you a riddle and if you can answer it correctly, I will carry the amulet to the Goddess Ate and present it to her. Should you fail, you will leave all my family and me and my friends in peace. You will never ever harass any of us again. Agreed?

--Agreed. Now let's get on with it, we have a long journey to the Goddess Ate.

-- What is greater than Jupiter?
What is more evil than the Goddess Ate?
What is more valuable than gold?
What is greater than the power of Magic?

* * * * *

"Tactus, look I think they are getting ready to open the gates."

"You're right. Oh. This is so exciting and we can see so well from up here."

The formation of the horses was taking place, the high strung animals were kicking up considerable dust with their hooves. The anticipation was creating a great deal of nervous energy for all.

In order not give any advance warning to those about to be attacked, silence was the order of the day. Slowly the large timbers securing the gates were carefully withdrawn.

Tactus was holding his breath.

Oh, I hope this all works. There go the gates, swinging wide. Now there's lot's of noise. Will they all do it?

And then it happened.

All 400 horses in the cavalry rotated on the spot and faced into the city. The gates were effectively blocked, no one could enter and none could leave.

The horses were beaten unmercifully with whips, the spurs drew blood from their flanks, but they resisted. The scream-like whinnying of the injured animals cut through Tactus like a knife.

"Tactus, you did it!" Shouted Viaticus.

The boy had no ears for what Viaticus was saying to him. All he could think about was the injury being done to the horses. Then he saw Ducis, magnificent in his breastplate suffering repeated beatings at the hands of the Centurion riding him.

It was then that Tactus saw the man withdraw his sword as if to inflict a wound in the animals side. The horse twisted sideways unseating the rider.

This is terrible, I must go and help Ducis, this is all my fault.

Before Viaticus could stop him, Tactus had slid down the ladder of the next rooftop and from there jumped to the ground. He disappeared into the crowd.

Chapter Sixty-five

There was great confusion when Tactus reached ground level. It was hard to see through all the dust kicked up by the horse's hooves and the noise was horrendous.

It was impossible for any movement through the gate to take place; they were jammed with animals all heading in the wrong direction. Confusion was everywhere, men shouted, horses whinnied and banners were being trampled underfoot. Chaos was everywhere.

I can't see Ducis. Where is he? I hope he hasn't been hurt. What would make the Centurion beat him so? Couldn't he see that hitting him wasn't doing any good?

Viaticus stood on the rooftop viewing the turmoil below. He'd lost sight of Tactus and feared the worst.

I must do something, but what? If they don't calm the animals people are going to get killed.

He touched the gold ring that Caecus had given him and thought.

What kind of magic is this thing supposed to bring? If ever there was a need for magic, now is the time, please give me a sign, something, anything.

Then calmness settled over Viaticus, it was as though a veil had been lifted; he knew instantly what to do. He made his way from the rooftop down to ground level and thought to himself.

No, this is no good, I need to be higher up, and no one can see me from down here. Maybe on top of that building over there.

He clambered up a ladder that had been conveniently left against the side of the building. He stood with legs spread apart and raised his hands high in the air.

Just then the clouds moved away and the moon shone brightly down upon the scene. A shaft of light lit Viaticus just as though he was on an illuminated stage.

And in a loud voice he shouted.

"STOP!"

Somehow his voice was heard above the din, faces turned toward this tall boy/man and they heard him say again.

"STOP!"

And the noise magically ceased, even the animals settled and stood calmly as if waiting for a message of great importance.

When all had focused their attention on Viaticus, he spoke. He did so with great presence and eloquence'

"Romans why is necessary for countrymen to fight against one another?

"Can you not see that even the animals know how wrong this is? Is it not a proper course for the affairs of the Republic that we all work together and not engaged in useless warfare?

"Misunderstandings have led us to this point but is war the only way to resolve these differences?"

Viaticus was so intent on what he was doing; he didn't notice Tactus climbing the ladder to join him. When he did, he smiled at his cousin thankful that he was safe and continued.

He spoke of the unfairness of the displacement of townspeople and yet acknowledged the debt owed to the Legionnaires.

It was as though the light that seemed to illuminate his body as he stood and spoke had bestowed the gift of rhetoric on him.

Finally be concluded by saying.

"Fellow Romans I say join together as one, meet with The Great Octavian and forge a better solution to all your grievances. Killing is not the answer."

A great roar broke the silence from the crowd and there was much embracing. The horses as if by magic cleared the entrance to the gate.

Outside stood a Century of Octavian's Cavalry, but they sat astride their horses with swords sheathed and spears pointed towards the ground. They had heard Viaticus's words and were moved. They had no intention of fighting.

A great cheer went up, the cavalry on both sides dismounted and each rider embraced his counterpart in a show of goodwill.

A lone figure on horseback appeared in the gateway and came forward as the crowd moved back clearing space for the young rider. A handsome young man of obvious importance given his lustrous musculata, shield and headdress.

A murmur was heard throughout the crowd, then a mighty roar.

"OCTAVIAN!"

He rode majestically to the center of the clearing and began speaking.

"As a member of The Triumvirate I come to echo the words of my young friend. And to pledge my word to find a peaceable means to settle the affairs of both sides.

"Romans must not fight Romans. We must join to make a greater Rome.

"I therefore declare this siege to be at an end."

Another ovation from the crowd, there was joy everywhere and in the excitement no one noticed Viaticus and Tactus climbing down the ladder and leaving the scene.

* * * * *

When they were well away from the celebrating crowd, Tactus asked.

"Where did you learn to talk like that? I was very impressed."

Viaticus simply shrugged and said.

"I just knew somebody had to do something and waiting for somebody else to do it didn't seem practical."

"But I've never known you to speak out like that. Did someone teach you that?"

Again he shrugged and held up his right hand.

"Maybe it was the power of this ring. Caecus gave it to me just before we left."

"Didn't he tell you what kind of magic it had?"

"No, as a matter of fact I'm not sure he said much about magic at all. But he must have, don't you think?"

"Seemed like it to me Viaticus."

"Strange isn't it, you can talk to animals and somehow I can talk to crowds."

"So you believe me now?"

"After this episode, how could I ever doubt you."

The smile of Tactus's face seemed to provide enough light for them to see there way through the dark.

* * * * *

Pico was falling behind Lucia as they made their way to the north wall.

"Come on Pico, hurry up or they'll leave without us."

"No they won't, I'll bet we'll be the first one's there and we'll have to wait."

He shifted the box to his other arm, it wasn't that it was so heavy but it was large enough that it caused his arm to ache. Particularly since he didn't want to carry it on edge. He was afraid that Oratio's tongue might roll around.

He wasn't sure that it really mattered but somehow it did seem disrespectful.

They walked along the path in silence and Pico thought.

I wonder what Oratio is going to say? I would think he'd be excited, I know I would be. It's really strange that Lucia doesn't seem to care at all and yet she seems to like Oratio a lot. I wonder why that is?

I can't believe Nog did that. I didn't know how I was going to get the box out of there. It's certain that I couldn't have done it myself.

I must make sure to thank him when we get back.

--You're quite welcome Pico.

--You're here with us Nog?

--Of course, I've told you a hundred times, I'm always with you.

--Perhaps not quite a hundred times Nog.

--Maybe not.

--I think you're a very smart Daemon.

--What is this, you want something else from me Pico?

--I was paying you a compliment.

--Hmmm, doesn't sound like you.

--Do you think Oratio is going to be pleased when he gets his tongue back.

--Well, considering I've never been without mine, I'm not sure how I'd feel if someone came up to me and asked "do you want your tongue back".

--You're being silly Nog.
--Careful boy.
--Why are you always so testy?
--If you had to be Daemon to someone like you, I daresay you'd be testy too.

Pico smiled to himself, comfortable in the certain knowledge that Nog was pulling his leg.

"Why are you so quiet Pico?"

"Just thinking."

"Want to tell me?"

"What?"

"What you were thinking?"

" I was just wondering why you don't seem excited at all about Oratio getting his tongue back?"

"I'm happy for him."

"That's all?"

"What do you mean?"

"It's just that you were so excited when he showed you the love poem. You remember, the scroll."

"Of course I remember."

"Weren't you excited then?"

"I suppose so."

"Why were you so excited?"

"There was something about the poem, I think I'd heard it before. But then how could I have, I wasn't even born when it was written?"

"Why does that matter?"

"Are you being stupid? Because I don't know why I remember and to me that's important."

"Since my brothers and I have left home, we've run into many strange things that can't be explained. Some I won't even tell you about because you wouldn't believe me.

"But, some of them involve magic, remember Sceleris? None of us questioned that. And the Chimera, ugh, he was ugly."

"I don't understand what you mean."

"You don't question magic, right?"

"Well no, everybody knows there's magic."

"Well then why can't you just accept these memories you have as being more magic. As I recall none of the memories you've told me about are bad, are they?"

"Well no, none seem bad."

"Why not just accept them as magic and be grateful?"

"You don't understand. These memories may involve my family somehow and I can't remember."

"Do you feel that you are without family Lucia?"

"Yes."

"You're not you know."

"What do you mean?"

"Family isn't just blood relatives. As far as I'm concerned, you're part of my family now and I'm part of yours.

"Since this whole thing has started just think how our family has grown."

Chapter Sixty-six

The Chimera was silent for a time and then said.
--That's a stupid riddle.
--Why, because you don't know the answer?
--Don't annoy me boy.
--Would you like me to repeat the riddle? Perhaps you didn't quite understand it.
--No, I don't want you to repeat it. I don't think I want to play this silly game.
--So you're just going to cheat now? Go back on your word, is that it?
--Just bring the amulet to me.
--Even if I wanted to, how would I do that? I can't see you. Why are you invisible this time?
--That's none of your business.
--You weren't shy about showing yourself the last time we met.
--That was different.
--How so?
--Never mind.
--I think I know.
--Know what?
--Why you're invisible this time.
--You couldn't know that.
--I think the Goddess Ate is punishing you for your failure last time.
--Just shut up.
--I knew it. I'm right, what's she going to do to you if you fail again?

The Chimera said nothing. Ludus looked down on the scene below. The priest was descending the stairs with a torch; a line of townspeople was forming behind him. Soon the pyre would be lit.

--Cat got your tongue Chimera?
--Release me from my promise. There's no answer to your riddle.
--Yes there is. And I have no intention of releasing you from your promise.

--I could just smite you as I did Pando, then who would save you?

--But I don't think you will. Surely then Ate would consider you a dismal failure again because you can't give her the amulet.

--Enough talk. I say you do not have an answer to the riddle. You're trying to trick me.

--And I say I do.

--Then tell me what it is. If you lie I'll kill you regardless of Ate.

--The answer you already know, are you sure you don't even want to try?

--Tell me boy.

--The answer is...

--Tell me you fool.

Ludus, obviously enjoying the Chimera's discomfort, paused and cleared his throat rather ceremoniously and said.

--The answer is 'Nothing'.

The Chimera spluttered in outrage.

--That's not an answer

--But it is the answer, just think about it.

> What is greater than Jupiter? Nothing!
> What is more evil than the Goddess Ate? Nothing!
> What is more valuable than gold? Nothing!
> What is greater than the power of Magic? Nothing!
> The answer is "Nothing'.

There was a cry of great anguish as the Chimera realized that all was lost. A cry so great that it stopped the funeral procession and everyone looked up towards the source of the sound.

And then it happened.

A bright flash that illuminated the Town Square as though it was midday followed by a sound greater than any thunder ever heard.

Fireballs rained from above striking many in the crowd below and igniting the pyre before the priest even reached it. The dry wood burst into flames, as did several of the rooftops of the surrounding building. Including the one Ludus was standing on.

The Chimera has exploded! Just like when Kashta threw the flaming coals in it's mouth. Only this time it's much bigger.

As a great wind came up and whipped the flames into a great fury Ludus made his way off the roof and got to the ground and into the pandemonium.

People were running in every direction, screaming, saying whatever prayers they could remember. Most seemed sure that the world was coming to an end and it certainly seemed like it.

Ludus saw the priest slapping wildly at his robes that had caught fire as a result of a fireball. He pushed the elderly man to the ground and rolled him in some standing water putting out the flames.

Ludus helped the old man stagger to his feet looking more like and old beggar than a priest in his tattered and mud spattered robe.

"Thank you my boy, may the God Jupiter bless you for your quick thinking. I know I do."

Ludus looked up to see the flames leaping skyward many feet above the rooftops as the gusting wind drove the fire to other buildings. There were live cinders and hot ash flying everywhere.

People were running without any thought of direction, people were being trampled underfoot. He thought.

I must do something, there's no order here and many people will die. What can I do? Wait, the wind is coming from the North, if I can direct them that way we'll be out of the fire's path.

Ludus grasped the priest's arm and said to him.

"Come with me, we must try to save these people."

The heat was beginning to become so intense that wooden structures were spontaneously bursting into flames.

"Our only hope is to try to get the people to move to the northern part of the city, away from the fire. If we can get through the wall we should be safe on the other side.

"Stop whoever you can and get them to understand that this is their only hope. Have them pass the message to the others, once we get the movement started, I'm sure everyone will follow."

The priest acknowledged what Ludus had said and between the two of them they succeeded in getting the mass of people moving north.

Ludus looked back on the Square, there was nothing more he could do and he had to meet up with the others.

* * * * *

Tactus looked skyward as he and Viaticus headed north, off to his left he saw a bright orange glow in the night sky.

"What do you suppose is causing that Viaticus?"

"I would guess it's some kind of fire, what else?"

"Shouldn't we go and see what's happening?"

"Don't you remember, we saw preparations for a funeral on our way down?"

"Yes, now that you mention it. But it looks awfully bright for a funeral pyre."

"That may be, but we have to meet up with the others and this head wind is making walking difficult enough without making any side trips."

"You're probably right Viaticus and besides it's been a busy night. Was it my imagination or did you hear it too?"

"Hear what?"

"A loud noise, it seemed to come from the direction of the fire. Like 'boom', you know."

"I think I did hear it now that you mention it."

"What do you think it was?"

"I have no idea, just another of those strange happenings we've been experiencing I guess."

The traveled along in silence leaning into the strong wind that seemed to impede their every step. Then Viaticus said.

"Tell me what it's like, being able to talk to animals, I mean."

"Well, it's not really like you and I talking. It's more of a case that we can understand what each other is thinking. I guess you really can't call it talking but I don't know what else to call it."

"It's funny, I never had any idea that animals could think, but I've seen the proof of that." Said Viaticus.

"Yes and I still can't believe how you got everyone to listen to you at the gate."

Viaticus pondered things and said.

"Like you, I can't quite explain it. It just happened."

Tactus said.

"I'm just happy that the siege is over, perhaps now we can get our parents back and go back to the way things were."

"Tactus, do you really believe we can ever go back to the way things were?"

* * * * *

"What's that in the sky back there Lucia?"

She turned and saw a bright orange ball low in the sky as if sunrise was about to occur. But she knew it was far to early for that.

"I don't know Pico. A fire perhaps?"

"Must be a real big one."

"If it is, it's going to get bigger with this wind. I must say I'm glad we're heading into the wind otherwise we might be choking on smoke."

"Pico do you have any idea how much further?"

"Not far Lucia. Are you getting tired?"

"No, I'm all right."

"Lucia could you carry this box for a little while, my arm is getting sore?"

"I'd really rather not."

"You're not afraid of an old box are you?"

"No, not the box."

"You mean Oratio's tongue, surely you're not afraid of that."

"I just think it's awful, that's all."

"It's just a tongue."

"Don't you be gross."

Chapter Sixty-seven

"That seems like a really big fire back there," said Pico.

"Yes it is, I just hope it's not an indication that the battle for Perusia has begun."

Pico swallowed hard.

Will the others get caught up in the battle if it is? Is that why it's taking them so long to get back here? Oh Lord Jupiter, please don't let anything happen to my brothers, or my cousins.

Lucia could see by the expression on Pico's face that he was near to tears. She tried to comfort him as best she could.

"Don't worry, the boys are smart, they know how to stay out of trouble."

"But where are they? What is taking them so long?"

Just then there was a scrambling sound coming up through the bushes. Both Lucia and Pico pressed their backs to the wall. She took Pico's hand. He didn't resist.

Then a voice, in a hoarse whisper.

"Pando, Ludus, anybody, are you here?"

"It's Viaticus." Cried Lucia

He and Tactus emerged from the thicket.

Pico rushed forward and embraced his brother and then his much larger cousin.

All of them began talking at the same time; finally Lucia raised her voice and said.

"One at a time. Otherwise I can't make sense of what you're saying."

Tactus spoke first.

"Where are Pando and Ludus?"

Lucia answered.

"We were the first to return and now you. Pando and Ludus have yet to get back." Then she noticed something about the two boys and she asked.

"What have you got all over you? It looks like soot or cinders or something?"

Viaticus responded.

"Exactly, that's just what it is. The whole town is ablaze it just hasn't reached here yet."

"Has the war started?" Asked Pico.

"No, there will be no war." Answered Viaticus.

"What do you mean there will be no war? Quickly, tell us what's happened?" Snapped Lucia.

Viaticus looked at the young girl, annoyed at the way she spoke and said.

"When Tactus and I were leaving, the two sides were embracing, Octavian appeared and promised to make things right between both sides. The gates were opened and provisions were made available to those inside," he said nothing of his or Tactus's involvement.

Pico then asked.

"If there's no war, then what started the fire?"

"When Tactus and I were making our way the South Gate, we saw a Funeral Pyre being prepared in the Town Square. It was a very large pyre, for some official or other.

"Then on our way back here we saw the flames leaping into the air and that terrible wind came up. I suspect that fire got out of hand and spread to the surrounding buildings."

"But the fire is not heading in this direction is it?" Asked Lucia.

"Not yet, but the wind seemed to be changing direction, if it does I'm afraid there won't be much left of Perusia," said Viaticus.

"What about Pando and Ludus? Maybe they're caught in the fire," said Pico.

"Pico, we must be patient and wait. We can't go back to look for them," said Lucia.

They all sat with their backs against the ancient wall listening as best they could for any sound that might signify that all was well with Pando and Ludus.

There was no such sound. Each was left with their thoughts about the events of this night.

The excitement that Pico had felt in recovering Oratio's tongue was now gone. He was worried about his brother and his cousin. He also thought about his home and the strange feeling he had when he entered it realizing it was occupied by total strangers. Now he wondered if he would ever see it again, let alone return with his brothers and parents to the life that they had once enjoyed.

It seemed like an eternity as they waited, but then a noise. Someone or something was coming towards them.

"Who's there? Called Viaticus.

"It's me you big horse."

"Ludus, for once I'm glad to see you." Said Viaticus.

The two embraced, then Viaticus asked.

"Where's Pando?"

Ludus flopped to the ground and looked up sadly at those crowded around him. The whites of his eyes shone in his grimy face he was close to tears.

"The Chimera attacked him."

Tactus and Pico were stunned. Ludus continued.

"I couldn't really see anything because the Chimera didn't make itself visible. When Pando refused to give up the amulet, the Chimera struck him with his tail and knocked him down.

"I thought he was just unconscious, but apparently the tail has something poisonous on it."

"Poisonous," cried Pico.

"That's what Kashta said."

"Kashta was there?" Asked Lucia.

"Yes and he carried Pando back to Caecus. He said it was Pando's only chance."

"Where did Kashta come from?"

"That's a whole other story Lucia. I think we should get out of here now and get to Caecus's farm before we're overtaken by the fire."

Just as he said that, the top of a tall poplar burst into flame nearby. They needed no further encouragement to clamber through the hole in the wall and begin their return journey.

* * * * *

Caecus felt the boy's forehead; it was still very warm. He gently lifted his head and poured a green potion between Pando's lips. Some spilled onto the coverlet of the bed.

"Do you want me to help with that?" Asked Kashta.

"No, I think he's had enough. Now we must wait."

"I got here as fast as I could Caecus."

"Do not blame yourself Kashta. You better than any other know how unpredictable the Chimera can be."

"Yes, and I worry about having left Ludus alone with the beast."

"You had no choice if we were to save young Pando. But do not underestimate Ludus, I sense that the Chimera may just have met it's match."

"When will we know if the antidote has been effective?"

"A matter of hours, by morning at the latest."

"Then Caecus, I should go back to Perusia and find the others, they mat need my help."

"No need Kashta. I can see that they are all well and on their way back here.

"Go, Black Prince, you need some rest. I will call you if there is any change."

* * * * *

Kashta headed towards the barn. It seemed that the wind was dying down and the clouds were clearing from the sky.

If things were different sleep could come easily on such a night. But who can sleep with this turmoil?

How is it that I have come to have such affection for this group of young people? Is it because they haven't lost their innocence? Or is it because they're filled with such promise?

Kashta entered the barn and saw Fortitudo nervously pawing at the floor of his stall.

--What's got you so unsettled this night old friend?

--I worry about the 'little toad' my Prince.

--As do I, but Caecus tells me that they are on their way back to the farm.

--That is good news. And they are all right?

--Not all Fortitudo.

--I don't understand.

--Pando has been injured.

--Injured how?

--By the Chimera. It was trying to obtain the amulet from Pando and of course he would not relinquish it. The Chimera became angry and lashed out at the boy with it's tail.

--Is Pando badly hurt?

--Not from the force of the blow but by a poison on the tail. Caecus has just given Pando an antidote.

--He will be cured then?

--We can only hope.

--Is there any word on what's happening with the siege?

--No, we await the return of our young spies for such news.

* * * *

"There are the lights to Caecus's farm just ahead," cried Pico.

He still held tightly to the box taking care that he didn't jostle it or in any way cause any disturbance for the contents. On the trip back everyone was so busy talking about the siege and the fire, no one had thought to even ask what was in the box or indeed why Pico had it.

They were tired, dirty and now hungry as they approached the front gate of Caecus's home. All were anxious to find out about Pando.

Ludus ran ahead, he couldn't wait for the others. He jumped the gate and ran towards the porch of the house. Stopping short when he saw the old man standing there waiting for them.

He always knows when we come and who we are.

"Welcome home Ludus."

"It's good to be back Caecus. How is Pando?"

"He's sleeping right now, but when the others get here you can all go and look in on him."

When finally all had arrived and greeted Caecus, he took them to the room where Pando lay asleep.

They stood quietly, lining either side of the bed, each looking into Pando's face.

Tactus thought.

Oh Pando, don't die. You look like you're asleep, surely that's all it is, and you're just asleep. Please wake up.

Ludus fingered the amulet on his chest.

Pando, the Chimera never got it, see. You should've been there, he just exploded, and I've got so much to tell you.

Pico clutched his box.

I did it Pando, you'll be so proud of me. Just wake up please. I want things the way they used to be, please.

Viaticus bent lower to look into Pando's face.

332

Cousin you must not die. Awake, please awake. You must help us all make things better.

Lucia had tears in her eyes.

Do not leave this place; you've many memories to make.

Caecus stood in the doorway and watched the scene before him. Then he saw the eyelids flicker.

What's going on here? Why are they all standing around looking at me? Oh yes the Chimera, am I dead then?

Then he spoke.

"You are all so dirty! You need a bath and you smell too."

Then there was great laughter, Pando was back.

Chapter Sixty-eight

All had retired for the evening each exhausted by the evenings work. All that is except Pico for whom sleep would not come.

He stood outside Caecus's door, waiting to be summoned to enter. Finally the old man spoke.

"I know you're there Pico. Why don't you come in?"

"I didn't want to disturb you Caecus."

"Sit down and tell me what you've brought me."

Pico sat across from the blind man, unsure of just how to begin this conversation.

"The best thing to do is just start Pico."

Unnerved, the boy put the box on the table in front of Caecus and pushed towards him.

"What is it Pico?"

He could contain himself no longer and blurted out.

"Oratio's tongue, I've brought you Oratio's tongue."

Caecus didn't seem disturbed by Pico's outburst, he just matter-of-factly asked.

"And how did you come by Oratio's tongue?"

"I took it from Lucius Antonius. When we were in Perusia."

"You mean you stole it?"

"I didn't really consider that I stole it. It never belonged to Lucius Antonius, it belonged to Oratio."

"But you broke into his house didn't you?"

"It wasn't his house, it was or is my house."

"I'm afraid it's nobody's house now, there are few houses left in Perusia."

Pico was saddened by this thought and said.

"Perhaps we will be lucky."

"Perhaps. But tell me what you want with Oratio's tongue?"

The boy was perplexed, at why was the old man asking him? Surely it was obvious.

"I thought you could use your magic and restore Oratio's tongue so that he could speak again and maybe even sing."

"Did Oratio ask you to do this for him?"

"No."

"Then tell me why you did it?

"When he told me of what happened to him it made me very sad. He lost so much, someone he was in love with and then to be attacked that way and to have to live without being able to speak. I just thought it so unfair."

"So you think Oratio wants to have the power of speech once more?"

"Wouldn't everyone?"

"Perhaps he is so well adjusted to his current condition that he doesn't want to go back to the way he was. Did you ever think of that?"

Should I have talked to Oratio before I did this? Surely he'd want to speak again. Am I wrong to have done what I did?

"I didn't say it was wrong Pico. But you must admit that it was not the reason you were sent to Perusia, was it?"

"How is it you read my thoughts?"

"Don't change the subject Pico."

"No it wasn't Caecus, I'm sorry. But I thought you'd be pleased with me."

"What you were sent in there for was much more important than Oratio's tongue, but you decided that you knew better. And in doing what you did you put your life and Lucia's in danger."

The boy was crestfallen; the euphoria of the night had evaporated.

"You're right of course Caecus, I just didn't think. All I wanted to do was help Oratio."

"Very commendable Pico, but you understand what I'm telling you don't you?"

"Yes I disregarded what I was supposed to do and I selfishly followed my own objectives at the expense of others."

"Good, now that we've straightened that out, push the box a little closer to me."

His gnarled fingers opened the lid of the box, just enough to slip his other hand inside.

"Hmm it seems to be surprisingly supple after all these years. It was a clean cut; we may have a chance of restoring

Oratio's tongue. But there is something that must be done first."

"What's that Caecus?"

His heart began to soar again; maybe it would all work out after all.

"We must first talk to Oratio and let him know what's happened. He must agree that this is what he wants done and we will be bound by his decision."

"Yes Caecus."

"It's far too late now, you must go to bed and we'll discuss it with Oratio after breakfast."

"We?"

"Yes since you are the author of this episode it is only fitting that you observe the results."

* * * * *

Because of Pando's condition, he was allowed to sleep in the house, the rest had accommodation in the barn. Pico made his way down the path past the fig tree.

"Nog come."

Then the sound. Pfffft.

Nog stood in front of him rubbing sleep from his eyes.

"Why do you find it necessary to wake me from a sound sleep Pico? It's been a very long night with more walking than I like."

"Don't be cranky Nog. Why didn't you just fly instead of walking?"

"Silly boy, did you forget how dark it got with the smoke and the clouds. I'd have crashed into something for sure and then where would you have been?"

"You're right."

"I asked you, why did you wake me?"

"I never said thank you for all your help."

"Don't you think that could've waited until morning?"

"Well, besides that, I wanted to talk to you."

"About what?"

"Caecus didn't seem very happy with what I did, you know, about getting Oratio's tongue back."

"I know, I was there."

"I keep forgetting that you're always with me. I'm not used to the invisible thing yet."

"You can get used to me being invisible but as for you, you can forget it. That was a one time arrangement."

"What do you mean?"

"I mean that I could be in hot water too for giving you that magic. So never again."

"I understand Nog, I do hope that I didn't get you in trouble. Would you like me to talk to Caecus? I'll take the blame."

"No. No, just leave things alone."

"Tell me Nog, wasn't it a good thing I did, helping Oratio I mean."

"If I didn't believe that I wouldn't have helped you. Remember."

"That makes me feel better."

"Good, now can I get back to sleep?"

* * * * *

Lucia tossed in her bed of straw. She was well away from all of the others; she didn't want to disturb them.

I'm glad that Pando is on the way to recovery and it seems that Oratio is due for a change too. And soon I'll have to make a decision with respect to the 'Cup of Forgetfulness'.

What should I do? Would it be simpler just to drink from the cup and wipe the fragments from my mind? Or, are the fragments better than nothing?

Is Pico right? Can these people I have met become an extended family for me? Or will they just disappoint me like all the others?

What about Oratio? Will the ability to speak change him? Will he leave this place? What is the connection I feel towards him?

So many questions, where will I find the answers?

* * * * *

--Pando, wake up you're not alone.

Pando stirred in his sleep, then deep in his brain he sensed.

--Pando, I want the amulet, bring it to me.

--How did you get here?

--That's not important, bring me the amulet.

--No, I will not.

--If you think what has just happened to you was bad, just keep up this attitude and you'll see what more I can do to you.

Pando reached his hand to his throat.

It's gone! Where did it go? Who has it? Not the Chimera. I can't remember. Did it somehow slip off my neck? Is it back in Perusia?

--Don't try to lie, you have it. Bring it to me.

Panic was gripping Pando. Not so much because of the Chimera's presence, as for the fact that the amulet was gone.

--I will burn down this farmhouse and everyone in it if you do not bring it to me. Do you hear?

--I hear, but I tell you I don't have it.

He frantically searched beneath the blankets in the event it had slipped off during the night. But it was not there.

--I will begin counting to ten. If by the time I reach ten you haven't brought it to me, I will I will create a fire so fierce that nothing, not a trace, of anything will be found.

Music, I must think of music. The loudest I can think of, anything to drive this beast away. But nothing is coming into my head.

Something is beginning to appear at the foot of my bed. What is it? It's the lion head; he's in the room.

Then Pando screamed. It was so loud the windows rattled and the next thing he knew he was sitting bolt upright is his bed. The image gone, his eyes wide open.

It had all been a dream.

Chapter Sixty-nine

Pico entered the kitchen, under normal circumstances he would be there to help Oratio with the clean-up. However, today would be anything but normal.

After Pico's discussion with Caecus the previous night, the boy was unable to get much sleep. Weariness burdened him. He could only hope that Oratio would be happy with what he had done.

He spoke to Oratio.

"Oratio that was a wonderful breakfast, even better than usual."

--Thank you Pico, I'm glad you enjoyed it. You can dry those dishes over there for a start.

"Caecus said the chores can wait. He'd like you to come to his room."

--Did he say why?"

"He just said it was very important."

--Well you can still dry the dishes."

"No, he said I was to come with you."

--Whatever for?

Pico answered with a shrug.

The two made their way to the old man's room, on the way nothing passed between them. Pico could feel his knees quake as they stood outside the door.

Oratio knocked.

"Come in."

They entered, two chairs sat facing Caecus on the opposite side of the table and in the middle of the table was a box. The box.

"Please close the door and come sit with me."

They did as they were asked. After a period of silence during which Pico had an urge to ask to be excused to relieve himself, Caecus began.

"Oratio I think you should know that our young friend here thinks very highly of you." He paused.

--And I of him.

"However, he has done something without asking your permission. He did this thing at considerable risk to himself and others, but I believe with the best of intentions."

Oratio gave a puzzled look at Pico.

--What was the thing that he did Caecus?

The old man pushed the box toward Oratio.

"See for yourself."

Tentatively Oratio reached for it, unsure of what to expect. He opened and looked inside and was stunned at what he saw.

Oratio just sat staring at what was inside the box. He knew immediately what it was.

--Pico, where did you get this from?

"From Lucius Antonius. I found out that he had it and when we went to Perusia yesterday, I got in the house and took it."

--How did you know he had it? And how did you know where it was?

Pico looked to Caecus and saw a half smile playing on his lips. But he said nothing. Pico responded.

"I had some help from a friend who had special knowledge of the situation."

--But just why did you do this?

"Because I felt so badly for you. Losing Aurelia, being beaten by those cutthroats and then losing your tongue, being unable to speak or sing it just wasn't fair.

"I just felt I had to do something and I thought if I did this perhaps Caecus could restore your tongue and your speech.

"I'm sorry if I did the wrong thing."

He was close to tears but struggled and managed to hold them back.

--Pico, Pico, I appreciate what you've done and the spirit in which you carried it out. You are very brave my friend.

Caecus spoke.

"The question is Oratio, are you prepared to undertake the treatment required to restore your speech? It won't be a pleasant experience.

"Are you unhappy enough with your current state to undertake this procedure?"

The room was silent as Oratio considered what had been said, then finally he said.

--Caecus, I'm very happy here and I've learned to live with my handicap. You have been a good and true friend, from the time of my misadventure. I would not want you to think that should I decide to go ahead with this, that my decision in any way indicates any unhappiness on my part with my life here.

"I understand that Oratio."

--I must say, in truth, I miss being able to sing and I'm almost ashamed to say, I miss the sound of my own voice.

A smiled spread over Pico's face and he said.

"Then you'll do it?"

--Yes my little friend, I'll do it.

Oratio put his arm around the young boy's shoulders and said.

--Pico you are a wonderful friend and I thank you from the bottom of my heart for doing this thing. It took courage and bravery and I'm lucky to have a champion such as you.

Pico was ecstatic.

It was all worth it. I just hope that everything will turn out well with the procedure. I can't wait to hear him speak and to sing.

Caecus was smiling at them both and then said.

"Well we may as well get on with it then."

Pico was surprised.

"You mean you're going to do it now, right away?"

"Unless you'd rather finish the dishes first."

"They can wait, they can wait. But do you mean that I get to help?"

"Of course. Let us prepare."

* * * * *

Ludus came into the room that Pando had been assigned. At first he thought he was asleep until Pando said.

"Come in Ludus, I'm awake."

"How are you feeling."

"Aside from a headache and the occasional bad dream, I'm fine.

"I won't stay long, I don't want to tire you."

"Never mind that, I want to know all about what went on with the Chimera. How did you escape? Do you know what happened to the amulet? Did the Chimera get it after all?"

"Slow down, so many questions. You must be feeling better."

"Please tell me Ludus, what happened to the amulet? That's the most important thing."

Ludus opened up the neck of his tunic and Pando was astonished at seeing the jewel around his cousin's neck.

"You have it. But how? I thought that if anyone other than me touched it they'd be turned to stone."

"So did I. But Kashta said that those that are 'true of heart' will be unaffected. So he told me to put it on.

"I guess that since he was bringing you back here he didn't want the beast to follow so I put it on."

"Kashta was there? I don't remember."

"Yes."

"But how did he get there, how did he know where we were?"

How do I tell Pando that Fortis turned himself into Kashta? He'll think I'm mad. I'm not so sure now that I really saw what I saw.

"Ludus, did you hear me?"

Ludus said nothing, unsure of just what to say.

"Ludus tell me."

"Pando, I don't think you're going to believe me but here goes.

"You remember that Fortis was with us, well when the Chimera hit you with it's tail and you were unconscious, Fortis suddenly changed into Kashta. It was truly weird."

"Not as weird as you think, I believe the same thing happened when I was on my journey to meet you and Viaticus. Except then Fortis changed shape into a bear and then a golden eagle.

"I've come to believe that Kashta is a 'shape changer'. Did you ever notice that we never see Fortis and Kashta together?"

Ludus reflected on what Pando had said.

"Come to think of it, you're right. We never did see them together."

"So that explains how I got here and where the amulet went but what about the Chimera and weren't you scared to be left alone with it?"

"Scared isn't the right word, I was terrified. But then I remembered this."

He held up his right arm and showed Pando the bracelet.

"Caecus gave me this before we left for Perusia. When I was alone with the beast, I touched it and something came over me. I can't really explain it.

"But I had an understanding of what the Chimera's intentions were."

"What do you mean?"

"Well, it never really wanted to take the amulet from us. I felt it wanted me to take the amulet and go with it.

"Remember, the Chimera is evil, you could hardly call it 'true of heart'. There's no telling what would have happened had the Chimera touched the stone."

"So you think the Chimera wanted you to take the amulet to someone or something else?"

"Yes."

"But who?"

"The Goddess Ate."

"The Goddess of Evil."

"Yes."

"But wouldn't she have turned to stone too?"

"Remember, it was she who stole the gem from Jupiter in the first place. I guess that she had enough power of her own to resist being affected."

"Makes sense. But then what did you do?"

Ludus gave Pando the whole story about tricking the Chimera with the riddle and what happened to the beast when it failed to solve the puzzle.

"Very clever Ludus, what made you think of all of that?"

Again he held up the bracelet. Pando nodded and said.

"So the Chimera dissembled again?"

"But far worse than the first time we saw it. My guess is that the Goddess Ate had something to do with it. I think she'd be very angry with the beast for playing my game."

"True, then what happened?"

"Unfortunately, with the dissembling of the Chimera being so violent and the Funeral Pyre being so large, the result was the burning of Perusia."

"Perusia is gone?"

"It looked that way to me, I was the last to leave and destruction was everywhere."

A look of sadness crept over Pando's face.

"Then my home is gone too."

"I'm afraid so, but we can be thankful that we all got back here safely."

"Ludus, you saved my life. If you hadn't been brave enough to stay behind and fight the Chimera, I could be dead now."

Ludus blushed and said.

"You would not have done less for me."

"True."

Ludus reached behind his neck and unfastened the amulet, passing it to Pando he said.

"Here Pando, you're the one that should have this."

Pando looked at the jewel sparkling brightly in the palm of his hand.

"I must return it to Caecus, surely we are done with it now."

Chapter Seventy

Oratio lay on a cot in Caecus's Room and watched as the old man made preparations for an event that might just change his life.

Have I made the right decision? It seemed so simple on the surface but now, I'm not so sure. What if the treatment fails? Could I be worse off than I am now?

I've gotten along just fine without speech, maybe I should change my mind, there's still time. But Pico would be so disappointed; he wants so much to help me.

I can't let him down. I think he has more courage than I do, I must go on with this.

Pico was standing wide-eyed beside Caecus, watching his every move. He jumped when Caecus said.

"Pico, bring me that blue bottle from the shelf behind you."

The boy did as he was asked. He was surprised at the weight of such a small vessel. As he handed it to Caecus, the old man said.

"Now, Pico, I want you to watch very carefully and count the drops, out loud, as they fall into the flask."

He did so and when the number reached ten, Caecus stopped, replace the stopper in the blue bottle and put it down on the table.

He took a glass rod and stirred the potion in the flask; a vapour appeared coming up through the neck of the container. Pico wrinkled his nose at the smell but said nothing.

Caecus spoke.

"Oratio, since there may be pain associated with what we are about to do, I've prepared this potion so that you will sleep and feel nothing until I'm finished.

Oratio seemed pleased. He turned and looked at Pico.

--My little friend, I just want to tell you that regardless of how all of this turns out, you will have my eternal gratitude for everything you've done for me.

Pico smiled and said.

"Don't even think about this not working Oratio. And you're very welcome."

I think it's a good thing he can't see my fingers crossed behind my back.

"I'm afraid this is going to taste a little bitter. But you must drink all of it and then lay your head back and let the potion do it's work."

Oratio almost choked on the liquid, it was more than just a little bitter. But he succeeded in drinking all of it and lay back awaiting the results.

They weren't long in coming. He looked into Pico's face and he became aware of a mist encroaching upon his vision. It started on the outer edges of his sight and proceeded until Oratio could see nothing of the boy's face. There was nothing but darkness, he could feel or hear nothing.

Caecus hovered over the still form of Oratio, prying open one eyelid.

"Yes, that's very good. I think we can begin now. Bring me the box Pico."

The sound of the old man's voice surprised Pico, so intent was he on watching what was happening to his friend. But he gathered himself and brought the box to the side of the bed and put it in Caecus's hands.

Somehow, I didn't think that this was how it would all be. I imagined that Caecus would simply say some magic words and the tongue would be restored. This looks much more complicated. How will Caecus be able to do this if he's blind?

"With your help of course." Said Caecus.

The old man opened the box and took out the tongue and held it up to the light, turning it over and over as he did so.

"Yes, yes, it looks fine. A surprise given that it's been lost for more than thirteen years.

"Come now Pico, I need your help."

"What shall I do?"

"I want you to open Oratio's mouth. You must take care that you hold it open. Any reflex action might cause him to do injury to this piece by accidentally biting it."

Caecus returned the tongue to the box and went back to the table for yet another dish that contained a yellowish liquid and a swab.

"Now Pico, open his mouth and hold it steady as I've asked you to."

Tentatively Pico pushed down on Oratio's lower jaw and was surprised at how easily it moved. This wasn't as hard as he had thought it would be.

But he wasn't prepared for what he saw when he looked into the cavity. The ragged root of the tongue shocked him.

How uncomfortable it must be to go through life with that in your mouth. Never mind being unable to speak, but to have a constant reminder of the attack in your mouth. That's awful.

Pico was surprised at the blind man's dexterity as he reached in and swabbed the root with yellow liquid.

"Hold that position Pico, we must allow some time for the potion to take effect."

While the boy did as he was told the old man removed the tongue from the box and began swabbing the raw edge with the same solution.

Pico tried not to look into Oratio's mouth, but for some reason it was almost impossible for him not to. He could see a foaming action taking place on the root and as he looked up at Caecus, he could see the same thing happening on the edge of the tongue.

"I think we're ready now Pico."

With that Caecus inserted the tongue into Oratio's mouth. There was an overwhelmingly putrid smell that was emitted as the two pieces of flesh met.

Even Caecus coughed.

He held the tongue in place for what seemed to Pico to be forever before he finally said.

"Good, but don't you move yet. I must get some cloth to bind up his jaw."

The smell, while it had almost sickened Pico, was now lessening but his hands were beginning to ache from holding the same position so long.

Caecus returned with a narrow white cloth strip. He carefully removed Pico's hands, for which he was most grateful, and tucked the tongue carefully into Oratio's open mouth.

Then gently closing it he took the white cloth strip and bound the mouth shut by winding it under the chin and up over the head several times.

When he had finished he stood upright and held out both of his hands palm downwards over Oratio's face. He uttered a series of mysterious phrases that Pico would never be able to repeat, then the room turned very dark, even though it was only midday.

Pico could do nothing other than stand in silence in the darkness until daylight was restored to the room.

"It is done." Said Caecus.

Pico swallowed hard, his mouth dry, likely because it was open throughout this whole procedure, then he asked.

"Did it work?"

"It will take some time before we know."

* * * * *

Tactus entered the barn and saw Kashta brushing Fortitudo.

"Good Morning Kashta."

"Good Morning little toad."

--Good Morning Fortitudo.

--The same to you little toad. I understand that you had a great adventure last night.

"Would you care to tell us all about it Tactus?"

He wasn't sure whether he liked being called 'little toad' or Tactus better.

Shyly he began.

"Well it was Fortitudo's idea really. He told me how those inside the walls would be likely to attack with the cavalry first and of course that they would be coming through the south gates. With Octavian's encampment on the south side that only made sense.

"Fortitudo suggested that if I could communicate with the lead horses inside, perhaps I could convince them to resist and not attack."

"Very enterprising," said Kashta.

"I was lucky, I found an old friend of Fortitudo's, a horse named Ducis, who just happened to be assigned to lead the charge.

"He said he would communicate with the other mounts, so really when you come right down to it, I didn't' do very much."

"You're very modest my boy," said Kashta.

Fortitudo nodded his head in agreement, then Kashta continued.

"It seems that the animals had more intelligence than their human counterparts in this whole thing. It wouldn't be the first time nor the last for that matter."

Tactus face saddened.

"What is it little toad?"

"The brave horses were beaten, badly beaten. I felt that it was all my fault. I was sure that Ducis was going to be killed."

"That is indeed unfortunate, but you must understand that in cases of mutiny, many participants die or are wounded. That's hardly something you could be responsible for."

"Why do you say 'mutiny' Kashta."

"Because that's what it was. No matter the motivation, it was mutiny. It takes great bravery to go against the majority when you believe your cause to be right.

"In this case the animals were right and they knew it, they also knew that there would be retribution for their action."

"That doesn't make me feel much better Kashta."

Chapter Seventy-one

"Pico, tell me how things went with Oratio. Is he all right?"

"I think so. Caecus gave him some kind of potion so that he wouldn't feel the pain of the operation. He's still asleep."

"Do you think I could see him?"

"I don't know about that. You'd have to ask Caecus."

I really don't know if I want to do that. I'm not sure of what to do about the 'Cup of Forgetfulness'. He's sure to ask about my decision and I haven't really made it yet.

"Did you hear me Lucia?"

"Yes, yes, I heard you."

"Well are you going to ask him?"

"Probably not much point if he's still asleep. Do you have any idea how long it may be before he awakens?"

"Not really."

"I Think I'll just wait."

Pico shrugged, turned and left her alone.

What is going to happen to me? I feel so alone. All I have are the people here on the farm but I don't really belong here.

My own family doesn't want me. Corripio is dead and Oratio lies unconscious. The country is in chaos and I don't know what to do.

She heard a voice behind her.

"Is it really all that bad Lucia?"

It was Caecus; she had not heard him approach.

Can I have no thoughts of my own in this place?"

"I don't mean to intrude, but if you talk to me about your concerns, perhaps I could help you."

"No one can help me. Why should they?"

"You have friends here. I think what you've witnessed since you got here should confirm that you are held in high regard by them all."

"They are friends yes, but that's not the same as family. Oh yes, I know that the parents of the boys are gone, but they have each other."

"We live in tumultuous times Lucia. Surely you don't think you are the only one to have lost loved ones or for that matter, been disowned by family?"

"Caecus, I know you mean well, but it doesn't make my situation any better."

"Then perhaps you should look at what you do have as opposed to what you lack."

"I have nothing."

"Not true. As I've said and I think Pico has told you the same thing. Everyone here is your friend. If you take a close look we are like a family. Blood is not the only tie that binds."

"Pico must have heard that from you."

"No, he said it because he truly believes it."

"I don't believe that Kashta thinks the same as you."

"Ah, Kashta. He is a forceful man but I think you mistake his directness for dislike. Like you he has lost his family and like you he lives in a place foreign to him. There are more similarities between you than you might think."

"But if he really likes me then why does he treat me as he does?"

"Again, another similarity. Like him you have a forceful personality. I think he is trying to make you aware of the negative side of that."

"Maybe."

"Then you do accept the fact that you are sometimes abrasive with others?"

"I suppose I am, but how else can I protect myself?"

"You mean 'protect yourself' from being hurt."

"Yes."

"Do you really believe that you might be hurt by your friends?"

"I haven't had much experience with friends."

"You have the opportunity to change that situation now."

"I think I understand what you're saying Caecus but I look at my life and wonder what's going to happen to me."

"You wonder what the future holds for you?"

"Yes."

"Fortunately for most, they have no way of knowing. So one lives on hope and expectations that the future will be good.

"It is said that 'good begets good and evil begets evil. You must understand that nothing very good ever happens by accident, you must work at it."

Lucia looked at the old man as she tried to absorb everything that she was being told. Then she asked.

"But where will I go, what will I do?"

"You are more than welcome to stay here and make this your home for as long as you want to or need to. As for what will you do? That's really up to you, there are many things you could learn here."

"Like what?" Immediately she regretted the way the words came out.

"You've shown a talent for medicines and the treatment of the sick."

"You mean become a physician?"

"It makes sense to me."

"Even though I'm a girl?"

"What difference does that make?"

Immediately she felt as though a great weight had been removed from her shoulders.

"Do you mean that I could work with you Caecus?"

"Of course."

"And learn all that you know?"

"Well perhaps not all Lucia," he said smiling.

Yes, this could be the answer. Oh I can feel my life changing, I'm sure that's what I feel. I can be good at this, I know I can.

"So do I Lucia."

She laughed and said.

"I can't keep anything from you can I?"

"Nor should you." He laughed, his laughter sounded strange, like the sound of a crystal bell.

"Caecus, may I go see Oratio?"

He looked at her for a moment while stroking his sparse beard, then he said.

"I don't see why not. In fact perhaps he could be your first patient."

* * * * *

Pando was just about recovered from his ordeal. Fully dressed, he was ready to leave his room when the door opened. It was Kashta.

"Well I can see that you're feeling better."

" I am and I can't lay in bed any longer. I need to find out all that's happened in Perusia."

"Come, let's sit under the fig tree and I'll tell you all I know Pando."

It was a beautiful sunny day as they crossed the farmyard. The sun felt good on Pando's back as he turned and asked Kashta.

"What day is it?"

"It's Wednesday, why do you ask.

"We went to Perusia on Friday and I don't remember anything after the Chimera."

"Not surprising, you had a very close call."

They sat under the tree, Kashta with his back against the trunk and Pando cross-legged in front of him.

"So tell me about Perusia."

Kashta was silent for a moment as if he was unsure of just where to begin.

"The last you remember is being struck by the Chimera's tail and that's what set everything in motion. At least as far as the fire is concerned.

"I asked your cousin Ludus to take the amulet from your neck and put it around his, I'm sure he's told you about that."

Pando nodded and said.

"He told me about the riddle and how the Chimera disintegrated as a result."

"Yes, and that coupled with the Funeral Pyre caused a fire that spread to surrounding buildings. At the same time a great wind came up fanning the flames and causing a wider spread of fire.

"All of your cousins and Lucia were fortunate to get to the north wall before the fire reached that point. As you know they escaped without harm."

"I'm curious Kashta, I saw the Pyre it was huge, why was it so big?"

"It was for a popular politician, a Councilor Fabius. Even in death, for a politician, bigger is better."

"And he just happened to die at that particular time?"

"Not really. It was rumoured throughout the city that Octavian would launch a strike against the city. If it was, everyone was certain that he would succeed and he would take over the city.

"In that event, Octavian would have put the whole city Council to death for siding with those that defied him. Fabius made the decision to end his own life instead. That way he could make it as painless as possible."

"Sounds like a coward's way out." Said Pando.

"Perhaps, but the fire ended up consuming just about everything made of wood. The only things left are some of the ancient stone buildings. The fire was so hot anything made of wood inside was destroyed.

"The Etruscan walls still stand as they have throughout the ages, but I'm afraid everything else is gone."

"My home too?"

"Yes."

Kashta could see the tears well up in the boy's eyes. Pando fought them back and said.

"There must have been great loss of life too."

"Yes, but it could have been much worse if it wasn't for Viaticus and Tactus. By helping to end the siege and getting the south gates opened, many people were saved that would've otherwise perished."

"What happens now?"

"Octavian is in Rome meeting with the Senate. Rumour has it that Perusia will be rebuilt if he has his way.

"The question is, will he have his way."

Kashta touched the boy's shoulder and said.

"If you knew Octavian, you wouldn't ask that question.

Chapter Seventy-two

Lucia entered Oratio's room very quietly, she could hear his heavy breathing.

He's sleeping so soundly even after three days. Caecus said he should be all right, but how can he tell until Oratio awakens?

He looks so pale and with his jaw wrapped the way it is, one might mistake him for being dead, except for the heavy breathing.

She moved closer to the side of the bed and looked down on the figure beneath the single sheet.

He seems familiar to me. Why is that? Tell me Oratio, what is it you mean to me?

As though he had heard her thoughts, his eyes fluttered open and widened as he recognized her. With some difficulty he attempted a smile.

She put a hand on his shoulder as though to reassure him. He struggled to get up, but she maintained a pressure on his shoulder to prevent any movement.

His hand appeared from beneath the sheet and moved to his mouth, motioning with his index finger, pointing to his lips.

"What is it Oratio? Do you want something to drink, is that it?"

He nodded his head. Instinctively, she went to the small table and poured some water from a jar into a clay cup.

When she returned to her patient, it was obvious that he'd be unable to drink with the bandage in place. Carefully, she untied the cloth and removed it. When she was finished she was about to take the cloth away but Oration caught her hand.

He motioned to her that he wanted the cloth. Puzzled she gave it to him. He fashioned it into a ball and held it to his mouth. Then he coughed and retched and spat into it.

Lucia averted her eyes not wanting to see the product of his effort. It was then she heard a voice behind her. It was Caecus.

"If you are truly to be a physician, then you will find it necessary to look at all aspects of your patient's condition. Including just what it was he coughed up."

She steeled herself and took the cloth from Oratio's hand. She opened the cloth and saw a greenish-black lump of mucus.

This is revolting, but if I must, I must. I don't know what I'm supposed to be able tell by looking at this mess. And the smell, it's almost overpowering.

"Yes, you're right it does smell, however, if you notice, there is no sign of blood. Therefore I would say that the procedure has been a success.

"You can give him some water, just enough to rinse out his mouth. It must taste very foul by now."

Again, Oratio nodded.

As she gave him a sip of water, Caecus said.

"Spit it back into the cup Oratio."

Lucia stood wondering just what she was supposed to with the cloth and its contents.

Caecus looked into Oratio's face and asked.

"How are you feeling old friend?"

--Aside from the terrible taste and feeling a little groggy, I think I'm fine.

"Good, good. Now I want you to remain silent for the next few hours. I don't want you to rush anything. We will test your ability to speak later in the day. However, only a little at a time. Do you understand?"

--Yes Caecus, but I'd very much like to get out of this room. I have work to do; it must be very nearly time for dinner.

Caecus chuckled and said.

"You've been unconscious for three days and we've not starved, so another day is not going to hurt any of us."

--Three days?

"Yes, so as far as I'm concerned you can get up and move around, just remember, no speaking until after I see you this afternoon, and only then if everything appears in order."

--Do you suspect that something may have gone wrong?"

"No, it's just that we must use caution and not test the work we've done too soon or too vigorously."

--I understand.

Caecus turned to Lucia and said.

"If I were you I'd dispose of that smelly rag."

She gritted her teeth and said.

"I plan on it. I have to say Caecus, that it's a little disconcerting to only hear one side of a conversation with a patient. How am I to learn anything that way."

"Perhaps you'll have to listen more carefully."

With that he turned and swept out of the room.

* * * * *

Kashta met Caecus as he came out of the farmhouse. Kashta asked.

"How's the patient?"

"I think the operation was successful. I'll know more later today."

"Good, has my young lady friend made any decision regarding the 'Cup of Forgetfulness'?"

"Not yet, but I have the sense that she will soon. Is there any news with respect to Perusia?"

"My understanding is that Octavian is due back from Rome tonight. He apparently has decided to take charge of the situation himself."

"I thought he might," said the old man.

"From what I've heard he is very grateful to our young friends and intends coming here to thank them in person."

"That would please them I'm sure Kashta. I think they all performed exceedingly well."

"I would agree Caecus. I think it would be fitting if we were to hold a banquet honouring Octavian and our boys."

"You haven't forgotten about Lucia's part in all this have you Kashta?"

"Not intentionally, of course, I meant in her honour too."

"Good, but I think the idea of a banquet will have to await Oratio's recovery."

"When do you think that might be?"

"I'll know better when I go back to examine him this afternoon."

* * * * *

Pico watched as Lucia left Oratio's room.

I wonder if he's awake? If I just peek in quietly, maybe he'll see me and call me in.

He stood by the open door; Oratio lay on his back with his eyes closed. Disappointed, Pico was about to leave when he saw one eye pop open.

--It's you Pico, come in.

"I don't want to disturb you, are you sure it's all right?"

--Yes, of course.

The boy moved to the bedside and looked down at his friend.

"How do you feel?"

--I'm not really sure just yet, I just woke up. But I'm sure I will be fine.

Oratio saw the troubled look on the boy's face and asked.

--What is it Pico? What's bothering you?

""I'd hoped you'd be able to talk. Does that mean the operation was a failure?"

--No, No, it's just that Caecus doesn't even want me to try until later today.

Pico seemed relieved at this and asked.

"Does it hurt much?"

--No, not at all. However it does feel strange.

"How do you mean?"

--Well after all the years without my tongue. It seems very odd. Like I have something in my mouth I need to swallow.

"Don't do that." He exclaimed.

--You don't have to worry Pico, I won't. It's just going to take a little getting used to that's all.

"I worry that maybe I forced you into this whole thing Oratio. You never once said that you were unhappy with not being able to speak…"

--Pico even though you never heard me express it, I wanted to be able to speak and sing again as much as anything in this world. But, when that seems impossible it is better to make adjustments and get on with your life as best you can than to dwell on what will never be.

"Suppose that it doesn't work? What will you do?"

--The same as I've always done I suppose. Just get on with life. However with one exception this time.

"What's that?"

--The knowledge that a true friend tried to help me.

* * * * *

Tactus gave Fortitudo his apple, he had remembered to bring one for Hector this time. So this time there was no grumbling.

--That was a very good apple Tactus. Thank you.

--You're quite welcome.

--So, are you feeling better now about everything that happened?

--Somewhat, but the pain I caused the animals still bothers me.

--Remember 'little toad', that all the horses are seasoned veterans. They have fought in many wars; pain and injury is nothing new to them.

--But not at the hands of their riders.

--But look at the result of their actions. A civil war was averted, many lives saved. You may never know how important your actions were.

--Fortitudo, I did nothing, it was all your idea.

--But I wasn't in a position to execute the plan and you were. Without you, who is to know what the final outcome may have been?

--Viaticus did more. If it wasn't for him winning over the men inside the walls it could have been a disaster.

--That may be true but I think all of you deserve credit for the things you did, you are a very brave group. The sad thing is that history may never know of your exploits.

--That's not so important Fortitudo.

--Tactus the world needs all of the heroes it can get. Particularly in times like these with chaos everywhere.

Chapter Seventy-three

Oratio was dressed and sitting in a chair in his room. He jumped as he heard a soft knock at the door.

He went to the door, opened it and found Caecus standing there.

"May I come in Oratio?"

--Please do Caecus.

The old man made his way to the chair that sat opposite the one Oratio had been sitting on. He did so without hesitation, anyone witnessing the scene would never suspect that he was blind.

"How are you feeling this afternoon?"

--The bitter taste is gone and my head is clear, aside from the strange sensation of having my tongue back, I'm fine.

"Good, before we proceed I must discuss this matter with you.

"You must know Oratio, that it is entirely possible that the return of your tongue will not initially mean that your ability to speak has returned as well."

--I don't understand Caecus.

"You must remember that you have not spoken in more than thirteen years. Speaking may be a skill you will have to relearn.

"It's just that I don't want you to be disappointed."

--I won't be, I'm very grateful for everything you've done for me.

"Well then let's begin.

"I want you to say a simple sentence. Something like, 'it's good to see you'. But I want you to do it in a whisper, without any strain, do you understand?"

Oratio nodded his head.

"All right. Go ahead and try, remember whisper."

Oratio's lips moved but no sound was forthcoming.

What's happened? I can't make a sound. Was this all a pipe dream?

"Oratio, calm down and try again."

Again the lips mouth forming the words but only a grunt was issued.

"That's it Oratio, just keep trying."

After the fourth try he finally was able to say.

"It's goooo to.."

"Go on try again."

"It's good to, to…" He whispered hoarsely.

"Yes, yes, that's it. Again."

"It's good to see you."

Oratio's face lit up in happiness as he broke into a broad smile.

"Better than I had hoped Oratio. Say something else."

"Thank you Caecus, this is wonderful."

"You are most welcome my boy.

"Now, you must be very careful, only a little speaking at a time and again only in a whisper. Say nothing to anyone for now otherwise you may cause damage.

"Do you understand?"

"Yes, but can't I even tell Pico?"

"Considering his part in all of this, I suppose that would be only fair, but you must swear him to secrecy."

"Yes I will."

"There's another reason for telling Pico."

"What's that?" Oratio whispered.

"Because now that you've regained your speech you can no longer communicate as you once did with Pico."

"I see and if I didn't tell him about our success, he'd be very hurt at my ignoring him. Or at least seeming to."

"Exactly. Now there is one other thing I would like to discuss with you.

"Kashta and I think it would be good if we held a banquet to celebrate the end of the siege and of course the fact that you've regained the power of speech.

"I think our young friends deserve a 'thank you' for everything they've done to help in both of these events."

"I think that's a wonderful idea, I could start right now."

"No, no, you're not fully recovered yet, I would not ask that of you. But perhaps three weeks hence. Could you manage?"

"Definitely."

"Good, I will leave you now so that you can rest and remember, say nothing to anyone save Pico.

* * * * *

Pico sat under the fig tree having a conversation with the invisible Nog.

"How is Oratio doing since the operation Pico?"

"I went in to see him this morning, he told me that it felt strange to have his tongue back. But he seemed sure that the sensation will go away."

"Is he able to speak?"

"Not so far."

"But he will be able to, won't he?"

"I don't know Nog. I certainly hope so."

"Caecus has left him now, why don't you go and see if anything has happened?"

"You're curious too?"

"Of course. Go ahead, I'll be right behind you."

Pico made his way to the kitchen door; he entered and stood uncertainly before the door to Oratio's room.

Nog prodded him in the back with his stick. Gingerly he opened the door and saw Oratio staring out the window.

"Oratio, it's me, may I come in?"

Oratio waved him in and bade him sit opposite him.

"How are you Oratio?"

He crooked his finger at Pico indicating that he wanted him to move closer. He did so.

"I'm wonderful." He whispered.

"You can speak." The boy almost shouted.

"Ssh, not so loud, we must speak quietly."

"Oh that's wonderful Oratio, I'm so happy."

"Thanks to you Pico," he uttered hoarsely.

"Why are you whispering?"

"Caecus's instructions. I'm not to talk too much right now. But I must tell you something and then I must rest."

"Of course, what is it?"

"You must tell no one of this. Caecus wants me to limit my speech and says it is better if no on else knows because they will insist on talking to me."

"I understand and I promise to tell no one. But I thank you for telling me."

"I appreciate what you've done for me but also you should know that I'm no longer able to communicate with you as we used to, I've lost that ability.

"I didn't want you to think there was anything wrong."

"Thank you for telling me. It doesn't matter anymore we'll be able to talk like everyone else now."

"Yes, but I'm growing tired, I must rest."

" I understand, I'll leave. This is wonderful."

* * * * *

Three weeks later

"What do you think this banquet tonight is all about Pando?" Asked Viaticus.

"A celebration I guess."

"Of what?"

"The end of the siege most likely."

"With Perusia all but destroyed and the population living largely in military tents, I don't see much to celebrate."

Pando thought for a moment and then said.

"It could've been much worse. The fire was an accident but if war had broken out as well, just consider the loss of life and there is no telling how far the civil war would've spread."

"True, but still, there were many that lost their lives. I regret that."

"Viaticus, you can take comfort in the fact that you saved many."

"Not me really, it was Caecus's magic." He said holding up the gold ring on his right hand.

* * * * *

Lucia caught up with Pico as he left the kitchen.

"Good morning Pico. Do you have time to talk to me?

"What do you want to talk about? I'm busy helping Oratio prepare for the banquet tonight."

"I wanted to talk to you about Oratio, you seem to be the only one that can communicate with him.

"What is it you want to know?"

"I just wanted to know what kind of progress he's making with being able to speak. Surely you must have asked him."

"All I can say is that Caecus said it may be a long process, but aside from that he's doing well."

"So you know nothing."

"I know many things Lucia but not as much as Caecus, why not ask him?"

I suppose if Caecus had wanted me to know he would have told me. He must have a reason for not doing so. Perhaps the period of recovery is going to be longer than I thought. I can only pray that this works.

I will say no more and just wait as patiently as I can.

Pico left her and returned to the kitchen. Oratio was puzzling at just what the menu for the banquet would be.

"What's wrong Oratio, you seem a little concerned?"

Oratio checked to make sure that no one was around that might hear, then he whispered.

"Just trying to decide on a main course. I was going to make 'Stuffed Dormice' but alas I don't have enough dormice."

"Oratio, you're teasing me. Who would eat dormice?"

"Pico it is a great delicacy, usually reserved only for the very rich. It doesn't matter anyway, because I don't have enough for everybody and it wouldn't be fair to those that wouldn't get any."

"I'd give up my share."

"Very generous I'm sure. Let me see, I guess it's going to have to be goat."

"Not Hector."

"No of course not, silly boy. I bought some from a neighbour."

"Even so, I don't think it's a good thing to serve. Hector would be very depressed if he finds out."

"You think so Pico?"

"Oh yes, he feels goats are very badly mistreated by being used as sacrifices. Just think how he'd feel about goats being eaten."

"Well this is a celebration after all, so we don't want to offend anybody, do we?"

"No."

"We could always have a vegetarian banquet."

"That would be kind of boring."

"Then what do you suggest my little friend?"

"We could always have your famous 'Sweet Cake."

Oratio chuckled and said.

"Somehow I knew that might be your suggestion. But that won't do for a main course and I already have something even sweeter planned for dessert."

"What is it?"

"You'll have to wait and see."

"If you make it Oratio, it'll be wonderful."

"Thank you Pico. Now perhaps while I'm trying to work out this menu you could set up the banquet table.

"But I must tell you that there will be some extra guests so you will need to set five extra places."

"Five? Who's coming?"

"Caecus didn't say. Some of his friends perhaps."

Pico left and entered the dining room. It was then that Nog appeared.

"Oratio said he had some dormice, I love dormice. Do you think you could find out where he has them? I haven't tasted any dormice for a hundred years."

"Nog that's gross. Why would anybody eat dormice?"

"Really Pico, they are delicious. Can't you just find out where he keeps them?"

"Then what? You'll steal them? You know you can't do that."

Nog's body sagged at the comment. Of course Pico was right.

"Sorry Pico, my appetite just got the best of me."

With that, he disappeared.

I wonder who can be coming? Is the banquet really for them? In all the time we've been here this has never happened before.

Maybe Oratio is right, Caecus must have many friends, he is after all very old.

* * * * *

Oratio sounded the cymbal summoning them all to dinner. It to took no further encouragement to get them to the table. The luscious smells had filled the house for the better part of the day; none had eaten much in anticipation of the feast.

Pico had done a good job setting the table; he had even gone to the garden and cut flowers and arranged them into beautiful bouquets.

They all stood in some wonderment at the table, then Pando asked Pico.

"How come we've so many places set little brother?"

"I just did what Oratio asked. He thinks maybe Caecus has some of his friends coming for dinner."

"How many?" Asked Ludus.

"Five extra."

"What about Oratio? Is he not joining us?" Asked Lucia.

"You know him Lucia, he said he'd be too busy serving. He might join us for dessert though." Said Pico.

"Where do we sit?" Asked Tactus.

Pico enjoyed being viewed as the one in charge.

"If you look you will see a small piece of papyrus at each place. On it is your name and that's where you sit."

They all began to circle the table finding their places. When they had done so, they stood behind their respective chairs, unsure of what was to happen next.

Then Caecus and Kashta arrived and took their place at the table. Curiously, they did not sit together; there was an empty chair between them in the center of the table.

When they had all taken their seats there were two empty chairs at each end of the long table.

Caecus arose, cleared his throat and began to speak.

"It appears that our guests of honour have been somewhat delayed, but I'm assured they will be here shortly.

"As we wait I would ask that Oratio serve us all some wine. While we have not made it a practice in this house to serve wine to those as young as you, this is a very special occasion.

"Just take care to sip it slowly."

Oratio appeared with a large flagon of wine and carefully poured each of them a small amount into the goblets set at each place.

When he had finished, Caecus stood and said.

"Before our guests arrive, I would like to make a toast to our young adventurers. Would you all please stand."

When they had done so, Caecus held up his goblet saying.

"To all you young Romans. You undertook with great bravery several dangerous missions.

"I am very proud of you all."

Just as they finished a sip of the wine, there came a loud knock at the door. Oratio rushed to answer it.

It was Octavian, dressed as they had not seen him before, gone was the armour, the shining musculata, he carried no weapon.

He strode to the table and took his place between Caecus and Kashta. Shrugging his cape to the floor, he began to speak.

"Thank you Caecus for inviting me here tonight. I've looked forward to meeting once again with these bright-faced young Romans.

"Who despite the adversity of being separated from their parents, recognized how important family is and the need to look after one another in the face of great danger.

"As a fellow Roman, I'm a proud of the part they played in helping to prevent a civil war and in helping to end the chaos in the Republic.

"But we can have more speeches after we enjoy what I'm sure will be another wondrous meal prepared by Oratio. Before we do however, I would like to introduce the other four guests who have an equal interest in the strength of family to that of our young friends here."

With that the door opened again and the other guests of honour entered. There was no sound; just gaping stares and then the room erupted.

"It's mother and father!" Cried Pico, his eyes filling with tears.

Ludus rushed to his parents and cried.

"I thought we'd never see you again."

Pando and Tactus joined Pico in hugging their parents as did Viaticus and Ludus with theirs.

There was great commotion, questions were flying from all involved, and it was a scene of great pandemonium.

Octavian held out his arms and quieted them as he said.

"There will be much time to catch up on all the things that have taken place with all of you. But now I would like to toast the two sets of parents and thank them for their forbearance. All of you have shown great courage."

They all lifted their glasses and shouted as one.

"Long live Octavian."

Oratio arrived with platters of food and the banquet began in earnest. They had a great variety of tasty roasted vegetables with seasoning such as no one had ever tasted before. Pico had been trying to guess what the main course would be when it suddenly arrived. Wild boar roasted to perfection.

Pando looked at Kashta and both laughed and to their great surprise so did Lucia.

More wine was poured for the adults and milk substituted for the young ones.

Pico's mother was amazed at the amount of food that her youngest son was eating and she commented.

"Well, Pico, I can see that you've finally developed an appetite. I'm very pleased to see you eating all those vegetables."

The boy smiled an angelic smile at his mother.

It's a good thing that nobody can see Nog sitting on my lap. I don't know how much longer I can stand it. His hairy legs are so itchy. I better give him some more eggplant.

Caecus stood and said.

"I'm sure you all join with me in thanking Oratio for such a wonderful meal."

All applauded the shy man standing in the doorway to the kitchen.

"I think we need to rest our stomachs before we consider having dessert. And while we do so, I think we should hear from the young people. I'm sure they have much to say. Viaticus, I've heard it said that you've become something of an orator, perhaps you might begin."

There was an audible gasp from both his parents. Fortunately, Viaticus didn't hear it.

" I do want to say how happy we all are to have our parents back once more."

The other four banged their hands on the table in approval. Viaticus continued.

"However, I must say that I think I speak for all of us when I say that too much is being made of what we did. For without the magic of Caecus, none of this would have happened."

He held up his hand and showed the gold signet ring.

"Without this gift from Caecus, I could have done nothing to help."

Ludus stood and echoed his brother's sentiments.

"If Caecus had not given me this." He said, indicating the bracelet.

"I would've been unable to trick the Chimera."

Pando reached inside his tunic and brought out the amulet, he held it up and it caught the light from the oil lamps.

"Without this I would never have found my cousins and I feel the amulet has protected all of us since the very beginning"

Pando made as to remove the jewel and return it to Caecus.

But Caecus arose and spoke.

"Pando I would ask you to continue to wear Jupiter's Stone a while longer, for I'm sure that there will be trying times ahead and I will take comfort in the knowledge of the protection it affords you.

"As far as the magic mentioned by the boys, I cannot deny that magic has had a part in all that has happened, it could not be otherwise.

"However, my young friends, you must understand that much of the magic is within you yourselves. It simply became a matter of believing, believing in yourselves and believing in your magic.

"Our world is full of magic both good and evil and either one can possess you. For the rest of your lives you must resist evil and cultivate the good.

"Therefore there is no reason not to accept our thanks for what you've done."

Oratio hovered at the kitchen door, finally getting Caecus's attention.

"Yes of course Oratio, you may serve dessert."

It was a most delicious cake of a kind none of boys or for that matter, no one else at the table had ever tasted.

It was covered in edible flowers of every colour of the rainbow. Oratio cut it and served everyone a piece and then retired once again to the kitchen.

There was a great smacking of lips and licking of spoons, it was an entirely delicious dessert. And Nog was having trouble getting his share. Pico was so anxious to eat his piece that he dropped his spoon. Nog caught it in mid-air, fortunately nobody seemed to notice as the cake on the end of it disappeared and the spoon returned to the plate to scoop up more.

Then Oratio came through the kitchen door, but this time instead of food he carried a Citara. He plucked it as he stood in front of group and it gave out a most beautiful sound.

Immediately everyone was overcome by the melodious instrument and fell silent. The music seemed to float throughout the whole building.

Then Oratio opened his mouth and began to sing in a voice at once strong and yet gentle in harmony with the sound coming from the Citara.

As they all listened to the words it wasn't long before they realized it was really a poem set to music. A poem of the epic adventures of the five boys and Lucia.

Each verse was a chronicle of one of the participants, beginning with Viaticus, the eldest.

They were amazed at how it all flowed into one whole story, finishing with Pico and the recovery of Oratio's tongue.

When Oratio finished there was stunned silence. He thought for a moment that they had not liked it, but only for a moment. Then there were loud cheers and clapping of hands.

Oratio beamed, they liked it.

Octavian was now standing behind the table.

"Oratio, that was as good as anything I have ever heard about you. Maybe even better than what I've heard. Thank you.

"I'm afraid that I must leave as I have other pressing business. But before I go there are a few other things I would like to share with you.

"First, the Senate has approved the reconstruction of Perusia, including financial assistance to those who suffered losses as a result of the fire.

"Second, a more equitable arrangement has been devised to reward the Legions without penalizing those who've worked hard to build up the City.

"Third, the property that was improperly seized in Rome will be returned to the family immediately.

"Now I must go and thank you all."

He was gone in an instant; the sound of horses could be heard leaving.

Caecus was still standing he was smiling.

"I know that you all have great deal to discuss, so I will leave you now so that you may have time together.

It seemed as though everybody was talking at the same time; there was so much to tell so much to catch up on. No one noticed the remains of the cake slowly disappearing into thin air.

Lucia went to find Oratio; he was stacking dishes in the kitchen.

"Oratio, your song was beautiful and your voice is so fine."

He blushed.

"Thank you Lucia."

"It's wonderful that you can speak again."

"Thanks to you and Pico."

"Pico really."

"I understand you have a big decision to make."

"Not as big as I once thought." She said.

"Have you made it?"

She ignored his question and asked one of her own.

"Do I seem at all familiar to you? I mean do you think you've ever met me before?"

"We both know that's not possible. But I must say you remind me of someone."

"Who?"

"Aurelia."

"The one you loved?"

"Yes."

"I feel very humble to be compared to her."

"No need."

"Why?"

"There was really only one of her, there will never be another."

"I understand that."

"So, have you made up your mind?"

"About the 'Cup of Forgetfulness?'"

"Of course."

"Yes I have. I've decided not to give up any of my memories because even those fragments are too precious to lose. Therefore I will not drink from the cup.

"I'm very glad."

"Why?"

"Because I would hate to think that any fragment you have of me might be lost to you."

She smiled and said.

"Never."

And so ends this story and the beginning of the end of the chaos in the land and the start of what came to be known as the Pax Romano, the greatest era of the Roman Empire.

Glossary

Term	Pronunciation	Definition
Almathea	A-mal-thee-ah	In Greek Mythology, a goat and foster mother of the God Zeus
Apedemek	Ah-ped-ee-mek	Nubian God, Lion of the South
Archimedes	Ark-im-ee-dees	Greek Mathematician and physicist
Ate	Ah-tay	Roman Goddess of Evil
Athena	Ah-thee-nah	Goddess of wisdom and useful arts and prudent warfare
Azazel	Ak-zah-zel	The Sacrificial Goat
Barbacan	Bar-bah-can	A Tower that is part of a defensive structure
Chariclo	Shar-ee-clo	Mother of Terisias
Charlatan	Shar-lah-tan	A flamboyant deceiver
Chimera	Chim-er-ah	Mythological fire breathing she-monster with a lion's head, a goat's body and serpent's tail
Citara	Sit-ar-ah	Ancient stringed musical instrument, like a guitar
Clitumnus	Clit-um-nus	Ancient God of the springs
Daimon	Day-mon	Spirit being
Fasces	Fa-sh-es	A symbol of a magistrate's power
Gladitoria	Gla-dit-or-ee-a	Schools to teach Gladiators
Lectica	Lek-tee-ka	A chair to carry people, lifted by four men.
Lictor	Lik-tor	Roman official who carries out the orders of a Praetor
Lupercalia	Lup-er-cal-ya	Ancient Roman Festival
Obsidian	Ob-sid-ee-yan	Granite glass
Pan	Pan	Ancient God of the fields, woods and shepherds. Has a man's body and a goat's legs.
Praetor	Pray-tor	Roman Judge or Magistrate
Proscription	Pro-scrip-shun	An act of the Senate allowing for seizure of property
Procurator	Pro-cur-ay-tor	A supplier of animals and gladiators for the games in Rome.
Pulse	Pulse	Edible seeds of plants, lentils, beans or peas etc.
Rhetoric	Ret-orik	Using language effectively to please or persuade.
Tabula	Tab-oo-lah	An ancient game of chance
Zeus	Zoos	The supreme God of ancient Greeks. Known as Jupiter in Rome.